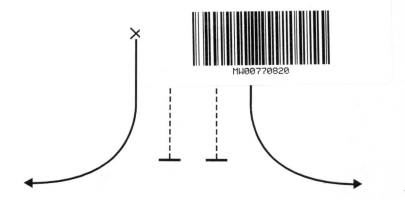

FALSE START

kandi steiner

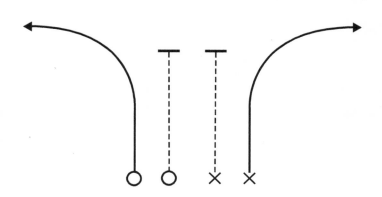

Published by Kandi Steiner, LLC
Edited by Elaine York/Allusion Publishing
www.allusionpublishing.com
Cover Photography by Ren Saliba
Cover Design by Kandi Steiner
Formatting by Elaine York/Allusion Publishing
www.allusionpublishing.com

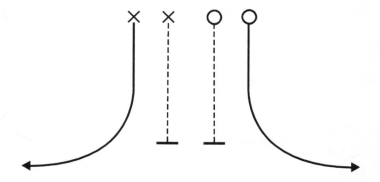

FALSE START

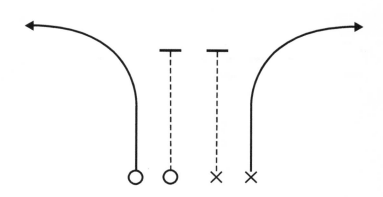

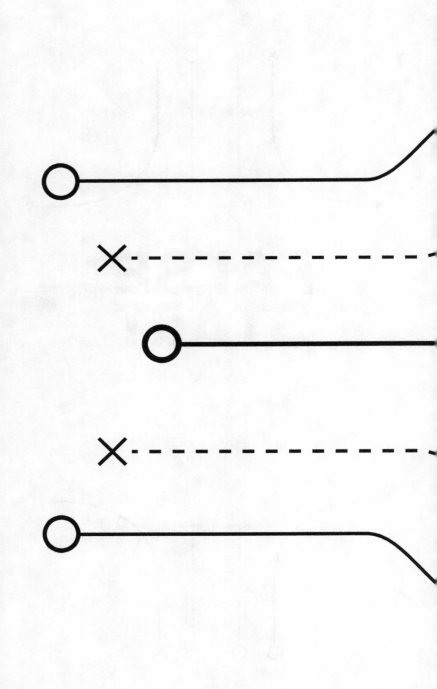

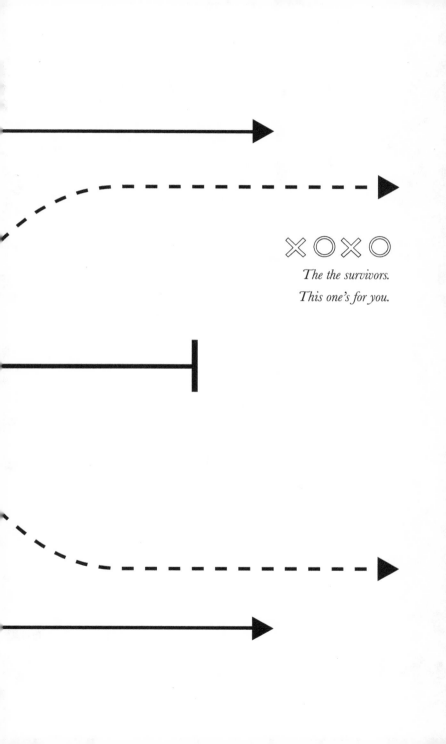

XOXO

The the survivors.
This one's for you.

NOTE FROM THE AUTHOR

Thank you for picking up *False Start*. I didn't realize how much I needed Kyle Robbins' story in my life, but here I am on the heels of one of my favorite books I've ever written. I hope you fall in love with Kyle and Mads just like I did.

There are subjects/themes of domestic violence and miscarriage in this book. While nothing takes place on page, I want you to be aware so you can take care of yourself and read in a safe way. There is also one scene containing voyeurism.

I also want to note that toward the end of this book, there is a brief scene of a court trial. I am not a lawyer, and trying to decipher what happens versus what would *never* happen in a courtroom is like trying to learn Latin in a day.

I have consulted with multiple lawyers and have tried to make that scene as realistic and reasonable as possible.

That being said, this is a work of fiction, and I love a little juicy drama. ;)

Therefore, I'm asking you to slip into a world of plausible believability with me and just enjoy the fun.

If you love *False Start,* fall in love with the rest of the crew (who you'll see much of throughout this book) in the rest of the Red Zone Rivals series. More on those books at the end of this one!

Happy reading,
Kandi

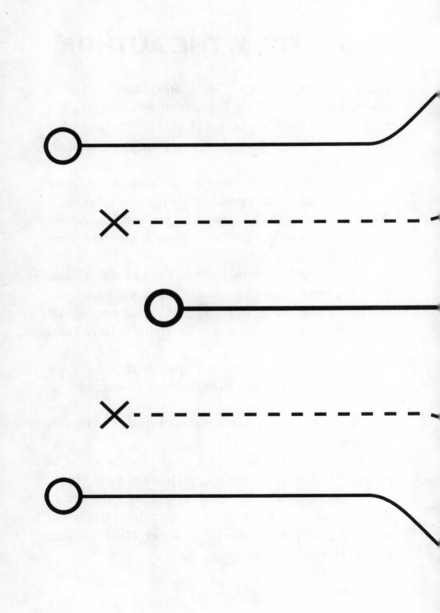

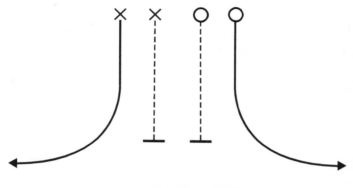

CHAPTER 1

Madelyn

I wondered how big his cock was.

It was an entirely inappropriate thought for a real estate agent to have about her new client, but standing in the middle of the vast mansion with marble floors, high ceilings, and a striking view of Mount Rainier, it was all I could think.

Because this smelled a lot like overcompensating.

My guess was the guy wasn't even serious. I'd been alerted at two in the morning by a real estate app that someone wanted to see this house, and since I hadn't slept through the night since I was a kid, I was easily the first agent to respond to the request. It was a nearly four-million-dollar home, which got my attention, because even if it was likely just a prank, the possibility of that commission was life changing and too good to pass up.

I'd also learned that in today's day and age, most people preferred to be texted rather than hounded on the phone.

So, I'd sent a text right away, saying I had availability today and sending over my times. My mystery client had picked the first one, and so here I was, tea in hand, standing in the middle of a seven-thousand-square-foot home and wondering who the hell could possibly need this much space.

I sighed.

It was probably a joke.

I'd dealt with enough of those in my five years as an agent. People loved to play that trick, pretending to be interested in buying just to see the inside of a nice house. Most of the larger homes required some sort of background check before allowing anyone in to see, some sort of proof that the client had real intent to buy. But, sometimes, like in this case, anyone could request a viewing.

The listing was new, and my guess was the sellers would learn their lesson to put some parameters in place soon enough.

I glanced at my watch, noting that the guy was already twenty minutes late. Of course, it could be a woman. It wasn't fair that I assumed it was a man. But judging by the house listing boasting a *man cave* complete with an indoor golf simulator, I guess you could say I had a pretty good hunch.

The name they'd given in the app request was *Nunya Biznaz*, which either meant this was *absolutely* some nosy prick who just wanted to see inside a mansion, or that it was someone high profile who didn't want the media snooping on their real estate inquiries.

Both were plausible in Seattle.

I was just about to break my text-only rule and call the guy when a loud engine alerted me to his arrival.

That overcompensating thought came rushing back.

Slapping a smile on my face, I let my stiletto heels carry me toward the front door, the soft *click-clack* a bit soothing as I did. I'd left the door open, so I stood in the foyer, ready to greet my client — who'd just pulled up the stone drive in a forest green Aston Martin that still purred even while idle.

The engine cut, and the door opened, revealing one long leg and a very large sneaker.

My theory on overcompensating went out the door when the man stood.

He towered over the tiny sports car.

In fact, I was trying to figure out how he fit in that car *at all* as he smoothed a hand over his long-sleeve shirt, his eyes surveying the house in front of him like it wasn't measuring up to be what he expected.

He was *insanely* tall, at least six-foot-seven, but built like a tank. His waist was lean somehow, but his shoulders broad, his arms thick and corded with muscle that strained against the fabric of his shirt. He wore a pair of light-gray joggers that stretched over thick thighs, thighs I didn't have to study long to know were just as muscular as his arms. He also didn't have to turn around for me to know he likely had an ass to match.

His hair was hidden under a beanie, but I imagined it matched the brown of the stubble lining his jaw. That wasn't *oops I forgot to shave* stubble, either. It was purposeful, neatly trimmed, the kind of stubble that drove a woman mad if she thought about what it would feel like brushing her neck.

My neck heated with that thought, one I hadn't had in years, a feeling I thought was dead stirring to life deep in my gut.

The man was dripping in sex appeal, from his casual attire to his hot sports car.

And though I wanted to be immune to it, I wasn't.

My thighs clenched, and I tried to fend off the electricity buzzing in my veins by standing a bit straighter as I waited for him to climb the steps. He wore sunglasses, even though it was too early for him to need them, and his thick lips were in a sort of unamused pout as he scanned the yard.

"Good morning," I said, my voice a bit raspy. It felt like it'd been that way for years now, as if all the lack of sleep and late nights crying had permanently changed it. "You picked quite a beautiful home to see today."

My smile felt even more forced, but I kept it plastered on as the man sauntered up the stairs, still looking around at the house. He walked with a swagger only someone with ridiculous money to spend could, like the breathtaking architecture of the home didn't impress him, like this wasn't even close to the nicest view he'd ever seen.

"I'm Madelyn Hearst," I said, extending my hand when he hit the top stair.

But as soon as he did, he finally looked at me.

And he jolted to a stop.

I noticed it, the shift in his demeanor that probably would have been lost on anyone else. But I'd learned how to read body language. I'd had to.

It was the only way I could survive against my ex-husband.

I saw his neck strain, noted how his jaw was suddenly tense, his hand rolling into a fist where he held onto his car key fob. He wasn't standing there with all that swag he just strolled up with. Instead, his face went slack, his breath shallow like he was seeing a ghost.

When he slowly took his sunglasses off, I understood why.

Eyes as bright blue as the hottest flames of a fire stared back at me, sheltered under thick, dark brows and lashes that had once made me jealous.

I'd know those eyes anywhere.

And the sight of them after all this time made me rip my hand back like I'd been electrocuted.

I backed away two steps, then covered my mouth with one hand.

And just like that, the power shifted.

His eyes flicked between mine, unbelieving at first, and then hurt, and then angry — all within seconds. Then, he took a deep breath, like he remembered who he was.

And the bastard smiled.

"Hello, Madelyn," he said.

And every memory of Kyle Robbins washed over me like a torrential rainstorm.

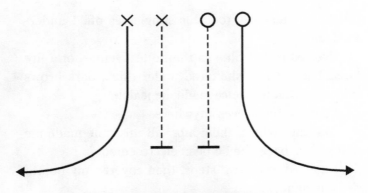

CHAPTER 2
Kyle

I couldn't fucking believe it.

Maybe only a few seconds passed, but it felt like I stood there for hours staring at Madelyn James — at a woman who used to be a girl who broke my fucking heart.

Wait, not Madelyn James.

Madelyn *Hearst*.

My nostrils flared with what that meant — that she was married, that she really did move on as easily as I thought she had once I was out of her life. I'd stalked her online for longer than I'd ever admit out loud after she so easily let me go, until the night I'd realized holding onto her, onto the idea of *us*, was pointless and hazardous to my health.

I'd blocked her, then.

And apparently, she'd gotten married and moved to the West Coast.

Now, she stood in the foyer of a mansion, her ginger hair resting in long, slightly curled waves over her shoulders. Her brown eyes were framed by thick black lashes, but they had dark bags beneath them. It didn't just look like she hadn't slept well.

She looked... exhausted. Bone-deep tired in a way I'd never seen her before.

Then again, I hadn't seen her in years.

It didn't matter that she wore a white blouse with some floppy bow wrapped around her neck, and a pencil skirt that hugged her slight hips. I still saw her in cut-off shorts and a spaghetti strap top, no bra, no makeup, her skin sun-kissed and begging to be touched.

She was small, even in the six-inch heels she wore. She'd always been petite, but this was different.

She was *standing* small, like she was afraid to lift her chin, like she wanted to shrink away and not be seen.

I knew what it was like to see a woman shrink in on herself, to try to become invisible. I'd seen my mother do it all my life.

This wasn't the Madelyn I knew.

A war of emotions rioted inside of me. I wanted to scream at her, to grab her arms and shake her and demand she tell me what happened all those years ago.

I also wanted to ignore her, to treat her like the scum of the earth — the way she made me feel when she walked away from me.

And more than any of that, I wanted to hold her.

I wanted to pull her into me, brush her copper hair from her face and ask what happened to my girl — because she wasn't here now.

This was only a shell of the Madelyn that used to exist.

"Don't tell me you don't remember me," I said, arching a brow. "You've never been pretty when you lie."

Her hand was still shaking a bit as she removed it from where it covered her mouth. She tried to stand a little taller, swallowing, her eyes finally lifting to mine. And again, I felt that war raging inside me.

I wanted to be a colossal dick to her and make her hurt.

But I also wanted to know why she looked so hurt already, wanted to wipe whoever made her feel that way from the face of the Earth.

Fortunately, I'd played the role of cocky, self-absorbed asshole for long enough that it was almost my true personality. So, I grinned at her discomfort.

"Of course, I remember you," she said weakly.

I waited for more, but nothing else came. She just stared at me, in shock or disbelief or both.

I blinked, and a scorching night from my youth flashed behind my eyes. I saw my hands tangled in that copper hair, saw the freckles that dusted her collarbone, saw how those warm brown eyes looked up at me shyly before I slid inside her.

I could still hear the exact gasp she let out when I did, could remember how her nails dug into my shoulders just slightly and her eyelids fluttered shut. It was the first time she'd felt a man that way, the first time she'd let anyone touch her like that.

It was the first time for me, too.

I'd had countless women since that night, and yet they were all forgettable in comparison. It was only that first time that still clung to me like tree sap.

As if she was lost in the same memory, Madelyn cleared her throat, turning on her heel and gesturing to the large pivot door that was already open and giving a view of the foyer.

8

"I'm happy to guide you through the home, if you'd like, or you can explore on your own," she said, leading the way inside. It was like watching someone put on a mask or slip into a costume too big for them. She was pretending like this was an everyday occurrence, like seeing me for the first time in years didn't shake her to her core.

Maybe it didn't.

That thought stung me like a wasp as I dragged my feet to follow. I swallowed it down, along with any feelings trying to stir their way to life, and I put my own mask in place.

"I doubt you can guide me anywhere in those," I said, letting my eyes rake down her lean legs and catch on her stiletto heels as I walked past her. It was easy to do, my strides three times hers.

I waited for her to snap back at me, because that's how it used to be. I was a mouthy motherfucker, and she was the poor girl assigned to babysit me when I was far too old for it. My parents didn't trust me, which pissed me off. So, I made it my mission to break the poor girl they chose to be my caretaker.

Unfortunately, it was her who broke *me* in the end.

But Madelyn didn't sass back. She didn't peg me with an insult three times as good as mine the way she so easily used to. Instead, she shrank even more in on herself, looking down at her shoes with her cheeks tingeing pink in embarrassment.

And I instantly felt like an asshole.

I paused, an apology on the tip of my tongue, but it dissolved like sugar when the knot in my chest reminded me of our history.

"Tell the truth — is this place worth the price tag?" I asked, waltzing past her and into the sitting area. It was an open-seating plan, the ceilings tall, the windows lining the back of the house stretching from the marble floors all the way to the wooden beams. The view of Mount Rainier was a cool one, I admitted to myself, but overall, the place didn't really impress me.

It felt like something built in the 80s and half-heartedly updated to try to feel modern.

"It's a lovely home," she said, and I eyed her over my shoulder, because her voice was so damn weak it didn't make sense.

She couldn't look at me, just kept her eyes on her shoes.

"The location isn't the best," she admitted. "If you want easy access to the Seattle nightlife. But if it's quiet solitude you're looking for, and privacy, then this is a great neighborhood."

I nodded, considering. And then a thought hit me.

"What if I don't like this one?"

"Then don't buy it."

"Will you help me find the right one?"

At that, she stiffened, finally lifting her gaze. "I..." She shut her mouth again, her eyes flicking between mine like I was a crossword puzzle clue she didn't quite understand. "You want me to be your agent?"

"Well, it beats the hell out of you being my babysitter."

Her lips popped open a bit, and then I swore she almost smiled before she looked down at her shoes again.

"If you don't like this one, I would be happy to show you other listings," she said softly. "I'd like to know more about what you're looking for so I can help find you the right house."

I turned to face her fully, folding my arms over my chest. "I thought you'd shoot me down."

She shrugged, glancing at me quickly before looking down again. "I need the commission."

Those words felt like little rocks pelted at my head. They stung, both because I hated the thought that she only considered putting up with me because of the money she could get out of me buying a house through her, and because I hated that she needed money enough that she had no choice but to agree to work with me when I knew damn well she didn't want to.

My stomach was a churning sea from the whole interaction. She was the last person I expected to see this morning, and yet now that I had seen her, I had this unrelenting desire to do whatever I could to see her again.

"Sounds like we're in business, then."

She nodded, but her brows knitted together like she'd just sold her soul to the devil.

I scrubbed my hand over my mouth, looking around the stupid house before walking the few steps that separated us. "Not this one," I said.

"You haven't even made it past the foyer."

"I don't need to."

She opened her mouth, then sighed and closed it again. Finally, I saw a bit of her fire emerge, saw her eyes harden and her lips purse together.

"Perhaps we should discuss what it is you're looking for before we see any other houses," she clipped, turning on her heels and walking toward the front door. "That way neither of us wastes our time."

"Is that your subtle way of telling me I wasted yours?"

"You're a big boy. Figure it out."

"There she is," I said on a laugh, and I caught up to her in four long strides. Then, I blocked her from taking another step.

She halted before she ran right into me, her eyes widening a fraction as they climbed up my chest to meet my gaze.

"I thought I lost you there," I teased. "All that looking at your shoes shit isn't the Madelyn I used to know."

Her chest rose on a long, slow inhale, her throat constricting with a swallow. Then, her eyes fell to my chest, losing focus, like she was on another planet instead of less than a foot away from me.

"The Madelyn you used to know no longer exists."

With the finality of those words, she slid past me, contorting her body so she didn't so much as brush against me as she did.

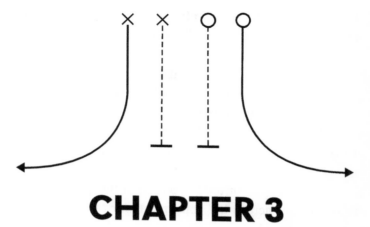

CHAPTER 3
Madelyn

I came to my senses once I'd driven about ten miles from the property, my breaths ragged and shallow as I chugged every last drop of water in the bottle I had in my car.

There was absolutely *no way* I could take on Kyle Robbins as a client.

I was firm in that decision, ready to text him and tell him so, and then immediately block his number. Maybe I'd give him a reference to someone else, as a last gesture of good will.

But when I pulled into my driveway and threw my car in park, my thumbs hovered over the keyboard on my phone screen, unable to touch down.

Because the commission I could make would be enough to change my life.

I'd been an agent for five years now, and I'd been getting by just fine. The first couple of years were the hardest, but it picked up after that, and I was making enough to do what I needed to do.

I paid my bills.

I saved every dime I could.

And most importantly, I took care of Sebastian.

I let my head fall back against the headrest at the thought of my six-year-old son, of the relentless drive I had to do anything and *everything* I could to protect him and make sure he was cared for.

The best way for me to do both of those things was to move him across the country, as far away from his father as I could.

But to do that, I needed more than I had saved now. *Way* more.

I didn't know how it happened, but somewhere in my real estate journey, I found a sort of niche — helping single mothers find homes for them and their children.

Maybe it was a way for me to protect others the way I wished someone would protect me.

But in that effort, my commissions had suffered. I was lucky to take home twelve-thousand dollars when I sold a house, and with how crazy the market had become, and how many realtors were fighting for business, I was closing maybe one house every two months.

It was decent money. I could get by. I could afford our house, our bills, and to scrape together a bit of a savings.

But if I helped Kyle buy a house, I would make close to two-hundred-thousand dollars when he closed.

That was life-changing money.

That was sell the house, pack our shit, and move across the country right now money.

My chest burned so fiercely I pressed a hand against the ache to try to soothe it, because I knew I couldn't turn that down.

If I knew one thing about my ex-husband, it was that he was a lazy piece of shit. The only reason he continued to harass me was because it was easy to do so. I was right down the street. I still needed his help to care for our child.

But if I could change those two facts, I knew he'd leave us alone.

That made my chest ache even more, because what kind of monster would want to take a child from his father?

But I'd rather be that kind of monster than the one who lets her son witness his father abuse his mother.

I hated that word. I hated the feelings it stirred up inside me, like I was a victim when I didn't sign up to be one.

But regardless of the fact that I'd managed to get a divorce, I still couldn't fully escape him — not when we had a kid together. The courts, at least, had the mercy to set strict guidelines in place for when he could see Sebastian and for how long.

He'd never laid a hand on Sebastian. He doted on his son, actually, which was the only reason I tolerated co-parenting with him at all.

And unless I had proof of his abuse, there was no reason for the court to restrict visitation. Even if I *did* have proof, it might not even matter. Judges tended to look the other way as long as the child was okay.

Proof.

That was fucking laughable.

How did you prove your ex-husband knew just how to intimidate you, with his words, his loud voice, his towering over you? How did you prove gaslighting and manipulation?

How did you prove that a seemingly kind, professional, caring veterinarian was actually a mean, grotesque sonofabitch?

In the court's eyes, Doctor Marshall Hearst was a stand-up gentleman and Sebastian's father, and that meant he had a right to his son just as much as I did.

A heavy sigh left my chest, and then resolution sank its claws in deep.

Kyle once used me and then left me behind.

Maybe it was time to return the favor.

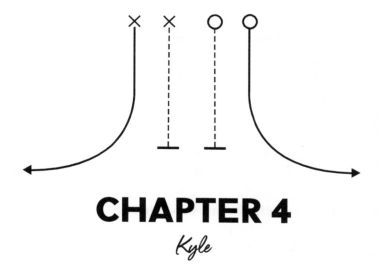

CHAPTER 4
Kyle

My phone buzzed with a text right as I pulled into the Badgers high school parking lot. I'd somehow survived rookie minicamp in May, but now I had about a month to get into the best shape possible before training camp started.

Just because I'd been drafted into the NFL and received a sick signing bonus didn't mean I'd be taking that field come kickoff.

I almost assuredly had a spot on the team, but I wanted a *starting* spot. I wanted playing time. I wanted stats that broke every Seahawks record. I wanted to put up such monstrous numbers every season I played that I had a spot waiting for me in the Hall of Fame at the end of it all.

It wasn't enough to be here.

I had to be the best.

So, I'd struck a deal with a local state championship high school to let me use their field and equipment for training. Braden and I had gone in on it together, both of us keen to show up in the best shape we could on day one of training camp.

Braden Lock and I played at North Boston University together, four years of grueling work that led us to a championship. We were a part of the best seasons that school had seen since the 90s.

I would miss it.

At NBU, we were serious, sure — but we also partied like our lives depended on it. We threw massive ragers at our team house, affectionally known as *The Pit*, and it wasn't strange for us to end up in bed with a girl or two at the end of the night.

Sometimes we rolled into practice hungover or still drunk, but a quick puke on the sideline would set us straight and we'd still be able to perform.

That wouldn't be the case in the NFL.

It didn't matter that I was a beast in college. I was nothing here in Seattle. I was a rodent. Even at six-foot-seven and two-hundred-and-thirty pounds, I was too skinny, too small, too *new*.

I had an iPad stacked with the team's playbook and film from the past three years to study, on top of a rigorous training schedule to get my body into shape.

Oh, and somewhere in there, I needed to find a place to live, too.

I pulled my phone from my pocket when I parked, chest sparking at the sight of an unfamiliar number. It was already being buried under a slew of social media notifications. I'd built a reputation for being active online, giving my fans an inside look at the life of a college — and now pro — football player.

I used to thrive off seeing those numbers climb, off posting a photo or video and watching it hit thousands of likes in seconds.

Now, it all felt like a numb annoyance I kept up with only because my agent, Giana Jones, used those numbers to land me sponsorships and licensing deals.

I slid my thumb across the screen.

Unknown: Hello, Kyle, this is Madelyn Hearst. If I'm going to be your real estate agent, we need to meet to discuss what you're looking for. And I reserve the right to make my decision after that discussion.

I smirked, licking my lips before I fired back a reply.

Me: So hostile.
Madelyn: You wasted my time this morning, and I won't put up with that if we're going to work together.

A flash of her at seventeen hit me square in the stomach, the way she'd boss me around, only to have me fight her every inch of the way. I'd done it to rebel against my parents at first, but the more I pushed her buttons and she pushed back, the more I did it for *me*.

Me: Dinner tonight?
Madelyn: Tomorrow night. 7PM at Rains. Please fill out this questionnaire before then.

She sent a link through, and when I clicked it, I found two-dozen questions waiting for me. I scoffed and shook my head.

Me: I don't have time to write you an essay.
Madelyn: Make time, or find another agent.
Me: There she is.
Madelyn: Don't be late tomorrow. I'll wait five minutes past 7 before I leave.

Tossing my phone in my gym bag, I slung the strap over my shoulder and climbed out of my car just as Braden pulled up in the lot a few parking spots down.

Where I had been anxious to start spending that signing bonus, Braden had his accumulating small interest in an investment fund. He still drove the same beat-up Camry he had in college, one I was surprised made the trip across the country to the West Coast.

"You do know that thing drastically impacts your score, right?" I said when he pulled his bag from the creaky trunk.

"My score?"

"Yeah. I'm a ten, obviously," I said with a smirk. "And you're a solid eight. But with that thing, a five, at best."

"Fuck off, Robbins," he said, but he grinned. I was thankful he was used to my antics, because not many people in my life put up with them.

I'd wanted it that way.

There was something comforting in building a shield, in pretending to be an asshole thirsty for attention. It kept most people away. It made them assume they knew all there was to know about you. It put you in the clown category, which meant when you had a shit day and wore it on your sleeve — no one noticed.

No one cared.

Add in the fact that I was pretty damn *good* at being an asshole, and it was the perfect defense for me.

But Braden was an exception. We'd roomed together at The Pit, and from the very first few nights, I knew he'd seen right through my bullshit. I'd hated it at first, and I was a first-class asshole to him to try to get him to bug the fuck off.

Lucky for me, he wasn't deterred.

Now, he was my best friend, and we were about to play our first pro season together.

"Just promise me you'll at least get a car made in this millennia before the season starts."

"Hey! This is a 2010."

I blinked at him. "And all the girls threw their bras, unable to control themselves."

I said the words in a monotone voice that made Braden grab a sock from his bag and throw it at me. I flung it back at him before we made our way toward the field, each of us slipping on our headphones to warm up and get in the zone.

As I ran through my usual routine — high knees, burpees, stretching and the like — my mind drifted back to Madelyn James.

Hearst, I reminded myself.

My teeth ground together as I did. She was married. That was a fact that should have just been something I easily accepted. Instead, it made me see red, like she should have asked me for permission first — or at the very least, *told* me.

Then again, this was the girl who'd turned her back on me along with the rest of the town I grew up in, who'd abandoned me when I needed her most.

Madelyn Hearst was my babysitter — when I was *fifteen*.

I hadn't needed a fucking babysitter, but my parents didn't trust me. Not that I could blame them, since

21

I threw a party the one weekend they *did* trust me. I was fourteen at the time, new to high school and desperate to make friends. And since I'd watched my parents drink like it was their job since I was born, I thought that was the way to do it.

Step one: get a shit ton of booze.

Step two: invite everyone I knew to the house.

Step three: tell them to bring friends.

It was an epic party, one that put me on the map at my high school. Of course, it also got my ass grounded.

I'd found it laughable when my parents had punished me, because my father was a proud alcoholic. As in, he *knew* he drank too much, and he took it as a challenge at every event to outdo his previous performances. He had a man cave at our house that had a full bar in it, and our outdoor entertaining space by the pool was even more of an alcoholic's heaven.

Most of the time, he was funny, and charming, and a goofball when he drank.

Sometimes, he was a monster.

And when he was, I was his favorite target.

Where my father got louder when he drank, my mother became numb — shrinking in on herself until she practically didn't exist.

And when my father screamed at me, when he told me I was worthless, when he backed those words up with physical reminders once I was big enough that he felt like I could take it?

Mom didn't do anything.

I was sharpened into a man by the blunt force of my father's fists, so when he told me I had a fucking babysitter as a fifteen-year-old sophomore in high school, I bucked like a wild mustang. It was stupid. It was unnecessary. And I was going to do everything in my power to drive every *babysitter* away until my parents gave up.

I expected some middle-aged woman with strict rules and a watchful eye.

Instead, I got Madelyn.

I could still close my eyes and see the first time she walked into our house, headphones draped around her shoulders and attached to the phone sticking out of the front pocket of her jean shorts. Her long copper hair was pulled into a messy ponytail, and when I'd scowled at her, she'd cocked a brow and smiled.

If I were a mustang, then she was the cowgirl ready to break me.

I snapped out of the memory when Braden threw a football at my head, my hands flying up to catch it just in time.

"Wake up," he said, jogging out onto the field. "Let's work."

Braden and I took turns running drills, one of us running a route while the other threw the ball. I was a tight end, he was a receiver, so we both fucking sucked at throwing the ball. But that made it more challenging for the one trying to make the catch, which was good practice.

After a few hours, when we were both sweating and out of breath, we dragged our asses to the sideline to stretch and cool down. When we were packing up our shit, Braden pulled his phone from his gym bag and let out a laugh.

"Well, not surprised to see that in the group chat."

I arched a brow. "What?"

He nodded toward my bag. "Check your phone."

When I did, I saw multiple messages from the group chat we had with some of our teammates from North

Boston University. And the first text of the day was from Clay Johnson, our safety who now played for Denver.

Clay: Don't make any plans for next weekend.

The text came through before a photo of Giana — my agent, his girlfriend — holding up her hand.

I didn't have to look hard to see it now sported a very large diamond ring.

The next text was a date, time, and location for the wedding, along with a promise that a more formal invite would be in the mail.

"For fuck's sake," I muttered, not even reading the rest of the texts that came through from my teammates after that before I shoved my phone back in my bag with more force than necessary.

"Try to contain your excitement, Robbins," Braden mocked with a cocked brow.

"*Next* weekend? Why the rush?"

"Did you forget he knocked G up?"

I blew out a breath, pinching the bridge of my nose before I picked my phone up again long enough to type out a congrats text.

"What's with the attitude?" Braden asked.

"I'm just tired of fucking weddings," I grumbled, my chest tight with the words. "Excuse me if I'm not excited to shell out more money for a fucking suit, fly across the country during an offseason that's already too short, and watch Clay and Giana stare into each other's eyes all lovesick."

It probably came off as me being an asshole, which was fine by me. But the truth was, I didn't want to attend yet another event where one of my teammates was celebrating finding the love of his life while I continued to be the butt of every joke.

They'd given me so much shit when I'd shown up to our quarterback Holden Moore's wedding without a date, making smartass remarks about me being in a relationship with Instagram. I'd covered up the sting of those remarks by fucking one of the bride's cousins in the bathroom.

I was about to be in my rookie season in the NFL. I'd worked my fucking ass off to get here, and all I wanted to do was spend my summer getting bigger, faster, *better*.

But whether I showed it or not, these guys were my family.

So, if they wanted me to come to their weddings and baby showers and whatever else they were celebrating, I'd be there.

Braden knew as much without me having to say a word, which was why he didn't judge me in that moment. He clapped my shoulder as if to tell me to shake it off before packing up his bag.

At the end of the day, I wouldn't have made it through college without my teammates — even if I was a pain in most of their asses while we were there.

So, with a sigh, I wiped the sweat from my neck with a towel before nodding at Braden. "Guess we should book our flights."

He gave me a knowing smile, slinging his bag over one arm. "I'll take care of it. Just you?"

He asked that question with more curiosity than jest, but it soured my stomach all the same.

"Yep," I bit out, already walking toward the parking lot. "Just me."

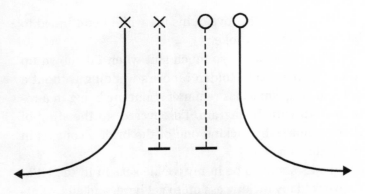

CHAPTER 5

Madelyn

My hands were embarrassingly sweaty as I sat at a corner table at Rains, quietly drinking my water and eyeing the door.

I prayed he wouldn't show up.

Almost as hard as I prayed he would.

My stomach flip-flopped with every minute that passed, with every tall man who entered the restaurant. I expected him to let me down, to show up late or not at all. But then there was the small part of me that wondered if he still had a little bit of that innocent kid I'd babysat left in him, if maybe that kindness still existed.

I snorted internally at the terms *kid* and *babysit*.

He'd been fifteen, and I'd been seventeen — counting down the days to my eighteenth birthday.

A softness washed over me then. *God*, we were so young, so naïve. We had our whole lives ahead of us then. Endless opportunities. Endless goals to achieve.

At least one of us had followed through on those.

My throat was thick with my next swallow, a flash of the last time I'd seen Kyle Robbins before this unexpected run in hitting me square in the gut.

The hard set of his jaw.

The accusation in his eyes.

The secret I thought I was keeping written out so clearly on his face.

He'd never talked to me again.

Until now.

I shook out of my memory just in time for him to blow in through the front door, and it really was like a stiff wind. Every head snapped in his direction, every mouth murmuring as I watched table by table get excited.

They recognized him instantly.

Kyle kept his sunglasses and ballcap on, speaking in a hushed tone to the waitress who then led him over to where I sat. I stood, folding my hands in front of my waist and putting on my best smile as he approached.

I knew when I asked him to come here for dinner that it was beneath him. I didn't know exactly how much money he made, but judging by his house budget, it was easy to guess that it was at least fifteen million, if not more.

I couldn't even wrap my head around that kind of money.

But seeing him strut toward me now, it was almost laughable how out of place he was. The rest of the room consisted of families celebrating birthdays, or couples grabbing a bite to eat when they didn't feel like cooking dinner. Rains was kind of like an upscale Chili's, and even in athletic slacks and a long-sleeve training shirt, Kyle looked too rich to be here.

The hostess gestured to the table once she was close enough, and then blessedly left us before Kyle peeled off his sunglasses and hit me with a sideways quirk of his mouth that made my stomach flip for entirely different reasons.

I knew that smile intimately.

"Madelyn," he greeted, his voice a rumbling promise. "You look beautiful."

I glanced down at the one nice dress I owned, the one without stains or tears in the fabric. It was navy blue, form-fitted and modest. I wore it to every important dinner I had. And when it came to showing houses, I had a whopping four outfits that I rotated between.

Not that I cared. I'd never been one for fashion. I would much rather spend my extra money on Sebastian — on a toy that would make him smile, or a new book to add to his rapidly growing collection. I loved that kid more than any dress, more than any*thing* in the entire world.

Still, I arched a brow when I looked up at Kyle again, because we both knew me in this dress was not beautiful, nor impressive to him.

I may or may not have done some social media stalking and googling before our meeting.

For research purposes, of course.

And *in* that research, I discovered the kind of woman who usually clung to Kyle's arm at charity events, or grinded on him in crowded clubs. They were all the kind of gorgeous you found on covers of magazines, the ones you scrolled past on social media thinking *there's no way this woman is real.*

So, him saying I looked beautiful right now in this dress that could have been worn by my mother?

Well, it felt more insulting than complimentary.

"You're on time," I said in way of greeting.

"Surprised?"

"Disappointed," I countered. "I thought this was a meeting that would be over before it started. Please," I added, gesturing to his seat before I took my own.

"Ouch," he said as he sat, the waitress butting in long enough to fill his water glass and top mine off. "Is the commission not enough to make it worth suffering through a few days with me?"

On the contrary, that commission was the only reason I was considering this at all.

One thing I'd learned about myself over the last eight years was that I was much better at facing my trauma behind closed doors. I wasn't the kind of person who found peace in facing my demons head on. I much preferred to write a letter I'd never send, or sing Celine Dion at the top of my lungs while I sobbed and stress-cleaned my entire house.

So, agreeing to work with the first boy to ever break me was not exactly at the top of my to-do list.

But it was a way out of the current hell I lived in — and I was *just* desperate enough to take it.

"Thank you for filling out the questionnaire," I said, opening the three-ring binder I'd put together on his preferences and ignoring his jab. "I do have a few questions before I can start culling homes, and I also want to reiterate that my time is valuable. If I feel like you're wasting it, I will drop you faster than an old picture frame with a nest of baby spiders on it."

"What a visual," he teased, sipping his water with his eyes dancing in the low light of the restaurant.

I flushed, looking down at my binder so I didn't fall into those eyes like I did as a young adult. I knew first-hand how easy that was to do.

The waitress came and took our food order, giving me a sacred moment to catch my breath and suck down some water. Once she was gone again, Kyle leaned forward, his elbows balanced on the table and those damned eyes on me.

"I won't waste your time," he promised. "One, because I respect you—"

I flattened my lips at that.

"And two, because I don't have time to waste. I need to be settled by the time the season starts, and I already have my hands full trying to get my body and mind in shape to play at the level I need to. Add in the fact that everyone and their fucking mom keeps inviting me to weddings, and you could say my availability is scarce."

I didn't miss how he sat back in his chair with a little more force than necessary when he added that, drinking his water with more gusto. I was surprised he didn't order a drink when he sat down. I knew why *I* didn't, but this was a pro athlete who I knew for a fact partied harder than a whole fraternity of college boys.

I'd seen the pictures, the videos from *The Pit* — whatever the hell that was.

"Do you have time to commit to seeing houses?"

Kyle's eyes flicked between mine. "Whatever spare time I have is yours."

I nodded, ignoring how my chest fluttered at the way he said those words. "Good. Now, I have a few questions."

"So do I."

That startled me, and I smoothed my hands over the napkin in my lap before folding them on the table. Of course he had questions. This was essentially like an interview. He didn't have to hire me as his realtor — despite the way I acted like the job was already mine.

"Okay, go ahead."

His eyes were like the sea. They always had been. Green in some light, blue in others, a deadly combination of the two when the sun was setting and casting his face in a warm glow. Right now, they leaned more in the deep blue direction, and they searched mine like he saw right through me.

He always had.

"You're married."

"That isn't a question," I pointed out.

"Your last name is different, but you don't have a ring on your finger."

I covered my left knuckles like I had something to hide. "Very observant, but still not a question."

"Why didn't you tell me?"

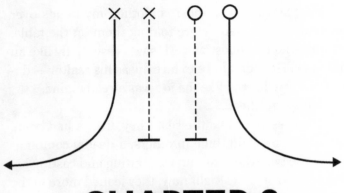

CHAPTER 6

Madelyn

I blinked, mouth falling open before I bit it shut again. "This is inappropriate and not necessary to our business. May I proceed with my questions?"

Kyle didn't like that answer. I saw it by how his jaw ticced, by how his eyes flicked to where I was still covering my ring finger like a secret.

But he sat back on a nod, waving his massive hand over the table as a sign for me to take the wheel.

I cleared my throat, reading over the notes I'd made in his file. "You didn't have any preferences on neighborhoods, which leaves a very wide expanse of land to cover. You really don't care where you live? Perhaps we should start in one of the more affluent and protected neighborhoods?"

"I can handle security after I buy," he said, dismissing the thought quickly. "What I care about more than anything is that I like the house."

"Right..." I said, flipping through my notes. "Which is going to be slightly difficult to find, considering your preferences aren't super specific. You want..." I scanned until I found that part of the questionnaire I sent him. "A pool, a dedicated space for a gym, a chef's grade kitchen, six bedrooms, a four-car garage minimum, and a nice view."

"See? That's plenty to narrow down choices."

"In Seattle?" I chuffed a laugh, closing the binder. "You'd be surprised." I paused a moment. "Okay, so, I understand the gym and the pool. When it comes to the kitchen, what are you specifically looking for?"

"I want something well-equipped for my nutritionist and chef to work in, as well as the kind of kitchen made for entertaining."

I nodded. "Okay, and then... six bedrooms. Any flexibility there?"

"No."

"May I ask why?"

"Because if my former teammates and best friends, who are the closest things I have to family, ever come to visit, they all have girlfriends or wives or fiancées. So, they'll all need their own room."

"Fair enough," I said, ready to move on, but he cut me off.

"And if my actual family ever comes, I need a room on the opposite side of the house from me to stick them in so I can avoid them at all costs."

My hands froze in my lap, my eyes on the tablecloth.

I couldn't even look at him, for fear of what I'd find in those deep blue eyes.

I was no stranger to his relationship with his parents. I could close my eyes and still remember the first time I heard his screams when his father came at him with a belt, could still see his mother's dejected face as she sat on the porch and pretended like she didn't hear it.

I guessed part of me hoped things had changed.

By that comment, I knew they hadn't.

The way Kyle was sitting now, all blasé, his arms folded across his chest as he reclined in the chair across from me, he seemed like he had the world in the palm of his hand. And in so many ways, he did. He was young, insanely hot, insanely rich, and a professional athlete.

But in those eyes of his, I could still see the boy I used to know. I could still remember his lopsided grin and carefree attitude. I could still remember how different he was when it was just me and him, as opposed to when his parents were around. I could still remember how hard I'd fought against my crush on him, how I'd made fun of myself for having the hots for a boy two grades younger than me who was so... annoying.

And yet, it'd been impossible to fight his charm. He'd been impossible to resist.

And I'd paid the price for falling.

Our food arrived, saving me from having to comment. For a few moments, we ate in silence, and then Kyle dropped his fork and took a long pull of water with his eyes on me.

"You never answered my question."

"You never asked one," I shot back.

He tapped the side of his glass with his long fingers. "Did you get married?"

"Yes."

"Why didn't you tell me?"

I tongued my cheek, dropping my own fork and sitting back in my chair before I dragged my gaze to his.

"Because at the time it happened, you had been out of my life for years."

"And whose choice was that?"

My jaw hardened at the audacity. "I think for the sake of remaining professional, we should keep our conversations to house-hunting and steer clear of reminiscing over the past."

"Are you married now?" Kyle asked. "That's a present question — not a past one."

My nostrils flared, my eyes dropping to the table once more. "No."

Suddenly, my phone began vibrating in my purse hanging beneath the table. I scooted back so hard the chair ground against the floor, fumbling for my bag and whipping the device out. I always put my phone on silent during work meetings, but I made sure the few important people I needed to have access to me could still get through.

When I saw my ex-husband's name on the screen, my stomach dropped.

"Excuse me," I said, ditching the table and all but running back to the hallway where the bathrooms were.

"Hello?" I answered.

"Sebastian's sick."

I blinked, and then let out a long breath, pinching the bridge of my nose. "I'm at a work dinner, Marshall."

"And your son is sick," he shot back, his voice violent already where mine was level and calm.

"Can you handle it?"

"He threw up everywhere — like, projectile vomited all over his bed. I don't have any spare sheets and I don't even know where to *begin* cleaning up this goddamn mess."

That was a no, I guessed.

I wanted to tell him to calm down, but I'd learned long ago that wasn't the approach to take with Marshall.

"I'll be there soon," I said instead, hoping the calm in my voice would transfer to him.

In reality, I knew he'd be happy just because he still had power over me.

One call, and I was doing what he wanted.

My stomach was in knots as I made my way back to the table, my feet moving slower than I wanted them to. I needed to rush, to get to my baby boy and take care of him.

But going to him also meant going to Marshall.

I did my best to stay away from him as much as I could. Other than dropping Sebastian off or picking him up, I didn't have to see my ex.

But with this, I'd have to go into that house I once lived in with him. I'd have to be within the walls, behind closed doors, alone with him — other than our child.

Nothing put me on edge quite like that did.

Marshall was careful. He always had been. He never outright hit me when we were together, and since our divorce, he found clever ways to bruise me without any physical marks being left on my skin.

Still, he was unpredictable.

"I'm sorry, I have a family emergency," I said to Kyle when I made it back to the table, pulling cash from my purse.

Kyle immediately stood, dropping his napkin on his chair. "What happened? Is it your mom?"

My chest squeezed violently.

"No."

Kyle frowned. "Your brother?"

"No," I gritted, and when I tried to put cash on the table, Kyle stopped me, his hand lightly finding my wrist.

The soft touch made a lump form in my throat.

Slowly, he slid his hand down to mine, folding my fingers around the cash and guiding it back toward my purse.

"Who, then? Your dad?"

God, why did he have to ask, why did he have to pretend to care?

"Sebastian," I said on a swallow, breaking contact with his hand. "Let me pay for dinner."

"Not happening." His eyes were still hard on me when he asked, "Who is Sebastian?"

I met his gaze. "My son."

It felt like all the air in the restaurant was sucked out with those words, and I kept his stare even long after it burned me.

"Son," he repeated. "You... you're a mom?"

My eyes watered when he asked. It was like he was hurt by that fact as much as he was amazed by it.

He had a lot of balls to have that reaction, since the last time he'd found out I was pregnant, he'd left me.

I licked my lips on a laugh, slinging my purse over my shoulder. "Yep. And before you ask, no, he isn't yours."

That made Kyle frown. "Why would I assume that?"

I closed my eyes, forcing a breath. Of course, he wouldn't assume I kept our child. I was just eighteen when he left. He was sixteen, for fuck's sake. We were both still kids ourselves.

Not that I'd been much older when Marshall had knocked me up, but in that scenario, he was the older one. He was more mature. He knew what to do.

Or so I thought at the time.

I cleared my throat, lifting my chin to meet Kyle's gaze even when it made me sick to do so. How he could be so callous, pretending like it never happened, made my blood boil.

Almost as much as it made my heart long to go back to that day, to force him to talk to me, to not let him go so easily. I was young, scared, and insecure — even though I masked that with a hard exterior.

We were both so good at pretending to be people we weren't.

The commission, I reminded myself.

I only had to stomach him for a short while, and then I'd have the key to my freedom.

"I will send you a list of houses in the morning. I have your availability here, and I'm sure we'd both like this to be over quickly, so expect a full schedule."

I bolted out of that restaurant like it was on fire, leaving Kyle Robbins to put out the flames.

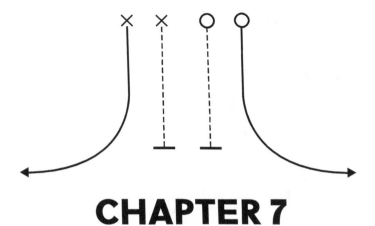

CHAPTER 7
Madelyn

I was terrified when I found out I was pregnant.

I wish I could say I was elated, that I cried tears of joy and dreamed of the child I was growing inside me and what they'd be when they grew up. I wish I could say I ran to my husband and celebrated.

The truth was that I fell to the floor in the bathroom, covering my mouth and shaking my head, convinced I wasn't actually seeing those two lines.

I was scared when I told Marshall. I was scared when we went to the doctors' appointments. I was scared when my mom talked me through what to expect and most of all, I was scared of being a mother.

I was scared I wouldn't be a *good* mother.

My fears never went away, but they did fade the moment the doctor put Sebastian in my arms. Suddenly, fear took a backseat, and the most primal feeling took its place behind the wheel.

I knew, no matter what, I would protect him with my life.

"Can we try to get the spoon *in* your mouth, Sebastian?" I teased from the other side of the kitchen island, reaching over to wipe up the bit of milk that had splashed next to his book. He had it splayed open with one little hand while the other unsuccessfully navigated spoonfuls of Honey Nut Cheerios into his mouth.

He giggled a little when I wiped up the milk and then tapped his nose with the rag. I was just thankful he was feeling better, that his little display of projectile vomiting at his father's seemed to be a one-night bug and not something that knocked him down for a week.

"You like that one," I said, nodding at the book.

"It's okay."

"Just okay?" I asked, continuing where I was packing up his lunch. "You've been laughing all through breakfast."

"It's funny, but I like the history books better."

I wrinkled my nose. "History?"

This kid was so much like me in so many ways — from the shape of his eyes and nose to the way I had to all but drag him out of bed in the morning — but his love for reading, for knowledge?

He didn't get that from me.

"What history books are you even reading?" I asked, trying to rack my brain for what I was reading when I was his age. I followed up that question by holding up a banana and a mandarin.

Sebastian looked up long enough to point at the orange, and then his nose was in his book again. "Well, like we just read a book about Abraham Lincoln."

"Ah," I said, zipping up his lunch cooler. "Honest Abe."

Sebastian's deep brown eyes widened. "You *knew* him?"

I loved the laugh that barreled out of me. It was the laugh only my son could conjure, one of pure surprise and adoration. "No, baby. He was a little before my time."

Sebastian seemed thoughtful as he digested my answer, and then he went right back to reading and spilling more of his cereal than he ate. "Well, I bet you would have been friends."

"You think so, huh?"

He nodded, and then around a mouthful of cereal, he added, "You both love to help people."

For a moment, I watched him, my heart squeezing painfully in my chest as I did. I loved him so much it physically hurt. I didn't know that was possible before I was a mom. I thought I knew what love felt like, but I had no idea. Not really.

Not until I had him.

"Alright," I said when he started slurping his milk from the bowl. "Go brush your teeth and I'll come in to help you get dressed."

"Can I wear my rock shirt today?!"

And by rock, he did not mean music. He meant geo.

"You wore that shirt twice last week," I reminded him.

He blinked. "Is that a bad thing? You wear the same clothes a lot."

He had me there.

"Not a bad thing at all," I told him, rounding the island to kiss his hair. "Now go brush those stinky teeth."

41

"I'm not stinky!" he protested as he hopped down from the bar stool.

"Hmm, let's investigate." I made a show of lifting his arm and taking a big whiff before I pretended to gag, and he giggled the deep-belly laugh that I wished I could bottle up and save forever.

Then, the angel that he was, Sebastian took his bowl to the sink, standing on his tiptoes to drop it inside before he grabbed his book and ran back toward his room.

I let out a happy sigh, running one hand through my hair as I watched him go. Then, I checked my watch, and my stomach sank.

I was meeting Kyle in an hour.

After our dinner, I'd almost been tempted to call the whole thing off. Being in close proximity with him after all these years was making my brain short wire. Add in the way he had looked at me when I told him I had a son, the way he looked almost like... like he was in *awe*.

It grated on my nerves even now.

Or maybe that was just a mask for the truth — which was that his reaction hurt like hell.

It was the reaction I wished I'd had from him when we were younger.

Instead, he'd just... left.

I'd been devastated at the time. It was the worst pain I'd ever felt — to have the boy I loved, the only boy I'd been with, walk away from me when I needed him most. I was content to do it all on my own, but I'd lost the baby a couple weeks later.

That had hurt worse than Kyle leaving.

I closed my eyes, covering my racing heart with a shaky hand in an attempt to soothe it. I hadn't let myself think about that time in my life in so long. I couldn't. I had to protect myself, my mental health and well-being. I had to move forward. I had to move *on*.

But now, I could search my memory and remember exactly who I was, exactly how I felt.

We were each other's best friends after that first summer together.

Then, we were something... more.

He was my first everything — first love, first intimate partner, first heartbreak.

Now, I hoped he'd be my first break in years.

He held the key to my new life in his hands, whether he knew it or not.

And when Sebastian called me back to his room and I helped him get dressed, when he celebrated tying his own shoes, when he smiled up at me like I hung the moon even though I was struggling to hold on... I felt my resolve thicken.

I would do anything to provide a better life for him.

Even if I had to rip off an old scab to do it.

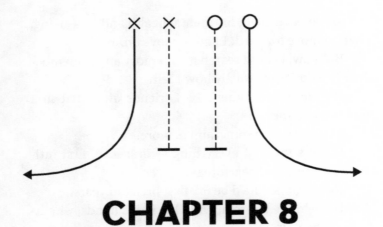

CHAPTER 8

Kyle

True to her word, Madelyn sent a list of house address-es, dates, and times the morning after our dinner.

I'd wanted to ask her a dozen things, starting with *what happened to your marriage*, and ending with *why did you think I would have assumed your kid was mine?*

Instead, I'd sent her a thumbs-up emoji, and now it was Tuesday and I was on my way to meet her at the first house she'd suggested.

My mind raced the entire way, much like it had ev-ery minute since she left me in that restaurant. Sitting across from her had been a unique kind of torture, the type that makes your stomach roil as much as it makes your chest light with excitement.

I needed to get away from her, from the rage and disappointment and hurt she dredged up in the trenches of my being.

But I also wanted to get close to her, to know everything about her life since she'd exited mine.

I felt like a crazy person, but when I pulled up the drive of the mansion she'd selected for us to see first, I put on my best mask and stepped out of my car with confidence.

It was beautiful — a stately home on Lake Washington with grandiose landscaping and the classic kind of rich vibe that made me feel like I needed to wear slippers and smoke a cigar. I'd flipped through the photographs, already fairly certain it wasn't the spot for me, but I didn't want to negate the work Madelyn had done.

I was going into this with an open mind, mostly because something about Madelyn told me she wasn't happy. And I didn't want to add to that.

In fact, for a reason I'd never understand, I wanted to be the one to fix it.

I was loading up my jokes when I shut my car door and headed for the grand entrance of the home. My phone buzzed in my pocket, and I paused, taking it out to see a slew of missed texts in the group chat.

Holden: Hate to act like your captain even now that we're on different teams, but has everyone booked flights and hotels for this weekend?

Clay: We love you, daddy!

Leo: Hey, that's my title.

Zeke: To Mary, maybe.

Braden: Correction — *Mary* is daddy. Leo is just shitstain.

Leo: *middle finger emoji*

I chuckled, reading on to see Braden had already booked our flights. The guys teased him about hiding his love for me and how we were so clearly a couple. It then went into Clay saying he was an expert in fake dating, if we needed him to help find us a guest.

I stopped long enough to thumb out a sarcastic response to a few of their jests, and then my phone was tucked away and I was headed inside.

It was wild, to think of how fast my friends had been locked down. Zeke Collins had fallen hard for Riley Novo our freshman year, although to his credit, he had been in love with that girl since they were kids. It wasn't his fault she was the only girl on the team, and then he was forced to room with her. Any man would have cracked under that.

Then, Clay simped for Giana, pretending to date her to get his ex back only to actually fall for G, instead.

Holden was the one I thought would stay strong. He was our quarterback, our captain, and nothing distracted him from football. That was, until our new coach's daughter had strutted into the locker room looking like an absolute snack. I was mildly jealous of that one. I would have given my starting position for a chance with Julep.

They got hitched in April.

Lastly, there was Leo Hernandez and Mary Silver. Those two fought like fucking cats and dogs when Mary found herself without any other choice but to live with us at The Pit for a few months. That was our senior year, the one where I started pulling my head out of my ass and acting like a grown man who wanted a shot in the NFL. I'd thought being a star on social media would get me my ticket in, but it was Holden who helped me see I needed to straighten up if I wanted a real shot.

And I could still remember how it felt to watch him that first time on the field as an NFL player. We were all gathered at The Pit, stunned silent when he lined up as quarterback during a pre-season game for North Carolina.

That had straightened me out real quick, and my singular focus shifted from fame, girls, and partying, to being and doing whatever it took to get my own spot in that league.

At least I still had Braden. I was pretty sure he was just as content being single as I was, his drive to be a beast in the NFL just as strong as mine.

The front door of the massive white house was unlocked, and I pushed it open with my eyes scanning the tall ceilings and rich woods when I did. The foyer opened up to a dining area and kitchen, which spilled into the living area. All of it was lit up with the natural light coming in from the large sliding glass doors in the back, and I ticked a brow up at the view of the lake.

"Not bad," I muttered to myself.

Still, it felt a little old fashioned for me. I tried to keep my mind open as I made my way farther inside.

"Good morning."

Madelyn's voice was soft and tentative, and I turned to find her joining me from one of the back hallways.

She had her arms wrapped around a binder hugged to her chest, as if it were a shield. Where she'd been in a pencil skirt and blouse last time she'd shown me a home, this time, she was in straight-legged dark green slacks and a long-sleeve black turtleneck. It hugged her slight frame and matched the heels she wore, the ones that helped her stand at least four inches taller.

Her copper hair was straight today, and the morning light off that lake warmed the gold in her brown eyes.

Fuck, she was beautiful.

"Good morning," I echoed, leaning a hip against the kitchen island where I stood. I folded my arms over my chest, looking around at the house. "Nice find. I dig the Spanish Revival style."

"I'm glad you approve. Care for a tour?"

"Lead the way."

I followed behind Madelyn as she gave me the overview of the home, listing off all the construction materials, square footage details, years it was made and updated, age of the appliances, and so on and so forth.

I listened intently, nodding and taking it all in as we toured the eight bedrooms, the two kitchens — one for the chefs, one for me — the six-and-a-half bathrooms, the three bonus rooms that she illustrated could be used for a gym or man cave or whatever else my heart desired, the four fireplaces, the two dining areas and living areas, the back yard with a garden and a pool and an outdoor cooking area.

I really was listening.

But I was also staring at Madelyn's ass and daydreaming about a life that felt almost like it never happened.

I remembered the way her torn-up jean shorts would hug that ass when she was seventeen, when I was a fifteen-year-old with raging hormones driving all of my decisions.

I remembered how I slowly grew from a pain in her ass to her friend, how we went from annoying each other to opening up to one another in ways we didn't open up to anyone else.

By the time I turned sixteen, she was my best friend.

One cold winter night, the two of us snuck into a house not even a quarter of the size of this one in the gated community a ten-minute walk from my parents' house. Its owners had just moved out, but it hadn't gone up for sale yet.

We'd thought *that* was a mansion, thought we were so fucking cool jumping into that dirty, freezing cold pool. It wasn't like we didn't have a nice, clean, decent-size pool at my house. It was just that this one was like a fucking waterpark. It had multiple slides and a diving board and a hot tub that sat a few feet higher than the pool.

Of course, it wasn't hot then, but we pretended like it was.

We'd gotten tipsy off cheap champagne we stole out of my mom's secret fridge in the garage, and I'd teased Madelyn about being the worst babysitter in the world, about how she was more trouble than I would have found if I was left on my own.

Then, I'd touched her for the first time.

I could still hear the way her breath had hitched when I did, how my heart had been hammering out of my chest thinking she was going to tell me to stop.

But she hadn't.

"So, what do you think?" Madelyn asked when we'd finished the tour, ending in the kitchen where we'd began.

I leaned against the counter again with a smile on my lips and that memory still playing vividly in my mind.

"Do you remember when we snuck into Waterford Lakes?"

Her eyes widened, cheeks flushing a light pink.

I laughed a little when she didn't respond, shaking my head. "We thought *that* was how the rich and famous lived. And now, here we are, grown ass adults touring a house at least four times the size."

Madelyn's jaw was tight as she looked at the floor. "That was a nice house."

"I seem to remember liking the pool quite a bit..."

I arched a brow when Madelyn's gaze met mine, and for a moment, I thought I saw the same heat and desire in her eyes. Did she remember what it was like to be two kids fooling around for the first time, all that excitement and nervous energy?

I thought maybe she would return my smile and let me take her down memory lane.

Instead, she swallowed, hardening even more as she laid out the binder with the house stats on the granite counter.

"They're asking for six point two," she said, leaving off the *million* part of that statement. "But I think we could offer six and get away with it. It's been on the market for two months now. I realize this is at the high-end of your range, but I thought you'd appreciate the lake view and the options for your gym."

I hated that she changed the subject, that she was being so cold with me. But I also hated that I *wasn't* being cold with her.

After what she did, after how she betrayed me... it should have been *me* who was pissed off.

Instead, I found myself scratching my head and trying to recall why I'd been so angry to begin with.

We were young. We were fucking *kids*. Of course, at that time in my life, I didn't realize it. Everything felt big. Everything felt like the end of the world.

Especially when my father made a fool of himself, enough so that the whole community turned their backs on us and forced us out of town.

Madelyn and her parents included.

I sniffed. "I do love the view, and the access to the lake. The pool is nice. I love all the dark wood. But..." I looked around, trying to figure out how to name what was off. "It just feels a little..."

"Old?"

I cringed. "Yeah."

She nodded, making a note in her binder. "That's alright, this will help me figure out what your style is, since you didn't really give me anything to go on there."

I chuckled. "I'm going to have to start wearing armor around you, with all these little jabs you love to throw."

"Have you gotten soft in your old age?" she teased, arching a brow at me as she shoved her sleeves up. "The Kyle I knew could dish it right back."

My chest sparked with the challenge, with how she was letting me in a bit. She was smiling. She was teasing. I saw just a glimpse of the girl I used to know.

But then my eyes caught on her left arm, on the dark coloring of skin above her watch.

There were four bruises.

And there was no mistaking they were from a hand.

"So, let's cross this one off. I think the next—"

"Who did that to you?"

My jaw was tighter than I'd ever felt it in my fucking life, my teeth grinding together hard enough to crack as I stared at those marks. They were a dark, nasty purple against her pale skin, the edges of them turning a sickening green.

Madelyn frowned up at me, and then instantly went white as a sheet. She tugged her sleeves down without even looking at the bruises she knew I'd seen.

"Oh, stop it," she tried, waving me off. "You know how clumsy I am. I just—"

"I swear to fucking *God*, Madelyn, if you try to tell me you *fell* and bruised your arm in the shape of a hand—"

That was not the right response, and I knew it by the way she shriveled in on herself. But it was like trying to ride a fucking bull, the way my rage was bucking wildly in my chest.

I inhaled a long breath, closed my eyes, and opened them again before tentatively moving toward her. I didn't dare reach out for her, not when she looked like a scared doe ready to race across a highway if I did.

"Look at me," I whispered.

I didn't miss how her eyes welled with tears, but her nose flared despite them, her chin lifting and eyes finding mine in defiance. "I'm fine."

"Who hurt you?"

"I'm not hurt."

"Who," I repeated, slower this time, the strain evident in my voice as I tried to keep my cool. "Did this?"

She sighed, shaking her head and looking away from me. Then, she rolled her lips together, eyes falling to the binder. "My ex."

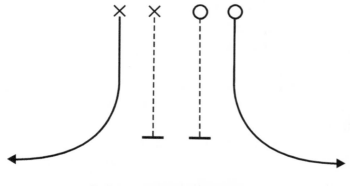

CHAPTER 9

Madelyn

He looked like I'd just thrown a bucket of ice water over his head.

Kyle stood frozen for a long moment, and then he nodded, over and over, like I'd just told him the NFL schedule for the year, and not that I had bruises on my arm from my stupid ex-husband.

His eyes found mine, and I thought I saw them break before they hardened into stone.

"He's dead."

Kyle was already turning for the exit, key fob in hand and shoulders tight as a bow string. But I reached out for him, my hand catching him by the crook of the elbow.

The moment our skin touched, fire licked along my spine, a thousand memories racing to be the first to reach me. But I snuffed them out, focusing on the matter at hand.

"Don't," I begged, voice cracking a bit. That only pissed me off, and I blew out a frustrated breath. "I'm serious when I say he didn't hurt me. I'm fine. But if you go acting like a big tough guy with a savior complex, you're going to make it a lot worse."

He spun to face me. "He can't be worse if he's not fucking breathing."

I sucked my teeth, letting my hands fall against my thigh with a slap. "You sound like an absolute brute right now."

I left out that it was *annoyingly* hot as hell.

"Your ex-husband *bruised* you," he pointed out, slowly and with punctuation like I was ignorant.

"I am aware," I shot back. "I am also aware that you are blatantly ignoring me when I tell you repeatedly that I am *fine*. You think I'm some poor victim stuck in an abusive situation? Why do you think I'm divorced?"

I waited for him to put the pieces together.

"I got out," I said. "But unfortunately, the state doesn't think I have enough proof to keep a well-respected veterinarian from his son. So yes, occasionally, I have to put up with his drunken temper. And yes, sometimes, he gets in a mark. But I am not a victim. I am a survivor, and these stupid bruises on my arm don't mean shit other than that there was a situation and I fucking handled it. So, if you would kindly back out of my personal business, we can get back to finding you a house. Okay?"

The bruises that had Kyle in a tizzy didn't even hurt — not anymore. Marshall had thrown a fit when I started to leave his house after getting Sebastian settled in the car. He was drunk and mad that I wasn't going to stand there and listen to him try to belittle me, which happened to be one of his favorite pastimes.

He'd tried to stop me from going, his hand squeezing tight around my wrist.

I'd pulled free and warned him to keep his hands to himself.

Fortunately, that was the end of it.

It wasn't often his temper got to that level. Usually, he used his financial power and his words to hurt me.

But this time, he'd gone just far enough off the rails to use his hands.

I'd snapped a picture of the bruises when they started to appear and hid it in a secret album on my phone, just in case.

I didn't know how much *proof* the court needed, but if this little incident could help me one day — I was going to make sure to use it.

For a long moment, Kyle and I just stared at each other — me with my chin lifted, not backing down, and Kyle with his chest rapidly rising and falling, his fingers curling into fists and then releasing over and over.

Finally, he let out a long sigh, pinching the bridge of his nose with one hand and holding up the other toward me. "I'm sorry."

"Look at me when you say it."

That made his head snap back like I'd slapped him, and the corner of his mouth curled a bit. It reminded me of when he was a bratty fifteen-year-old, and I was sent to straighten him out.

I was halfway to it.

And then I had to go and fall in love with him.

"I'm sorry," he said again, his blue flame eyes locked on mine this time. "Not for wanting to kill his punk ass," he clarified, holding up one finger. "But for thinking you need anyone, least of all me, to save you."

We were back to staring at each other, and now it was *my* chest rapidly rising and falling.

I cleared my throat. "As I was saying, the next house—"

"Let me help you."

I looked up at the ceiling before letting my hand slap against my thigh. "Didn't we just arrive at the conclusion that I don't need your help?"

"I said you didn't need saving," he said, his voice dropping an octave.

Then, he stepped into me, and all the air in the room split like an atom, leaving us in the tight, unbreathable space between.

"Everyone needs help sometimes, Mads."

I closed my eyes at the nickname, wetting my lips and willing myself not to let my memories get the best of me. My body was already a traitor, chills racing up my arms, my heart fluttering at the way it sounded rolling off his tongue in his new, older, deeper voice.

"How much?"

I blinked my eyes open. "How much what?"

"How much do you need to be free of him?"

And just like that — all the ooey gooeyness was gone.

I scoffed, pushing past him. "Wow."

"I'm serious," he said, and this time, it was him stopping me from storming out. His hand caught the inside of my arm, but it was gentle, enough that it took a half shrug to break free of the grip.

"Absolutely not, Robbins," I seethed. "I am not now, nor have I ever been, a charity case. When this closes,"

I added, motioning to the binder still clutched in my other hand. "I'll have money. And don't you *dare* try to rush it," I threatened, pointing my finger into his chest. "Because I'll light you on fire and dance in the ashes. I am not a weak, helpless thing. I can handle myself. And if you respect me at all, you'll honor this."

He opened his mouth, and I already saw that he was about to argue.

"This isn't up for debate," I said. "We are doing business together. *Fair* business. The only money I will take from you is the commission I rightfully earn after finding you the house you want. Do you understand?"

Those last three words came out the same way they did when I had to get stern with Sebastian — which wasn't often, but enough that I had the severity of them down pat.

Kyle's nose flared, his lips curling into a devilish smile.

Something told me he *liked* that tone I used.

Something told me it sent him down memory lane the way him using my nickname had done for me.

"I understand," he finally said. "But I have a proposal."

I arched a brow.

"Business," he clarified, holding his hands up in surrender before I could even aim.

I looked at my watch, then back at him. "We have thirty minutes until this next showing, which means we need to be on the road in ten. Talk fast."

"Date me."

My jaw might as well have been a mop, for how fast it hit the floor.

"Hear me out," he said before I could tell him to take a hike. "I understand you wanting to take care of yourself. I know better than most people that you can do it, too," he added. "But I haven't seen you in years, Madelyn. Isn't it kind of crazy that we would bump into each other on the opposite side of the country the way we did?"

I waited, not sure where he was going with this, but decided I'd let him finish before I turned him down.

He inched closer, taking up even more oxygen when he did. "I want to protect you — whether you need it or not. And I feel like I was put here to do that. If your ex is going to be in your life, he's going to respect you." He paused. "And Sebastian."

Fuck.

My heart swelled, doubling in size, and no matter how I tried to tamp it down, it bucked against my resistance.

"Besides," he added, stepping back a bit, which allowed me to take my first deep breath. "Everyone and their fucking mom on my former team is getting married, and like I told you at dinner, my teammates are like my family. I'm so fucking tired of going to these things stag."

The admission was meant to sound grumpy. I knew because I saw it so many times when we were growing up.

But it landed flat.

It landed like he was hurt, like he was lonely.

Just like he had been back then.

"My proposal is that, from here on out, until we close on a house — you're my girlfriend to everyone who isn't you and me. No one else knows the truth but us."

It was *me* who opened my mouth this time, but he held up a finger to stop me.

"I get to do my part in keeping your..." He swallowed, jaw tense, and then chose his words carefully. "*Ex* in line. I get to keep you and Sebastian out of harm's way. And you pretend to be my girlfriend so my friends will lay off the jokes and take me seriously for once."

He stopped talking for a moment, and I shocked even myself when I didn't immediately say *thanks, but no thanks.*

He stepped into my space again, and this time, he reached out and gently wrapped his fingers around my wrist, as if he wanted to erase the bruises with just that touch.

I closed my eyes against the sparks that ignited every cell in my body.

"Madelyn," he pleaded, and he waited until I looked at him to continue. "This is a deal that works for both of us, and you know it. Tell me you wouldn't sleep better at night knowing that a six-foot-seven, two-hundred-and-thirty pounds and counting professional athlete has your back."

My heart pounded harder, faster, the sound echoing in my ears.

Was I actually considering this?

"Besides — this would guarantee that I wouldn't rush buying a house. I wouldn't be in a hurry to get you your commission if I knew I could watch over you in the meantime."

"I don't need—"

"I know you don't need me," he said, cutting me off. His eyes flashed with something achingly familiar when he added, "But I need you."

I swallowed past the wad of sandpaper in my throat, searching his gaze as I tried to find something, anything, to say to that.

"Come on, Mads," he said after a while, one corner of his mouth ticking up mischievously. "What do you say? Do we have a deal?"

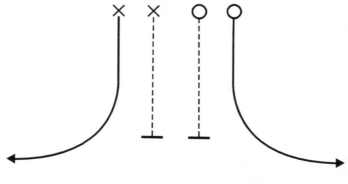

CHAPTER 10

Kyle

It was a dumb fucking idea.

I knew it, and had I stopped long enough to consider what I was proposing before I actually opened my mouth, I likely would have shoved the idea down and never spoken it out loud.

As it was, seeing those bruises on Madelyn's arm had my brain short circuiting.

I didn't care about being logical.

I only cared about making sure she was okay.

The truth of that made me frown a little as I waited for her to respond, because the first time I'd seen her after all those years, I'd wanted to hurt her. I'd wanted her to feel the pain she'd put me through.

Now, I was trying to keep her from pain.

I was a walking contradiction.

"Well?" I probed again when she didn't answer, the word echoing in the empty foyer where we stood.

Madelyn's soft brown eyes flicked between mine, and then she blew out a breath, shaking her head and looking up to the ceiling.

"I can't believe I'm saying this, but... fine."

Inside, I threw a fist into the air in victory.

On the outside, I simply smirked.

"But I have conditions," she added with a finger pointed straight at my chest. She was using that thing like a damn weapon today.

"Name them."

"No fighting with Marshall."

Marshall.

So that was the fucker's name.

Madelyn must have seen how tense my jaw was because she arched a threatening brow. "I mean it. If you go fighting him, it's going to cause more issues for me. So, be the six-foot-seven bodyguard all you want, but do not goad him, do not call him names, and do not lay a finger on him."

"I won't," I promise. "Unless he lays a finger on *you*."

Madelyn's brows tugged inward, just a little, as if she didn't understand why I would care if he did. But she listed her next condition before I could think too much on that reaction.

"No one lays a finger on me. You included."

It was my turn to cock a brow.

"We can... *pretend* all you want," she said with a wave of her hand. "But let's not forget the reality. We aren't even friends, let alone anything more. Don't go holding my hand or touching my back or trying to sneak in a kiss."

The way she listed out those demands made it so hard not to laugh. Her little cheeks were growing redder by the minute, the blush creeping down her neck, too. She could barely look me in the eye when she said *kiss*.

"Madelyn," I said, leveling her with a gaze that I hoped told her she was being ridiculous. I took a tentative step toward her. "Come on. We're adults, and we *used* to be friends. I think we can handle some fake kissing."

"Absolutely not."

"No one is going to believe we're actually together if you won't let me touch you, least of all your ex."

She chewed on that, then swallowed and crossed her arms over the binder she still had, crushing it to her chest like a textbook.

It made me flash back to when I was a sophomore and she was a senior, when I saw her walking the halls and had the irresistible urge to hold her hand, to claim her for everyone to see.

"Fine," she gritted out. "But *minimal*, you understand? No tongue."

"No tongue," I conceded with a wry grin. "My turn to list a condition."

"You don't get conditions. This was your idea, remember?"

"Exactly — which means I get to make some rules, too. And my number one rule?" I cracked my neck. "I don't want you around Marshall without me there."

She blinked at me. "You don't want me around *the father of my child* who I co-parent with."

It was a deadpan statement, not a question.

"Nope."

"He's Sebastian's *dad*."

"I don't give a fuck," I shot back without hesitation. "Did you hear what I said? Unless I am with you, you're not to be around him."

Distantly, I was aware I was overstepping. Madelyn had survived this long without me here to do shit about it. She could handle herself.

But that didn't stop me from wanting to help her now that I was here.

I watched her digest what I'd said. At first, she looked appalled, like she was about to slap me hard across the face and walk out of this house.

But then, she softened, her chest rising on a deep inhale before she slowly let it go. And that's when I saw it.

Relief.

It was *relief* in her eyes.

She may have been strong enough to take care of herself *and* her son, but that didn't mean she didn't like the idea of someone else wanting to protect them, too.

"First of all, do not get the impression that you *ever* get to tell me what to do," she said sternly. "Second of all... okay," she conceded softly. "But I don't know how that's going to work out. We trade off at least once a week, sometimes twice."

"Any time you need me, I'll be there."

"What about football?"

"We have a while until camp. Right now, it's technically off-season. So, like I said," I repeated, inching toward her with my eyes locked on hers. "Call me, and I'll be there."

Madelyn held my gaze for a long pause before she tore her eyes away and nodded.

Her face fell a little then, and she shook her head, eyes falling to her feet. "This means you have to meet Sebastian."

I couldn't explain why, but my heart both broke and swelled at the sound of those words. I could tell Madelyn was scared. But I also could feel my own excitement.

I wanted to meet her son.

I wanted to know the child she had made.

"I can't break his heart, Kyle," she said, her wet eyes finding mine. "I can't."

Shit.

I nodded, scrubbing a hand over my face. "Listen, what if we agree to be friends when this is all said and done?"

She tilted her head at me.

"We can just tell Sebastian we're old friends, that we went to high school together. That's technically not a lie," I reminded her. "That wouldn't raise any red flags. In fact, Marshall would probably prefer that, right? For Sebastian to just think we're friends?"

Madelyn sighed. "He'd lose his shit if I said anything else."

"Exactly. So, to Sebastian, we're friends. And when you're safe and away from your prick ex-husband, then... we just *stay* friends. Sebastian won't know the difference."

"Except as soon as I get your commission, I'm moving across the country."

Those words slammed into my chest like a WWE wrestler with a metal folding chair in tow, but on the outside, I acted like they didn't faze me at all.

"Good," I said. "Get a guest room for when I visit."

She huffed out a laugh at that, shaking her head and furrowing her brows as she studied me. "Why are you doing this?"

"I told you, I'm tired of going stag to every wedding I'm invited to. My former teammates give me too much shit, and I want to shut them up."

"I've seen the girls you post online," she shot back. "You could take one of them."

"Trust me. My friends would see right through it. If anything, they'd give me even *more* shit if I brought a girl they thought was just the flavor of the week. But with this, with us... we could make them believe it's real."

She flattened her lips like she still didn't believe me.

But I couldn't say more than that.

I wasn't ready to admit to her that, regardless of what she'd put me through, I'd always have love for her. I'd always want to make sure she was safe.

I didn't much care what *I* got out of this deal.

I only cared that she would be okay — and I'd be there to ensure that.

"When is this wedding I'm supposed to go to with you, anyway?"

I cringed a bit. "Next weekend."

"Next *weekend*? And where is this wedding, exactly?"

Another cringe. "Colorado."

She laughed. "You're joking, right? I can't just *leave the state* next weekend."

"Why?"

Madelyn stuttered for a moment before groaning. "I don't know. Marshall is kind of incompetent. Even when he takes Sebastian for the weekend, I like to know I'm right down the street."

"Let's bring him with us."

"Yeah, okay. Because Marshall would be okay with that." She shook her head, but I saw her wheels spinning. "My mom has been begging to see her grandbaby. Maybe I could get her to fly in."

My heart squeezed at the mention of her mother.

I had such mixed feelings when it came to her. I loved her, loved the girl she'd raised, loved the generosity she'd shown me as a shithead kid.

But I also remembered the way she'd turned her back on my parents when they needed a friend.

When they needed forgiveness.

"I'll pay for her to fly in, if she's willing," I offered.

Madelyn glared at me, then cursed. "I don't have anything to wear to a wedding, Kyle. I *definitely* don't have a nice enough dress to attend a professional football player's wedding."

"Trust me — my friends aren't like that. You could show up in a trash bag and they'd love you for it."

"You calling me trash, Robbins?"

"If you're trash, then I'm a dumpster diver."

She paused, frowned, and then laughed so hard she bent at the waist.

I made a face and looked up to the sky, embarrassment heating my neck. I couldn't even try to come back from that. It was a stupid and awkward comment, but it was also the kind of jokes we'd say to each other as kids.

We were weird together.

That was what I loved most about us.

"You're really serious about this," she mused.

I swallowed, nodding. "I am. In fact," I said, fishing my wallet from my pocket. I plucked one of the many credit cards out, the American Express that earned me flight miles. "Here."

She eyed the card between my fingers and then cocked a brow at me.

"Go get a dress. Get shoes, too. Get a bag, get your hair done, whatever you want."

Madelyn tongued her cheek. "I'm not taking your fucking credit card."

"Fine, then let me take you shopping."

Again, she let out an incredulous laugh that told me she thought I was acting insane.

And maybe I was.

If anyone in this world could make me crazy, it was this girl.

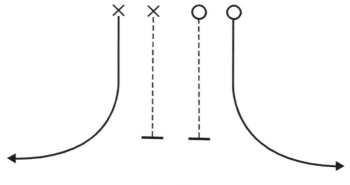

CHAPTER 11

Madelyn

I couldn't believe I'd agreed to this.

Two days after the house showing, a stylish white woman in her late thirties with platinum blonde hair and breasts the size of balloons was guiding me around an almost-empty boutique, plucking dress after dress from each rack we passed. Her name was Larissa, and when she picked a dress, she'd hold it up against my neckline and tug the fabric over to one hip, tilting her head from side to side, and then either put the dress back on the rack...

Or hand it to Kyle.

Kyle, who seemed all too happy to follow behind, his muscular arms serving as a shopping cart.

For the most part, I ignored him — focusing on Larissa's questions as well as forcing each new breath into my lungs. And while I couldn't believe I'd agreed to this little shopping trip, it was the other deal I'd made with the devil that was haunting me.

In that vacant mansion on the water, I guess it had made sense. I'd been standing too close to Kyle. His cologne must have made me dizzy. That was the only explanation for why I would have ever agreed to pretend like we were dating.

I didn't owe him a damned thing. After what he did to me, leaving me behind when he *knew* I was pregnant with his baby, the only thing he deserved from me was a swift kick to the balls.

But when he'd seen the bruises on my arms, he'd lost his mind.

A chill swept over me even now as I remembered the way he'd carefully held me, his eyes shielded under furrowed brows as they assessed me for damage. And then, his jaw had tightened, his resolve set.

He wanted to protect me.

And while I'd been quick to point out that I could take care of my damn self, thank you very much, I couldn't deny that seeing that protectiveness wash over him had done something to me.

I liked the thought of someone having my back.

I *loved* the thought of seeing Marshall squirm when he realized he couldn't touch me — not with a beastly NFL tight end watching his every move.

Still, there was no way I was signing onto any deal with Kyle.

At least, that's what I thought — until he twisted the game to work in his favor. I knew if I didn't agree to this, he'd buy the first house I showed him just to make sure I was taken care of.

That infuriated me as much as it made my heart melt like a Creamsicle on a summer day.

I let out an audible groan as my thoughts warred with themselves in that little boutique. I hadn't felt this confused and ruled by unpredictable emotions since I was pregnant.

"Everything okay there?" Kyle asked from behind me.

"There's not even a single thing that's okay about this."

He chuckled. "Oh, come on. Have a little fun. You've got a personal stylist, a credit card without a limit, and a hunky football player carrying your shit. It could be worse."

"You and I have very different definitions of what constitutes as *fun*."

"Okay, I think we have plenty here to get started," Larissa said before Kyle could respond, and she spun on me with a dazzling smile. "Let's get you a fitting room."

"Let's," Kyle said behind me, and I didn't have to turn around to know the bastard was beaming at my discomfort.

I subtly flipped him the bird behind my back as I smiled at Larissa, who turned on one heel and led me toward the back of the boutique.

The dressing rooms were more like the closets of the houses I'd been showing Kyle throughout the week. Each one was brightly lit, with multiple full-length mirrors that let you view every angle of yourself — including ones you never wished to see. There was an elegant chaise lounge, a table with a bottle of champagne on ice and two flutes, and two large leather chairs.

There were also countless accessories everywhere I looked — high heels of every shape, color, and height propped around the room, purses and clutches hanging from hooks, jewelry daintily displayed on well-lit tables with a black velvet backdrop. I was thinking to myself there was no *way* Larissa would have been able to sneak in here to do all this when a young man frantically swept in with another pair of heels, setting them carefully by a mirror before he smiled at me and darted out again.

I was still looking around the room wide-eyed when Larissa began to take dresses from Kyle's arms, hanging them one by one around the massive room. I let myself walk to the nearest one she'd placed, a rich brown, floor-length number that felt as bohemian as it did elegant. I ran my fingers over the buttery soft fabric, subtly fishing for a price tag.

There wasn't one.

Which told me that the kind of people who shopped here didn't ever need to think twice about the price of something before purchasing.

When Kyle's arms were empty, he plopped down in one of the oversized leather chairs, crossing an ankle over the opposite knee.

And I didn't care that he looked like the sports god he was in that moment. I didn't care that his chestnut hair was perfectly mussed, his eyes taking on a sea-green hue in this light. I especially didn't care that even in navy blue joggers and a heather gray t-shirt, his jacket slung over the arm of the chair he was in now, he looked as rich as the fabric in my fingers felt.

He was highly mistaken if he thought he was staying in this room while I tried on dresses.

I arched a brow at him that told him as much, and the brat arched one right back at me as Larissa popped the bottle of champagne and poured two glasses — handing one to him and offering me the other.

"I'll let you two get settled," she said. "I'll be right outside, and when you're ready in the first dress, just pop the door open and I'll come in to help accessorize. Please let me know if you'd like the temperature adjusted at all, and of course, if you get hungry or would like anything other than champagne, we're at your disposal."

I was still glaring at Kyle, subtly shaking my head as he cockily sipped his champagne. I managed a thank you and a smile aimed at Larissa, who really was an absolute angel, before I was folding my arms and leaning my weight on one hip.

"Alright," Kyle said once Larissa had left us, and when she closed the door behind her, the massive dressing room suddenly felt like a tight closet. He rubbed his hands together. "Which one first?"

"That's for me to know and you to find out at the same time Larissa does," I said, pointing a finger at the door. "Out."

"Oh, come on," he goaded, spreading his hands out wide. One still held on to a half-full glass of champagne. "There's plenty of space in here."

"Out, Robbins."

"I'll be good, I promise," he added, clutching the champagne flute under his chin in a prayer motion. "I'll close my eyes and everything."

I tapped one foot, folding my arms and giving him one slow blink that I hoped would get my point across.

His smile knocked my next breath loose in a rattle, the way it spread so wide and effortless across his too-stupidly-handsome face. He sighed, standing, and then tilted the flute toward me. "Fine. But it's your loss. I'm great with zippers. Bra clasps, too."

He winked, and I rolled my eyes hard enough to make my lids flutter. "Get out before I call this whole thing off."

His hands went up in surrender at that, and once he was outside the dressing room, I let out a puff of a laugh, shaking my head.

He was just as infuriating as he had been as a bratty kid.

I couldn't help but think about that time in my life as I undressed and pulled the first dress from its hanger, the brown one I'd been admiring. It felt like a mixture of silk and the highest thread count of Egyptian cotton as I slipped into it, and all the while, I thought about that summer nine years ago.

I'd been excited about the job, one my mom had told me about after talking to Kyle's mom. They were good friends back then, ran in the same circle, and when Mom told me what they were paying for babysitting their son, I had jumped at the chance.

I was saving for college, just like my older brother had to do. Our parents took great care of us, but they didn't have the kind of money to pay for tuition for two kids.

Of course, I had been a bit surprised when Mom originally told me about it all. I'd laughed, actually. I knew Kyle. We went to school together. Sure, he was younger than I was, but I knew him. Add on the fact that our parents were friends, there'd been more than a couple parties where we'd been at the same place at the same time.

Because of that, I knew he was fifteen. He wasn't a baby.

Although, he sure acted like one that first day I showed up at his house.

I could still remember his scowl, could recall exactly how much of a brat he'd acted like until I proved to him that I wasn't deterred. The more he acted like a child, the more I treated him like one. And somewhere along the way, he went from trying to get me to quit, to trying to get under my skin for another reason.

He had a crush on me. It was easy to see it.

What wasn't easy was admitting that I had a crush on him, too.

It was embarrassing. His pestering turned into flirting, and I'd go home every night groaning and trying to slap some sense into myself. I was going into my senior year. He was a *sophomore*. His stupid jokes shouldn't have made me laugh. His messy hair and goofy, lopsided grin shouldn't have made my stomach tie into knots.

But they did.

When the school year started back up, I wasn't his babysitter anymore. We were just two kids at school. He turned sixteen, kept growing even taller than he already was, and filled out that lanky body with muscles that made my teenage-brain short circuit.

The more that year went on, the more the joking between us drifted into something more.

At first, it was just hanging out after school. Sometimes, he'd walk me home after he got done with football practice and I finished up with yearbook. Sometimes, he'd text or call me when my parents thought I was asleep.

And sometimes, he'd show up at my window, a new mark on his body and a somber, haunting look in his eyes.

I never asked questions, not on nights like that. I'd just open my window and let him inside, tossing a pillow and blanket onto my floor without a word.

Fall turned to winter, and Kyle turned into my best friend.

Then, on a cold winter night when we were just two kids getting into trouble and sneaking into an empty house, he turned into something more.

I blinked, holding my eyes shut and shaking my head to clear the memory. Hastily, I pulled on the dress, not so much as giving myself a once-over in the mirror before I ripped the dressing room door open. I was desperate to get out of my head and focus on the task at hand.

Larissa buzzed over to me the moment the door was open, clapping her hands together and fussing over how beautiful I looked. She immediately ran in to grab shoes, and my eyes drifted to Kyle.

Just in time to watch his Adam's apple bob hard in his throat.

His eyes washed over me, slowly, trailing a heated blaze from where Larissa was carefully strapping my ankles into a glittering pair of heels up to where the fabric gaped between my breasts. It showed a healthy amount of my chest, my collarbone framed with the delicate straps, and I saw Kyle's gaze snatch there before his eyes flicked up to meet mine.

"Do we need to get you a bib?" I tried to joke, though my voice was softer than I would have preferred. "You're drooling a bit there."

But Kyle didn't joke back.

It was like looking at me in this dress, he was shocked silent.

And that made my throat dry up like the Sahara Desert.

"Isn't she *stunning*?" Larissa probed, continuing to accessorize me.

I watched her drape a long, delicate chain around my neck, the gold bar at the end of it settling in the gap of the dress at my chest. When my eyes found Kyle again, he was subtly shaking his head, his eyes drinking me in again.

"Always has been," he said, his voice almost too low for me to hear.

He looked at me, and I tore my gaze away, turning to face the mirror, instead.

We all agreed the brown dress was an option, but there was no way Larissa was letting me get out of this hellish ordeal that easy. She wanted to see me in *all* the dresses she'd plucked off the racks, and I had no choice but to oblige.

In the end, it came down to three: the brown one I'd first tried on, a form-hugging black number, and a frosty blue one that draped like starlight down to the ground and had a slit so high it made my cheeks flush the first time I stepped out in it.

But it also made me feel beautiful.

I put them all on again, modeling them one at a time with full accessories for Larissa and Kyle. When I walked out in the blue one for the second time after the first two were seen again, Larissa's eyes glistened and she clasped her hands under her chin.

"Oh, Madelyn," she said.

Kyle stood, hastily smoothing a hand over his stomach like he was wearing a suit and not a t-shirt. He was quiet as his eyes washed over me, his hands finding his pockets like he didn't know what else to do with them.

Like if he didn't tuck them away, he might reach for me, instead.

I felt the heat from his gaze like a roaring bonfire, and by the time his eyes reconnected with mine, my neck was flushed a bright pink.

He swallowed, shaking his head. "God*damn*, Mads."

Larissa's eyes bulged, her head snapping toward him like she couldn't believe that was his response. She'd expected him to call me beautiful, maybe. Or gorgeous.

But his response was so him that I couldn't help but laugh, covering my face with my hands.

When I peeked through them, I saw him grinning.

I tried not to overanalyze the way my heart was fluttering when I disappeared inside the dressing room again, ready to get the hell out of this dress *and* this store. But when I went to unzip the back, the zipper wouldn't budge.

I cursed, fussing with it until I realized I'd lodged it in part of the delicate blue fabric.

That made me curse again, and I maneuvered so I could watch myself in the mirror as I tried to undo my mistake. When my shoulders started aching from the awkward angle, I sighed, deciding my pride wasn't worth tearing a dress that was likely more expensive than my mortgage.

I opened the dressing room door just a crack, peeking out, and Kyle's gaze snapped from his phone up to me.

"Where's Larissa?"

"She ran up to the front to help another customer," he explained. "I told her we'd bring all this to the counter." He frowned when I muttered an expletive under my breath. "What's wrong?"

"Zipper's stuck."

At that, Kyle beamed, standing and tucking his phone away before spreading his arms wide like he was God's gift to the world. "My specialty."

I glared at him. "I'll wait."

"Come on," he said on a hearty chuckle. "I've got you."

When I didn't respond, he walked closer, lowering his voice.

"You really want to stay stuck in that dress for who knows how long to wait for her to come check on us? I'm right here," he reminded me, as if forgetting that fact was possible with him towering over me and smelling like a mixture of teak, turf, and the woods after a rainstorm. "Let me help."

I bit my lip, craning my neck out a little farther to search for Larissa. When I didn't see her, I looked back up at Kyle, who arched a brow.

I groaned. "Fine."

I didn't watch his victorious smile for longer than a second before I opened the door wider and let him step inside. I'd intended to keep that door open, but when I turned and Kyle walked up behind me, the door closed of its own accord, no doorstop propping the weighted thing open.

It shut with the quiet click of the lock, but it might as well have been a gun blast for how my ears rang.

"I'm glad you picked this one," Kyle said, his voice drowned out by how my heart was beating in my ears.

He reached for the zipper, one hand holding the fabric taut as the other maneuvered the contraption. "The blue is…"

He didn't finish that sentence, just shook his head, and I watched him in the plethora of mirrors all around us. His eyes were fixed on where his hands worked, and my *attention* was fixed on where I felt the slightest brush of his skin against the back of my neck.

Every second dragged with him so close behind me, my body buzzing and all too aware of the subtle heat rolling off him. When he finally got the fabric free, the zipper lurched down an inch, and I sucked in a breath that made us both freeze in place.

Kyle's eyes snapped to mine in the mirror, and then that gaze dropped to where my chest was struggling to take a deep breath.

He wet his lips, swallowing once before he slowly started sliding the zipper down.

His knuckles brushed against my spine as he did, and my eyelids fluttered shut at the touch.

Neither of us said a word, the only sound being the soft *snick* of the zipper as Kyle carefully guided it all the way down to the small of my back.

My chest was on fire with how hard it was to breathe, and then I felt the warmth of Kyle's breath against my ear.

"Maybe we should practice."

I swallowed, trying to wet my mouth so I wouldn't cough from the desert dryness when I attempted a response. "Practice what?"

I opened my eyes, finding Kyle staring right back at me with just a slight tilt of his lips.

"Flirting," he said, and his knuckles found my spine again, this time running *up* the length he'd just traced down.

I shivered, feeling every centimeter of that touch until he found one of my straps and carefully, slowly, slid it off my shoulder.

"Touching," he said softer, and my heart stopped when he bent and lowered his lips to the sensitive spot just behind the shell of my ear. "Kissing."

My next breath shuttered out of me, and I ripped away from his grasp, folding my arms hard over my chest to keep the dress in place.

"Ha-ha, so funny," I deadpanned, hoping I came off as agitated or annoyed rather than the shaking mess of nerves he'd turned me into. "Next, you'll say we need to practice horizontal dancing."

Kyle quirked a smile. "That wasn't on my list, but I'd be happy to add it."

I rolled my eyes, thankful for the distance that was allowing me to find at least *some* semblance of my dignity again. "Okay, Casanova. Thanks for your help. Now, get out."

He laughed a little, sliding his hands in his pockets as he backed up on a shrug. "I'm serious, you know."

"I'm sure you are."

"Better for us to get comfortable when no one is around. Wouldn't want my friends to see that pretty blush on your cheeks the first time I kiss you in front of them."

My eyes widened, my cool fingertips floating up to touch my cheeks that were as hot as an oven.

That made me scowl, and I resorted to shoving Kyle the rest of the way out of the room while he laughed.

When I was alone again, I pressed my back against the door, one hand flying up to my forehead as I closed my eyes and internally groaned.

What have I gotten myself into?

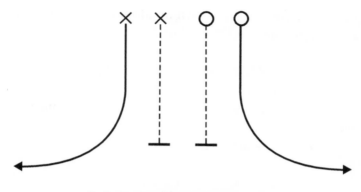

CHAPTER 12

Kyle

The next day, I sat in my car with a bag full of rocks in my lap, but they might as well have been in my stomach.

I was about to meet Sebastian for the first time.

When Madelyn and I had made this plan, I'd peppered her with questions about her son. I wanted to know everything — what he liked, what he *didn't* like, anything I could find out to get to know him a little before we actually met.

For reasons I couldn't articulate, it mattered to me that his first impression of me was a good one.

It mattered to me that Madelyn was trusting me to meet him. Period.

It'd been surreal, to listen to her talk about her son, to know she was a mom at all. I'd watched her so closely as she detailed everything about him, the way she lit up with pride, how her smile seemed genuine for the first time since the day I'd shown up at that house and ran straight into my blast from the past.

Today was a big deal. It meant a lot to her, to *me*.

And as if all that wasn't already enough to make my gut heavy with a mixture of emotions, I'd pulled into the park and immediately received a phone call from my agent.

About me being seen with Madelyn.

"There are no pictures, though?" I confirmed again, my heart thundering in my ears at the thought of having to tell Madelyn about this.

"No pictures," Giana echoed. I could hear her typing away in the background. "I mean, there was one, but it was blurry and far away, and the only part of the woman they could see was one leg. Not really the kind of gold the press will pay for."

I let my head fall back against the headrest. "Thank fuck."

I'd been lucky with the media so far, most of it dying down soon after the draft. There was team press, of course, but that was on our terms. For now, I was just a rookie tight end. I wasn't hot enough to be in any kind of spotlight.

But apparently, I wasn't free of the claws of the press on a slow news day.

There was a pause on the other end. "Okay... clearly, this girl isn't a one-night stand. If she were, you wouldn't be so concerned."

"She's not," I said with a swallow, lifting my head again to search the park for her. We'd decided to meet in a neutral place for my first time being around Sebastian. She'd be here any minute now.

The week had passed in the strangest blur.

From the moment she crashed back into my life, I couldn't escape my thoughts of Madelyn. Add in the fact that I'd seen her almost every morning to look at houses, and that I'd had to endure the sweet torture of watching her try on evening gowns, and you could say I was going a bit mad.

Part of me wanted to hold onto the anger I had for her for so many years.

The bigger part of me couldn't even remember why I'd been so mad.

I'd blacked out that chapter of my life long ago, but I never forgot how Madelyn had been acting weird toward me even before my parents' party, before the incident... and I'd been upset with her for not talking to me, for not coming to that party when I really needed her to.

Then, my father had crossed a line in his drunken, asshole state of being, and Madelyn had sided with her parents, writing me off before I even had a chance to talk to her.

I'd been so pissed back then.

But now that I was older, I could understand.

Madelyn was a family girl. She always had been.

"Okay..." Giana prompted. "Is that all I get?"

"For now? Yes."

She huffed. "If it's someone you want help in protecting, I can't do that if you leave me in the dark."

"You'll meet her at the wedding."

"Ah, so that's why Clay added a plus one for you," she mused. "You know, that was a pain in the ass to do. We already gave final numbers to the caterer."

"Hey, you're the one throwing a wedding in two weeks. Don't blame me for your mistakes."

"That's fair," she conceded. "Okay, fine, so I'll meet her then. For now, my recommendation is a security team with decoys ready to confuse any greedy paparazzi that might want to stick on you. Especially for the airport when you and Braden head this way with your mystery guest."

I groaned, scrubbing a hand over my five o'clock shadow. "I hate this."

"Welcome to the NFL. It's not just your social media that gets to tell the story anymore. Any bastard with a camera gets to weigh in, too."

I nodded. "Thank you, G."

"You know how you can thank me?"

"I'm not telling you who she is."

"Ugh!" She pouted. "Fine, but can you give me something? Tell me how you know her, or what level of serious it is. Oh, tell me your tropes!"

I blinked. "I am not going to even pretend to know what that means."

"Okay, so, in romance books, a trope is—"

"Gotta go, G. See you next weekend," I said, cutting her off when I noticed Madelyn across the park. Giana whined a bit when I ended the call, which made me smirk.

That girl and her damn smutty books.

She was going to have a field day with Madelyn. I needed to prepare my fake date for that.

But right now, I wasn't thinking about the wedding.

Right now, I was too focused on where Madelyn was smiling and walking toward the swings we'd agreed to meet at, hand in hand with a little boy who looked just like her.

For a moment, I let myself sit in the privacy of my car and watch them. Madelyn released Sebastian's hand, letting him run full speed toward the slide while she hovered close to the swings. She folded her arms over her chest and looked around.

She seemed as nervous as I was.

My gaze floated to Sebastian, to the way his smile lit up his entire face as he zoomed down the bright yellow tube slide. He tumbled into the wood chips at the bottom, and then popped up on a laugh, running right back up the stairs to go again.

He looked so much like her, it was like an ice pick to my chest.

Even from this distance, I could see how the shape of his nose mirrored hers, how his hair had the same coppery tone to it — though his was a bit browner. And I knew once I got closer, I'd see more and more evidence of their relation.

She was a mom.

I couldn't explain why that made my next swallow harder to take, or why my chest fired up with the need to protect them both. But I didn't overanalyze it before kicking my door open and climbing out of my Aston Martin.

Madelyn noticed me when I was twenty or so yards away. She didn't smile, but she did offer a slight wave of her hand in greeting. It was a warm summer day in Seattle, the kind the locals wait all year for. It was just after noon now, seventy-eight degrees with not a single cloud in the sky.

Because of that, I had the fortune of seeing Madelyn in a pair of shorts and a tank top.

They weren't the same as what she used to wear. No, those had been ripped-up jean shorts and tank tops so small they might as well have been bras. Now, she wore a more conservative outfit, the shorts cutting her off mid-thigh and the tank top a bit baggy on her.

She still looked as hot as ever, though.

"Hey there, friend," I greeted when I found her. And just because I loved the particular shade of pink her cheeks turned when I flustered her, I reached one hand for her hip and lowered my lips to her cheek.

"Let me guess — practice?" she mused when I pulled back, tucking her hair behind one ear. That blush I was aiming for bloomed beautifully on her face.

"Indeed, and you did great. Look," I said, thumbing the pinkness on her skin. "Barely a blush. A plus."

Madelyn rolled her eyes, and then she frowned a little, her gaze on Sebastian.

"You ready?" I asked her.

She let out a long breath, and then turned to face me head on, her shoulders square. "To him, we are friends. Now, and after all this is done. Okay? This is serious, Kyle."

"I know."

"I mean it," she echoed.

"I know, Mads."

She paused, swallowing. "No matter what happens, we cannot hurt him. This is a big commitment and I understand if it's too much to make. You can call this whole thing off. But you can't meet him and then... and then..."

I stepped into her, careful not to push too close. I knew she was in a nervous state, and I only wanted to calm her — not agitate her more.

"I'm in this," I said with absolution. "It was my idea, remember? If anyone is wanting out, it's you. And considering the fact that you don't want me to just say yes to the next house you show me — which I'd make sure was out of my budget just to up your commission — my guess is you're not backing out, either."

"You're a real jerk for doing that, you know."

"Well, I need a date to this wedding."

"More like you need to insert yourself into a situation you should just leave alone."

"Shut up and let me take care of you."

Madelyn sighed, but the way her eyes held mine, the way the corner of her mouth lifted just slightly, I wondered if deep down, she liked the sound of that.

I wondered if as much as she fought me on it, she wanted someone to take care of her — even if just in this small way.

Sebastian came running toward us with his hands waving crazily over his head. He skidded to a stop at my feet, and Madelyn bent to his level, ruffling his hair.

"Did you see that?!" he asked, a bit breathless. "I went down the slide on my stomach!"

"I did see that," she echoed, plucking wood chips out of his hair now. "And you set a new record for how fast you could dirty a new shirt."

He looked down at the shirt in reference, one that said, "I'm a Book Dragon, Not A Worm." It had a dragon blowing fire and sitting on top of a stack of books like it was golden treasure.

He was beaming when he looked back up at his mom. "Two for one!"

I chuckled a bit, especially at how Madelyn nodded like she had taught him what that phrase meant and now regretted it a little bit. When that little laugh left me, it drew Sebastian's attention to where I stood.

Just like I'd predicted, I saw their similarities even more now that I was standing a foot away from him. His eyes were hazel, green and brown battling for dominance, but they were the same shape as Madelyn's. There was something about his smile that mirrored hers, too.

My chest ached the longer I looked at him, and when I glanced at Madelyn, she offered me a small, understanding smile.

"Sebastian, this is my friend, Kyle."

I didn't know what I expected, but it wasn't for the kid's eyes to go as wide as baseballs, nor would I have put "crush my legs in a fierce hug" on my bingo card. But that was exactly what he did. And when he pulled back, he jumped up and down excitedly.

"Mommy never has friends!"

Madelyn and I were silent for a beat, and then a loud laugh burst out of her, and she covered her red face with both hands before shaking her head and looking up at me.

I grinned, arching a brow at her before I bent to one knee so I could be on her son's level.

"Well, good thing I moved to Seattle, then, huh?"

He nodded excitedly.

"It's nice to meet you, buddy," I said. Then, I offered him the black velvet bag in my hand. "I heard you like rocks."

His eyes shot wide again, and then he took the bag and ripped at the strings tying it closed.

"Wow!" He gasped, showing it to his mom next. "Look! Calcite, topaz, obsidian..."

It was my turn to have my eyes grow twice their size, because the fact that he knew those words and could pronounce them nearly perfectly shocked the shit out of me.

He shook his little head, looking back at me next. "Thank you."

"Of course. There's a magnifying glass in there, too. And some seashell fossils."

"Whoa!" He dragged the word out, digging in the bag. "Do you wanna come to our house and look at them with me?"

I peeked up at Madelyn, who smiled and petted her son's hair again. "Maybe another time. For now, why don't you hand those to me and I'll hold them while you play."

"Okay," Sebastian said. I didn't know why, but that shocked me, too. He didn't whine, didn't throw a fit. He trusted Madelyn, trusted that when she said later, that meant it would happen. And for now, he was content to do what she asked. "Can Kyle play, too?"

"You'll have to ask him," she answered.

I stood, dusting off my hands. "Oh, I don't know..." Then, I gave him a grin. "Last one to the merry-go-round has to push!"

I took off on a slow jog, and Sebastian froze before all but throwing the bag of rocks at Madelyn and sprinting after me. I made him work until we were almost there, then I pulled back a little, letting him beat me. He flew onto the merry-go-round and jumped up and down in victory before holding onto the safety bars as I grabbed the outside edge and gave it an easy spin.

"Faster, faster!" he called.

And then he laughed, and my stomach hollowed out again.

His laugh reminded me so much of the way Madelyn used to laugh, it was like going back in time.

Almost an hour passed like that, me chasing Sebastian all around the park while he made up games for us to play at each and every piece of equipment on the playground. Our only breaks were to run over to Madelyn long enough for him to have a snack or a drink of water, and then we were off again.

Madelyn watched from a blanket she'd laid out under a tree, something between joy and terror marking her face.

Eventually, Sebastian begged his mom to play with his rocks, and she let him take them over to a sand pit and pretend to dig for them. I sank down next to her on the blanket with a grunt.

"Tired already?" she teased. "Maybe he's all you need to get your stamina up for the season."

I shook my head. "I wish I remembered what it was like, to have endless energy like that."

She smiled. "He's a good kid."

"He is," I agreed. "And you're a good mom."

Madelyn's smile softened a bit at that, her eyes flicking between mine before she looked down at where her feet were at the edge of the blanket.

"He looks like you," I added. "Laughs like you, too."

"Poor kid," she joked, shaking her head. "That laugh got me made fun of a lot in middle school."

"Well, by high school, I assure you — there was nothing to make fun of."

She cocked a brow, and I shrugged.

"It was one of my favorite sounds. I loved how you'd

hold it back until you had no choice but to let it free, like you'd try to be annoyed by me but then I'd somehow win."

Madelyn rolled her eyes. "I was mostly laughing *at* you, not because you said something funny."

"Didn't matter, not when I got what I wanted. That laugh... all smoky and sexy without you even trying."

"Oh, my God, Kyle," she said, covering her face with her hands. "Stop. You're so stupid."

"I'm serious. Used to be my goal, to get that laugh out of you at least once a day." I paused, waiting until she uncovered her face. "Think I might need to bring that goal back front and center, actually. Think I might like to hear you laugh more now."

Her eyes sparkled a bit when they met mine, a thousand questions dancing in her curious gaze.

But when her attention snapped somewhere behind me, she froze.

All the playfulness left her in an instant.

"Shit," she whispered.

I turned to look over my shoulder, wondering what the problem was since Sebastian was playing in the opposite direction where we could see him and he was fine.

But when I cranked my neck, I saw a red-faced man storming toward us.

And there was no mistaking who it was.

He was older than Madelyn, that was easy to see from the get go. His medium-length brown hair had that whole salt and pepper thing going on at the edges, his eyes crinkled with crow's feet, his freshly shaved jawline a bit soft. One look at his gait told me he held himself in high esteem. He walked the way only an overly confident man could.

I could admit he wasn't ugly. But he was... average. About what I would expect to see if I pictured an almost forty-year-old veterinarian.

"I take it that's your darling ex-husband?" I asked, cocking a brow at Madelyn when I looked back at her.

The joke died a bit when I saw the worry in her eyes. She masked it, feigning indifference, but I could see it.

She was scared of him.

Fuck, if that didn't piss me off more than anything in my entire life had.

"Hey," I said, calling her attention. For a long second, her gaze was stuck on where he was charging toward us. I didn't dare touch her with him watching our every move, but I called her name. "Mads."

Her eyes snapped to mine.

Slowly, I took a deep breath, nodding my head toward her to do the same. "I'm right here," I told her. "I've got you. Okay?"

Madelyn just swallowed.

"You are safe," I said, softer this time. I covered just the edge of her hand on the blanket with my own, angling my body so the touch was hidden from Marshall's view.

It was like touching an electric fence.

"You don't have to do this alone," I said.

Finally, she pulled a fresh breath through her nose, nodding, her eyes slipping to where my hand covered hers before she slowly found my gaze again.

And in that moment, in that particular light, she looked like that girl I fell in love with years ago — her brown eyes golden in the bit of sun sneaking through the trees, the freckles on her cheeks dark enough to draw a map between them.

I smiled.

She smiled.

Then, I climbed to my feet, cracking my neck before I turned to face Marshall. He was just a few yards away now.

His stride slowed a bit when he realized how tall I was, and that made my fake grin even easier to slap into place.

Alright, motherfucker.

Let's play.

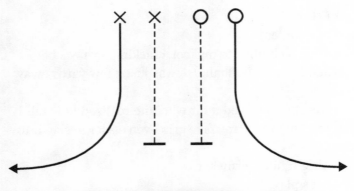

CHAPTER 13

Madelyn

The muscles in Kyle's back were as tight as a bow string, and I watched him subtly crack his neck like he was preparing for a fight.

I prayed it wouldn't come to that, but with my ex, there was no telling.

I hoped Marshall would be smart enough not to start something in a public place. I hoped the fact that our son was here would stop him. But I couldn't be sure.

He'd put his hands on me with Sebastian in the next room before.

"What the fuck is going on?" Marshall asked when he made it to our blanket. He was in his scrubs and white coat, which told me he was likely on break. His veterinary practice was relatively close, and it wasn't unusual for him to take an hour to go home for lunch.

How this man could be trusted to help or save *any-thing* was beyond me.

But at least him being on break from work meant he wasn't drunk. He always had an issue with his temper, but when he drank, that's when it became dangerous.

He tried to storm past Kyle, but Kyle side-stepped and angled his body in-between us like a human barrier.

"Hey, man," Kyle greeted, extending a hand for Marshall's. "We were just having a picnic. Nice of you to join us. I'm Kyle."

Marshall eyed his hand like it was poison before ignoring it completely, his narrowed eyes snapping to me. "Madelyn, who the fuck is this?"

"I'm Kyle," Kyle repeated. "I just told you that. Is your hearing bad, or are you just stupid?"

My eyes shot open wide at the same time Marshall blinked up at Kyle with a scoff. "What did you just say to me?"

"Wow, your hearing really is shit, isn't it?"

I tried to intervene, stepping around Kyle so Marshall could see me. "Kyle is an old friend of mine," I explained. "He just moved to Seattle."

"Old friend," Marshall deadpanned, his eyes slicing to me and then to Kyle and back again. "I'm sure he's a very good *friend* of yours."

Before Kyle or I could react, Sebastian was running up to us. I schooled my features enough to pin both men with a warning glare to keep their shit together before I turned just in time to catch Sebastian as he barreled into me.

"I'm a plane!" he exclaimed as I scooped him up into my arms with a spin.

"Oof, when did this plane get so heavy?" I teased, pretending like it was difficult to hold him. It was getting harder, that was for sure, but he was still my little man.

Sebastian was breathing heavy from playing, the new bag of rocks Kyle had given him safely secured in his little fist. When he saw Marshall, his face went absolutely blank. He didn't light up with excitement at the presence of his father, nor did he cower or show any negative emotion.

I didn't know whether the lack of emotion should have made me happy or absolutely devastated.

On the one hand, I wished he had a relationship with Marshall that he loved, one that made him excited to see his father. On the other hand, I was simply glad to see he wasn't afraid of the man, that Marshall's wrath had been tamed enough for our son to not understand the full extent of it.

Although something told me he knew, even if he'd never bore witness to it.

Kids just *know*.

Sebastian offered his dad a small smile, and then he gave me a questioning look before leaning a head into the crook of my neck and shoulder.

"Hi, Daddy," he said quietly. I could feel his entire body tense with the words.

"Hello, my boy," Marshall greeted. He glared a bit at Kyle as he stepped around enough to hold out his fist to Sebastian, who bumped it with his own fist before clinging to me again.

"It isn't Daddy's day," he whispered to me. "Is it?"

I shook my head on a smile. "No, sweetheart. Your dad is just stopping by to say hi." I carefully dropped him back to the ground. "Why don't you go play on the monkey bars. We're going to go soon, okay?"

Sebastian nodded, looking up at his own father warily, like he wasn't sure he should leave me with him.

That made my stomach lurch.

Then, I watched my son's eyes find Kyle, who winked at him and offered an, "I got this" smile. Sebastian beamed up at him in return, and then he handed me his bag of rocks.

"Okay, Mommy," he said, and then he took off in a sprint toward the bars.

My eyes found Kyle's.

No fighting, I hoped that gaze said.

But I was pretty sure there was a silent *thank you* in there, too.

Marshall took a big step toward me, calling my attention. "Who do you think you are, introducing our son to some random man without asking me first?"

"I'm pretty sure she doesn't have to get permission from you for a damn thing," Kyle said.

"She does when it comes to our son," Marshall shot back at him.

"He's a friend," I said. "And that's how he was introduced to Sebastian, too. You've introduced him to plenty of your *friends*," I reminded him pointedly. "So, I'm sure you can understand that this isn't an issue."

Marshall fumed, his hands rolling into fists.

Because that little comment confirmed just what *friends* meant.

I could see it from how red his face was that Marshall never thought he'd see the day I had big enough balls to date again. And it didn't matter that this was all fake.

The satisfaction of seeing him spiral out of control was very, very real.

"You have no right," he started, pointing his finger at me as he took another step. But that step must have brought him too close to me for Kyle's comfort, because he clapped a hand hard on Marshall's shoulder to stop him.

"Come on, buddy," he said like he was talking to a kid. "Let's take a walk."

He didn't give Marshall a choice. His grip was so firm, Marshall turned against his will and walked a few steps away before he shrugged Kyle's hand off him.

My heart was in my throat as I watched them, trying to read lips all while also keeping an eye on Sebastian to make sure he was okay. Fortunately, he was playing with another kid on the playground, seemingly oblivious to what was occurring over here.

I let my gaze slide back to the men, and my stomach coiled into a tight knot.

Kyle towered over Marshall, his stance tall and confident as he listened to Marshall spew whatever vitriol he was so happy to let loose. Where Marshall was animated, Kyle stood completely still and unaffected, like a grown man listening to a child throw a tantrum.

But I didn't miss the subtle ways he *was* reacting.

I saw how his muscles were tense — from his shoulders to his fingertips. I saw how his nose subtly flared, how his jaw flexed, his breaths leaving him in slow, controlled waves.

If I hadn't asked him to play nice, I had a feeling my ex-husband would already be laid out on the ground.

I couldn't explain why that made me want to melt into a puddle, and also climb Kyle like a tree all at once.

I shook off the thought, internally cursing myself just as I watched Kyle take one meaningful step into Marshall's space.

I couldn't make out what he was saying at first, but when Marshall tried to interrupt, Kyle raised his voice just enough for me to hear him.

"The *only* reason I'm letting you live is because I care enough about that woman to do what she asks me to," he said, and when his finger pointed right at me, I felt it like a bolt of lightning to the heart. "But slip up even *one* time," he continued, shaking his head as a damn near evil smile spread on his stupidly handsome face. "And I will risk it all. Understand? I will risk it *all*."

It was a subtle threat, but a poignant one.

Those words said he would protect me, even if it meant risking me being upset with him.

It said he would risk his career, risk jail time...

Risk it *all*.

I swallowed down the lump in my throat, pressing a hand over where my heart was racing rapidly in my chest.

Kyle lowered his voice to say one other thing, and then he clapped Marshall on the shoulder and started walking back to me.

This time, all pretense of *just friends* was gone.

Because Kyle walked right up to me, framed my face in his massive hands, and pressed a long, slow kiss...

To my forehead.

Heat spread like lava over every inch of me the longer he held his lips there, branding me as I closed my eyes and fought against the shiver that chased that heat. I tingled from that point of contact all the way to my toes.

It was more powerful than if he would have shoved his tongue down my throat and hiked my leg up, than if he would have pinned me against the nearest tree and had his way with me.

Because that kiss claimed me. It sent a message to my ex-husband.

But it was also innocent enough not to cause questions for my son.

The fact that Kyle understood how important *that* part of the equation was made me weak in the knees.

"I've got you," he whispered against my skin when he broke the kiss, and then he pulled me under his arm, smiling at Marshall just as he rejoined us.

Marshall was still pissed — that was easy to see. But something Kyle had said had sobered or scared him enough that he didn't push any further than he already had.

"I'm picking him up at 6 PM sharp on Sunday," he said, his gaze hard on mine.

"Wonderful. We'll see you then," Kyle interjected, his smile growing as he tucked me more into his side.

Emphasis on the *we* made Marshall vibrate with rage, but he smoothed his hands over his scrubs and tugged on the lapel of his white coat like he wasn't bothered, and then he left.

As soon as his car pulled away, Kyle turned, framing my arms in his hands as his eyes searched me like Marshall might have bruised me when he wasn't looking.

"You okay?"

I nodded, clearing my throat and stepping away from his grasp. I *needed* that distance. My head was spinning in a way that was dangerous the longer he held onto me.

"I'm good," I said with more confidence than I felt. "What did you say to him?"

Kyle shrugged. "I just made it clear that I'm not going anywhere, and that if he wants to live, he'll learn to keep his hands to himself when it comes to you."

My heart skipped a beat.

God, why did hearing him say that turn my insides to goop?

I hoped I was convincing when I rolled my eyes and smirked up at him, hoped he couldn't see right through me. "So much for subtlety."

"Did you hear how many times he asked who I was even after I told him?" Kyle asked, pointing a thumb over his shoulder. "That guy is too stupid for subtle."

I tried to fight it but couldn't win against the laugh that broke free from my chest. Kyle smiled in victory when I gave in to it, and then Sebastian was running over to us again.

"Can Kyle come over and play?" he asked me as soon as he was in front of our blanket. "I want to show him Titan!"

I was surprised by how much I wanted to say yes to that request, but I squelched the desire. I obviously needed some space to think clearly again.

Apparently, watching Kyle Robbins serve as a knight in shining armor obliterated all my feminism and turned me to mush.

"Not today, little man. But soon, okay?"

Sebastian looked ready to pout when Kyle bent to one knee in front of him.

"Who's Titan?"

Sebastian's cheeks went pink, and he looked at the ground before softly replying. "My gecko."

My heart broke at how disappointed my son looked that I'd said no, but Kyle didn't miss a beat.

"A gecko?! That's so cool! I can't wait to meet him. I'll have to look up presents for geckos. Do you have any ideas? I gotta make a good first impression if he means so much to you."

Sebastian grinned a little. "Geckos don't get *presents*," he said on a giggle.

"Why not? Everyone likes gifts. Come on, what should I get him? Does he like... toy cars?"

Sebastian laughed. "No!"

"Does he like soccer balls?"

Another laugh. "No! He's a lizard!"

"Well, help me out then!"

"He likes crickets," Sebastian offered, and as soon as he did, Kyle snapped his fingers.

"Crickets it is."

Sebastian was placated, though he still looked a bit sad.

"Trust me," Kyle said, looking my son right in the eye. "I'm not going anywhere. We'll have all the time in the world for Titan and anything else you want to show me."

Sebastian's little brows pulled together, like that concept was foreign to him. Then, he smiled so big it showed off two front teeth he was going to lose soon, and I had to look up at the sky to fight off whatever emotion was trying to strangle me.

I told Sebastian to start packing up our picnic. He loved to help clean up — always had. And as he worked on folding the picnic blanket, I ran a hand through my hair, shaking my head a bit before my eyes found Kyle.

"I guess we're really doing this."

Kyle smirked, his glass-like eyes looking a bit more blue than green with the sky stretching out behind him. "I guess we are."

My stomach fluttered at the wing tips of a hundred butterflies with the way he looked at me, but I quickly put a lid on that.

I was thankful for his help. It was sweet. It was kind. It was a way to give me a bit of peace while I worked on finding him a house, and then I'd have my commission and Sebastian and I could leave, and Kyle could go back to his superstar life.

This is temporary, I reminded myself.

And I'd *keep* reminding myself until those stupid butterflies died.

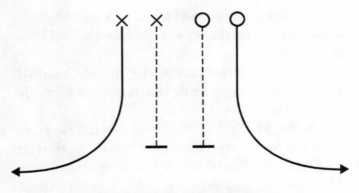

CHAPTER 14

Kyle

"Why do you look so nervous?"

Braden turned to look at me from the driver's seat of his beat-up piece-of-shit car the following Friday. I'd considered hiring a driver along with a few decoys for this trip to the airport, but when Braden offered to drive, I realized there was no better way to fly under the radar.

There was no way in *hell* anyone would think an NFL player was in this car — let alone two.

"I don't," was my answer.

"The only one looking at your sorry ass right now is me," he said pointedly. "And trust me when I say you look like you're two seconds away from being caught cheating on a math quiz."

I cracked my neck, hanging one arm out the window and watching the trees pass. "You know how I feel about weddings."

"Sure it has nothing to do with this mystery *guest* we're picking up?"

"Madelyn."

"Ah, so she does have a name," he said, shifting his grip on the wheel. "You know, you could have given me a heads up. Now *I'm* the only one going stag to this thing."

"I didn't exactly see this coming," I said.

Braden was quiet for a moment. "You want to talk about anything?"

I flattened my lips when I looked at him, and when my gaze slid out the window again, he chuckled.

"Come on, man. You haven't posted her on social media. Say what you want, but for you?" He shrugged. "That's a big deal."

"I'm private when it comes to things like this."

"Things like what?" he probed. "Things that are real?"

I laughed, both because I wanted to hide the way I hated how that motherfucker saw right through my shit, and because *technically*, what was going on with me and Madelyn was everything *but* real.

It was fake. It was pretend. It was me not taking no for an answer when it came to protecting her and her son.

But looking at houses with her, watching her try on dresses, spending time with her and Sebastian…

Fuck.

I was having a real hard time not blurring the line.

I heaved a deep breath, turning to face Braden. He was the closest thing I had to a best friend. When it came to the guys on my college football team, we were like family. But in *my* family, we didn't talk about feelings.

So, even when the guys opened up to *me*, when they let me in on what was happening in their lives...

I had a hard time doing the same.

But I knew now after meeting Sebastian — after facing off with *Marshall* — this little plan I'd schemed up wasn't something trivial.

I was already in over my head, and I had a feeling I'd need a friend to help me through it all.

"Don't make a big deal of this," I said to start. "And don't say a fucking word to anyone else — not Clay, not Zeke, not Leo, definitely not Holden."

Braden's brows bent together the more names I listed. "Okay..."

I ran a hand through my hair as the GPS told Braden to hook a left. "Madelyn and I knew each other growing up," I said. "She was my babysitter."

"Um..."

I held up a hand to stop him. "Just let me get this out. Okay? This shit makes me so uncomfortable I already have hives." I shifted in my seat. "It's a long story. She's only a couple years older than me, but my parents didn't trust me home alone after I threw a massive party. Our parents were..." My stomach turned. "Friends, or something similar to it, anyway. So yeah, she was charged to watch me."

Braden licked his lips on a grin. "This is way better than I imagined."

"Just wait," I said.

And then I told him everything I could stomach telling him.

I told him about how we went from me being a brat and her being a bossy babysitter to being friends, and then... more.

I told him how my family had moved, and I hadn't seen her since.

I left out *why* my parents had moved.

I skipped forward to the house, and quickly filled him in on the last couple of weeks. And when I told him about the bruises on her arms, I saw his hands tighten on the wheel.

To my surprise, when I told him about how I'd proposed a fake relationship, he didn't seem shocked.

Then again, after Clay and Giana, I guessed we had practice in that area.

"So, you're pretending to be her boyfriend so that piece-of-shit ex-husband of hers knows his place," he filled in for me. "And she *thinks* you care enough about not going to another wedding single that she's also doing you a favor in all of this."

I nodded, though my throat was tight.

Because I actually *did* care — but Braden didn't need to know that part.

He whistled, shaking his head as we turned onto her street. I didn't know where Marshall lived, but I knew he was close by. I glared at every house we passed as if I could stare through the walls and kill him with just a passing look.

"Your secret is safe with me, man," he said. "But I gotta say... good luck keeping this from Giana. You know that girl. Not much gets past her. All those smutty books she reads give her superpowers to see right through shit like this."

"I'm hoping she'll be too distracted by her own wedding. And pregnancy."

"Too distracted to see North Boston University's most notorious bachelor smitten over a girl she's never met?" He laughed. "Yeah. Again — good luck with that."

I smirked, because I knew he wasn't wrong. Giana would be watching us in that studious way she assessed everyone. It was part of what made her a good agent.

It was also part of what made her a pain in my ass.

But when we pulled up to Madelyn's house, all those nerves I'd been feeling scattered, and a warm calm settled in its place.

Because I had a feeling I'd have no trouble at all pretending Madelyn was really mine.

Madelyn

I rolled my suitcase out to the curb when the car pulled up, hoping I looked steadier than I felt.

My hands weren't shaking. My smile felt easy, unforced.

But inside, I was freaking the fuck out.

I was about to get in a car with Kyle Robbins. A car that would take us to the airport. And then we'd get on a plane.

And then we'd be at a *wedding*.

Together.

As a couple.

I blinked, wondering if I really was existing in the longest dream ever. There was no possible *way* this was my reality. Two weeks ago, I was just living my usual life and routine. I was taking care of Sebastian. I was working my ass off to sell houses. I was dealing with my ex-husband the way I had been for years.

Now, I was playing dress up with the first boy I ever loved.

When Kyle climbed out of the car, his massive frame towering over the thing as he walked around it and toward me, my breath hitched in my chest — reminding me exactly how real this all was.

God, he was so handsome it hurt.

It didn't matter how many times I'd seen him over the past couple of weeks. Every time I did, he shocked me with how tall he was, how broad his shoulders were, how muscles stretched over every inch of him. I was never quite prepared for the cocky grin he always threw me, or the way his hair was always carefully styled to look like a woman had just run her hands through it.

"This is it?" he asked, taking the carry-on sized luggage from my hand. He tossed it into the trunk without an ounce of effort.

I shrugged. "I don't need much."

His mouth quirked up at that, and then, he snaked an arm around the small of my back, pulling me into him.

He did it without hesitation, like he'd done it a million times before.

Suddenly, I wished I'd taken him up on all those practice rounds he'd offered.

My heart stopped before kicking back to life in an unsteady rhythm, and Kyle used his free hand to tilt my chin up. He smiled, one brow arching as if to say, *you ready for this?*

Then, he lowered his mouth, and pressed a feather-light kiss to my lips.

I didn't mean to, but I sucked in a breath at that touch, at the first kiss we'd shared in years. It didn't matter that it was short and sweet, the kind of kiss you greet someone with.

It sent heat rushing down my spine.

It sent memories flashing behind my lids.

It sent fluttering wings free in my stomach, and my fingers curled into a fist where I didn't even realize I was holding onto his shirt.

When he pulled back, he smirked down at me, lazily — like that kiss had meant nothing to him. Like it was easy. Like it was fake.

And I reminded myself quickly that it *was* fake.

For a moment, I stood there, staring up at him with my mouth open like a guppy, my breaths shallow and short. Something shifted in Kyle's expression then, like he was searching for whatever emotion he thought I was feeling.

I quickly wiped my face blank, inhaling a deep breath and tucking my hair behind one ear as I put distance between us. "Ready?"

"I was about to ask you the very same thing," he said. Then, he frowned, looking behind me. "Where's Sebastian?"

Warmth spread through me again, but I dumped a bucket of ice water over it.

"School," I answered. "My mom's flight just landed. She's got plenty of time to get settled, and then she'll pick him up later."

Kyle's face went a bit ashen at the mention of my mother.

Probably because the last time he'd seen her was the night before he found out I was pregnant.

And then he'd left.

Yeah... let's just say I couldn't exactly tell my mom *who* I was going to this wedding with. I'd been very adamant about the time she flew in so I could avoid her finding out at all costs.

She was just happy to hear I was dating again, and aside from the adorable kind of prying all mothers did, she was leaving me alone about the details.

For now.

I knew if this went on for too long, she'd want answers. And there was no way I could tell her Kyle Robbins was back in my life.

I *definitely* couldn't tell her that we were dating — which was why reminding myself this was all temporary made it a bit easier to breathe.

The kiss was fake. What Mom doesn't know won't hurt her. And soon, this will all be over, anyway.

But holding up my end of the bargain had my chest tight as Kyle opened the back seat door and helped me inside. Him pretending to be my boyfriend around Marshall was one thing.

Me pretending to be his girlfriend around a wedding full of his old college buddies?

This was a whole new level of *what the fuck did I get myself into?*

As soon as Kyle climbed into the passenger seat again, the guy in the driver one turned around to face me.

"Hey, I'm Braden," he said, extending a hand with the widest, most dazzling smile I'd ever laid eyes on.

He was hot — the kind of hot that makes you a little breathless to be in close proximity.

Kyle I was used to. I could still see him as the little brat I used to fight with. But Braden was an NFL player.

I was in a car with two freaking NFL players.

I was about to be at a wedding *full* of them.

I shook his hand with an awkward smile, my heart working overtime again. "Madelyn."

"She packed lighter than you," Kyle teased Braden when we released hands. He turned to me next. "I can't convince this guy to use his signing bonus to get a car from this decade, but he has no problem buying a new pair of shoes every day and insisting they all need to come with him on a long weekend trip."

"You're just salty because I dress better than you," Braden quipped, throwing the car into drive. "Always have."

"It's four nights," Kyle said. "You have two *giant* suitcases for *four nights*."

"Well, we might be hiking!" Braden said, as if that was all the defense he needed. "And then there's the rehearsal dinner, the groom's brunch, the wedding itself, whatever we end up doing the next day — which *could* be hiking. I'll be hitting the gym every day, we might play football while we're there — what? Don't look at me like that. We might!"

Kyle barked out a laugh, razzing his friend as my eyes lost focus once we pulled onto the highway.

What the hell am I doing?

My hand gripped the seat below me, my chest aching with the pressure of each breath. I thought I might actually be hyperventilating when I felt a pair of sea green eyes on me.

Kyle had pulled the visor down, and he was staring at me through the mirror of it.

When our eyes met, time slowed, the sound of traffic and the radio and Braden continuing to defend his packing all fading until everything was muted.

Relax, he mouthed in the mirror.

I glared at him, and he smiled.

Then, he reached one massive hand behind him and squeezed my knee.

I stared at that point of contact, fire licking along the inside of my thigh. And when I glanced at him in the mirror again, I saw his eyes sparkling.

And for some reason I couldn't understand even if I dissected it, I *did* relax.

I took a breath. I smiled. I shook my head and flushed as Kyle squeezed my knee once more before removing his touch altogether.

Something about the way he looked at me told me this wasn't serious enough for me to freak out over.

Something in those eyes of his told me to have fun.

Fun.

I couldn't even remember the last time I'd done anything like this. I used to love to take long weekend trips, to travel, to meet new people.

Sometime in the span of my brief marriage and time of being a mother, I'd lost that.

I'd lost *me.*

But until the plane landed back in Seattle on Tuesday, I didn't have anything to do or anywhere to be other than right here with Kyle Robbins.

My blast from the past who turned everything upside down.

Maybe I didn't have to think too hard about it all. Maybe I didn't need to stress about being underdressed or out of place or states away from my son.

Sebastian was safe with my mom.

Work was on hold until next week.

Right now, regardless of what I was wearing, Kyle had his eyes on me with all kinds of mischievous promises dancing inside them.

And my only job was to pretend to be his girlfriend.
I smiled.
Yeah...
I could work with that.

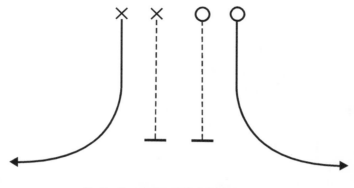

CHAPTER 15

Madelyn

How silly it was of me to assume we'd be taking a commercial flight to Denver.

I'd certainly expected some type of security once we got to the airport. I had also presumed we'd be in premium economy seats, if not first class.

What I had *not* expected was a private turboprop.

We didn't park at the airport and drag our luggage inside. Instead, we drove right to a hangar where the plane waited for us — along with the pilot, a flight attendant, and a grounds crew waiting with glasses of champagne.

Kyle and Braden took a glass without blinking, not even bothering to move for their luggage in the trunk of the car. I went to reach for mine, but a man with pale skin, silver hair, and kind eyes stopped me — offering me a smile as he handled the luggage and nodded for me to join the others.

I felt so out of place, I wanted to crawl out of my skin.

It wasn't that I hadn't traveled to some nice places before or had some upscale experiences. Marshall was a veterinarian. He made a nice salary and used to like to spoil me when we were together.

Usually after he roughed me up.

It was his favorite way to apologize — by not actually apologizing at all, but rather buying me something or taking me somewhere.

My parents were also decently well-off, and they had taken me on many of their travels when I was younger.

But it was never anything like *this*.

I was still standing shocked-still and staring at the plane waiting for us to board it when a glass of champagne was propped right in my eye line.

"If I remember right, you love bubbles," Kyle said, his voice low and teasing.

He cocked one of those gorgeous, thick brows of his when I looked at him, a smirk curling on his lips.

I took the glass from him with my cheeks heating. "That's a very specific memory to hold onto," I noted with an arched brow of my own.

"Oh, trust me," he said, hooking his arm around my waist. Again, he did it so effortlessly, like his hand belonged hooked on my hip and pulling me into him. "I remember everything about that night."

He smiled with the words, but they hung heavy in-between us when I dragged my gaze up to his. I was so small in his arms — even more so than I had been when we were younger.

I felt his body against mine like a fortress and a warning all at once.

That night.

That night we were just two kids getting into trouble. That night we snuck into the pool of a vacation house, when we spent the night drinking champagne we stole from Kyle's parents, when we crossed a line that had already been so thin it was impossible to see.

That night we went from *just friends* to something more.

The more the memory resurfaced, the more both of our smiles dropped. The heat and the questions swirling in Kyle's eyes were too much for me to bear.

I tore my gaze away and took a sip of my champagne.

When the crew was ready for us, they helped us board the plane, continuing to serve us as they went through the brief safety instructions. Then, they took our empty champagne flutes, and we were taxiing down the runway, ready for takeoff.

I looked around at the plush leather seats, the luxurious interior of the plane that could have seated eight, but just had the three of us.

I wondered what it was like to book something like this without thinking twice about it.

Kyle and I were seated next to each other, our seats in the back of the plane facing the cockpit. Braden sat across from us.

They were both massive, sprawling beings — their legs almost too tall even with the expanded leg room we had on this plane. I listened absentmindedly as the two of them joked around with each other, all while being entirely too focused on where Kyle's arm brushed mine on the arm rest, on where his knee pressed against mine.

And when we took off, my stomach plunged.

Because as the plane soared up into the sky, Kyle covered my hand with his own.

And he didn't move it.

"So, Madelyn," Braden said when we were at ten-thousand feet. "Kyle said you grew up together."

I blinked, hoping Braden didn't see how intently I was staring at where Kyle's hand was holding mine before I brought my gaze to him.

"We did," I said, smiling. "And you two went to college together?"

"Unfortunately," he said on a sigh. "I had to live with his smelly ass for a couple of those years, too."

"You're welcome for all the breakfasts I made you," Kyle piped in from beside me.

The flight attendant interrupted us long enough to take a drink order.

"You?" I asked, not meaning to sound so incredulous when I added, "Cooking?"

Kyle pressed a hand to his chest in mock offense. "I'm an excellent cook, I'll have you know."

"He's particularly well-versed in smiley-face pancakes," Braden chimed in.

I chuckled, shaking my head. "I cannot picture Kyle cooking anything without burning it."

"I've come a long way from the Easy Mac days," he said, nudging my arm. "I'll show you. When we get back, I'll cook for you and Sebastian."

My smile faded, stomach tightening at how easily he offered that.

I knew it was probably just for show in front of his friend. He had to sell the lie that we were a couple, after all. That was probably why his hand was still holding mine even after the flight attendant gave us our drinks.

He didn't remove his hold on me, just took the cocktail she offered him in his other hand.

That shouldn't have made me dizzy, but damn if it didn't do just that. Because with Kyle's hand around mine, it didn't feel the way Marshall's always had. It didn't feel like a tether, like a restraint, like a form of control.

It was warm, comfortable, and familiar.

It was sweet with pride, as if I were some sort of catch — like claiming me in that small way in front of his friend made him sit a little taller.

"What was Kyle like when you were growing up?" Braden asked.

I blinked out of my thoughts and back to the moment when I answered. "A brat."

He laughed at that, and Kyle smirked, not denying it.

"Did he tell you I was his babysitter?" I asked Braden.

"He did, actually," Braden said. "I'm not surprised. I took that job once he went to college."

Kyle flipped him off as I laughed.

"So, what do you like to do when you're not letting this one drag you to a wedding halfway across the country," Braden asked.

"Oh, I'm in real estate."

Braden nodded. "That's cool, but what do you like to do when you're not working?"

I didn't miss how Kyle's eyes slid to me then, how he leaned in like he wanted to know the answer to that question, too.

"Hang out with my son, mostly," I said. "He's a curious kid, loves to explore. We spend a lot of time outside."

"What do you do for you?"

Those words came from Kyle, and I tilted my gaze up to meet his.

I swallowed, wishing I had an answer for him, but I didn't.

The truth was that Sebastian had become my world when he was born — even more so when I left Marshall. I worked hard to provide for him, and when I wasn't working, all I wanted to do was spend time helping him learn and grow.

I loved to watch him experience something for the first time. I loved answering his questions and helping him think of even more to ask. I loved when it was just the two of us on a lazy, rainy day, cuddled on the couch and watching *Cars* for the fifteenth time.

When I didn't answer, Kyle's expression shifted, and Braden muttered something about needing to make a call. He moved to the couch toward the front of the plane, and I didn't have time to analyze the fact that he could make a call from a freaking airplane before Kyle was tilting even more toward me, his ankle crossing over the opposite knee.

"You used to write."

I swallowed. "I used to do a lot of things."

"Do you still write?"

"No."

"Do you want to?"

I smiled, looking down at my lap. I realized we were still holding hands, and I glanced to make sure Braden wasn't watching us before I pulled my hand from Kyle's.

He frowned as soon as I did.

"I don't know," I answered honestly. "I think I missed it, for a while. But I haven't felt that way in a long time."

I didn't expand on what *that way* meant. Maybe he knew. Maybe he could look right through me and see that inspired was the last thing I've felt over the last several years.

"You love being a mom," he said, not so much a question as an assessment.

I nodded. "More than anything in the world."

"Sebastian is a great kid. You..." He swallowed. "He's lucky to have you."

My heart hollowed out with him looking at me like that, with him saying those words like he... like he wished he was a part of the family equation.

Like he had regrets.

And I couldn't fight it any longer.

I couldn't hold back the question that had been eating me alive since I was eighteen.

"Why did you leave?"

I whispered the words, my voice shaking and giving away the nonchalance I tried to fake with the question.

Kyle's jaw tensed, his marble eyes holding mine. "You know why, Mads," he croaked.

He looked hurt that I'd asked him, that I'd made him say that.

But not as hurt as I felt having him admit that to my face.

I blinked, and I thought I was holding a poker face, but I felt a tear trickle down my cheek. My bottom lip trembled, and my breath lodged in my chest when Kyle reached over and thumbed that tear away.

"I didn't have a choice," he said, his voice lower than before, his voice cracking with the words. "If I had — it would have been you. My choice would have always been you." He swallowed. "Even if you didn't choose me."

He ripped his hand from where it held mine, scrubbing it over his face as he looked out the window and leaned away from me like I was on fire.

I frowned, confusion overtaking the hurt I felt before as I dissected his words.

I didn't have a choice.

What the hell did that mean?

My mind raced with the possibilities. Did his parents not give him an option to stay with me and our child? Surely, they would have wanted him to stay and hold responsibility. Mr. and Mrs. Robbins were well-known and well-respected in our community.

My heart stopped in my chest.

They were well-known and well-respected.

But would they still have been, if their teenage son knocked someone up?

I covered my mouth with one hand, staring at the back of Kyle's head before my gaze dropped to my lap.

Is that why they left?

Even if you didn't choose me.

I frowned again, thinking about the last time I'd seen Kyle. We were at school, walking toward each other in the courtyard. I'd frozen when I'd seen him, not sure what to expect now that he knew about our predicament.

I had wished for him to run to me, to hold me, to assure me it would all be okay, and he was right there with me no matter what.

Instead, he'd taken one look at me, scowled, and stormed in the opposite direction.

I didn't find out until later that he had cleaned out his locker. And I didn't find out from *him* that he and his family were moving.

I put the pieces together once they were already gone.

As if that experience hadn't plagued me as a teenager, as if I hadn't lost sleep wondering what had happened all those years ago, as if I hadn't endured the most horrific loss of my life — alone...

Now, I had an extra layer of confusion to add to the mix.

I didn't have a choice.

But he did. He could have chosen to talk to me. He could have chosen to tell me if his parents had made the decision for him. He could have run away.

We could have run away. Together.

As a mother myself now, I knew how foolish that idea was even as I thought it. But it didn't stop me from wondering. It didn't stop me from wishing he would have at least *talked* to me.

I thought about Kyle's father, about the nights he would drink too much, lose his temper, and take out all his life's frustrations on his son.

Had he threatened Kyle?

Had he...

I closed my eyes, the thought souring my stomach.

Had he *hurt* Kyle... because of me?

I searched my memory of that last day I saw him, trying to remember if Kyle had worn any physical signs of the abuse I knew he'd suffered at his father's hand.

But all I remembered was the hard stone of his gaze.

And now, I wondered if I'd misinterpreted it all.

Even if you didn't choose me.

What did *that* mean?

I'd thought he was upset with me for getting pregnant. I thought he blamed me for ruining his life.

FALSE START

I thought he was running from me because he didn't want me.

Now, I had no idea what to think.

But I had a weekend with him to find out the truth.

And that was exactly what I intended to do.

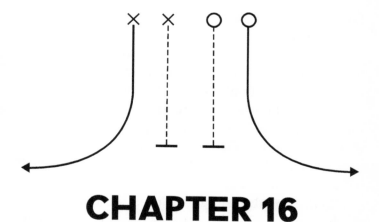

CHAPTER 16

Kyle

It was the calm before the storm.

I felt it as we walked into the hotel lobby of a boutique luxury hotel in downtown Denver. There was no press waiting when we arrived, which meant somehow Giana had kept the wedding under wraps — at least for now. It also seemed like she and Clay had hired a full staff of security. They were everywhere, from where the black car dropped us off to where we walked now to check in.

It felt like we slipped into our own little bubble of the world when we walked through those revolving doors, and it was quiet in the lobby. Peaceful.

But I knew that wouldn't last long.

Someone had already taken our luggage, and without anything to hold onto, Madelyn folded her arms over herself. She looked around at the high-hanging chandeliers, the lush gem tones of the rich furniture, and the impressive textures of the walls and floors — marble and wood, everything polished to shine.

I told myself I was putting on a show when I carefully threaded my hand over her forearm and pulled her to a stop, waiting until she looked up at me.

Her soft brown eyes were wide as they swept over me, and the corner of my mouth ticked up before I tucked her hair behind one ear. My knuckles grazed her neck when I did, and I didn't miss the goosebumps that paraded over her skin.

God, I loved that sight. I loved the thought that maybe that little flush on her cheeks wasn't completely pretend.

"How are you?" I asked.

"Good," she said, and then forced a smile. "Great."

I arched a brow. "What was that rule you made when we were younger?" I asked, and then hung a hand on my hip and tried to imitate her. "No lying. Lying is the highest offense punishable by purple nurple."

I couldn't help but chuckle when I said it, my imitation of her voice leaking out of me like a deflating balloon. It had been hilarious the first time she'd said it to me — even more so when she'd followed through on that promise and twisted my nipples so hard I yelped the first time I'd tried to lie to her.

But Madelyn didn't even smile.

Her eyes were a bit hollow as she said, "Sometimes the truth has worse consequences than that."

I frowned, my heart stuttering, and everything she'd said on the plane came rushing back to me.

I felt it again.

It was the calm before the storm.

This exact same feeling had washed over me on that fateful weekend when I was sixteen, the weekend that everything changed.

I had been sick back then, a tornado of teenage hormones and emotions. I could feel Madelyn pulling away from me. I could feel her rationalizing how I was too young for her, how she was about to go to college and do something with her life while I was stuck in high school for another two years.

She'd stopped answering my texts. She'd stopped picking up my calls. At school, she avoided me in every way she could.

When I found out about the party my parents were hosting, that's when the first bit of wind blew. That's when the storm announced its impending arrival.

I didn't know why I felt that way, only that my gut was telling me something and I wanted to listen. I called and texted Madelyn repeatedly, begging her to be there.

But she didn't come.

Not until the next morning, when everything had blown up.

I'd been staring out my window in a daze after the longest night of my life, my lip split and starting to scab from trying to control my father. He'd shown his ass in the worst possible ways, in ways that I knew couldn't be erased with a simple apology.

But then I saw her.

Madelyn parked her car in front of our house, and I swallowed, watching as she walked toward the door with her arms crossed hard in front of her chest. She didn't look up at my bedroom window the way she usually did. She just kept her eyes on the door.

I waited.

I waited for my parents to call me downstairs, to say that Madelyn was there to see me.

I waited for Madelyn herself to bound up the stairs and into my room, to throw herself into my arms and say she was sorry she hadn't been there.

I waited for mercy, and it never came.

Instead, I heard voices downstairs, and thought it was just her being polite to my parents before she came up.

Then, I saw her leave.

She was only a couple steps across our lawn when I barreled downstairs, wild-eyed and panicking. I'd sprinted for the door, but my parents had stopped me — Dad with a hard hand on my chest, Mom with her eyes flooded with tears as she shook her head.

I'd looked between them and knew before they said a word that Madelyn had turned her back on us.

On me.

"I'm sorry, son," Dad had said, and the way his eyes stuck on my split lip, I wondered if he was apologizing for more than one thing. "She doesn't want to see you."

Mom had folded in on herself, crying even more, until Dad gently nudged her and she nodded, her eyes finding mine.

"She's asked us to tell you..." She shook her head, more tears spilling. "She's asked that you stay away from her."

My entire world had crashed down with those words.

I pushed past my parents, one of them spitting apologies while the other one tried to stop me. I didn't know which was which. I pushed until I reached the door and yanked it open, but Madelyn was already gone.

My father took my phone then — as punishment for my behavior the night before, but also as a mercy.

He knew as well as I did that I wouldn't have been able to leave Madelyn alone, not even when she asked me to.

It was the longest weekend of my life.

And on Monday, my dad took me to school long enough to get my shit.

And we moved.

A distant laugh from check in snapped me back to the moment, and I glanced over to find Braden working his charm on the attendant handing him his room key. I swallowed, trying to erase the memory of the past as well as Madelyn's question from the plane.

Why did you leave?

She knew. She *knew* why. She'd told me to stay away, and then my parents had put states between us, robbing me of any choice after.

But if that was the case... then why did she ask?

I couldn't explain it, but it put all my senses on edge. It made me want to get her alone to talk, made me want to drag up that dark memory that clearly still hung over both of us.

It also made me suspicious.

Because all this time, I'd thought she'd turned her back on me.

But she asked why *I'd* left, as if it hadn't been her to do so first.

And suddenly, all I could think was that I didn't trust my parents. I never had.

And I was analyzing every detail of that day under a magnifying glass, looking for new clues.

When I turned back to face Madelyn, I held her gaze, as if I could look through those eyes and find the truth. "Once we get checked in, you can go nap, if you'd like," I offered.

She chuckled. "Oh, God. I haven't napped in years."

"Really?" I smiled a little. "You used to love naps. And you'd wake up from them and immediately start writing, like your dreams would fade if you didn't capture them right away."

"No time to nap when you have a kid," she said, looking down at her feet.

I tilted her chin up with my knuckles. "Hey, Sebastian is with your mom. He's good. And *you* have permission to relax this weekend."

Madelyn's eyes searched mine, a soft line appearing between them. Then, that gaze slid behind me, and she smiled a bit.

"I have a feeling there won't be any *relaxing* happening," she said.

And before I could reply, I was tackled from behind, barely catching the heavy sonofabitch who mounted my back and clung onto my shoulders.

"Aw, shit! The party has arrived!"

I recognized Leo's voice before I even shrugged him off me to confirm it. His feet had barely hit the ground before he hit me with a fierce hug, both of us clapping each other hard on the back.

"Damn, what are they feeding you up there in Washington?" he asked when we pulled back, punching my pec. "You're almost as buff as me."

"Please," I scoffed. "I've always been bigger than you and you damn well know it."

"Eh, depends on what we're talking about," he said with a salacious wink, and I rolled my eyes before pulling him under my arm and ruffling his hair like he was my kid brother. The motherfucker loved to brag about the size of his dick — one he let sling between his legs like a proud bull when we were in the locker rooms at NBU.

To be clear, I was just as cocksure and had no shame when it came to being naked. I was packing and proud.

But Leo Hernandez was a fucking freak of nature.

"No, really, it's good to see you, man," he said when I released him, and then his eyes slid to Madelyn, and both of his eyebrows inched up into his thick hairline.

He glanced at me, then back at her, and then shoved me out of the way.

"Excuse this rude motherfucker," he said, extending his hand for hers. "I'm Leo."

"Madelyn," she said, taking his hand.

"Nice to meet you. Blink twice if you're in danger or being held against your will."

Madelyn smiled a bit at that, and I ground my teeth, gritting out a smile of my own.

It was a joke. This was what we *did*. We razzed each other practically nonstop.

But fuck, I was tired of being the butt of this particular joke.

A cool hand sliding into the crook of my arm made me blink and release the tension in my jaw, and then I looked down in time to watch Madelyn nuzzle into my space. She looked up at me with a heart-stopping smile, one that slapped me with more memories of the past.

"Never felt safer, actually," she said.

Then, she tilted up onto her toes, trailed her arms up around my neck, and pulled me down into her for a kiss.

Time slugged like a train pulling into a station, steam erupting from the depth of my being when she pressed her lips to mine. They were warm and soft and perfect — just like I remembered them.

And this kiss put the one I'd given her in front of her house to shame.

That had been brief, a little peck of a greeting that I did without even thinking. Braden *knew* the truth. I didn't have to put on a show for him, but damn if that was going to stop me. I'd stolen that kiss. I'd kissed her like we were used to it, like we'd done it a thousand times.

But this...

This was Madelyn fitting every inch of herself to me in a seam. It was her arms around my neck, and us both inhaling when my hands found the small of her back and pulled her even more flush against me.

It was her hands trembling where they tangled in my hair.

It was a low and throaty groan I didn't mean to let loose when I wrapped my arms all the way around her, when I felt her shaking in my grasp.

She didn't just hold her lips to mine and then pull away. She kissed me once, twice, a third time, each one more sensual than the last. And I met her kisses eagerly, nipping at her bottom lip until she opened her mouth on a slight gasp — one I captured with my mouth on hers again.

My hands trailed up over her rib cage, her arms, sliding north still until I cradled her face in my hands.

I didn't give a fuck if Leo was there anymore.

I didn't care about putting on a show.

I knew Madelyn initiated the kiss because that was her role. She was here pretending to be my girlfriend.

But nothing felt fake about this.

I deepened the kiss even more, ready to let that woman consume me for all eternity. But she pressed her fingertips against my chest gently, just enough to tell me she wanted me to stop.

I pressed my forehead to hers, breaking the kiss even while my heart battered my rib cage and begged me to carry her upstairs to the first room I could find.

Madelyn's eyelids fluttered open when she pulled back, and then she flushed a dark crimson, burying her face into my chest like she'd just realized we'd put on a show.

And what a show it must have been.

Because when I looked back at Leo, he was smirking and shaking his head like we'd proven our point.

And he wasn't alone.

Everyone was there.

Zeke and Riley, Clay and Giana, Holden and Julep, and now Mary was hanging on Leo's arm. Braden was walking over from the lobby desk with an intrigued grin.

Everyone else was silent, shocked, and gaping at us.

"Well," Holden finally said, breaking the silence as he put an arm around his wife. His grin was the kind only a superstar quarterback could have — all teeth and dimples. "Seems we have a lot of catching up to do."

It was absolute chaos after that.

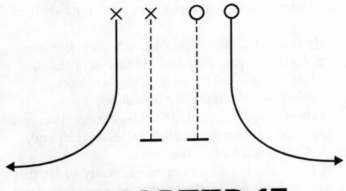

CHAPTER 17

Madelyn

My face was on fire after that kiss — along with every other inch of my body.

I hadn't allowed myself long enough to think before I made the move. All I could process was how Kyle had looked when he'd first proposed this absolutely insane idea, how he'd said I'd be doing him a favor by coming to this wedding with him.

"I know you don't need me, but I need you."

I'd thought it was bullshit when he'd said it. I thought he was just trying to control the situation. But seeing his face after Leo made that seemingly harmless joke, I realized there was more depth to the statement.

He really was tired of being stag at these weddings.

He really was tired of all the jokes.

And the moment I'd pressed up on my toes to kiss him, I'd felt the weight of the world slip off his shoulders before he wrapped me in his arms.

That kiss...

It was still burning through me like raw electricity, my body humming with the desire to continue it.

His hands in my hair...

His lips claiming mine...

The little groan that no one else could hear, but I felt like a brand imprinting me for life...

I tried not to read too much into it, tried to remind myself it was all fake as I buried my face in his chest.

And now, his entire friend group was gaping at us.

The first to speak was a tall, lean blond with dimples and a dazzling smile. I'd tried to do a little research before I came, and I was almost certain it was Holden Moore, a quarterback for the North Carolina Panthers.

"Well, seems we have a lot of catching up to do."

He arched a brow at Kyle with the words, and then, we were hit with a blast of sound like a bomb had gone off.

Everyone started talking at once, greetings flying every which way.

Kyle was ripped from my grip into the arms of a very attractive man with rich brown skin and a jet-black fade. I thought to myself that it was likely Zeke Collins, if I had done my research properly, but before I could analyze, I was pulled into a hug, myself.

"Oh, my God. It's so nice to meet you!"

The girl hugging me was as short and petite as I was, but her hug felt like that of a bear. When she released me, she held onto my arms, her gray-blue eyes searching mine. She had long, brown curly hair and wore a pair of gold-framed glasses almost too big for her face.

"I'm Giana Jones," she said. "Soon to be Giana Johnson," she added with a little dance. "I'm Kyle's agent. I've heard so much about you, and yet not nearly enough because Kyle is stingy with tropes."

I blinked, trying to keep up.

I was also breathing a little more shallowly after her saying Kyle had told her so much about me, mind racing with what he might have said.

"It's nice to meet you," I finally replied. "Thank you for inviting us."

I cringed internally at how weird that sounded, but before I could fold in on myself, the three girls flanking Giana introduced themselves.

There was Riley Novo, petite like Giana and me with long brown hair and the most beautiful bronze skin. She was athletic, that I could tell even in the joggers and warm-up jacket she wore, and she introduced herself with a firm handshake.

Julep Moore was next, and with the name alone, I put together that she was Holden's wife. She had the kind of smile that warmed you from the inside out, but the kind of eyes that told me she had ghosts from her past that would forever be a part of her.

I could tell because I carried spirits of my own.

We shared a look of understanding after she hugged me, and then I shook the hand of Mary Silver. Mary had the body of Aphrodite, except instead of hers being pale white, it was covered with the most stunning array of tattoos. Her makeup was flawless, her long, wavy blonde hair the kind you see in commercials, and one look at her spaghetti strap olive-green velvet dress and the combat boots she'd paired with it made me want to raid her closet and be her best friend immediately.

After our introductions, I chanced a glance at Kyle, who was laughing with the guys. His eyes flicked to me, and my cheeks warmed again when the corner of his mouth tilted up just an inch, like he was replaying our kiss and wondering where the hell it came from.

As if I had a clue. I felt like I'd been possessed.

"I have to tell you, we were all a little shocked to hear Kyle was bringing someone with him," Julep said, calling my attention back to the girls. "This is the first time he's introduced us to a girlfriend."

"That's because it's the first time he's *had* one," Riley chimed in with a smirk.

The comment sent a mixture of emotions through me. I hated the first thing I felt, a lash of jealousy thinking about the women he'd been with, the parade of them he'd likely had in his bed throughout the years.

But the next sensation was a distinct and penetrating sadness, knowing how alone he must have been to have behaved that way in the first place.

Riley put her arm around me, leading me toward the lobby bar. "I heard you grew up together. We should swap stories. You tell me all the embarrassing ones from high school, and I'll tell you about the time he had to shave my name into his head."

"That game was rigged!" Kyle yelled from behind us, which made all the girls laugh.

Then, they were threading their arms with me and with each other, and we strolled up to the bar like a burlesque troupe.

I was quiet while they ordered us drinks, Giana promising me I would love the fruity gin one she was having the virgin version of. I'd forgotten she was pregnant until that comment, and I noticed then that she had a little bump under the flared, plaid skirt she wore.

My chest hurt a bit as I stood there watching them all, the way they so easily laughed and joked with each other. I could tell they were best friends.

I'd never had anything like that.

"So, how did you and Kyle meet exactly?" Julep asked once we all had cocktails.

I cleared my throat, stirring mine. "We went to high school together."

"I heard you were his babysitter," Mary said, tilting her martini glass toward me. "I've had that job before, too. We can commiserate."

"Babysitter?" Julep asked.

"Long story short, his parents didn't trust him after a massive party he threw his freshman year, and they offered to pay me to basically keep him in line. I'm only a couple years older than he is," I said.

"Oh, God. I bet he *hated* that," Riley said. "I can picture him throwing fits."

"He was an absolute horror the first month or so," I confirmed, and I didn't know why, but a smile spread on my face as I took a sip of my drink. "Although, I think he secretly liked when I bossed him around."

"That tracks," Mary said. "He called me daddy when I lived with him."

I nearly spit out my drink. "Lived with him?"

"Against my will, trust me," she said. "Long story short, I had no place to live, and the guys let me stay at The Pit for a while."

"Okay, but can we get back to the most important question here," Giana said, waving her friend off. Her eyes lit with excitement when she turned to me. "How did you reconnect? How long have you been dating?"

"Yeah, and how do you put up with the smell of his cleats?" Riley added.

140

I laughed with the rest of them, even as my heart started pounding in my chest.

Kyle and I hadn't talked about any of this. We hadn't made a plan.

I didn't want to say anything different than what he might be telling the guys right now, so I tried to get as close to the truth as possible.

"I showed him a house. I'm a real estate agent in Seattle. We went to dinner to catch up and…" I shrugged. "Here we are."

"Second-chance!" Giana said on a dreamy sigh. "I love that one."

Riley rolled her eyes. "Sorry about G. She can't help but romanticize everything, due to her consuming approximately four smutty books a day."

"If you're looking for recommendations, I have a Spicy Books for Beginners list," Giana said to me with a wink.

"So, you're in real estate?" Julep asked. "I have an unhealthy addiction to home renovation shows. What made you get into the business?"

I blew out a breath, trying to keep up with the pace of conversation that felt kind of like an interrogation. "Honestly, I was just trying to find a job I could do while also taking care of my son."

There was a brief pause from the group, and I waited for it — for the reaction I'd had from many girls my age when I told them about Sebastian. Sure, I'd met moms who were as young as I was, but more often than not in Seattle, I was the youngest.

And more often than not, girls my age couldn't imagine having a kid yet, and they also couldn't hide their pity when they found out *I* had one. It was like they felt sorry for me, like I was missing out on partying and living it up the way they were.

If only they knew that partying was the last thing I wanted to do. If only they could understand that having Sebastian had changed my life for the better.

I loved him more than I loved anything or anyone in the world.

And where it might have seemed boring or like an obligation to most women my age, I cherished every moment I got to spend with my kid. I lived for our adventures, for our lazy days, for our nights we laughed so hard that tears ran down our cheeks.

I waited for someone to do the awkward, "Oh, you have a kid? That's so sweet!" thing, but instead, Giana jumped for joy and abandoned her glass on the bar so she could grab onto me.

"You have a *son?!* Oh, my God! Show us!"

The girls all gathered around me as I pulled up my phone and showed them my background, which was Sebastian grinning at the camera from where he was bundled up and making a snow angel.

I was met with a chorus of *AWWW* before Julep was begging for more photos, and Mary was asking his name, and Riley was asking what sports he played, all while Giana tried not to cry.

"Okay, I need all your advice," Giana said, one hand on her belly and the other reaching for her mocktail once I'd put my phone away. "Because your girl is very knowledgeable when it comes to books, PR, and wrangling that one over there," she said, pointing to a brunet beast of a man I assumed was Clay Johnson. "But being a mom?" She shook her head. "I'm clueless."

"Honestly, I think we all are. We just do our best to figure it out as we go," I said. "You'll be great."

Giana's eyes watered, and she fanned her face. "Sorry. These stupid hormones have turned me into an absolute mess. Oh!" She covered her mouth on a gasp. "Single mom! Another of my favorite tropes. Has Kyle met Sebastian yet?"

I couldn't hide how I melted at that question, and all the girls saw it, because when I nodded, they squealed and surrounded me, begging for details.

But then, a large, warm hand wrapped around my hip from behind, and Kyle sidled up next to me, tucking me under his arm with a kiss against my hair.

I felt that kiss all the way down to my toes.

"Alright, I think it's time I get my date up to our room before you four scare her onto the next flight out of here," he said, winking down at me with a smile that made me melt even more into his side.

I told myself to get a grip, to remind my stupid body that all of this was for show.

But apparently, with that man's hands on me, my brain just didn't work properly.

The girls let out a chorus of jests at his expense.

"Boo!"

"You're no fun, Robbins."

"We were just getting to the good stuff!"

When Kyle only responded by chuckling and pulling me even more into him, the girls conceded, and I didn't miss the looks they gave each other.

Giana pulled me from Kyle's grasp long enough to wrap me in another hug.

"Go get settled. We'll see you at the rehearsal dinner tonight. There will be plenty of time for us to steal you away again."

"Good luck with that," Kyle said, sliding his arm around me once more. "I'm pretty selfish when it comes to this one."

I looked up at him, heart tripling its pace when I saw the sincerity in his gaze.

God, he's good at this.

When I looked back at the girls, they wore a mixture of emotions. Giana looked like she was about to burst, her eyes doubling in size and hands clasped in front of her heart. Julep and Riley were exchanging glances like they couldn't believe what they were seeing, and Mary was watching Kyle with an eyebrow ticked up in half-amusement, half-suspicion.

Kyle slid his hand down the inside of my arm, threading his fingers with mine. I stared at where he held my hand until the moment he tugged me away, and then I smiled over my shoulder at the girls, giving them a wave.

As soon as I turned around, I heard one of them squeal, and then they were chattering away — and there was no need to guess just *who* they were talking about.

"You survived," Kyle said when we rounded out of view and were walking toward the bank of elevators. He didn't drop my hand, even though no one was around to see us. "Sorry about all that. My friends are... a lot," he said on a smile that told me he loved that about them.

I'd only been in their presence a half hour, and already I understood why.

"They're..." I smiled, shaking my head as we stepped into the elevator.

"Crazy? Overbearing?"

"Lovely," I said, looking up at him. "I've... I've never

had anything like that."

His smile slipped at my admission, his brows furrowing together. Then, the elevator doors slid closed, muting the noise from the outside world as it shot us up toward our floor.

And the moment we were alone, it felt like all the oxygen had been left in the lobby.

I was suddenly very aware of how close we stood, of how good he smelled, at how my lips still tingled with the memory of his pressed against them.

Kyle's gaze dropped to where he still held my hand, his Adam's apple bobbing in his throat. Then, his eyes flicked back up to me.

He made no move to break the contact.

"That was some kiss down there," he said, arching a brow. His smile returned when my cheeks burned at his words, and I could only imagine how red my face was.

I wanted to bury it in his chest like I did before, but instead, I covered it with my free hand on a groan.

"Too much?"

"Not at all," he said quickly. "I'm just surprised by the gusto without any practice."

I dropped my hand, glaring up at him with a teasing smile. "You say that like we haven't kissed before."

"We haven't in years, and never like that."

Those words hung between us for only a split second before the elevator doors opened.

Kyle tugged me out, still holding my hand.

"Well, I'm proud of you," I said, hoping to lighten the tension threatening to suffocate me.

"Proud?" Kyle asked as he thumbed a card out of the small envelope he had in his hand. He still didn't drop mine as he did.

"Yeah," I said, lowering my voice to a playful whisper. "When we were younger, you couldn't kiss me without popping a boner. And look at you now."

I nudged his ribs with the tease, which made Kyle's jaw hit the floor before he barked out a laugh.

"You're going to pay for that comment," he promised.

And even though we both laughed, goosebumps swept over me, my clearly disturbed mind running through all the ways I wouldn't mind him making me pay...

But his laugh died as soon as he opened the door to our room, and when I followed his gaze, my smile slid off my face like a runny egg.

It was a beautiful room, spacious and modern with soft jazz playing from a speaker on one of the nightstands. We had a view of the city, the mountains stretching behind it in the distance.

But there was a real big problem.

Because it only had one bed.

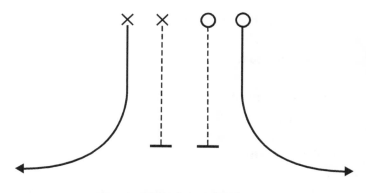

CHAPTER 18

Kyle

I hung up the phone with a sigh, scrubbing my hand over my face before I balanced my elbows on my knees and stared at the ground between my shoes.

I was afraid to even look at Madelyn.

"I swear," I started, wringing my hands together. I finally lifted my eyes to hers. "I booked a two-bedroom suite."

Madelyn was still frozen in the same place she'd been when I made the call down to the front desk. She was standing next to her suitcase by the window that looked out over the city, her knuckles white where she held the handle of it like she was ready to bolt.

I ran a hand through my hair, picking up the phone again. "I'll call for a cot. They don't have any suites available, but—"

"Kyle, you're like eight-feet tall," she said, and I breathed a little sigh of relief when she let go of the grip she had on her suitcase. "You're not sleeping on a cot."

147

I was still holding the phone, ready to dial the front desk as she looked around the room with her little mouth twisting to the side.

"This couch is huge," she said, gesturing to the sofa in the little seating area our room had. "I can sleep there easily. We just need some sheets and a blanket."

"Not happening, Mads."

I didn't mean for the words to growl out of me the way they did, didn't mean to sound like a bossy fucking prick. But there was absolutely no way I was letting that woman sleep on a couch.

When she looked at me, her expression told me she knew better than to argue.

We were both silent for a moment, and then she let out a sigh, running her hands through her hair and relinquishing the grip she had on her suitcase completely. She walked over to where I sat by the phone, forcing a smile that didn't quite reach her eyes.

"Look, we're adults. That bed is ginormous," she added with a sweep of her hand.

"Is that a word?"

"Sebastian says it is, so yes."

I smiled.

"We can handle sleeping in the same bed for a few nights," she said, and she might have actually believed those words.

At least, until the moment they left her mouth.

Because when they did, she swallowed, her neck flushing the prettiest pink as she looked at the bed and then dragged her gaze back to me.

"Yeah," I said, and then cleared my throat, because the word came out like a fucking squeak. "Yeah," I repeated, voice normal again. "It'll be fine. We can put a line of pillows between us."

Madelyn arched a brow. "A pillow fort. We're pretty well versed in building those."

"Oh, God. Leave the building to me, okay? We all know what happened the last time you played architect."

She reached behind her for a decorative pillow and launched it at me, sticking her tongue out when I caught it effortlessly.

"It's not *my* fault! You farted and brought the whole thing down!"

I rolled my lips together, but it was no use — the fact that this gorgeous, grown ass woman just said the word *farted* and then blushed about it made me lose it.

A laugh barreled out of me, and then Madelyn was grabbing another pillow to throw at me. Before she could, though, I stood and swooped her up over my shoulder like a defenseman trying to get to the quarterback. I hauled her toward the bed and dropped her down into it, her hair splaying across the white comforter when I did.

"You better sleep with one eye open tonight, Robbins," she threatened, leaning up on her elbows to glare at me.

I dropped down on top of her, fists hitting the bed on either side of her head, mouth dropping until I was just a few inches above hers.

"Or what?"

I knew instantly that I'd taken it too far.

I was eating up the fact that she was showing a little bit of who she used to be, that her feistiness was coming out the more time we spent together. Razzing each other used to be our favorite way to communicate.

But she wasn't smiling anymore.

She was staring up at me with wide eyes, her breath shallow in her chest, lips parted.

This wasn't just a friendly gesture.

This was flirting.

And there was no one around to pretend for.

Fuck.

I tried to play it off, laughing and pushing off the bed to stand. I reached a hand down for hers. "Alright, let's unpack. You can plot how to kill me while you put your panties in a drawer."

She rolled her eyes as I helped her stand.

And I hoped like hell I hadn't just ruined whatever progress we were making.

Madelyn

We unpacked in silence.

My heart finally stopped racing about halfway through, and then Kyle put on a playlist — a mixture of rap from the 90s, 00s, and 10s. I felt like I took my first real breath when "So Fresh, So Clean" by OutKast came on.

I bobbed my head to the beat, singing along in my head as I hung my dress for the wedding. Every now and then, I'd glance at Kyle, who was busy unpacking his own things.

My heart rate spiked again when I blinked and saw him on top of me on that bed, that wicked gleam in his eyes.

Or what?

I shivered, closing my eyes and shaking my head. He was just playing around. It was a joke.

But it was so close to how we *used* to be, how we used to flirt and test the friendship boundary between us with little stunts like that.

It could have been innocent.

But we both knew it wasn't.

I needed to clear the air, to get things back to comfortable between us. Otherwise, I was going to crawl out of my skin.

We had a whole weekend together, and I didn't want to spend it walking on eggshells.

"Your friends seem really close," I said, and then covered my mouth with a yawn, shaking it off. I'd been tired from the moment I woke up this morning, but between flying, the chaos in the lobby, and the adrenaline spike from Kyle pinning me on the bed — I was downright exhausted now.

Kyle smiled from where he was tucking some athletic shorts into one of the dresser drawers. "I told you — like family."

"Mary said she lived with you at one point?" I cocked a brow.

"Aw, don't be jealous, Mads," he said, crossing to where I was still working on unpacking. He'd finished up, tucking his empty suitcase into the closet. He plopped down on the couch to watch me. "She was all Leo's, from the moment she moved in."

I rolled my eyes, but then frowned a bit, glancing at him and then focusing on smoothing out the wrinkles in the tops I'd brought.

"All of the girls had... interesting stories to tell about you."

Kyle quieted, crossing an ankle over his opposite knee. "I'm sure they did."

"I found it quite odd," I admitted. "It just seems like the Kyle they knew is..."

"Different from the one you did?"

We locked eyes for a moment, and then I went back to unpacking.

"I was going through a lot," Kyle said. "I just didn't think making friends was important. I focused on football and on growing a social media following. I knew having a big audience could help sell me to a team. It also helped with getting paid, even in college. I made my own money with all the Name, Image, and Likeness deals that I could get."

"Your parents weren't helping you?" I asked, genuinely shocked.

Kyle's jaw hardened. "I didn't want their help."

My mouth was dry as I thought of how to respond but came up blank.

Kyle's father was one of the most complicated creatures I'd ever known in my life. He was respected where we grew up, always serving as a leader — at our schools, at our church, at a whole slew of community initiatives.

But I knew what happened behind closed doors.

I knew that when he drank too much, he turned into someone unrecognizable. And I knew that when that happened, Kyle seemed to always be in the way.

My stomach cramped as a flash of memories hit me — bruises on Kyle's skin, cuts on his eyebrows and mouth.

I was there for him back then.

But now, I could relate.

I understood him in a way I wished I never had to.

When I tucked my suitcase away in the closet, I covered another yawn, stretching my mouth wide. "I'm excited to see you with your friends," I said. "It's nice to get a glimpse of who you were after..."

I swallowed, not sure how to finish that.

After you left?

After you left me?

"What about you?" Kyle asked. "I don't think I'm the only one who's changed since high school."

I smiled on a sigh as I sat on the edge of the bed. "My life has been pretty boring compared to yours."

"Doesn't seem boring to me, especially not with Sebastian."

Kyle smiled on that remark, but it twisted my gut.

"He's everything to me," I whispered, looking at my fingers in my lap.

I'd peeled half my nail polish off on the plane ride here, and I cursed internally, knowing I'd look like a kid next to all those beautiful women I just met in the lobby. No doubt, they'd have perfect manicures.

"How did you and Marshall meet?"

I chuckled, looking up at him. "You really want to know that?"

His jaw ticced. "Yes."

"You're still a shit liar," I said on a laugh. I shook my head, shrugging. "It's nothing romantic. I was out at a bar that I had to use a fake ID to get into. He was there with some friends. He saw me trying to drink away my problems, and came over pretending to be an undercover cop, and then he was making me laugh, and then..."

I swallowed, not wanting to finish that sentence, and realizing I didn't need to.

Kyle was smart enough to fill in the blanks.

"You got married pretty quickly," Kyle guessed. "You must have really fallen for him."

I snorted. "Getting married was not my idea. But, I got pregnant, and Marshall is old school, so..."

I didn't dare look at Kyle. I didn't want to see his reaction to that.

I yawned again, covering it with the back of my wrist before I shook my head. "I'm not being fair, I guess. I really did fall hard for him." I paused. "It's just that now, I realize I fell for who he was making me believe he was, not who he actually is." I sniffed. "Hard to find anything kind to say about a man who..."

I sucked in a breath, not able to finish the sentence.

And when I let that breath out, Kyle was beside me, his large frame sinking into the mattress and making me lean into him a bit without meaning to.

He covered my hand with his, squeezing it.

And I knew from that alone that I didn't need to say another word.

He understood.

Another yawn found me, and I laughed a little, eyes watering as I shook it off. "Sorry."

"You should take a nap," Kyle said on a smile.

"No, no. We need to go meet up with your friends. I'll just splash some cold water on my face. I—"

I tried to stand, but Kyle grabbed me by the hips and pulled me back down onto the bed.

He let go of me as soon as I was sitting, but I felt the imprint of his hands on my skin like he'd branded me.

"Look at me," he said, and when my eyes slowly trailed up to meet his, he grinned in a way that made me feel like a teenage girl with a crush again. "I'm going to get out of here so you can have some quiet. Call your mom, check in on Sebastian, and then take a nap."

"But—"

"I'll have some tea sent up around five, that's plenty of time for you to shower and get ready for the night. You still like Earl Grey? Honey and milk?"

My lips parted.

He remembered the kind of tea I loved?

He smiled a little when I didn't respond, and then his hand reached forward, tucking my hair behind one ear. "When's the last time you took a nap?"

I finally closed my lips on a swallow, then shook my head. "I can't even remember."

"See?" He held up his hands and splayed them wide over the room. "Look at this. You're in a fancy hotel room with this *ginormous* bed all to yourself for a couple hours. Take a fucking nap, Mads. You deserve it."

My eyes stung, and I blinked several times to keep them from watering. "What about you?"

"I have five rowdy teammates downstairs to keep me occupied," he said, standing and moving to the window.

He pushed a button and the blackout curtains slowly lowered, instantly making the room dark, save for the lights we'd turned on. He put those out one by one, until only the lamp on one of the bedside tables was lit.

"I'll be back around six," he said, grabbing his wallet and a hotel key from the table. He tucked them both into his pocket before walking over to me again. "Take a nap. Take a shower, or hell, a bath — did you see that tub in there?" He grinned. "Drink your tea, enjoy some peace and quiet, and then you can face my crazy friends for a night."

He laughed with the joke, but I couldn't even smile in response.

My chest felt like it was going to explode.

He was taking care of me.

He was giving me something I hadn't had in years — alone time, without pressure to take care of Sebastian or the house or work.

My eyes pricked again, and this time I couldn't blink, because I knew if I did, I'd set the tears free.

Kyle leaned down, and with my breath still held captive in my throat, he pressed a kiss to my forehead.

We both stilled.

He froze like he didn't actually mean to do that, but like he couldn't help it.

I kept still so my tears wouldn't stream down my face.

Kyle stood and cleared his throat. "See you in a bit," he said, and then he rushed out the door like he was late.

As soon as he was gone, I closed my eyes, two parallel rivers of tears staining my cheeks.

I called my mom.

I talked to my son.

I changed into a fresh pair of underwear and oversized shirt.

And I crawled under those expensive sheets to have the best nap of my life.

CHAPTER 19
Kyle

A few hours later, I slid my key card over the sensor on our hotel room door, opening it slowly and quietly just in case Madelyn was still asleep.

I was greeted by the soft sound of music, something old and familiar sounding, though I couldn't quite place it.

Tossing my wallet and hotel key on the desk, I took in the room.

The bed was a mess, the comforter and sheets twisted up and pillows piled up like she'd made that fort around her even though I wasn't here.

The tea I'd sent up was on the nightstand, a kettle as well as two mugs. One was untouched while the other had just a sliver of tea left in it. I lifted it to my nose and inhaled, smiling at the way that scent brought memories back.

I promptly closed my eyes and shook my head on an internal curse.

Keep it together, Robbins.

I knew when I had lowered my lips to her forehead earlier — without an audience to pretend for — that I was in deep shit.

This was all pretend. This was me doing what I could to protect her while selfishly using the situation to avoid being solo at another wedding.

Holding her hand in front of my friends? Fair. Stealing a kiss or two? Also fair.

But showing that kind of emotion when no one was around to see it?

It was dangerous.

I expected Madelyn would probably tell me so, too, as I followed the sound of the music. Now that she'd taken a nap and had some tea, she was probably overanalyzing that move I'd made and wondering what the hell I was thinking.

I was fully ready for her to lay into me just like she had that day I'd proposed this scheme at the house showing. I could hear her already, the way her voice would grow stern as she pointed her finger at me and reminded me we weren't even friends, let alone anything more.

But when I made it to the bathroom, I thought I'd find her doing her hair or makeup in the mirror.

Instead, I found her in the bathtub.

It was only a split second. I turned the corner, ready to ask her how she was feeling, and my eyes had shot to where she was sprawled out in the water. Her eyes were closed, her head resting on the back of the tub, a thin layer of bubbles just barely hiding her breasts from view.

I jolted back out of view, praying she didn't hear or see me. For a long moment, I stayed like that, back pressed against the wall and heart hammering out of my chest as I waited for her to yell at me.

But she didn't.

Instead, a full sixty seconds passed with just that soft music crooning and the sounds of water gently splashing.

And then, a moan.

I froze, eyes wide and heart picking up its pace. My fingers rolled into fists at my sides as I forced a slow, steady exhale.

Madelyn whimpered, the sound of the water splashing picking up pace a bit, and then she let out another long, deep moan.

Fuck.

She was touching herself.

I closed my eyes with my nostrils flaring, pressing my back even more into the wall to keep myself from bolting into that bathroom and doing something I'd regret.

I needed to leave.

I needed to slowly back away and take my stupid ass right back out the door.

But I was rooted in place, straining to hear another sweet sound over the music.

My cock was already rock hard, pitching a tent against my joggers. I listened to the water splashing, and then stilling, to the sound of labored breathing over the jazz until another low moan ripped from her throat.

I couldn't swallow past the knot in my throat, couldn't breathe properly with how hard my heart was beating.

And instead of walking away, I slid along the wall slowly, silently, until I could peek through the crack of the open door above the hinges.

All I could see at first was her foot, wet and dripping water on the tile floor. Her toes curled, a chorus of soft, whimpering sounds floating up from her lips.

Christ.

My cock begged for me to relieve it as I followed the line of her leg up, finding her head still tilted back in ecstasy, her lips parted, a line between her brows as her hands worked under the water.

I closed my eyes.

Time to leave, you fucking creep.

And I was doing just that.

I was turning around, ready to walk out when I heard her murmur something that stopped me in my tracks.

I strained to hear against the thumping of my heartbeat in my ears.

A moment later, she moaned again.

She moaned *my name*.

"Kyle," she breathed. "*Yes*, just like that."

A stronger man would have walked away. A smarter man would have gone into the hallway and waited ten minutes before knocking and loudly announcing their return.

But in that moment, I wasn't smart *or* strong.

I was helplessly driven by the lower half of my brain, and when it came to that woman, I was weak as fuck.

Madelyn gasped as one of her hands slid up to palm her breast, and I caught just the glimpse of her dark nipple before she covered it and arched into the touch.

I couldn't take it.

Swiftly, I reached into my joggers, one palm wrapping around my aching cock as I suffocated the groan I wanted to let loose as soon as I was touching myself. I kept my eyes locked on what little of her I could see through the slot above the door hinges, pumping myself in long, slow strokes as my eyes feasted on the sight of her.

She wet her lips as one hand squeezed her breast hard, and then that foot that was dangling over the tub found purchase on the edge. She pressed her weight into it, bucking her hips until she was lifted out of the water.

And then her pussy was above the bubbles, above the water, pink and glistening as she ran her fingers in tight circles over her clit.

I bit down hard on my lip to keep silent, fucking my hand faster to match her rhythm. She found the friction she was looking for out of the water, and her thighs quaked as she circled her clit and let out a whimpering moan.

"Jesus Christ," I whispered, so low it was barely a sound at all. I rolled my fist over my crown, flexing my hips into the touch as my breath grew shallower.

Madelyn's face was red now from straining, and she lifted her hips as much as she could, the hand on her breast moving down between her legs. She let out a hot, short breath as she plunged one finger inside herself, and a searing fire licked along my spine at the sight.

She was fucking her fingers, writhing in that water and chasing a release. Her chest heaved with every breath, her wet hair stuck to her lips and neck as she worked. She moved those fingers over her clit faster and faster, and I stifled another grunt as I matched her pace with my climax within reach.

"Yes," she whined, biting her lip. "Yes, Kyle. *God, yes.*"

"Oh, fuck," I growled, and I knew it was loud enough for her to hear, but she didn't stop. She bucked wilder, and I squeezed my eyes shut as I came, spraying the door with my release and curling my other hand into a fist to fight from making another fucking sound.

My release was short-lived, an explosion of pleasure and then a mind-numbing overdrive of sensation. I pulsed out the last of it, cursing when I saw the mess I'd made.

I needed to clean it up, but my selfish ass was too greedy.

I had to see her finish first.

I slowed my pace on my cock, shivering a bit when my fist covered the wet, sensitive tip as I brought my gaze back to Madelyn. She was close, her face beet red, legs trembling and breasts heaving with every ragged breath she took.

"Come on, baby," I silently encouraged. "Let me see you come."

As if she'd heard me, Madelyn went absolutely wild, touching herself with fervor as she writhed and bucked and moaned.

But then, she stopped.

Abruptly, she let herself fall back into the water, her hands flying up into her hair as she let out a frustrated groan.

I blinked, unsure of what was happening until she dragged those hands over her face and shook her head. She sank down into the water next, blowing bubbles underwater until she re-emerged and pushed her wet, copper locks back from her face.

Then, she was pulling the plug.

Fuck!

Hastily, I grabbed a tissue off the bedside table, cleaning my mess and my cock before I tucked it away again. I could hear Madelyn getting out of the bath as I silently tiptoed over to my key card and wallet before sneaking back out into the hallway.

I let out a loud breath of relief when I was outside, pressing my back to the wall and pinching the bridge of my nose.

"What the actual *fuck*, Kyle?"

I shook my head, sighing and looking up at the ceiling with my hand dropping down to slap against my thigh.

She said my name.

The memory of it made me close my eyes on another silent curse.

But then, my brain was hyper focused on the fact that she hadn't come.

It was like she *couldn't*.

And it made me absolutely feral with the need to take over and prove I could get her there.

When I felt marginally put together again, I slid my key card over the sensor again, this time loudly announcing my presence as soon as I pushed through the door.

"I'm back," I said, tossing my wallet and hotel key on the same desk I had before. "Are you decent? Because if so, I can go back out and wait for you to get naked."

I hoped the joke came out without the shake I swore I felt in my voice. I stayed by the foot of the bed, pretending like I was taking in the scene for the first time as Madelyn swung out of the bathroom in nothing but a towel.

She was still dripping wet, her face flushed and her smile a little strained. "In your dreams, Robbins," she said.

"My teenage dreams, for sure," I shot back with a wink.

She rolled her eyes, and I thought I saw her shaking a bit as she ran a hand over her wet hair and let out a long exhale.

"How long do I have before we need to go?"

I checked the time on my phone. "About an hour."

"Perfect. You need to shower? I can do my makeup in here."

My throat was tight when I nodded. "Yeah. I'll be quick."

"Take your time," she said, moving her stuff into the main bedroom where a large, floor-length mirror was.

She sank down right on the floor, legs crossed under her towel. For a second, she frowned at her reflection, sighing like she looked like hell when it was the exact opposite. Then, she looked up at me, her expression a bit solemn, brows folding together.

"Thank you," she said.

She didn't need to say what for. I could see it in her eyes.

She needed that time alone.

That time to rest, to wake up slowly and drink tea, to listen to music and touch herself in a bubble bath.

She probably hadn't done it in years.

I nodded, clearing my throat. "I'll be quick," I said again, which made me wince at the dumb repetitiveness, and Madelyn smiled, cheeks flushing a bit more when she turned back to her reflection.

I bolted for the shower, shutting the bathroom door behind me and ripping off my clothes like they were made of pine needles.

I ran that water as cold as it would go before I stepped under the spray.

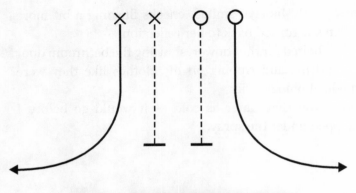

CHAPTER 20
Madelyn

Kyle was uncharacteristically quiet after his shower, and we got dressed and ready mostly in silence.

I didn't mind.

It was hardly *ever* silent in my life.

Besides, I was still slightly frustrated after my bath.

It was nothing new for me. Somewhere over the last couple of years, I'd lost the ability to make myself get off. I'd tried everything from toys to porn, but I could never turn my brain off long enough to fully release.

I was mildly aware it likely had to do with my ex-husband. Nothing about our sex life had been fun — especially since he loved to weaponize intimacy in a way that made it feel more like a chore than anything else. But maybe part of me was in denial about that. Maybe I just didn't want to deal with it.

Maybe I was pissed he had any semblance of power over me still, so I refused to acknowledge it at all.

After my nap, I'd felt stirred up. Maybe from the day's events, maybe from that *kiss*.

The water had been so warm and inviting, and the more I soaked, the more I ached for a release.

But I couldn't get myself there.

And what frustrated me almost as much as that fact was that I'd thought of Kyle in the process.

My cheeks heated as I worked on getting ready, the memory of my fantasy still bright behind my eyelids. I'd wondered what it would have felt like if that kiss we'd faked earlier had lingered. I'd imagined what could have happened if when he jokingly pinned me on the bed, he hadn't just laughed it off and left me to nap.

What if he would have stayed, pressing into me, his thigh gliding between mine.

What if he would have noted how faint my breath was, if he would have called me out on it.

What if he would have kissed me again — without anyone to perform for?

The insistent ache between my legs that I hadn't been able to take care of in the bath flared to life once more, and I cursed against it, focusing on the task at hand.

I took my time with my hair and makeup — as if that would somehow suddenly make me good at doing either. I had only a very basic knowledge that I picked up mostly from watching YouTube videos of teenagers.

My hair wouldn't curl, so I just straightened it, and in the end, my makeup was no more than moisturizer, concealer, a brush of shadow over my eyebrows and some mascara. I added a bit of lip gloss that I was fairly certain was four years old to finish the look.

I got dressed in one of the few dresses I owned, a very simple black dress my mom had purchased me as a gift for Christmas last year, and then sat on the edge of the bed to strap into my heels.

I was doing just that when Kyle rounded out of the bathroom, his eyes on where he was fastening a button around the wrist of his gray-blue button-down shirt.

My hands stilled where I was buckling my shoe, eyes scanning him from head to toe.

His hair was still a bit damp from the shower but styled with just the right amount of mousse. He had that swoop going, the one that reminded me of the boy I used to know. His tan skin and bright blue eyes blazed against the color of his shirt, and the way the cream slacks he'd paired with it hung off his hips made it impossible for my gaze not to snag there.

Kyle looked up, and I snapped my attention back to my heel, finishing the clasp before I stood and grabbed my clutch.

When I dragged my gaze to Kyle again, he was staring at me with his lips parted.

I tried not to flush at the sight of his eyes on me, at the way his Adam's apple bobbed and the muscle in his jaw ticced. He didn't rush his gaze after I caught him staring, either. He took his time like he had nothing to be ashamed of, letting his eyes wander over every inch of me.

His eyes finally found mine, and he arched a brow on a whistle.

"Damn, Mads."

The words were almost a whisper, they were so low, and they made goosebumps parade across my skin.

We were silent in the elevator on the way down to the lobby, Kyle checking the time on his watch. We also stood three feet from each other.

But the moment we hit the lower floor, Kyle looked at me, extending his arm with a crooked grin. "Let's give them something to talk about."

I blushed, looping my arm through his and letting him guide me into the lobby.

We didn't make it two steps before Giana grabbed me by my free arm and tugged hard enough to turn all three of us in the opposite direction.

"This way!"

She dragged us with enough force that we didn't even get the chance to argue or ask what was going on. Instead, Kyle and I shared curious looks before trying our best to keep up.

Clay jogged up behind us a moment later, looking over his shoulder before he grabbed Giana's hand protectively.

"Cops are here handling it, and hotel security has the front under control. We should be good this way."

"What's going on?" Kyle asked as we wove through some doors that I was fairly certain guests weren't supposed to access.

"Media got wind of the wedding," Giana grumbled.

My heart stopped in my chest, and I flicked my eyes up to Kyle, who pressed his lips together in a flat line.

The media.

I hadn't even *thought* of that.

I felt stupid for that fact, but before I could think too much on it, Kyle unlinked our arms so he could grab my hand, instead.

The moment he wrapped my hand in his, he gave it a squeeze, his eyes holding mine.

I've got you, that look said.

I swallowed down the knot in my throat as we hustled through the inner working of the hotel, following a path that clearly Giana and Clay were familiar with. We finally moved through a large kitchen that I assumed was for room service, and as soon as we pushed through the door that led outside, we were ushered into a waiting black car.

Kyle released my hand, and his palm slid to my lower back, instead. He shielded me with his entire body, and I felt the heat from him like an electric current in my bloodstream until the very moment he helped me into the car and slid in behind me.

There was no one at the back — at least, no one close enough that I could tell. I had braced myself for photographs, for flashes and people screaming at us. Instead, it had been completely silent, and once we piled in the car, the only sound was the labored breathing from all four of us.

"I don't think anyone got anything," Clay said, peeking out the tinted windows as the driver took off. He immediately turned to Giana, folding her hands in his and searching her eyes. "Are you okay?"

She grinned at him before kissing his knuckles. "Oh stop, I'm fine, you barbarian."

She dropped their hands to rest on her stomach, pressing Clay's palms flat against the small bump there, and he sighed with relief.

They pressed their foreheads together, closing their eyes, and I tore my gaze away.

Which left me looking up at Kyle.

His lips were pinched shut, his brow furrowed, eyes assessing me. "I'm so sorry, Madelyn. We... I didn't think..."

I squeezed his hand. "I'm okay."

He nodded, his jaw tight.

Then, as if it was the most natural thing in the world, he pulled me under his arm and kissed my temple, his next exhale warming my skin.

I tried not to overanalyze the media aspect too much as we drove across town, Giana and Clay finally letting go of each other and striking up conversation. But I couldn't help but spiral.

If someone got a picture of us together...

I shivered even at the thought. What would happen? What would my parents say? Would I lose all my privacy? Would they try to bother Sebastian?

The thought made my stomach tighten, but not as much as the next one that crossed my mind.

What would Marshall do?

I swallowed, hating that I was afraid of him. I could handle myself, but that didn't mean I wasn't still scared.

The rehearsal dinner was at a beautiful restaurant in the middle of the city. There didn't seem to be any paparazzi when we arrived, but Giana still asked the driver to take us around to the back. I could tell she was in public relations from the way she calmly handled everything, like she'd anticipated every possible scenario and was now enacting her second or third backup plan with ease.

We were greeted by the staff, who led us to the rooftop location of the event.

I promptly lost the ability to breathe when we entered.

It was an open terrace, half of it under a sheltered roof, and the rest open air. Edison lights were strung from one corner to the other, and candles flickered on every cocktail table in sight. Cream linens and soft piano music coming from a musician in the corner helped set the ambiance, but not as much as the backdrop.

The sun setting behind the Rocky Mountains, Denver illuminating slowly with lights flickering on more and more as the sky grew darker.

I didn't realize I'd walked straight out to the railing until my fingers curled around the banister, and I gaped at the brazen gold of the setting sun against the cool blue of dusk rushing in on its heels.

It was beautiful.

And for some reason, it made my eyes water.

I felt completely out of control of my emotions. This one day — no — the last two *weeks* had been so much... I didn't know how to sort through it all.

Kyle coming back into my life, everything going on with Marshall, then the deal, shopping, Kyle meeting Sebastian, Kyle defending me against Marshall, the plane ride, the fake kissing and touching that felt more real than I'd ever admit out loud, the hotel room, the way he saw what I needed without me saying a word...

My heart started racing the more I thought about it all, and then, there was a warm, steady hand at the small of my back again.

"Wow," Kyle breathed, sliding up next to me with his eyes on the sunset. His arm snaked around me, fingers curling on my hip and holding me close.

I shut my eyes against the panic.

When I opened them again, Kyle was smiling at the mountains. He looked at me next, and that smile faltered.

He looked around us like he wanted to make sure no one was watching, and then he leaned down, lowering his voice.

"We can leave. We can go right now. I'll—"

I kissed him.

I silenced whatever words he was going to offer next with my arms sliding up around his neck, pulling his mouth down to mine.

He stiffened only for a split second before he was gripping me to him, both of us inhaling the kiss like it was everything we needed.

I told myself I did it for show.

I told myself I was just holding up my end of the bargain.

And I swore to myself it wasn't because, in that moment of panic, I knew kissing him would make me feel calm again.

And it did.

My heart rate steadied, lungs expanding easier when he slid his hands up my arms to cradle my face and hold me to him. He kissed me slow and softly, his lips covering mine in sensual, methodic kisses that made me feel like he was exploring me, like he was mapping out every centimeter of my lips.

I couldn't be sure how long we stood there losing ourselves at that railing with the sun setting behind us, but eventually, Kyle pulled back, tucking me under his arm again with his lips coming right to my ear.

"If you don't stop, I'm going to have a situation," he said, his lips against my skin.

I frowned, confused, but then watched as he subtly used his free hand to adjust himself in his slacks.

Fire licked along my spine.

I'd turned him on.

I felt the heat blasting my neck as I peeked up at him with a grin. "Oops."

He dug his fingers into my side as I laughed, but then he dropped his mouth to my ear again.

"I need to apologize to you. Or, rather, I *should* apologize... but I'm not sure I'm sorry."

I frowned. "Apologize? For what?"

"I heard you earlier."

I froze, my next exhale lodging in my throat as a zip of excitement ran all the way down my spine.

He heard me?

"You said my name."

Oh, my God.

He heard *me.*

Whatever steadiness he'd given me with that kiss was obliterated, and I felt my heartbeat in my throat as he sucked the lobe of my ear between his teeth.

"I also know you left yourself... unsatisfied," he rasped.

My cheeks flamed — not from embarrassment, but from arousal at the thought of his admission. A small part of me wondered if I should be appalled, if I should feel angry or violated.

But I didn't. Not even a little bit.

Intrigue filled me, instead.

"Don't worry," he added with another nip of my earlobe. "I can help with that."

My next breath shook out of me, chills racing all the way down to my toes.

I angled my chin up toward him, our mouths centimeters apart, my heart beating out of my chest. When our eyes met, his nostrils flared, his fingertips tightening where they held my hip.

I wanted to know more.

I wanted him to tell me exactly what he'd heard, what he'd seen...

What he'd do next.

His throat bobbed, hand sweeping across my chin before he gently wrapped it around the back of my neck. When he wet his lips, lightning struck me to my core as if his tongue had been between my thighs, instead.

But before either of us could say another word, we were practically tackled from behind, Leo Hernandez popping up between us and hooking his arms around both our necks.

"Alright, you lovebirds. Save the snogging for the hotel room and come party with your friends."

"What, are you English now?" Mary asked, offering me an apologetic smile as she shook her head at her boyfriend.

I hoped like hell I had a convincing, normal smile on my face as Kyle reluctantly put distance between us, the smile on his face seemingly just as strained. I hoped no one could see the way my legs trembled with every step we took toward the bar.

Because inside, I was burning.

And when Kyle slid his arm around me when we rejoined his friends, the smirk on his lips told me he knew it.

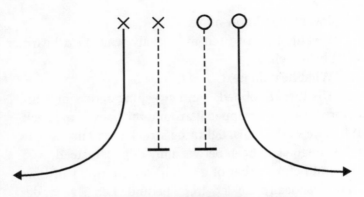

CHAPTER 21

Kyle

I don't know what I expected from Madelyn at the rehearsal dinner, but it was far from what I got.

Ever since we'd reconnected, she'd had a guard up. She'd been standoffish, quick to shut me down whenever I tried to get her to loosen up and have some fun. She'd fought me on nearly everything, it'd seemed.

But tonight, she was flowing like a river — free and beautiful, shaping the earth to curve around her and pulling everything and everyone into her current.

I watched her talk to my friends at the bar, listened to her laugh with the guys when we sat down at the table and they told her stories of our time in college.

I leaned in when she shared stories of her own, like how she'd ended up in a karaoke battle with a local radio station DJ one night when she was out drinking with her friends.

I tried to focus on the guys when she was on the dance floor with the girls, tried and failed not to watch her too long over the rim of my glass as she wound her hips and rolled her body in time with the beat.

She fit in like she'd always been a part of our group, like she'd spent the last five years with us, too.

It put a dull pain in my chest, one I couldn't decide if I liked or not.

Maybe it was the nap she had. Maybe it was being states away from her responsibilities.

Maybe it was being around me again.

The selfish part of me hoped it was the latter that let her feel safe to cut loose, to laugh and dance and sass my friends.

That was the Madelyn I knew.

God, I'd missed her.

The thought hit me with a roil of my stomach as I drained the last of my tequila when it was time to shut things down, my eyes on where Madelyn was taking a selfie with Mary and Julep. They took a normal one first, all of them smiling. Then, they did some type of smoldering look before breaking out into a fit of laughter.

"I like her."

I blinked, turning to find Zeke to my left. He was drinking water as usual, sober since the day I'd met him, and he set his glass on the bar before leaning against it.

"How long have you two been seeing each other?"

I folded my arms over my chest. "It's complicated."

"How so?"

"Let's just say we have history."

He chuckled. "I know all about that."

I smirked a little. I guessed he *did* know about that, considering Riley hated his guts after a rough patch they'd gone through in high school.

"Whatever happened between you two, it seems you've put it to bed," he assessed.

I frowned. "Not really. Can't put it to bed if you don't talk about it."

"What's stopping you?"

I swallowed past the sticky knot in my throat, my eyes still on Madelyn across the room as the last song played.

"Fear of what she'll say," I admitted, turning to look at my friend. "Fear of what *I'll* say in return."

Zeke nodded, clapping my shoulder. "When the time is right, you'll work it out. For now, it seems like you two are doing alright." His eyes were sincere as he looked at me. "She's good for you, man. I can tell."

"Yeah. For once, I'm not annoyed by your antics," Holden added, sliding up on the other side of me.

"I haven't seen you pull your phone out *once* all night," Leo chimed in, and then I was surrounded by my asshole friends who couldn't help but rib me.

But I smiled through it all, because they were right.

I hadn't reached for my phone. I hadn't even thought about posting in days.

And Madelyn *was* good for me.

My heart stammered a bit at the realization, because it was all under pretense.

I was helping her, keeping her safe from Marshall until we could find me a house, get her commission, and get her far away from Seattle.

She was just pretending to be mine, putting on a show for my friends as her part of our little deal.

But even as I thought it, something niggled in the back of my mind that maybe there was something more to it, something more to *us*.

I could still hear her saying my name in that bathtub, see her chest rising and falling as she chased a release she never quite found...

I smirked, eyes heating when Madelyn's gaze slid
to me from the dance floor. The music had stopped, the
party over, and I didn't miss how her cheeks reddened
the longer I stared.

I can help with that, I'd promised her.

It was a tease, a way for me to confess without making it too serious.

But her breath had hitched when I'd said it.

Her skin had erupted in chills when I'd breathed
the words against her neck.

And now, all I could think about was getting her
back to that hotel room with one bed to see if she'd let
me make good on my promise.

"Alright, ladies and gentlemen," Clay said, calling
attention to him and Giana in the middle of the room.
"We want to thank you for celebrating with us tonight,
and for getting together on such short notice to celebrate our wedding."

"We can't wait to continue celebrating with you tomorrow," Giana added, one hand absentmindedly cra-
dling her small bump.

"Our time is up here, but... the night isn't over yet,"
Clay added, and then he nodded his head at Braden,
who appeared with a box full of glow sticks in one hand
and a flashing volleyball in the other.

Madelyn joined me at the bar just as I laughed and
said, "Oh, shit," under my breath.

"What's going on?" she asked.

I smirked, arching a brow at her, but it was Clay
who answered as the rest of us erupted in a mixture of
cheers and groans, depending.

"It's Ravey Ball time, bitches!"

Half an hour later, we were at a sand volleyball court on the outskirts of the city.

It was dark, save for the lights from the surrounding buildings and a lone streetlamp overhead. But in no time, we were all wearing glow stick necklaces and bracelets, and the volleyball flashed every color of the rainbow as Braden and Clay volleyed back and forth while we waited for the last of the crew to show up.

Giana had picked up a couple of twelve-packs of hard seltzers and beer on the way over, and I sipped from one as I watched Madelyn with an amused smile.

She was next to me, one foot on the bench as she stretched. She hadn't picked up a beer when everyone else did. Instead, she'd been doing jumping jacks and high knees — in a dress, mind you — and now she was stretching and swinging her arms, a determined look glossing over her eyes.

Those eyes flicked to me the longer I stared. "What?"

"Nothing."

She narrowed her gaze even more.

"Just love to see you're still as competitive as you were when you were in high school," I said, holding a hand up in surrender.

"I'm not competitive," she said, cracking her neck.

"Uh-huh," I mused. Then, I finished my beer and leaned in close enough for my next words to sweep across the back of her neck. "And I'm not still thinking about you in that bathtub."

She froze, and even in the darkness, I could tell she was blushing.

But she swatted me across the chest after only a split second, and I barked out a laugh, jogging over to where everyone was gathering by the net. Madelyn followed, standing next to me with her arms crossed.

"Alright, a quick rule refresher," Clay said, tossing the ball up and catching it. "There will be two captains. We'll alternate picking people until we're in two teams of five. Giana is sitting out, for obvious reasons."

"Go team!" she yelled from the sideline, doing a fake cheerleader kick.

Clay smirked and shook his head before his attention was back on us. "She'll be in charge of blasting the music and will be line judge, should we need one. Winning team needs fifteen points and to win by at least two. Otherwise, regular rules of volleyball apply."

Madelyn nodded, bouncing on her toes as I tried and failed to stifle a laugh.

She elbowed me in the ribs.

"Braden, Madelyn — you're captains."

Braden frowned. "Why us?"

"Because you're the only single one here and Madelyn is our guest of honor."

She didn't even hesitate. Madelyn strode up to stand next to Braden, pointing at Riley. "My first pick."

She and Riley high-fived each other as I gaped at her with my jaw on the court, and the guys bent over laughing at my expression.

"That's just cold," I said.

"Oh, don't be a baby. I'll get you next time," Madelyn said.

"What if Braden picks me?"

"Holden," Braden said, and I turned my look of betrayal on him. He just shrugged. "Sorry, man."

I shook my head, tonguing the inside of my cheek as I crossed my arms over my chest. I pretended to be offended, but really, I couldn't help but smile as Madelyn stepped fully into her element. And when she called me to be on her team next, I walked slowly over to join her, dropping my voice low enough so no one else could hear.

"Enjoy being the one to call the shots now because that'll be my role when we get back to the room."

She stilled, swallowing.

And when she called out Clay's name, I smiled at how it came out in a squeak.

When the teams were set, we split up on the court, Giana blared EDM music so loud we couldn't hear each other even if we wanted to — and the game began.

The first few volleys were a mess. Ravey Ball meant you couldn't hear your teammates calling out if they were going for the ball, which meant we were running into each other and slamming down into the sand more than we were successfully hitting anything. Add in the fact that it was dark other than the flashing ball, and you couldn't tell you were about to hit someone until it was already too late.

I didn't mind the few times I ran into Madelyn, our bodies tangling as we rolled down into the sand.

I also found it amusing how pissed Madelyn was getting, especially when we fell behind by two. She painted on her game face, and when Riley served the ball, I knew my girl meant business.

We scored five unanswered points before the serve switched to Braden's team.

Giana cheered from the sideline, though we couldn't hear her over the music. Back and forth, we battled it out, playing volleyball in the dark in the same clothes we wore to the party.

The girls didn't give a fuck they were in dresses. Mary tied her long one up by her hip to stay out of her way while Julep pinned hers together between her legs with a safety pin, creating makeshift shorts.

The guys had all stripped out of their shirts, me included, and half of us had our slacks rolled up to just under our knees. Leo had tied his tie around his head, looking like a Teenage Mutant Ninja Turtle.

When it was 12-14, us, Madelyn huddled us in the middle.

"Alright, this is it," she screamed over the music. "Watch each other. Be smart. Wave if the ball is yours, and don't call ones you can't get. This is our set."

Riley and Clay nodded in determination. I watched Madelyn with that ache in my chest re-emerging, and when I looked at Mary, she was smirking at me like she knew something I didn't.

We threw our hands into the middle, launching them into the air on a *win!* before we all took our places.

It was Clay's serve, and he launched it perfectly to Leo.

Leo volleyed it to Mary, who hit the ball straight up, right in line for me to spike it. I hit it hard over the net and straight down, but Zeke caught it in time, sending it up into the air again. Their team volleyed it twice, and then it was sent up in front of Holden.

Who was jumping, and ready to spike.

It happened so fast I couldn't register it, couldn't block it, and the ball zoomed past me toward the open space of court.

I cursed.

But then there was a blur of movement, and the ball soared high into the air.

Madelyn was sprawled out in the sand for only a second before she popped up again, getting out of the way, and Riley jumped to hit the ball to me next.

I hit it as hard as I could, and this time, it landed in the sand on the other side of the net with Braden unable to stop it.

We erupted, Mary and Clay high-fiving each other as Riley wrapped Madelyn in a fierce hug. When she pulled back, I swept Madelyn into my arms and up onto my shoulders.

"You fucking dove for it!" I screamed over the noise.

"And you're surprised?" she asked, arching a brow down at me before she held her hands up in victory.

Giana turned the music down enough for us to gloat properly, me running around the court with Madelyn straddling my neck as the rest of our team did a synchronized dance in the middle.

After a few laps, I grabbed Madelyn's hips in my hands, carefully helping her down.

Every inch of her body dragged against mine as I did, and when she was standing again, we were both breathing heavily, my hands on her waist, hers braced against my bare chest.

Around us, my friends teased each other and laughed and called for another round.

But we were still, her eyes dancing between mine as I swallowed and fought the urge to pull her closer.

All the noise had faded to the background, Madelyn's skin hot where I held her.

She wet her lips, pressing up on her toes and sliding her arms around my neck.

"Don't I get a kiss for that game-winning point?"

My chest sparked with possession, and I gave in, fisting my hands in her dress and pulling her flush against me.

"I think it was *me* who scored the winning point," I combatted, nose flaring as I stared at her lips.

Those lips curled into a soft smile before they were touching mine, and I tasted her next words.

"Technicalities," she whispered.

And I kissed her.

I sucked in a long, deep breath when I did, and Madelyn melted into my embrace, a whimper escaping her throat when I deepened the kiss. I slid my hands up and over her arms until I cradled her face, and then I tested that rule she'd made about not using any tongue.

I slicked mine against her lips, seeking access.

And she opened.

The moment my tongue swept across hers, she trembled, and I felt a shock of electricity shoot straight down to my cock. Her hands twisted in the hair at the back of my neck, holding me to her, her body arching against me as I wrapped her fully in my arms.

"Alright, alright, get a room, you two," Braden joked as he jogged past us, and Madelyn broke the kiss, burying her face in my chest.

Braden caught my eye as he passed, arching his brow with a cocky grin, but my attention was pulled back to Madelyn as she backed away.

I snatched her hand in mine before she could go too far, and I held onto it until we slid into the back of one of the cars waiting to take us all back downtown.

My hand moved to her knee then, fingers wrapping around to the inside of her thigh as goosebumps raced from that point of contact all the way up under the hem of her dress.

I didn't know what the fuck we were doing anymore.

But I knew there was nothing *fake* about what I had planned for when we got back to that hotel.

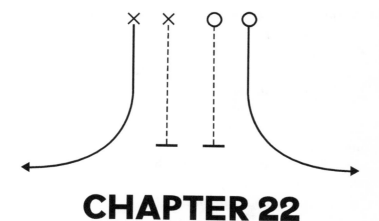

CHAPTER 22
Madelyn

It was late when we got back to the hotel, everyone hugging and saying their goodnights in the lobby before dispersing.

My adrenaline was still high when Kyle and I stepped onto the elevator. I felt a ghost of a smile on my lips as the events from the night played in my head, and I found myself racking my brain for the last time I'd had that much fun.

I came up empty.

Something in my stomach tightened the longer I thought about it, especially when I replayed how welcoming everyone had been to me. Giana, Riley, Mary, and Julep made me feel like I'd always been a part of their friend group. The guys made me feel like I'd always been a part of Kyle's life.

That made my stomach tighten even more.

Because, in a way, I had been.

Memories of the past slid down my spine like ice water, and when the elevator doors slid open, I blinked back to the present.

Kyle was quiet now, and he didn't move to put his hand on my lower back or touch me in any way when I stepped onto our floor. He just followed behind me silently, holding the door open for me once he'd scanned our key card.

The energy immediately shifted as soon as we stepped inside, and both our gazes locked on the bed.

I can help you with that.

His words drifted back to me, and a shiver ran over my skin as the door clicked shut behind us.

Kyle pulled his wallet from the pocket of his slacks, letting it drop onto the desk before he grabbed the back of his neck. His eyes slid from the bed to me, and I swore my face was hot enough to melt metal.

"Do you want to take a shower?"

My eyes bulged at the question, heart kicking in my chest, and Kyle chuckled. He took one small step toward me, but it was enough to suck all of the oxygen out of the room.

"That wasn't me inviting myself to join you," he said with a smirk, one of his gorgeous eyebrows ticking up into his hairline. "Although, it would save water…"

I rolled my eyes on an exhale of a laugh, a little of the tension melting away when I did. "Oh sure, *now* you're environmentally conscious? I know what you drive," I shot at him.

That made his grin double.

He nodded toward the bathroom. "You go ahead, I'll take second. I'm going to get some ice."

"Ice?"

"Yeah," he said, pulling the door open before looking back at me. "For your water."

He left before my jaw popped open, and I stood there gaping at the closed door for a full minute before I dragged myself into the bathroom and ran the shower as hot as it would go.

He remembered that?

When we were younger, when he'd sneak over to my house in the middle of the night to sleep on my floor instead of in his home, he would see me in my rawest form. I usually had on panties and a tank top and nothing else. Sometimes I would be wearing a face mask, sometimes I'd be rubbing lotion on my legs, sometimes I'd be jumping on my bed — a nightly routine I used to do to shake off some energy.

And I always had a tall glass of water on my bedside table, with as much ice crammed into that glass as I could manage.

I tried not to overthink it too much as I took a quick shower, washing my face and brushing my teeth before I wrapped myself in a towel and made my way back to the main room. Kyle's eyes flashed when I emerged, his gaze dropping to the water still dripping down my legs before he cleared his throat and slipped inside the bathroom to take his own shower.

I hadn't planned on sleeping in the same bed with Kyle.

I hadn't planned on even being in the same *room* with him.

Now, I was staring at the pair of panties and the silk camisole nightgown I'd packed to sleep in like they were enemy number one.

I muttered a curse as I hastily put them on, combing my hair with my fingers and scrunching out as much moisture as I could with my towel before I climbed into bed. I pulled the covers up to my ears and laid on the far edge of the bed, practically hanging off it as I stared up at the ceiling and willed my heart to beat steady.

It's fine, Madelyn.

You're both adults.

This bed is huge, and it's just sleeping.

You slept in the same bed with him plenty of times when you were kids.

I snorted out loud at that last thought, because he'd always slept on my floor — until the night everything changed.

And when we did share a bed, it was anything but innocent.

My heart hammered harder as I listened to the water slapping against the tile where Kyle was in the shower. I tried to convince myself he was just going to come out of that shower, climb into bed, turn out the lights, and we'd go straight to sleep.

But my logic laughed at me.

I heard you.

A shiver ripped through me, making me shake like a leaf.

He'd heard me in the bathtub.

He knew I'd been... *taking care* of myself.

He also knew I hadn't made it to the finish line.

My cheeks flamed when I considered that he'd heard me say his name in my attempt, and I groaned, burying myself deeper into the covers.

I can help with that.

The way he'd rumbled those words in my ear, the way his eyes had sealed the promise when he pulled back and pinned me with a dark smirk...

I stopped breathing as a realization hit me.

Did I want *him to follow through with that promise?*

A week ago, I was threatening him to behave himself, warning him not to use tongue when he kissed me.

Now, I was thinking of all the other things that tongue could do.

And after the plane ride, I had more questions than ever burning into my skull. I wanted to talk about what happened when we were younger. I *needed* to know how he could leave me, knowing I was carrying his child.

I needed to know if he even knew at all, or if all this time...

Kyle shut the shower off, and the absence of the rushing water made me blink, my thoughts on the past evaporating as my heart picked up its pace in my chest again.

I stared at the ceiling listening to the sounds of him brushing his teeth. Then, he padded into the room, using a Q-tip to clean his ears as he opened one of the drawers he'd unpacked his things into.

He was wearing nothing but a white towel wrapped around his waist, and that towel was far too small for the beast of a man that he was.

I followed a drop of water all the way down the middle ridge of his abdomen before I snapped my gaze back up to the ceiling, my throat closing in. When Kyle was focused on the items he was pulling from the drawer, I peeked over again, marveling at the muscles in his shoulders, his back, his thighs.

Then, without warning, he dropped the towel.

"Kyle!"

I pulled the covers over my eyes and shut them tightly as a throaty laugh rumbled through the room.

"Caught you looking," he teased as the memory of his perfectly sculpted ass burned itself into my brain.

"I wasn't *looking*," I argued.

"Then why are you so upset?"

"Because you flashed me!"

"You can always flash me back if it'd make you feel better to get even."

I did a quick check to make sure he had clothes on, then I peered at him over the edge of the covers with my eyes narrowed, earning me a laugh that warmed my insides.

He didn't pull on more than a pair of briefs, and after putting his phone on the charger and flipping the extra safety lock on the door, he shut off the lights.

And then the bed dipped with his weight, a flash of cold air sweeping over my skin as he pulled back the covers and slid under them.

I couldn't swallow the lump in my throat, couldn't hear anything over the sound of my heartbeat in my ears.

But I could feel him.

It didn't matter that I was hugging the edge of the bed, I could still feel the heat of his body, could smell his body wash and hear the groan he let loose as he settled into the sheets, stretching a bit before he lie still.

The blackout curtains snuffed out the city lights, and even after my eyes adjusted, I could barely see a thing in the dark room.

But I felt every subtle move Kyle made, my ears trained on the sound of each breath.

"You have plenty of room," he said, his voice low and gravelly. "Scoot over."

"I'm good."

There was a soft laugh in the darkness. "Madelyn, you're about to fall off the fucking bed."

I swallowed, shimmying a bit until my ass was no longer hanging off the mattress. Even though I only moved a couple inches, I felt even more of his heat, and every nerve in my body buzzed to life.

"I put your water on the nightstand," he said.

"Thank you."

The words were a squeak, which made me cringe a bit, but then silence fell over us, Kyle's breathing evening out a bit.

"Goodnight," I said.

There was a long pause before he spoke. "Goodnight."

I didn't close my eyes, didn't dare move even a centimeter. I just stared up at the ceiling with my eyes unable to see anything, trying to subtly take deeper inhales without letting Kyle hear how hard it was for me to breathe at the moment.

In for four, out for eight. In for four, out for eight.

I repeated the mantra in my head, feeling my heart settle a bit the longer the silence stretched between us. I thought I heard Kyle's breathing change, too.

Maybe he really is going to sleep.

I didn't know if it was relief or disappointment that I felt the longer we laid there without anything happening. Eventually, the cage around my chest loosened, and my breaths started coming easier, more natural.

The memories of the day faded, tucking themselves into files in my brain as my eyelids grew heavier. They fluttered, and then shut, and I rolled onto my left side, away from Kyle, curling into myself a little as one arm slid under my pillow.

I didn't realize how tired I was until that moment, all the adrenaline from the day slowly leaking out of me with each breath. The hotel bed was so comfortable. I let out a long, contented sigh as I settled in, letting the memory foam take my weight.

I was almost asleep when I felt a subtle movement on the other end of the bed.

I swallowed, body stiffening as I listened to the slight rustle of the sheets.

He's probably just rolling over, you weirdo. Go to bed.

I was too hyper-focused, and I rolled my eyes at myself, burrowing deeper into the covers.

Until I felt a large, warm hand at the small of my back.

My eyes shot open, heart stopping for a full ten seconds before it kicked back to life in my chest. I was completely still as Kyle rubbed his knuckles against my skin.

When I didn't pull away or say anything, he splayed his hand, running his palm up and over my hip.

Oh my God.

Goosebumps exploded over my skin, my next breath lodging itself in my throat. There was another dip of the bed, a shift of weight, and then a rush of heat.

Kyle pulled me flush against him, his chest against my back, legs curling behind mine. His forehead pressed against the top of my spine, and a long, shaky exhale ghosted over my skin as he rolled his hips into me.

I gasped.

I felt every thick, hard inch of him against my backside, and the soft, almost imperceptible groan he let loose made me shiver.

I didn't dare say a word. I didn't dare move an inch.

My heart was pounding out of my chest, and Kyle pressed a featherlight kiss to the back of my neck before his hand on my hip was traveling, gliding over my thigh and down to my knee before his fingers slid to the inside of my leg and trailed up at a torturously slow pace.

"Mads," he whispered, and I heard him swallow, felt his hand hesitate where it was traveling up.

I didn't respond.

But I opened.

Every cell in my being buzzed under his touch as I spread my legs, my ass still nestled against his hard-on as I did. The motion sent his hand sliding farther north, the rough warmth of his palm skating against my upper inner thigh.

One thick fingertip brushed against the lace edge of my panties, and I shook violently, nipples hardening into peaks.

Kyle paused there, kissing the back of my shoulder as he ran his fingertip over the lace. He trailed up to my right hip, dragged that gentle touch down to the left hip, and then went back to playing with the edge along my inner thigh.

I was still at first, frozen, afraid to so much as breathe.

But the more he toyed with that edge, the more I squirmed beneath the touch, opening my legs wider and bucking my hips to reach for his touch.

His breaths were short puffs of air on my neck, his heart thumping loud enough for me to hear.

I reached behind me, blindly feeling until my fingers ran through his hair. I held him to me, rolling against his erection with all my awareness centering on where his fingertips just barely brushed my panties.

"I didn't just hear you earlier," he husked against the shell of my ear. His touch was still just a tease against my thigh. "I watched you."

Another gasp left me.

"I watched you touch yourself, listened to the way you moaned."

I should have been shocked. I *wanted* to be shocked. I willed myself to break away from him and scream at him and storm out of the room.

But I was so turned on by the thought, by knowing he was watching me without me knowing, that he'd seen me writhing in that bath water trying to find relief.

"It was intoxicating," he continued, his breath ragged against my skin. "I couldn't look away."

"Kyle," I breathed, arching against him, and he groaned with a buck of his hips.

"I heard you say that, too," he murmured in my ear. "You were thinking of me."

"Yes."

He cursed, his teeth sinking into my shoulder.

"I fucked my hand as I watched you," he admitted, and the shock only lasted a second before a rush of power swept through me.

The thought that he couldn't resist himself, that he risked getting caught because he was so turned on...

"When you gave up..." he continued, and his fingers slid between my legs, toying with the sensitive skin just next to where I wanted him. I chased his touch, but he pulled away, continuing his tease. "I had to force myself out of this hotel room to keep from bursting into that bathroom and taking over."

My next breath shuddered out of me, and Kyle kissed just below my ear.

"Let me touch you, Mads," he begged, teeth sinking into my shoulder. "I want to hear my name on your lips again. But this time, I want to earn it." He bit the lobe of my ear, making me hiss and roll against him. "Let me get you there. Let me hear the way you moan when you come."

The words lit me on fire.

I arched against him, turning my head just enough to capture his lips with my own. He groaned when I kissed him, both of us inhaling a long, deep breath.

Then, I covered his hand with my own, and I slid it firmly between my legs, gasping when he cupped me, and the heel of his palm gave just the right amount of friction to make stars explode behind my eyelids.

That gasp was oxygen to the flame.

Kyle sucked in a breath, kissing me harder as his hand covered me. He pressed his palm where I needed him, rubbing up and down before he snaked his middle finger under my panties. He groaned when he felt how wet I was, gliding his fingertip just barely between my lips before he pulled it back out.

I whimpered at the loss.

"You've been uncomfortable all night, haven't you?" he mused, grinning against my mouth before he kissed me harder. His finger slipped under my panties again, and this time, he pressed inside me just a half-inch as I shook and gasped into his mouth. "How long have you been this wet for me?"

I moaned in lieu of an answer, rolling against his touch. I covered his hand with my own and made him push inside more, and then I was rolling onto my back, wrapping my arms around his neck and holding his mouth to mine as I bucked against his touch.

It had been so long since I'd been touched like this — slowly, softly, reverently.

It had been so long since I'd been touched like this by *him*.

My body responded to every lash of his tongue against mine, my core heating as he dove his hand all the way under my panties and curled that thick finger deep inside me. I cried out when he did, and he swallowed that cry with his mouth, kissing me hard.

"I need you to tell me what you want, baby," he said, sliding his finger in slow and withdrawing just the same. "Do you want me to tease you, to make this last?" He ran his fingers up to my clit, applying pressure and rubbing side to side in the perfect rhythm to make me fucking lose it. "Or do you want that relief you've been craving all night?"

"Get me there," I breathed against his lips, rolling into his hand. "Get me off."

His lips curled against mine in a smirk, and he applied more pressure, rubbing me hard as I shook and reached for the orgasm that was within reach. "That's my fucking girl."

But he pulled back before I could catch that spark, his hand sliding up to cup my breast with an appreciative groan.

"God, I've missed touching you," he breathed against me, low and needy.

The words made my heart catch, but only for a moment — because in the next breath, Kyle was ripping the covers off us, his fingertips sliding under the band of my panties. He tugged hard when I lifted my hips, sliding the fabric off my legs and flinging it somewhere behind him.

It was still so dark, I could barely make anything out as he braced himself on top of me, his fists sinking into the mattress by my head. He dropped his mouth to mine, our tongues dancing as a bolt of electricity shot through me.

Kyle wrapped one arm around my back, and then we were flipping, the world spinning until I settled on top of him.

He grabbed my hands, tugging me up.

"Sit on my face, Mads."

My eyes shot wide, but he was already maneuvering us before I could argue, before I could tell him that I'd never done this before. He shimmied down and helped me climb until my thighs were straddling his head, and then he grabbed my ass in two handfuls, groaning as he shook my cheeks and gave my left one a little smack.

"Hands on the headboard," he commanded, and I barely had time to brace myself before he wrapped his hands around my thighs and pulled me down.

"Oh, *fuck.*"

A desperate moan ripped out of me the moment his tongue lashed my clit, and Kyle groaned at the sound, making me spread wider for him as he did it again. He didn't ease into it, didn't play with me or tease me.

I asked him to get me there, and he was ready to deliver.

He held me to him as he feasted, running his tongue up and down before he sucked my clit with just the right pressure to make me tremble and grip the headboard tighter.

"Play with those pretty tits, baby," he rasped against my clit, and then he was sucking it again, making me writhe and buck against him. "Come on my tongue and let me hear you say my name again."

"*God*," I cried. I ripped my camisole overhead, rolling both nipples between my fingers as soon as they were free. I gave in to my urge to move against him, my climax mounting as I rode his face.

I'd been worked up all day, and the overwhelming sensation of *Kyle Fucking Robbins* touching me, licking me, tasting me... it was already enough to drive me over the edge.

And he read me like a book, picking up on all the ways I moved against him until he found the perfect rhythm, the perfect pressure.

When he slid that thick finger inside me again, curling it in time with his tongue against my clit, I became ravenous.

I arched and bucked like a wild bull, palming my breasts as all my awareness fell to where I was fucking his face and his hand. Kyle didn't slow, didn't stop, didn't pull away. He opened his mouth and flattened his tongue, one finger working inside me while his other hand grabbed my ass and showed me how to rock against him.

"Oh, God. Oh, *fuck*," I cried, and then I took over, rocking against his tongue as he fucked me with that finger and coaxed my orgasm to the surface. "Kyle," I breathed. "Yes, *God*, yes, yes, *yes*."

He moaned, and the vibration of it was the last little piece to send me spiraling.

The universe sparked behind my eyes, bursts of light invading my vision as the most intense pleasure washed over me like a tidal wave. All the blood in my body rushed to where his tongue worked mercilessly against me, and I bucked wilder, not wanting it to end. His name left my lips over and over again, breathy at first, and then in a scream. I felt him grin against my core the louder I got, but I couldn't find it in me to be even the least bit ashamed.

I rode out every last drop of that climax, shaking with the pent-up energy of hundreds of orgasms I'd tried to give myself in the last year but couldn't quite reach. It dragged on for what felt like hours, and by the time the final wave left me, I was so weak I collapsed.

Kyle caught my weight, helping me roll off him until I was sprawled out in the sheets on my back, my chest heaving, sweat slicking my skin.

"That was the hottest fucking thing I have ever seen," he said, and then he was kissing me like he wanted to soak up every little moan I'd just given him.

I tasted myself on him, and that was enough to make me fire up again.

As my orgasm receded, reality slowly washed back in, making my heart beat unsteady in my chest as Kyle slowed his kisses. They went from feverous to tender, from needy to soft and sweet. He took his time, kissing along my jaw and down my neck before he'd claim my mouth again.

I willed my mind to still, begged myself not to overthink anything.

It was just a little fun.

It was just a harmless hookup between two consenting adults.

It didn't have to mean anything.

But when he wrapped me in his arms, spooning me and nuzzling into the back of my neck with a content sigh, my chest seized.

It didn't matter how I tried to downplay it. The truth was impossible to ignore.

This changed everything.

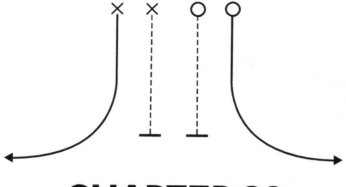

CHAPTER 23

Kyle

I fell asleep curled around Madelyn, and when I woke the next morning, the first thing I did was reach for her.

All I found was an empty bed.

I creaked one eye open and then the next, squinting a bit at the soft light streaming in through the hotel window. The blackout curtain still covered most of it, but there was about a six-inch slit letting in the morning rays.

That strip of light cast a light pink glow on where Madelyn sat at the desk.

Half of her copper hair was piled in a clip on top of her head, and the other half was a ratty mess curling around her ears and neck. She had slipped back into the silk nightgown she'd had on last night before I'd stripped her. One foot was on the floor, the other was perched on the edge of the chair, and she balanced her chin on her knee as she wrote in a notebook.

I stilled.

She was writing.

I sat up as slowly and quietly as I could, not wanting to disturb her. She had a soft smile on her face as the pen dragged along the page, and at one point, I thought I saw her cheeks turn a bright pink.

I watched her for a stolen moment of time, emotions battling for my attention as I did.

Part of me was wrapped up in last night, in how she'd fit in with my friends so seamlessly and made it so easy to pretend she was mine.

Part of me was still existing in the precious slot of time where I'd had her writhing on top of me, her cunt on my tongue and my hands gripping her ass and helping her ride my face.

But the loudest part of me was screaming, like a man falling deep down into a dark hole with no end.

Because whatever game we were playing had been shot to hell last night.

And now, I had no idea where we went from here.

Madelyn's pen paused over the page, her brows sliding together before she peeked over her shoulder and found me staring at her.

The moment our eyes locked, I felt both of our hearts stop.

She swallowed, and my chest tightened.

"Morning," she whispered, and I couldn't explain it, but just that soft rasp of her voice had me yearning to hold her.

I offered a lopsided smile. "Good morning, gorgeous."

Her cheeks flamed, and she dropped her pen, stopping long enough to pour a cup of coffee on her way over to me. I hadn't realized there was a carafe next to her. She must have ordered room service.

"I don't know how you like it," she said, the mug steaming in her hands. "Your coffee."

"Well, you must be a psychic, because this is exactly how I like it."

"Black?"

"No." I shook my head, taking the mug from her hands and setting it on the nightstand before I grabbed her and pulled her into my lap. "Delivered by you in a nightgown."

She laughed as I wrapped my arms around her and kissed her neck, dragging my stubble along the slope of it as she wiggled in my lap. When I pulled back, I kept my hands on her hips and searched her eyes for a sign of how she was feeling.

I didn't have to look long to know she had her own internal war going on.

"Thank you," I said after a moment. "For the coffee. But it's supposed to be *me* taking care of *you*."

She arched a brow. "Is that so?"

"It is."

A shy smile found her lips, and her gaze fell to where her hands were balanced on my chest, silence washing over both of us.

"You were writing," I mused.

Her little nose scrunched before she peeked up at me through her lashes. "I was."

"Feeling inspired?" I smirked, squeezing her hips. "I saw that blush. Just what were you writing about, Miss James?"

She was giggling at the tease, but when I said her name, the smile slipped.

"Hearst," she reminded me.

"Nah, fuck that," I said. "He doesn't deserve to have his name on you."

"So, you're just going to call me by my maiden name?"

"For now."

I held her gaze even when it widened, even when her eyes darted between mine like she was trying to analyze what I meant by that.

"Did it feel good?" I asked, and I chuckled a bit when her neck flashed a deep red. "Writing, I mean."

"Oh," she said, her eyes falling to her hands on my chest again. "Yes, actually. It felt... like coming home."

I smiled at that. "I love your writing."

"You only loved it because half the time I was writing about your stupid ass," she said with a roll of her eyes.

"Fair. I wonder if anything's changed. Maybe I should go take a peek..."

"Absolutely not," she said, and she pulled at my shoulders like she could stop me from getting up if I wanted to. But I let her, savoring the way it felt with her thighs straddling my waist.

I swept her messy hair behind one ear on a smile, and she lifted her gaze to meet mine.

A million unspoken words hung between us.

I didn't know where to start. I wanted to ask if she was okay after last night, if she was upset it had happened.

But I knew just from her sitting in my lap that that wasn't the case.

Which left me wondering what this meant for us now. It was clear we weren't just pretending anymore.

But it was also clear she was guarded.

I wondered if she was feeling guilty for what happened when we were younger. I wondered why I didn't feel the same anger and pain when I looked at her now. I wondered where that grudge had gone that I'd held onto for so long.

Because suddenly, I didn't give a fuck what happened when we were kids.

I just wanted a clean slate.

I wanted to start over, right here, right now.

When I opened my mouth to tell her that, I paused, frowning, thinking about the plane ride here and what she'd said.

Why did you leave?

The question had perplexed me when she'd asked it. She knew why. She knew what happened with my father. Hadn't that been why she'd come to our house the next day and told them she wanted me to stay away from her?

My phone ringing jolted me from the thought, Madelyn flinching a bit in my lap when the loud vibration sounded through the room. I kept one hand on her as I reached for my phone on the nightstand with the other. The nickname CAP covered the screen, and I tapped the green phone icon to answer.

"Holden," I greeted, eyes flicking to Madelyn. "To what do I owe the pleasure of a phone call from you at the ass-crack of dawn?"

"It's almost ten in the morning."

I blinked, pulling my phone back and blanching when I saw the time on the screen and realized he was right.

I hadn't slept this late since college.

When I didn't say anything, Holden chuckled on the other end. "Get your lazy ass in the shower and get dressed. We've been summoned."

"Summoned?"

"Boys brunch and round of golf before the wedding tonight, remember? We're meeting in the lobby in half an hour."

My eyes slid to Madelyn, but she showed no sign of emotion one way or the other.

"The groom really wants to get his ass handed to him on his big day?" I clicked my tongue. "Masochist."

Holden laughed a little on the other end. "See you downstairs."

When we hung up, I tossed my phone on the bed, hands resting on Madelyn's hips again. The comforter was bunched between us, and I hoped it was thick enough to hide the fact that I was rock hard and aching to fill her.

Not that I was embarrassed by that fact — quite the opposite, actually.

But thirty minutes wasn't enough time for me to take her the way I wanted to, not after all these years.

"You better get going," Madelyn said when I didn't attempt to move her off me.

I sighed. "You'll be alright without me?"

At that, she cocked a brow on a short laugh. "I've managed to survive this long."

She climbed off my lap long before I wanted her to, but before she could go far, I grabbed her wrist, standing and pulling her into me. My hands slid back into her hair, angling her face up to look at me before I bent and pressed a long, slow kiss against her lips.

I sucked in a breath when our mouths met, one she echoed as her fingers curled around my wrists.

"I want to talk later," I said when I pulled back, my forehead against hers.

She nodded, and I noted how her throat constricted with a thick swallow.

Reluctantly, I released her, internally cursing my former teammate as I hustled through a shower and hastily got dressed. It was his wedding day. I would do whatever he wanted me to.

But it was going to be torture waiting until tonight to talk to Madelyn about what was happening between us.

When I was ready, I slid my wallet into my pocket and grabbed my cell phone. I was halfway over to where Madelyn was writing at the desk again when *her* phone rang.

One glance at the screen had her dropping her pen immediately, and she propped the phone in front of her, smiling widely when the call connected.

"There's my favorite boy," she answered, and I stopped in my tracks, knowing it was Sebastian on the other end.

"Hi, Mommy!"

Her eyes watered at his little voice, and my heart seized in my chest.

I took a step, wanting to say hello, but when her gaze flicked to me, she went ashen.

And she held up a hand out of frame to stop me.

I swallowed, nodding and trying to force a smile as I gave her a pathetic two-finger wave to let her know I was heading out. She nodded, turning her smile back to the camera as Sebastian started chattering away.

Then, I heard another voice.

Her mother's.

She asked about where to find something, but I didn't catch what it was. I just grabbed my room key and slid out the door with my throat closing in.

Madelyn didn't want her mother to know she was with me.

That told me louder than words that she was still holding on to our past.

And when I shut the door behind me and made my way to the elevators, I couldn't escape the anger and hurt that gripped me by the throat.

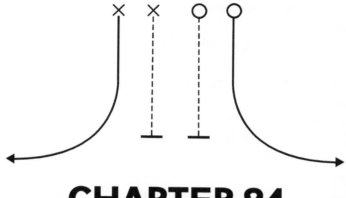

CHAPTER 24
Madelyn

My eyes were glued to the door once Kyle pushed through it, and I flinched a bit when it latched closed.

He'd wanted to say hi to Sebastian, but my mom didn't know I was with him.

My guess was now he knew that, too.

I closed my eyes on an exhale, and then I was beaming at my son, listening to him tell me about how excited he was to go to the museum with his nana today. He was talking with his hands, his eyes all big and wide and his voice entirely too loud for this early in the morning, but I smiled and nodded and listened intently.

I'd been away from him only twenty-four hours, and yet I already missed him.

Sebastian had become my entire life.

I couldn't remember what it was like before I had him, couldn't recall who I was back then. What had my priorities been? What did I do on a Saturday? Did I have dreams or aspirations that didn't revolve around my son?

My stomach dipped a little at that, because this morning when I'd woken up with Kyle curled around me, his body so warm against mine I'd had to kick the covers off, the first thing I'd done was dig in my bag for a notebook and pen.

And I'd spent the morning writing.

It wasn't the next great American novel, by any means. In fact, I was fairly certain every word I'd written was terrible.

But I'd written.

I'd *wanted* to write.

I couldn't remember the last time I'd felt that desire inside me. I'd forgotten what that part of me felt like.

I thought it had left me long ago.

"Sebastian, sweetie, why don't you go feed Titan, put on your jeans and t-shirt Nana laid out for you, and put your sneakers on like a big boy," Mom said when Sebastian finished telling me about the movie they watched last night. "We need to get going soon."

"And brush my teeth!" Sebastian added, clapping as if that was the most exciting thing in the world.

I chuckled.

"That's right. And you better brush them good, I'm going to do a breath test," my mom said.

"Love you, Mommy!"

"I love you most," I chimed back. I blew him a kiss, which he caught and smacked against his cheek before running out of frame.

Then, my mom's eyes were on me, and I knew before she said a word that she could read me as easily as a children's book with fourteen-point font.

"Long night?"

I hoped my cheeks weren't as red as they felt.

My mom smirked a bit when I didn't answer, and then shook her head, glancing down the hall to make sure Sebastian was out of hearing range.

"I'm glad you're enjoying yourself," she said. "You deserve that."

"Do I?"

Mom knew my guilt like no one else did. I felt like I should be able to do more to get Sebastian away from Marshall, felt like I never should have ended up in this position to begin with. Sometimes, my life felt like one long line of mistakes.

Then again, I couldn't imagine a life where Sebastian was never born.

Everything happens for a reason, they say. And if he was the reason for all the hell I had to endure, I'd do it ten times over.

"You're too hard on yourself," Mom said. "But whoever this man is that you are keeping a secret, something tells me he sees what I see in you. What everyone else sees, too." She paused, her eyes sincere. "You're a great mother, Madelyn. You're driven and caring and strong."

I almost snorted at that.

I did not feel *strong* most days.

"You're a catch," she finished, and then she let out a long sigh and gave me a pointed look. "If only I knew just who you'd been caught *by.*"

I swallowed, looking down at my fingernails. I had to stop my nervous habit of picking the polish off so I wouldn't show up to this wedding looking like a nervous wreck.

"I'm with Kyle."

I couldn't look at the screen for a full ten seconds after I said it, and when I did, the mixture of shock and concern on my mother's face made me drop my gaze again.

I waited for her to say something, maybe, "*Kyle who?*"

But she knew.

"I didn't realize you two still spoke," she finally said.

"We didn't. Well, not until very recently, anyway. I took a house showing from one of the real estate apps I'm on and..." I looked at her. "He showed up."

"I see."

We were both silent for a pause, and then everything poured out of me — the way it always does with my mom. She'd been my best friend since I was a kid. Dad and I were never that close, especially because he was more married to his job than to my mother.

But with Mom and me, the words had always come easy. I went to her with everything — good, bad, and in-between.

"I'm sorry I didn't tell you," I started. "But, for obvious reasons, I wasn't sure how you would take it."

"And how are *you* taking it?"

I let out a laugh, a sigh, and then shook my head with my eyes glossing over. "I feel like I woke up in the Twilight Zone."

Mom was patient while I filled her in on everything, starting with the house showing and dinner. I told her about the deal he'd proposed after he'd seen the bruises on my arm, told her about shopping and the park with Sebastian and everything that had transpired in the last twenty-four hours.

Well — not *everything*.

But by the time I finished speaking, her gaze had softened, and she was leaning in in the way that told me if I was there with her, she'd have a hand on my arm squeezing gently.

I looked a lot like her — same brown eyes, same button nose, same tired smile.

"It sounds like he's grown up quite a bit."

I nodded, but then frowned. "That's what I don't understand, Mom. Kyle has been so... *strange.*" I shook my head. "When we first reconnected, it was like he was mad at *me*, like it was somehow me who was the bad guy in our situation. That changed after he saw what Marshall had done to me."

"I want to walk right down the road and give him a piece of my mind for that."

"You know it wouldn't do any good," I said on a sigh. "And you also know I can take care of myself. I have a plan."

Mom's mouth twisted to the side. She and Daddy had offered several times to use their savings and give Sebastian and me a fresh start somewhere new.

But I wanted to do this on my own.

I *needed* to save myself.

"I asked him on the plane yesterday why he left," I said, my voice a whisper now. "And he said he didn't have a choice."

My eyes found Mom's, and though my hands were shaking, I knew I couldn't back out now.

"Mom... what happened at the party that night?"

Her face went white when I asked.

Everyone in our little suburbs knew about that party. Everyone knew something had happened, though the parents were tight-lipped about *what* exactly. All I knew was that come the following weekend, Kyle and his parents were gone. They'd moved.

Or had they been run out of town?

"That's an old story that I don't think we need to dredge up," she said.

"Please."

Mom looked away from me, tucking her hair behind her ear. "No one even wanted to go to that party, if I'm being frank," she started. "The Robbins liked to think they ran that town, and because of the money they had, I guess they did in a way. They helped a lot with the church and the PTA. They were the first to step up and donate whenever we had a cause. But... *Lord*, they were a pain to be around. Lynette had the backbone of a salamander, and Michael..."

She looked at me in the way that said she didn't need to finish that sentence — and she really didn't. I knew *exactly* the kind of man Michael was. He was well respected in the community, a leader at the law firm he was a partner at — the one my father worked at with him — and a seemingly stand-up guy.

But he was also a hot-tempered man with a short fuse and a bad drinking habit.

He was like Marshall.

I shivered a bit, nodding for Mom to go on.

"The first bit of the party was fine. The food was great, drinks were flowing. But we were all kind of biding our time until it felt like we'd stayed long enough to make an excuse to leave. The kids left around eleven — some of them going to a sleepover while others headed home or out to meet up with their friends. Kyle was the only one who stayed."

I swallowed.

He'd asked me to be there, but I hadn't been ready to face him. I hadn't been ready to tell him I was pregnant.

And I couldn't be around him and pretend I was fine.

I'd tried to be normal around him that week at school, but he knew something was off. He kept begging me to talk to him, but I needed time to process. I needed to figure out what *I* wanted, what I would say when the time came.

"About an hour later, your father and I decided to leave. We went to say goodnight to Michael and Lynette." Her eyes lost focus. "Michael was drunk — which was par for the course. We tried to laugh it off when he said we were losers for leaving so early. But then he got mouthy with your father, something about work." She went a bit green then. "He seemed to be insinuating that your father was having an affair with someone at the office."

"He would never!"

"I know," she said, holding up a hand. "I knew then, too. But Michael thought it was hilarious. Your father shoved him a bit, which made Michael laugh, and then he grabbed my ass and said a crude comment about how if I were *his* wife, he'd be too busy to stray."

I gaped at the screen.

"He... *what*?"

Mom nodded, letting out a long sigh. "It all happened so fast after that. Kyle stepped in, trying to get his dad to calm down and go upstairs." She paled. "Michael wound up and hit him right in the jaw with all of us watching. I can still hear it."

She covered her lips with her fingertips, and I mirrored her, shaking my head.

When he came to school on Monday, he had a split lip that was crusted over and healing. I remembered it now, that detail that I had catalogued before being overrun with heartbreak when he'd turned away from me.

"Everyone was up in arms. We threatened to call the cops if Michael didn't go upstairs and sleep it off."

"Did you? Call the cops, I mean?"

"We weren't going to originally, but later, we just couldn't stand it. We got home and couldn't stop thinking about what had happened. But when your dad called, I guessed someone else had beat us to it. The cops were already on their way, showed up about an hour after the party ended, according to the Moores."

The Moores had lived across the street from Kyle.

I blinked, wetting my lips and trying to process it all. "What happened when they came?"

"No one knows. Clearly, Michael wasn't arrested. No one pressed charges, or anything. But we were all pissed — obviously. We had plans to talk to Michael and Lynette about stepping down from their positions in the church and with the PTA. But then..."

"They left."

She nodded, her brows softening as she watched me take it all in.

Oh, God.

My eyes welled with tears. "Mom, what if... what if Kyle never knew I was pregnant?"

She frowned at that. "Honey, you *told* him you were."

"No," I said, the word wet and garbled. "I told his parents."

Mom's face slackened. "What? But you—"

"Told you I'd told him, I know. Because I thought I

did. I showed up that morning, I knocked on the door, and Michael and Lynette answered. They said Kyle was sleeping but they saw how upset I was and I... I told them." My eyes were blurring more and more by the second. "Mrs. Robbins hugged me. She told me it would all be okay. She told me they'd tell him as soon as he woke up and have him come to the house."

I sucked in a breath, my heart racing.

"But he didn't. And he didn't answer my calls. And when I saw him on Monday, he looked like he hated me. He... he turned away from me like I'd hurt him. But what if that wasn't about the baby? What if it was because I wasn't there for him, because I hadn't..."

I could barely keep up with how fast my brain was working.

"What if he didn't *know*?"

My mom leaned toward the camera, but Sebastian came barreling out of his room and down the hall, doing his battle cry that usually led to him running into my legs full-force and wrapping his little arms around them.

Mom painted on a smile at the same time I did, and Sebastian leapt into her lap.

"I'm ready! And look, I tied my shoes up just how you showed me!"

He leaned back far enough to kick his feet into the air, and Mom and I shared a look before we both smiled at him.

"Wow, you sure did!" Mom said. "Okay, blow Mommy a kiss and then go use the restroom and we'll get going."

"Can I get a bag of rocks at the gift shop?!"

If it weren't for the lump in my throat, I would have laughed at that.

"We'll see how good you are," Mom said.

Sebastian blew me a kiss, which I caught with as much focus as I could, pressing it to my cheek with a smile. He leapt up and ran toward the bathroom, and Mom turned to me.

"Okay, here's what you are going to do," she said calmly. "You're going to hang up this phone, take a deep breath, wash your face, and lie down on the floor for ten minutes."

"Mo—"

"Ten. Minutes," she repeated, holding up a finger. "And *then*, you can gather your thoughts, and talk to him."

I nodded, my eyes filling with tears again. Kyle had gone to golf and brunch with the guys before the wedding. I likely wouldn't see him until it was time for both of us to get dressed and go. I couldn't drop this on him right when we were supposed to walk out this door, fend off the media, and be happy for one of his best friend's *wedding*.

It would have to wait until tonight.

And just like last night, a sickening realization washed over me.

Because I knew before it even happened that this conversation would change everything.

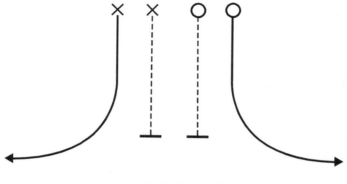

CHAPTER 25

Kyle

"**S**hit."

I hooked an arm around Madelyn's waist, pulling her back into the elevator before anyone realized we had even stepped off.

"Forget something?" she asked, her eyes wide as I punched the number for our floor.

"No," I answered, cracking my neck. "Paparazzi is crowding the door again."

As soon as we got back up to our floor, I checked the time on my watch, cursing when I realized we didn't have more than forty-five minutes to get to the venue. I quickly called Holden, who informed me the stupid bastards with cameras were also crowding the back of the hotel.

"There's no getting around them," he explained. "The venue is heavily guarded with security, so they're only on the perimeter, but the hotel..."

I nodded, thanking him and ending the call before I faced Madelyn.

Fuck, she was breathtaking.

It had been one thing to see her in that frosty blue dress when I'd taken her shopping for it, but it was another thing entirely to see her dressed in it tonight. Her hair was pulled back and pinned in an elegant way that made all my attention go to the long slope of her neck. Her makeup was light, but it accented her brown eyes and full, pink lips.

The blue fabric sparkled like starlight from where it hugged her neck to where it slit at her thigh, the skirt of it shimmering with every step she took.

When I'd touched her last night, the lights had been off in our room. It was pitch black.

I made a vow that when I touched her *tonight*, I'd savor every inch, not just with my hands, but with my eyes, too.

"We can't get around them," I said, and her eyebrows slid together. She didn't say a word. She hadn't said much at all since I'd returned from golfing. All her playfulness was gone, and her face was subtly somber, like she was lost in a memory.

I tried not to get anxious about it. We had a wedding to go to, and then I could talk to her after and find out what was on her mind.

"We have two options. One, we can walk out together, and I'll shield you from them as much as I can."

She was already shaking her head. "I don't... I can't deal with them trying to find out who I am, or digging into me, or..."

Madelyn's fingers covered her lips, her eyes widening even more.

"Sebastian," I finished for her — but I wondered if it was her son she was worried about, or her stupid ex-husband.

I wanted to remind her she didn't need to worry about him, not with me around, but right now wasn't the time.

"I know, I was thinking the same thing. So, our second option is for me to walk out by myself. I'll hog the attention, make a big show of things, and you should be able to sneak out the back without anyone knowing who you are or where you're going. I'll have them pull a car around for you now."

Madelyn nodded, but my throat was tight as I made the call.

I didn't want to leave her alone, even for just a short car ride.

"Security is locked at the venue," I told her, framing her arms in my hands. "I'll be there as soon as you get through."

"I will be fine," she said on a grin. "Stop acting like I'm some helpless damsel."

"Oh, trust me — I am well aware that you're the dragon, not the damsel."

She pinched my side at that, and then I pulled her into me, pressing my lips to her forehead and holding them there on a long exhale.

"Twenty minutes tops," I promised. "Then, I'll be stuck to you for the rest of the night."

"Oh, my God. Will you just *go* already," she said, pushing me off her.

I smiled, but as my eyes searched hers, I could still see all the evidence that something was off. "You okay?" I asked.

Her expression softened, but she nodded. "I'm okay."

I didn't feel the confidence in her answer, but the fact that she wasn't shutting down told me that there was nothing to worry too much about right now.

She'd talk to me about whatever was going on when she was ready.

And if there was anything I wanted to prove to her now that she was back in my life, it was that I was patient.

That I wasn't going anywhere.

My stomach tightened when I finally left her and ran for the elevators, ready to put on a show for the paparazzi and give her enough time to sneak out the back.

What's next for us?

I'd had such a mixture of emotions when she'd swung back into my life — anger being the most prevalent one.

Now, I could barely feel that rage at all.

She'd hurt me — that was the stone-cold truth of it. But now that I had her back in my life, I found myself less and less inclined to dredge up the past.

Maybe her parents had pressured her into coming to my house that day.

Maybe they'd seen my father hit me and didn't feel safe with their daughter being around us.

Maybe they thought I'd become the same man my father was.

Maybe *Madelyn* didn't have a choice at all.

I'd been so young, so ruled by my anger then...

But I could choose to let it go now.

I could choose to start fresh.

I couldn't wait to talk to Madelyn after the wedding, to set it all straight and figure out where her head was.

But for now, I had a performance to make.

I walked through the lobby with a cocky smile, my shoulders squared, and a swagger in my step. And when the doors slid open, I was blinded by a blur of flashing lights.

"You all waiting for me?" I said loud enough for every one of them to hear.

And then I posed for pictures and answered questions, hamming it up the way I used to in college until I was sure enough time had passed for Madelyn to get out safely.

A half hour later, I was sitting next to Madelyn in the fourth row of white chairs facing the Rocky Mountains with the sun dipping behind their peaks.

And I was doing my best not to sob like a baby.

I didn't know what the fuck was wrong with me, but the lump in my throat was all I could focus on as I watched Clay lose his shit when Giana appeared at the end of the aisle.

Holden was the only other one with him, as he'd agreed to get certified and be their officiant. And even *he* looked emotional as he squeezed Clay's shoulder, a smirk painting his lips like he knew exactly what our teammate was feeling in this moment.

Considering he'd just had his own wedding a few months ago, I supposed he really did.

"Alright," Holden said. "Everyone on your feet for our beautiful bride."

We all stood, Giana and her father paused at the edge of the aisle. The song changed, shifting into an instrumental version of "New Year's Day' by Taylor Swift, and then Giana started walking again.

She was gorgeous.

Her dark, curly hair was framing her face in a wild halo, her freckles more pronounced under the glow of the setting sun. She wore a cream-colored lacy dress with dramatic sleeves. It was fitted right under her bust, which accented the slight baby bump she had.

It was wild to remember her as the soft-spoken, shy little thing who had tried to wrangle us on the field freshman year. Watching her grow into the spunky, powerful agent she was now was something I felt lucky to have witnessed.

When I looked at Clay again, it was just in time to see him lose the fight against his emotions.

He pinched the bridge of his nose as his shoulders shook, Holden smirking behind him and clapping him on the back. When he finally gained a little composure, Clay looked up again, his eyes red and blotchy as he watched Giana walk toward him.

I heard a sniff, and when I looked over my shoulder, I found Madelyn watching Clay with her eyes glossed over. She blinked, and a single tear rolled down her cheek before her eyes flicked to mine.

She laughed a little, shaking her head as if she were embarrassed.

I couldn't help the smile that spread on my face, nor could I deny the way my chest tightened the longer I watched her.

I reached out, sliding my thumb over that tear and across her cheekbone. She leaned into my touch, closing her eyes briefly before she was looking at Clay and Giana again.

When we were asked to take our seats, I threaded my fingers through hers, pulling our hands to rest on my knee. I smoothed my thumb over her wrist as I held her, memories of when we were young pulsing through that touch.

The wedding ceremony was short and sweet, Holden cracking a few jokes before he told his version of the story of how Clay and Giana became a couple. We all laughed as he recalled the way Clay had been a broody asshole all sour over his ex-girlfriend, and then he'd jumped into a relationship with Giana. We hadn't known it was fake at the time. Hell, nothing *ever* seemed fake between those two.

That made me squeeze Madelyn's hand.

Nothing felt fake about her being here with me, either.

"I vow to always remind you to put yourself first sometimes," Giana said when it was time for them to share, her eyes glossy as she looked up at Clay. "And to believe in you even when you don't believe in yourself. I promise to always be there at the end of every game, win or lose, and to never let you sink too deep inside that head of yours."

Clay smiled, swallowing as Giana continued, and when it was his turn, he kept one of her hands in his while the other held a small notebook that he'd written in.

"I vow to always keep the house stocked with Cheetos," he said toward the end, which made all of us laugh — that girl *loved* Cheetos. "I promise to kick anyone's ass who doesn't take you seriously in your career, and I swear to continue stealing your books and studying every scene you tab and highlight until the day you stop reading."

"That will be never," she quipped, and we all laughed again.

The vows went from silly to sweet, from being just about the two of them to being about their family, about that baby growing inside Giana's womb. Then they were both crying, and the rest of us were doing our best to keep our shit together until Holden declared them husband and wife. We cheered as Clay dipped Giana in a dramatic kiss, and once she was upright, he bent to his knees and kissed her stomach, too.

They danced down the aisle as the music picked up tempo, and then we all dispersed, making our way to the patio where cocktail hour was taking place.

I held fast to Madelyn's hand as we walked. "So, you going to throw down for the bouquet toss?"

She arched a brow at me. "I wasn't planning on even participating, if I'm being honest."

"Ah," I said, leaning down to whisper in her ear. "You're scared, huh?"

Madelyn scoffed, but I didn't miss the way chills swept over her skin. "No, I've just already done the marriage thing."

My nostrils flared.

"And you won't again?"

"I didn't say that," she whispered, her neck reddening as her eyes flicked to mine.

I tried and failed to contain the hope those words ballooned inside me.

"Well, if that's the case, and you're *not* scared, then..."

She paused our walk, narrowing her eyes at me as she pulled her hand from mine and folded her arms over her chest. "Are you challenging me, Kyle Robbins?"

"Haven't I always?"

She shook her head, but a smile curled at the edge of her lips.

And I knew before it even happened that the other girls didn't stand a chance to catch those flowers — not with my girl wearing that determined look I knew so well.

"A hundred bucks says that bouquet is mine," she said.

I chuckled, pulling her under one arm and steering her toward the bar.

"Oh, come on, Mads," I goaded, voice low behind the shell of her ear. "I think we can think of a better wager than *that*."

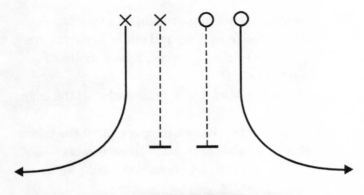

CHAPTER 26
Madelyn

I had to admit — it was quite fun hearing Kyle's friends tease him for being such an asshole in college.

"I don't understand," I said, sipping the white wine in my hand as we stood around a cocktail table. Giana and Clay were taking pictures with what was left of the sun, and the rest of the wedding party was — well, partying. "Why did you challenge her to a game of five hundred, anyway?"

"It wasn't *me* who challenged *her*," Kyle defended.

"He's right, actually. I was the one who called the game," Riley said, arching a brow at Kyle behind her own wine glass. "And I did it because he was a little prick who needed to be put in his place."

There was a fizzle of laughter at the table, and for a second, I thought it might have hurt Kyle's feelings. But he flattened his lips and rolled his eyes, seemingly fine.

"I found her on a dating app," Kyle explained. "And I *might* have been a bit of an asshole when I did. Riley heard me making jokes, and then she challenged me. But *she* made all the terms. It wasn't me who said if she lost, she had to sleep with me. That was her."

Zeke gritted his teeth. "I've never come so close to killing someone."

"Wait — why were you on a dating app?" I asked Riley, pointing between her and Zeke. "I thought you two were together."

"They weren't at that point. And honestly, they should fucking thank me — because it was crystal clear after that night that Zeke had feelings for Riley. I helped them get out of their own damn way." Kyle pointed at Holden and Leo next. "Helped you two fuckers, too."

Holden's expression was level when he retorted, "You have a funny way of *helping*."

"Oh, come on — admit it. Every time you saw me with Julep or got close enough for me to make a comment about her, it got under your skin. It made you move your damn feet instead of dragging them. You two would probably still be skating around each other pretending to be annoyed if it wasn't for me."

"Funny, Robbins," Leo said, tilting his head before sipping his tequila. "I thought you were a tight end, but you're awful defensive right now."

Kyle flicked him off while everyone else laughed, but then he let out a long breath, his eyes falling to the table and then flicking over to where I stood beside him.

Something caught in his expression when our eyes met, his brows furrowing. He searched my gaze in a way that made me feel like maybe I wasn't hiding my emotions as well as I thought I was. The conversation with my mother from earlier was still buzzing loud in my ears, and the weight of what I had to tell Kyle later sat on my chest like a pile of bricks.

"You know what," he said, watching me for a moment longer before he turned to face his friends. "You're right. I owe you all an apology."

That shocked the table silent.

"Riley, I shouldn't have been such an asshole to you. You were a great player from the moment you stepped on the field, and if I'm being honest, I was intimidated by you. I was also pissed to have to share the limelight when I felt like that media attention and those deals I was making were all that I had at the time."

Riley's jaw visibly slackened at that admission, and she looked at Julep and Mary with questions dancing in her eyes before looking at Kyle again. "Thank you."

Kyle nodded, his mouth tugging to the side before he looked at Julep. "I'm sorry most of all to you, Julep. That night at The Pit when you were drunk... I shouldn't have had you in my room — not even if to prove a point to my stupid roommate who couldn't get his head out of his ass," he added with a pointed glare at Holden. "But I promise you, I never would have hurt you or done anything to cross the line. I was just... fucked up, if I'm being honest."

He paused, sucking in a breath with his eyes on his drink now.

My throat tightened the longer that silence stretched, the more I realized how hard it was for him to say all this. I wanted to reach for him, to comfort him in that moment, but everything about his body language told me he needed space to get through what he needed to say to his friends. So, I stayed by his side, my gaze steady, letting him know I was there for him without saying a word.

"I didn't have the best family life," he admitted, and he swallowed hard before his eyes found me.

I nodded softly, keeping my eyes locked on his.

"But no one knew that — not at NBU, anyway." He looked at his friends. "I may have shown it in an asshole way, but I care about you guys. I always have. And if I ever annoyed you, if I ever pushed you, if I ever made you want to punch me in the jaw — it was because I was desperate for someone to recognize my existence." He tongued his cheek. "Sometimes, I just needed to know that someone still knew I was alive and gave a shit."

I covered my mouth with my hands, closing my eyes and hoping like hell that I didn't let a tear sneak free.

For a long time, no one said a word.

Then, finally, I heard a clap on a shoulder, and I opened my eyes to find Holden embracing Kyle in a fierce hug.

"There's a reason you were invited to my wedding," he said, pulling back but still holding onto Kyle's arms. "And to this one. There's a reason no one ever tried to kick you out of The Pit."

"We saw you," Leo filled in. "Even when you tried damn hard to make that impossible to do. I'll never forget when I fell apart over Mary, and you were right there for me."

Kyle nodded, his eyes sliding to Mary on a grin. "I don't have anything to apologize to you for," he said with a wink. "Still think your tattoos are sick. Still think you're one nasty girl. And would still call you Daddy if I didn't think Leo would break my jaw for it."

The tension at the table shattered, everyone laughing as Mary side-stepped Leo and threw her arms around Kyle's neck. She kissed his cheek, and one by one, I watched Kyle's friends embrace him.

I felt like I was snooping on a private moment, and at the same time, like I had been a part of everything they'd just talked about.

Like I was already in the family, too.

"Alright," Julep said with a clap of her hands. "Now that we've had our cry for the night, I think it's time to dance."

The rest of the wedding night was magical.

I audibly gasped when we walked into the reception area, seeing how beautifully everything was decorated. It was a large cabin-like venue with A-frame windows larger than anything I'd ever seen showing off the mountains in the distance. The sun had set, Edison lights hanging from one end of the room to the other, and every detail was elegant and refined.

My personal favorite was the book wall, where mine and Kyle's names were written in gold script on the spine of a fake book. When we opened it, it had our table number in it.

Each table also had photos of Clay and Giana, as well as a chapter or two from Clay's hideously written "book" about their love story. Apparently, it was part of what he called his "grand gesture" to get her back after he messed up, and each table told a little of the story — photos included.

We ate dinner with all the tension from cocktail hour completely gone, and then everyone was on the dance floor. Clay and Giana left only long enough to cut their cake and visit with the older guests of the wedding who were sitting along the perimeter of tables.

The bouquet toss happened about midway through the night, and though I pretended that Mary and Riley had to pull me out against my will, I didn't miss the way Kyle covered his laugh with one hand as he watched me gain my stance and prepare for the throw.

That thing was *mine.*

I hiked up my dress in both my hands, ready to dive like I did for the volleyball last night, if necessary. But I didn't have to. Giana tossed the bouquet of flowers made from book pages up in a perfect arc —

For Riley.

Shit.

I thought about losing the bet with Kyle for a split second, but my pride won out, and I jumped in front of Riley — who was somehow even more petite than I was.

She blinked in surprise when I snatched the flowers, and then all the other girls cheered and surrounded me.

The guys joined us then, and Leo poked Mary's side. "You didn't even try!"

"When are we going to have time to get married?" she barked back at him. "I'm running the shop and you're about to play your first season in the NFL."

He wrapped an arm around her neck and pulled her close, his mouth against her ear. I don't think he realized I could still hear him when he said, "Am I going to have to put a baby in you to tie you down the way Clay did with G?"

Mary flushed a deep red, and so did I, tearing my eyes away from them.

"Riley, you didn't try too hard either," Kyle assessed. "After all, I know how you fought for the ball when we played five hundred."

Riley shrugged, looking over to Zeke. "Bouquet toss is for women who aren't already married."

There was a long pause.

And then a chorus of demands for her to explain.

She laughed, leaning into Zeke before holding up her left hand. "None of you idiots noticed the ring?"

Giana and Clay had run over at this point, and Giana gasped before clutching Riley's wrist in her hands and studying the dainty yellow sapphire.

Immediately, she started sobbing.

"Oh, my God! I've been so focused on the wedding I didn't see! I'm the worst friend ever!"

Clay consoled her with a chuckle as Riley leaned into Zeke again. He put his arm around her, and she looked up at him like he hung the moon. "We eloped."

"Of course, you two would elope," Julep said. "Is this just because you didn't want to have to wear a frilly dress, Novo?"

Zeke sucked his teeth and leveled a look at his friends. "This girl wore her damn leggings."

"We were hiking!" Riley defended.

The chaos continued through the night, and I found that I really *had* started feeling better. Everything that had happened earlier with my mom was compartmentalized and shoved away for the moment. Kyle and I danced and laughed, and when the guys pulled him away for shots, the girls tugged me over to the photo booth.

The night was winding down when the DJ put on

a slow song, and Kyle slid his hand into mine, dragging me out to the middle of the dance floor. We smiled at each other as his hands found my waist and mine threaded around his neck, both of us finding rhythm in a slow sway.

"It's kind of crazy," he said, shaking his head as his eyes washed over mine.

"What is?"

"Two weeks ago, you were just a memory. And now..."

I swallowed. "I can't believe how fast this has all happened. I mean, I *hated* you. I never wanted to see you again. And then you showed back up in my life, and... it just feels like a whirlwind. One moment I'm just your agent, then I'm your fake girlfriend, then you're meeting my son, and then I'm here and nothing feels fake anymore and I just... I don't..."

"I know," Kyle said, thumbing my jaw with his brows furrowed. "We can slow down. We can pull back. We can be just friends, whatever you need." He paused, chewing his bottom lip. "Are you ever going to tell me why you hated me?"

I closed my eyes, my throat impossibly tight.

"Is it because of what happened with my parents that night? Did... did *your* parents make you say what you did?"

I frowned. "What do you mean *say what I did*?"

His jaw tightened. "That you wanted me to stay away from you. That you never wanted to see me again."

My breath caught in my throat.

Because that confirmed what I suspected.

His parents never told him I was pregnant.

They told him I wanted him gone.

And then, he left.

I felt myself hyperventilating, each breath harder to take than the last as it all sank in.

Oh, God.

"I know you were mad at me before the party though," Kyle added, speaking faster like he was onto something. "You were off that whole week. I tried to talk to you, but you wouldn't let me in. And then—" He framed my face. "What did I do? What happened?"

I shook my head, tears blurring my vision. I was so overwhelmed, so devastated, so... *angry* — but that emotion wasn't strong enough to trump the others, not right now.

I buried my face in his chest, trying and failing not to fall apart.

"Mads," he croaked, holding my head to him. "You're breaking my fucking heart right now."

"Not as much as I've already broken my own."

"*Talk* to me," he begged.

I shook my head on a sob but held onto him just as tightly. "Not here."

Kyle pulled back, holding my gaze a moment before he nodded. Then, he wrapped his hand around mine and tugged me off the floor, leading the way to our table where my clutch and his jacket still were.

"Where are you going?" Mary asked when we whizzed past her and Leo, her brows furrowing when she saw my no-doubt blotchy and tear-stained face.

"I'll see you all in the morning," Kyle promised, and then he hooked his arm around my waist. "I need to get my girl back to our room."

My girl.

Our room.

My head spun with it all as much as my heart squeezed with what I was about to have to tell him.

And I only had a short car ride to figure out how.

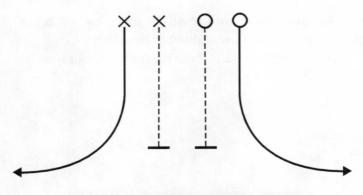

CHAPTER 27

Kyle

My stomach was tied into the tightest knot by the time we made it back to the hotel.

I held Madelyn's hand the entire drive. She didn't say a word, but she also didn't pull away. She just sat beside me, her eyes trained out the window, silent tears streaming down her cheeks before she'd thumb them away.

I didn't know what to think. My brain *wanted* to race, but I couldn't even begin to guess what was going on. I had to wait for her to tell me, for her to let me in.

All I could surmise was that it had something to do with that night.

It had something to do with why she told me to stay away from her.

I wanted to know. I *needed* to know. And yet, at the same time, I was sick even thinking about it. Going back to that time in my life was like sticking my hand in a hot fire. I didn't want to relive the pain — but I knew the only way for us to move forward was for us to face our past.

Blessedly, the media had gone by the time we pulled up to the hotel doors. Still, I shielded Madelyn with my suit jacket just in case there was someone sneaking around trying to get a photo. I rushed her to the elevator, holding her hand all the way until we slid inside our room and the door shut behind us.

Immediately, we were engulfed with the heaviest silence I'd ever felt.

I laid my jacket over the back of the desk chair, my eyes on Madelyn as she sat on the edge of the bed like she was in a daze. Her eyes were wide and unfocused, her fingers curling into the comforter as if it was all that held her to this Earth.

I didn't rush her. Instead, I left her alone for a moment — just long enough to get ice from down the hall. I poured us both two tall glasses of ice water when I returned, and Madelyn took a long drink of hers before setting it aside.

"Tell me what happened that night," she finally said, her voice low and cracking. "And the next morning."

I swallowed. "You know what happened."

She shut her eyes tightly and shook her head just once, fast and hard. "I need to hear it. I need you to tell me everything. Don't leave out a single detail."

My heart protested in my ribcage, lungs squeezing painfully. My entire body was ready to revolt at the thought of having to go back to that dark time in my life.

But I'd do anything Madelyn asked me to — even if it meant bleeding out right here at her feet.

I sat down beside her on the bed, giving her enough space to make her feel comfortable while also being close enough to give myself the courage to speak. I folded my hands between my legs, staring at them as I spoke.

"I was upset with you," I admitted. "Something was wrong that week. I knew it, and you wouldn't talk to me. I think I knew you were going to break up with me, and I..." I cleared my throat. "I felt so out of control. All I wanted was for you to be there with me that night at my parents' party. I wanted you to let me in. I wanted a chance to fix whatever I'd done wrong."

Madelyn didn't blink, but two tears slid down her cheeks and hit her dress.

"In hindsight, I'm glad you weren't there," I said on a sigh. "Because you would have had to witness what my father did — to your mother, to your father..." I swallowed. "To me."

She did close her eyes then, and I watched the way her chest rose and fell in a slow, steadying breath.

"The next morning, when all the dust was settling, I didn't realize how bad it really was. Not until you showed up."

My throat was thick with emotion that I could barely contain.

"I saw you from my window. And, *fuck*, Mads," I said, shaking my head and looking right at her. "I can't explain what I felt when I did. I was relieved, happy, hopeful, and yet shaking like a fucking leaf, too, because I didn't know if you'd ever be able to love me again after what had happened. The way my father had treated your mother, the things he'd said, and then..."

Madelyn looked like a zombie beside me, like she was listening but was incapable of any reaction.

"I just... I thought you and I could make it through anything," I confessed. "I waited in my room just thinking of how you'd open the door, how you'd see me and your face would crumple, and I'd run to you and you'd hug me and we'd hold each other and whatever you'd been angry at me for that week would just disappear. It wouldn't matter. It..."

Goddamnit.

I scrubbed a hand over my mouth and looked away from her, my eyes on the ceiling as I tried to regain my composure.

"When you didn't come, I ran downstairs. And my parents told me what you'd said to them, what you'd asked of me."

"They said I wanted you to stay away from me," she whispered, the first words she'd said since I started speaking.

I nodded.

"It fucking killed me," I said through the thickness in my throat. "My parents knew it would. They said we were going to move, that I wouldn't have to live in the hurt. They told me to pack my things. And when I saw you on Monday, when I showed up to get my stuff from school... I thought maybe you'd run to me. I thought maybe they were wrong, that you'd change your mind, that you wouldn't let your parents control you. But I saw it in your eyes. I saw how..."

I cursed, nostrils flaring as the memory resurfaced.

"I saw how fucking *scared* you were of me. It was like you saw my father when you looked at me, and that gutted me more than anything."

Madelyn covered her mouth with her hand and shook her head, her eyes squeezing shut.

"I hated you," I whispered. "I did, Mads. I hated you with everything that I was for *years*. Until I saw you again." I laughed then, the sound just a huff of air leaving my chest. "And then I realized that the only reason I could hate you was because I couldn't see you, couldn't touch you, couldn't remember what it was like to be in your presence. And the moment I was around you again, all that was eviscerated. Because the truth is I can't do anything but love you."

Those words broke her, and I hated it — the way her shoulders shook, her hands covering her face as little sobs left her. But it was the truth, and she needed to hear those words as much as I needed to say them.

"I'm about to prove you wrong," she said after a moment, dropping her hands into her lap. Her red, blotchy eyes met mine. "You're going to hate me after what I tell you."

My chest hollowed out.

"I never could—"

"You will," she argued. "Because I didn't tell your parents that I wanted you to stay away from me, Kyle. I told them I was pregnant."

A blink.

A heartbeat.

And then my stomach bottomed out.

The room turned upside down. My entire *world* turned upside down.

My pulse kicked loud and heavy in my chest, in my ears, and I stared at Madelyn willing myself to comprehend what she'd just said.

But it felt like she'd spoken to me in a foreign language, or like she'd garbled out some nonsense that didn't equate to anything.

I didn't breathe for the longest moment.

And then, I sucked in a breath that burned my lungs and made my eyes sting. I opened my mouth to speak, but no words came. My lips trembled until I pressed them together again, and Madelyn broke at the sight of me, rolling her lips together as her eyes welled with tears that spilled down her face.

"You..." I started, but stopped immediately, my stomach flipping so violently I nearly lost my dinner. I stood, shaking my head, hands flying into my hair as I walked away from her in denial.

When I was on the opposite side of the room, I froze, numbness invading every inch of me as I tried to process.

I turned slowly to face her, and I didn't know what hurt more — the crushing weight on my chest or the sight of her falling apart.

"I wasn't mad at you that week," she said, her voice trembling as she fought back tears. "I was terrified of losing you."

"Losing me?" I let out a breath, shaking my head in disbelief. "Why... *how* could you ever lose me?"

"You were sixteen," she cried. "You had your whole life ahead of you. You had football and a dream."

"I had *you*, Madelyn."

She shook her head, crying again as she looked at her hands. "I was just a kid, too. We both were. I had no idea how you would take it. I was afraid you'd hate me, that you'd be mad at me for stealing your life away."

I was already shaking my head and walking toward her when she put up a hand to stop me.

"Wait," she said, then she forced a deep breath. "I just... I needed time. So, I told my parents, and they told me no matter what I decided to do, they'd support me.

I went to tell you, but your parents said you were sleeping. They saw how upset I was... I was crying..."

My hands curled into fists at my side.

"So, I told them, and... and they said they would tell you when you woke up, that they'd have you call me. They hugged me and swore it would all be okay."

"Fuck!" I dragged my hands through my hair again, and then I couldn't stand to be apart from her any longer. I knelt in front of where Madelyn sat on the bed, folding her hands in my own and kissing her knuckles as she looked down at me.

"I'm so sorry, Kyle," she cried. "I should have told you. I should have—"

"You *did*, you tried. You trusted my parents to tell me and..." I went wide-eyed. "Oh, God. Madelyn, when you saw me at school on Monday..."

"I thought you hated me," she sobbed. "And then you left and—"

I climbed up to sit next to her on the bed, pulling her into my arms and holding her to me in the tightest hug I could manage. One hand cradled her head against my chest, the other wrapped around to hold her to me, as if my arms could put the pieces back together, as if I could heal her when I now understood I had been the source of all her pain.

"I lost the baby," she cried into my chest, her hands clinging to the fabric of my dress shirt. "And I lost you. And I lost *myself*. And now, realizing you didn't even know... I... I..."

Fuck.

I couldn't help it.

I broke.

Clutching Madelyn to me even harder, the first sob wracked my body, and that made Madelyn crack wide open, too. She clung to me, both of us crying like we were kids again, like this conversation and this room had transported us back to that time in our lives.

"Mads, I am so sorry," I croaked, my chest splitting open with every word. "I'm so sorry you had to go through that alone. I'm so sorry I didn't force you to talk to me, that I let my stupid anger get in the way of me running to you."

"It's not your fault."

"It's not yours either."

And maybe that was what hurt the most.

I pulled back, framing her face with my hands and swiping away the fresh tears I found there.

"You're not mad at me?" she asked pathetically.

"Are you fucking kidding me?" I shook my head, locking my eyes on hers as I bent to her level. "I'm furious, Madelyn, but not at you. Never at you."

As if acknowledging my rage allowed it to burn brighter, I felt my chest squeeze in the way it did before I got into a fist fight. I saw red at the thought of my father. I had no doubt he was the one who told my mom what would be said to me. And then I cursed my mother, who no doubt didn't have the spine to stand up to him and say no.

Both of them were fucking dead to me, but I could deal with them later.

Right now, the only thing that mattered was this woman in my arms.

"They stole you from me," I whispered, stomach curdling at the realization. "They stole our child from *us*."

Madelyn closed her eyes, freeing more tears as her hands covered mine where I held her face. She leaned into my touch as if it was the only thing that could save her.

"We can't go back and change any of that," I said, voice cracking again.

A baby.

A child.

I was a father.

Madelyn was the mother to my child.

My throat constricted, and Madelyn swiped away the tears that slid down my jaw.

"We can't go back and do anything different," I finally said, forcing a long inhale and exhale. "We can get angry, and sad, but none of that will change what happened."

Madelyn nodded, her bottom lip wobbling.

"But we can be together now," I said, tilting her chin up.

"How?" she whispered. "You're about to be a rookie in the NFL, Kyle. I... have a kid, one who *isn't* yours. I have to get away from Marshall. I have to—"

"Fuck all of that," I said gruffly. "Fuck any excuse your brain is trying to give you right now. You're a survivor, Mads, and I get it now. I understand why. You've had to survive on your own your entire life, and now, you have Sebastian depending on you, too."

She let out a little sob at that.

"But listen to me," I added, bending to hold her gaze again. "You don't have to do this alone. Not anymore. Not ever again. You're *mine*, Mads. You always have been. I lost you then, but I refuse to lose you now. Whatever you need, I'll give it to you. Whatever we have to do, we'll do it — together. No more letting anyone or anything get between us, you hear me?"

She nodded, her arms wrapping around my neck.

"From this moment on, it's you, and me, and Sebastian. Okay? We will figure it out. We will find a way. But I'll be fucking damned if I ever let you go again. I'll lay down my life before I let you walk alone. I'll walk away from everything else if I have to — Seattle, the team, football, my family — but never you. Do you understand me? Never, *ever* you, Mads."

The words were still leaving my lips when she pressed her mouth to mine, and I crushed her to me, one hand in her hair and the other flat against the small of her back. As if neither of us could bear to sit any longer, we were moving, standing, clinging to one another like a lifeline.

I breathed her in, everything that she was, everything that we never had the chance to be.

And I swore on my life right then and there that I'd make it right with her.

I'd make it all right again.

Madelyn deepened our kiss, pulling me to her like even a centimeter of space between us was too much. She climbed into my arms, and I held her waist as she wrapped her legs around me. Every kiss was urgent and needy, every touch burned like the hottest flame.

"Kyle," she sighed into my mouth, her tongue dancing over mine. "I need you. I need—"

I silenced her request with my mouth, one arm still holding her tight to me as the other weaved into her hair and tugged with just enough pressure to make her gasp and arch her neck for me.

I knew what she needed. What we both needed.

And I was all too eager to lose myself in her forever.

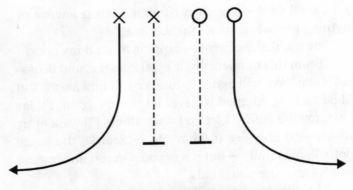

CHAPTER 28
Madelyn

Every kiss Kyle pressed against my skin was intentional and sure, as if he could see all the broken fragments I'd become, and he was hell bent on piecing me back together.

Tears still stained both of our faces as he clutched me to him, and I gasped into his mouth when his hands curled into my hair, tugging with just the right force. My hair was still pinned up from the night, but Kyle's fingers slid between the bobby pins and gripped what he could find until he became too impatient.

Then, one by one, he plucked each bobby pin from my hair.

"Mine," he husked against my mouth, and then two pins clattered to the floor. "Always mine, Mads."

With every pin he pulled, my hair fell more around my face, and when the last one was gone, he massaged my scalp with his massive hands, eliciting a groan from me as I tore at the buttons on his dress shirt.

250

Where I was in a hurry, Kyle took his sweet time.

He let me strip him out of his dress shirt, allowed me to thumb the top button of his slacks through the slit and slide his zipper down. But he didn't match my greediness.

Instead, he hooked one finger under the strap of my dress, sliding it off one shoulder and kissing along the collarbone he'd exposed before he trailed back up to my lips. One hand slid down to palm my ass as the other reached for the zipper of my dress, and just like he had in that dressing room when I'd first put it on, he slowly unfastened it, drawing a hot trail of fire with his knuckles in the process.

"Even when I hated you, there were so many nights I dreamt of this," he murmured against my lips. Chills raced over my skin when the zipper of my dress was all the way down and Kyle tugged at the fabric until it fell into a heap at my ankles. "I dreamt of growing up with you, of hearing how your moans would change, feeling how your sighs would warm my skin when I found just the right spot."

As if he'd cued me, I whimpered at the feel of his thick thigh sliding between my now bare legs. His slacks were still hanging from his hips, the belt unbuckled and the top line of his briefs showing through, but that thick warmth of him pressed against the thin lace of my panties in the sweetest way.

He cupped my ass in his hands and rolled me against him, and white light flashed behind my lids.

I shook so violently my legs gave out, but Kyle was there to catch my weight.

"That still gets you, doesn't it?" he mused with a smirk, and then he rolled me against him again, that grin growing when I moaned and clung to his shoulders.

His chest and arms and abdomen were a sight to marvel at, every muscle lean and defined the way only a professional athlete's can be. I dug my nails into his triceps as I held on tight, and the hiss he let free when I did lit me up from my core.

"I could get you off just like this," he promised, and I knew he was right. Every time he ground his thigh against my clit, fire stroked my belly, low and hot. "I could make you come without even getting you undressed."

I didn't know if I wanted to fight him or beg him to do just that. I was already wound so tight from the last two weeks of emotion and tension. I needed to release like I needed to breathe, but while my brain was fuzzy and focused on every thrum of pleasure he was stroking out between my legs, my hands were tearing at his pants again, begging him to be bare with me, to make this last.

With a grin and a swift kiss against my lips, Kyle granted my wish.

He pulled back with his eyes still devouring me, holding my gaze as he stripped off what was left of his clothing. It was all I could do to keep my breath steady as I watched him, as I noted all the ways he'd changed, and yet all the ways he was still the same.

His body was that of a man now, the muscles lining his abdomen and thick thighs more pronounced. When his cock sprang free from his boxers, I sipped in another breath, biting my lip at how big he was, how I'd known him intimately before and yet I had never known *this* version of him.

Where the years had sculpted him into an athletic, high-performing specimen, they'd softened me. I had silvery scars across my stomach, my hips, my breasts. I was a mother now.

Kyle didn't seem deterred by that reality.

In fact, he seemed ravenous, as if just being parted from me long enough to take off his clothes was too long. As soon as he was naked, he was on me again. One of his massive palms enveloped my modest breast, and his mouth devoured the other, his tongue swiping around my nipple before he covered it and hummed at how it felt to taste me.

"Kyle," I breathed, which made him more fervent, and *fuck* if seeing this man bent over and licking me wasn't the most powerful sight. I didn't miss the way he trembled slightly, like despite all the words he was casting, he was still a little nervous, too.

That made me absolutely feral.

I stepped out of my dress, kicking one heel off and then the next. But before I could slide my panties down, Kyle gripped me by the hips to stop me.

"Allow me," he said, and then he was kissing a slow, torturous trail down every inch of my stomach until he rested on his knees in front of me.

My chest rose and fell with every haggard breath, my hands roaming from his shoulders into his hair. He smiled against my left hip bone when I fisted my hands into those silky strands, and then his thumbs slid beneath the thin band of my thong on either side, and he tugged it down my thighs, centimeter by centimeter.

"Fuck, Mads," he breathed when the fabric was gone, and he sat back on his heels, staring at my pussy like it was his deliverance.

I didn't feel one ounce of embarrassment, not one inclination to hide.

I stood there, bared to him, and soaked in the electricity he sent soaring through me the longer his eyes washed over every inch.

"You are so gorgeous," he said, his voice low and sincere. Those fiery blue eyes flicked up to watch me as his hands wrapped around to cup my ass again, and then he pressed a soft, supple kiss just above my clit. "My pretty fucking girl."

I bit my lip, widening my stance without him saying a word, and that made a brilliant smile stretch on his face.

"You want more," he mused, and he lowered his mouth again, this time sticking out his tongue and flicking *just* the tip of it right above where I actually wanted him to taste me. I didn't know if I loved or hated the tease, but my hands were in his hair again, trying to pull him where I knew I'd feel the spark.

But Kyle stopped me, arching his neck and locking those hungry eyes on mine before one palm began sliding up the inside of my thigh.

"Patience, Mads," he teased, and then he cupped me, both of us moaning together when he slid one thick finger between my lips.

I shook around him, and the sight of him on his knees with his hand between my legs nearly sent me over the edge. He dove that finger through where I was wet and aching for him, cursing under his breath when he just barely brushed my entrance before retreating again.

"Drenched," he breathed, and I noted the way his Adam's apple bobbed hard in his throat. "This makes me so fucking hard, Madelyn. Knowing I do this to you."

He slid that thick finger through again, and this time, his thumb caught my clit at the same time. He circled it with just the right amount of pressure to make my legs quake, and I let my head fall back, a gasp shooting out of me.

"Come here," he growled, and then before I knew what was happening, he had one of my thighs hiked up over his shoulder. I had no choice but to grab ahold of his shoulders to keep from falling, and he kissed along the inside of the thigh he'd wrenched up before his mouth descended on my pussy.

And he devoured me.

There was no gentle play anymore, no tease of his tongue or caress of his finger. He covered me with his hot, wet mouth, licking and sucking my clit as that expert finger stretched me open. The combination made me cry out and shake, and I couldn't get enough oxygen, couldn't moan loud enough to convey how it felt.

Kyle Robbins was on his knees for me.

Kyle Robbins had his finger deep inside me, curling against my belly, his tongue working my clit in a perfect rhythm.

Kyle Robbins was *mine*.

"I can't," I gasped, heaving, my chest aching with every breath. "Kyle, I..."

"Give it to me," he commanded, and then he was sucking my clit again, another finger joining the first. "Give me the first one tonight, Mads. Come on my tongue."

"*Fuck*," I cried out, but the words were permission — and it didn't take me long to obey.

I didn't care how I looked. I didn't care that Kyle was witnessing me completely unravel for him, that I was wild and unhinged as I ground my pussy against his mouth and held him to me. I bucked against each roll of his fingers inside me, sinking so I could feel him deeper, and whimpering when he rewarded me with a satisfied groan at the feel of me giving him all my weight.

So long, I'd dreamed of a man who could touch me like this, who could make me feel so wanted, so cared for, so safe and yet so free.

So long, I'd wondered if I'd ever feel pleasure like this, if I'd ever know what it was like to be touched by a man who knew exactly what he was doing.

And now that I had it within reach, I let go.

"Yes, *yes*, Kyle, right there." I rolled my lips together, face hot as I grappled for the spark playing at the edge of my awareness. "Don't stop."

"Never stopping, Mads," he promised — and then he picked up the pace. His fingers curled inside me to the deepest spot, and the held them there, coaxing my orgasm like he was the master of it. His mouth covered my clit, and the hot swipes of his tongue turned into a steady sucking that drove me to ecstasy.

I ripped apart.

Every stitch that had carefully held me together since the moment I lost him was eviscerated, along with my ability to stand. I came like it was the first and the last time, like it was the end of my life and my body had one last chance to feel *everything*.

My hands curled in his hair. My hips bucked and rolled. My legs gave out, but Kyle held me steady, licking up every last wave of my release.

He consumed me, every part of me, and I never wanted to live outside of him again.

It felt like the longest orgasm to ever exist as I rode out each rolling spark of electricity coursing through me. Kyle never relented, either — he fucked me with his fingers and his mouth until the last moan leaked out of me, until my hands slackened in his hair and my legs began to shake so hard from the effort of standing that he carefully helped me into the bed.

He laid me down, maneuvering me up and up until my head hit the pillows, until he was sliding between my legs and kissing me as my breaths attempted to even out.

I tasted myself on him, and hot need rippled through me.

Mine.

I didn't care that I felt like I could sleep for a year. I didn't care that the sweet euphoria of release was trying to lull me into a coma. I fought against it, reaching for that part of me that yearned for more, and I deepened every kiss Kyle pressed against me.

My hands were in his hair again, my legs spreading wider, and when I felt his hard length warm and insistent against my slick core, I moaned deep and needy.

Kyle hissed, pressing his forehead against mine and slowly rolling his hips. Every time he did, his thick length slid between my wet lips, coating him in the orgasm he'd just given me. It was as if he was savoring it, as if he were memorizing every second of tonight before he was inside me again.

But I was impatient.

I reached between us, nipping at his bottom lip when I found his cock and stroked it from base to tip. He was soaked from me, and that made me even hotter, even more needy to feel him.

God, he was even bigger than I remembered. I'd seen his bulge, felt it pressed against me last night when he'd touched me and had it pressed against my backside. I knew he was thick and long and curved in a way that would hit *just* the right spot inside me, but to have him in my hand, to feel the way that beautiful cock twitched in my palm...

It was otherworldly.

"Mads," he croaked when I squeezed my fist around his crown and pumped him slow, slicking every inch of him until I knew he'd slide inside me with ease.

His hands slid under my back, fingers curling over my shoulders as I lined him up at my entrance. He pulled me down onto him, just the tip of him stretching me, and we both let out long, throaty moans.

"Wait," he said.

I paused, both of us breathing hard, his eyes locked on mine where he hovered above me.

"If we do this," he said, swallowing. "If you let me have you..."

"I'm not taking it back, Kyle."

He closed his eyes, forehead dropping to mine as he shook his head like he couldn't believe those words were true.

"Claim me," I begged, arching into him. "Leave your mark. Get back what's always been yours. *Ruin* me, if that's what it takes." I slid my hands into his hair and made him look at me before I kissed him hard, my next words vibrating against his lips. "Have me in every way you want, Kyle, because I'll only ever belong to you."

He let out a hot breath through his nose, like those words had seared him from the inside, and then his mouth captured mine in a punishing, exhilarating kiss.

And he flexed his hips, filling me, a groan ripping from his chest as I moaned and dug my nails into his back.

We were home again.

We were whole.

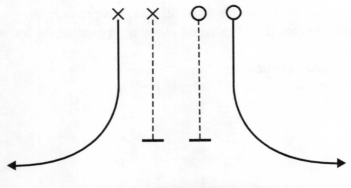

CHAPTER 29

Kyle

She was made for me.

Every cell in my body screamed that irrefutable truth as I flexed inside her, both of us gasping and moaning and closing our eyes as the ecstasy of that connection consumed us.

I was hyperaware of everything in that moment — the way Madelyn's nails marked my back with little crescents, how her breath caught in her delicate throat, the way she squeezed around me when I flexed just a little deeper, and how sweet her moan was, how it danced with the guttural groan that ripped from my chest.

"*Fuck*, Mads," I cursed, shaking my head and burying my face in her neck. I kissed the flesh there, tasting her as I withdrew my hips just an inch before driving in again.

I wanted to bury myself so deep in her that we became one.

I wanted to erase every man who had been with her since me, every year that has separated us.

Something incredible happened this weekend, as if the moment we got on that plane together, we slipped into another universe where nothing and no one else mattered. We faced our past. We learned the truth. We couldn't fight our feelings for one another anymore because there were no distractions.

This was meant to be.

We were meant to be.

"You're perfect," I murmured into her neck as I rocked my hips, out and back in, slow and steady. "Absolutely perfect."

The moment she locked her heels behind my ass and urged me in deeper, I took the cue, raising up onto my palms so I could look down at her as I slid out and back in. She was molded to fit me, her walls slick and tight as they hugged every inch each time I flexed inside her.

The view was almost too much — her metallic hair a mess against the white pillows, her cheeks and neck the most beautiful shade of red, her breasts bouncing with every thrust of my hips. One of her hands gripped my shoulder, the other flying to cling to the sheets by her head. She held them for only a moment before that hand moved to palm her breast, rolling her nipple between her fingers and thumb.

"*Yes*, baby," I praised, licking my lips before I dropped them to her chest. I covered her other breast with my mouth, circling her bud with my tongue. I sucked it with just the right pressure to make her moan and squirm. "You look so fucking pretty playing with your tits like this."

"Kyle," she breathed, and the way she flushed even harder told me my words both lit her up and embarrassed her.

I'd work to cure that, no matter how long it took.

Something told me her pleasure had been pushed to the wayside for far too long. She'd learn soon enough that with me? It would always be front and center.

She would always be my number one priority.

"Come here," I rasped against her neck, dropping down so I could maneuver my arm between her back and the mattress. I held her against my chest, rolling until she was on top, until my back was against the headboard and she was straddling my lap.

I was still inside her, and when her hands found my shoulders for balance, I flexed my hips just enough to drive in another inch.

I knew she'd feel me deeper this way, knew it would also leave room for me to play with her clit and coax another orgasm out of her.

"Ride me, Madelyn. Let me see you wild and undone and taking what you want."

Her eyes were heavy and heated as she stared back at me, lips parted, chest heaving. Her thigh muscles engaged, lifting her off my lap until only the tip of me was inside her, and then she sank back down.

In the most slow, torturous pace.

"You love feeling every inch of me, don't you?" I mused, smirking as she threw her head back and let out a moan once she was fully seated. "Naughty fucking girl."

I spanked the side of her ass, and her eyes flew open, connecting with mine in a mixture of shock and pleasure. I gripped her ass in both hands, helping her lift and slide back down again, and we picked up the rhythm, her rolling her hips to catch friction against me while I rocked in as deep as I could each time she sat in my lap.

"God, look at you," I said, shaking my head as she took over the pace. I let my hands roam, cupping her breasts in my palms and groaning at how they were the perfect handful. I slid my hands down next, one finding her hip as the other traced the faint lines on her stomach.

Instantly, Madelyn stilled, her brows furrowing as she covered that hand with her own to stop me from tracing the scars.

I met her worried gaze with one of nothing but admiration, lifting her hand to my lips to kiss each knuckle before I moved us back to run the length of those scars together.

"These are beautiful, Mads. You're so strong, so fucking sexy."

For a moment, I was sure she didn't believe me.

So, I snaked one hand between her legs, thumbing her clit while my other hand slid up and over her breasts until I could wrap it around her throat.

"Look at me," I commanded, and when she did, I squeezed with just enough pressure to make her moan, working her clit in a smooth, slow circle.

She bucked against the movement, riding me with more passion, telling me she was close.

"You," I repeated, rocking my hips up to meet hers. "Are." Another flex, another roll of my thumb. "Sexy." A squeeze of her throat. "Every inch of you. Every scar. Every mark of motherhood. I've never been more turned on in my fucking life, Madelyn. You're the only one who undoes me like this."

Madelyn let out a whimper, squeezing her eyes shut and riding me harder, faster, her hands braced against my chest to help her set the pace.

I kept that pressure on her neck, kept my thumb teasing her clit until I could feel her slowing, losing control, so desperate for her release she didn't know if she should move faster or stop moving altogether.

When she couldn't keep the pace, I took over, bending my legs so she could rest against them as I bucked my hips. I fucked her hard and deep and mercilessly, my grip on her throat never relenting. And when she caught her second orgasm, I smiled in victory, feeling the way she hugged my cock, the way her entire body quivered with the release.

It was the most intoxicating sight, watching her lose control. Her breasts bounced wildly as she rode me, her head tilted back in ecstasy, mouth open and crying out my name. I kept that bruising pace until the moment she went lax in my lap, until she crumpled against my chest, panting, sweating, clinging to me, her pussy still tightening around my cock in little pulses.

"That's my girl," I praised, kissing her hair.

I let her rest for a moment, just barely moving in and out of her. My cock was throbbing now, desperate for a release, but I waited until she caught her breath.

When she started kissing me, started lifting herself off me and dropping back down, I gave in to my own need.

Flipping her onto her stomach, I kissed and sucked and licked a trail up her thighs, biting the lush round apple of her ass before I straddled her from behind. Gripping her hips, I arched that ass up for me, giving her a light spank before I positioned myself at her entrance again.

And when I slid in this time, we hit a new depth.

I knew she felt it, too — likely even more sensitive from her second release. She cried out my name, fingers twisting in the sheets as I withdrew and flexed inside her again.

"I'm close," I promised. Hell, the truth was I could have come just from eating her out, from tasting her and feeling the way she trembled through her first orgasm.

My balls were tight with the need to release, my cock so sensitive that every thrust inside her felt like I was already climaxing. She was all I could feel, all I could hear, all I could see. She was all that existed.

Pulling her up off the bed and onto her knees, I flexed inside her again, palming her breast with one hand while the other tilted her face toward me so I could capture her mouth with mine. She moaned into the kiss, and I fucked her hard with three bruising pumps before I finally caught fire.

Light burst behind my eyes, her name rolling off my lips and against hers as I buried myself deep. I was on fire. I was numb. I was engulfed by everything that she was, everything we *could be* together.

I lost myself in her, riding out the most powerful orgasm of my life while she kissed me and gripped my hair in her fist.

Neither of us wanted it to end — as if once it did, we'd be thrown back into a reality where we couldn't exist together.

But I refused to let that happen.

I hoped she felt it with every last thrust. I hoped she'd never remember what it was like to live without me ever again. I hoped she realized as much as I did that there was no going back.

Even after I'd finished, we stayed connected, kissing and slowly fucking each other as my cum leaked out of her. When I did carefully remove myself, I instantly swept her into my arms, kissing her all the way to the bathroom before I ran her a hot bath.

I helped her settle in, knowing the way she hissed when she sank all the way into the water meant she'd be sore tomorrow. I did my best to ease that pain, caressing her with the washcloth between her legs and over her breasts before I slid into the water behind her.

She sighed, resting against my chest as I massaged her shoulders and kissed behind her ear.

I had full intention just to wash her and comfort her, to make her feel good and then put her to bed. But the little minx started slipping and sliding against me, her hand snaking back between us until she could wrap it around my cock and stroke me back to life.

Before long, we were sliding into round two, neither of us wanting to sleep until we'd had our fill.

When we finally did surrender to our fatigue, we slid into bed together without a stitch of clothing between us. I curled around her as she snuggled into my arms, and when I felt her start to weep, I closed my eyes, pressing soft, soothing kisses to her spine and the back of her neck. I held her tighter, letting her know I was there without a word being spoken, letting her know I wasn't going anywhere.

Pain. Loss. Longing.

Every tear she let loose was made of all three.

My chest ached with the same emotions, along with anger I knew I'd have to face in the morning. We'd survived the unthinkable. *She* had gone through it alone, thinking I'd turned my back on her, thinking I...

I shook my head, forcing a calming breath and holding her tighter.

Tonight wasn't the time.

In the morning, we'd talk. In the morning, we'd make a plan. But right now, I just wanted to wrap her up in my arms, make her feel safe, and kiss her until her breaths evened out and sleep took her under for a blissful peace.

I didn't know what happened next, but I knew one thing for sure.

From this moment on, we were a unit.

From this moment on, it was us against the world.

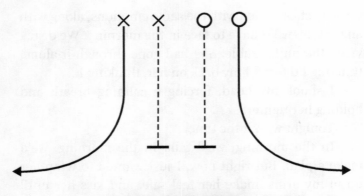

CHAPTER 30
Madelyn

Kyle wrapped me in his arms once my bags were unloaded from Braden's trunk the next night. He pressed his lips to my forehead and held them there, his giant frame enveloping me, his heartbeat calm and steady in his chest.

"I'm going to miss you," he said, and the words made tears prick my eyes as much as they made me smile.

"It's two days," I reminded him. I had houses to show and work to catch up on, as well as swim lessons with Sebastian. Kyle had training with Braden, both of them eager to get into the best shape possible before training camp started in just a few weeks.

"Too long," Kyle murmured, and then he kissed me in a way that made me feel how much he meant that.

The front door to my house opened, and Kyle and I broke apart, him shoving his hands in his pockets and me tucking my hair behind my ear.

My mom stood as a shadow in the frame, the light from the living room shining behind her.

Then, there was the sound of little feet storming through the house, and Sebastian bolted out of the front door and ran straight to me.

"Mommy! Mommy!"

My emotions were about as stable as a chair with two legs missing, and I fought against the urge to cry as I swung him up into my arms with a grunt.

"My goodness, what did you eat while I was away? I think you've grown two feet and gained twenty pounds!"

Sebastian giggled and buried his face in my neck, his arms wrapped around me. "You're silly, Mommy."

I kissed his hair, eyeing where Kyle was watching us. There were so many emotions sprawling across his face, but I couldn't name a single one before he smiled and hid them all.

"Hi, Kyle!" Sebastian said, beaming at him.

"Hey, buddy. How was your weekend?"

"Good. Me and Nana went to the museum."

"You did, huh?" Kyle bent to Sebastian's level when I put him back on the ground. "Well, I bet that was pretty cool. Did you see dinosaurs?"

Sebastian nodded proudly. "Uh-huh. And there was a whole room of bugs!"

"Bugs! I bet there were spiders. I love spiders."

Sebastian's eyes went wide as saucers. "You *do*? They're so scary!"

"Nah, just misunderstood. If we ever catch a spider inside together, I'll show you how cool they are, and we can get it outside safely instead of killing it."

Sebastian nodded emphatically, looking up at me as if to say, "*Did you hear that? This guy likes spiders!*"

"I brought you something," Kyle said, and Sebastian and I *both* looked at him in surprise and curiosity. I'd been with Kyle nearly the entire trip. When had he had time to get anything?

But he dug into his pocket and fished something out, holding it in his fist in front of Sebastian.

"Do you know what a meteorite is?"

Sebastian shook his head.

"Well, it's debris from outer space."

"*Space?*"

Kyle nodded. "Like a comet, asteroid or meteor. And there are some places in the world where meteorites have been found. Do you know where Argentina is?"

Sebastian shook his head again, hanging onto every word Kyle said.

Kyle pulled out his phone and clicked on the maps app, showing my son the large country.

"And right here, there's been discoveries of what they call *Campo del Cielo* — a group of iron meteorites." Kyle unfolded his hand then, revealing a small, lumpy object that looked like a cross between a rock and a heap of metal.

"Whoa!" Sebastian carefully took it from him, and then gaped even more, his eyes snapping up to Kyle. "It's so heavy!"

"It is, isn't it? There was a store in Denver run by two pretty amazing women who have the same love for rocks and gemstones that you do. They travel the world and collect them. When they told me about this one, I thought it would be perfect for your collection."

Sebastian jumped up and down, his eyes on his new toy like it was the best present he'd ever been given. "Thank you, thank you!"

He wrapped Kyle in a hug so fierce it nearly knocked him over, and Kyle let out a laugh, hugging him back before standing.

My heart was in my throat, my eyes welling.

"Alright, time to get ready for bed," I said through the emotion, smiling to keep the tears at bay. "Why don't you go brush your teeth and get into your jammies and Mommy will come tuck you in?"

"Can I sleep with my rock?!"

I bit back a laugh. "You can put it on your nightstand, okay?"

"Okay! Bye, Kyle!"

Sebastian ran inside, and I held up a finger to let my mom know I'd be there in just a second. With one last longing look at Kyle, I leaned in for a brief kiss on his cheek.

"Two days," I promised.

"Longest days of my life, no doubt."

I chuckled, waving goodbye to Braden. I could see how badly Kyle wanted to take my suitcase, how much he wanted to walk me inside. But my mom was still here, and I'd asked him on the flight to give me some time to explain things to her. Sure, she knew now who I had been with, but there was so much to catch her up on, so much she didn't know yet.

Kyle and Braden waited until I was inside the house before they drove off, and I dropped my suitcase at the door, hugging my mom quickly before telling her I was just going to put Sebastian down and I'd be back.

I could see the questions mounting in her eyes.

Sebastian took a half hour to calm down, excitedly telling me about his weekend with Nana, and also studying his new meteorite. He then transitioned into how excited he was for swim lessons that week.

After reading to him a little bit, he finally started to simmer, and he laid his head in my lap as I read one of his favorites — *Grumpy Monkey*.

"Mommy," he said when we were almost done.

"Hmm?"

"Did you have a good weekend?"

I smiled, running a hand through his hair. "I did."

"Good," he said decidedly, curling up into me more. "You seem happier. I like when you're happy, Momma."

I squeezed my eyes shut but couldn't fight against the tears I'd been warding off all night. One slid down my cheek, and I thumbed it away, shutting the book and leaning down to kiss my son's forehead.

"Goodnight, my handsome little man."

"Goodnight, Mommy."

After turning on his night light, I slipped out of the room, shutting it quietly behind me and taking a moment with my back pressed against the wall in the hallway to collect myself.

It was no use, though, because as soon as I walked into the kitchen and found my mom pouring us two cups of tea, I lost it.

"Oh, sweetie," she said, and she wrapped me up in a hug, holding me while I sobbed in her arms like I was nine again. All the emotions from the weekend won out, and in the safety of my mother's embrace, I let myself feel them all.

Eventually, when I'd calmed, Mom sat us down at the island and nudged a steaming cup of peppermint tea toward me. I took the first sip, took a breath, and then filled her in.

I was so angry I was shaking by the time I finished telling her what Kyle had told me about his parents. And though she was doing her best to keep me calm, I could see the rage simmering in her eyes, too.

"Selfish," she spat, shaking her head. "That man was always so selfish. He was probably worried about their reputation, about what everyone would say."

"Didn't he kind of already ruin that on his own that night though?"

Mom flattened her lips and gave me a sorrowed look. "You'd be surprised how many people were willing to look the other way when it came to his behavior. When you're a partner at a prominent law firm and have your hands in the church, the school, and other charities... well..."

I closed my eyes, gripping my teacup firmly. "He didn't know, Mom," I choked out. "Kyle never knew. And now..."

"I know, honey. I know." She pulled me in for another hug, and when she released me, her eyes were soft and assessing. "What happens now? I mean... I saw the way he looked at you out there, the way he held you." She shook her head on a soft smile. "He seems just as gone for you as he was at sixteen."

I smirked, but my chest was so tight the smile didn't reach my eyes. "I don't know," I said honestly. "I had a plan, you know? Save up commissions, move Sebastian and me across the country and away from Marshall, start over new... but now?"

"Plans change, my dear," Mom said, but she looked as worried as I felt. "Just... be sure before you make any big decisions, okay? I don't doubt that Kyle is a good man, but he's a professional athlete. Being in a relationship with him also means being in a relationship with the media, with the *world*."

My next swallow was impossible to force.

"Sebastian," I whispered.

My heart cracked.

Kyle and I had stayed up so late last night, we'd slept until well past even the late checkout Kyle had requested. There was no time to talk, no time to discuss what came next. We'd packed our things hastily and jumped on the flight home.

But Mom was right.

In our little oasis in Colorado, it seemed like nothing mattered but Kyle and me.

Back in reality, I was staunchly reminded of every little factor that would weigh into our decisions.

"Nothing has to be figured out right now," Mom said with finality. "You go take a shower and get some sleep. There will be plenty of time for discussions when you see him later this week."

I nodded, dragging myself off the barstool as the exhaustion from every crashing emotion settled in.

"Thank you for this weekend, Mom," I said, grabbing her hand and squeezing it tight. "For everything you do for us."

"Oh, honey. I wish we could do more. Your father and I have lost sleep so many nights wishing you'd let us give you the money to help you move the way you want to." She sniffed, but then smiled a bit. "Then again, I guess everything happens for a reason, doesn't it?"

I heard what she didn't say.

If I was already gone, I never would have run into Kyle.

I never would have learned the truth.

And as much as I didn't know where we went from here, as much as it hurt to discover we'd lived in a painful lie for years... I wouldn't give up this weekend for anything. I wouldn't trade what it felt like to hold him and kiss him and have him inside me again for a safe nest on the other side of the country.

The universe had led us to this point, to this collision, to this truth.

I only hoped it had a plan for what would happen now.

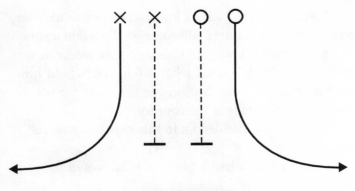

CHAPTER 31
Madelyn

A few days later, I stretched my legs out from the Adirondack chair in our backyard, watching as Kyle chased Sebastian with his arms loaded up with water balloons.

Sebastian was laughing so hard he could barely run in a straight line, and he certainly wasn't going fast enough to keep Kyle from catching him. But Kyle pretended like he couldn't catch him, lobbing water balloons close enough to break and splash Sebastian's feet and legs without actually hitting him.

It was the perfect summer day in Seattle, the kind where everyone was outside enjoying the sunshine. Kyle had ribs on the grill — the grill he'd purchased, because I certainly never used one — and he seemed to have just as much energy as my son, judging by the way they'd played all afternoon long.

My heart beat steadily as I watched them play, calmly — which was interesting, considering the conversation I knew was coming. Kyle and I had decided to tell Sebastian about us.

I waited for my stomach to knot, for my chest to seize, for my body to rebel and remind me that this could all go up in flames at any moment.

But everything about Kyle felt safe. Secure.

Comfortable.

As if no time had passed between us.

As if the only future ahead of us was one where we were together.

There was still a lot to figure out, that we both knew. But we were content to take things slowly — especially since, so far, it had felt like a whirlwind between us.

"Catch, Mommy!"

I blinked out of my thoughts just in time to see a bright red water balloon sailing through the air toward me, but my reflexes weren't fast enough to catch it. I put my hands up, but all that did was provide the perfect popping point.

My nails.

Water drenched me, and Sebastian died in a fit of laughter as Kyle struggled to keep his own at bay.

I stood, tonguing my cheek and wiping my wet hair out of my face. "Oh, think that's funny, do you?"

I took off in a sprint, bending to gather a few water balloons out of the large tin bucket before I was chasing them both down and launching balloons as hard as I could.

It was an all-out war then, and twenty minutes later, we were all soaked, our faces red from laughing, our stomachs growling as we sat down at the picnic table outside and Kyle served us dinner.

He sat down next to me once everyone had a plate and something to drink, and his hand slid confidently over my knee under the table, squeezing.

It sent chills parading over me, the delicious kind that made me cross my legs and squeeze my thighs together.

For a while, we just ate and laughed about the water balloon fight — Sebastian particularly stuck on how he had wrangled me into the whole ordeal. But after a while, when the conversation had slowed, Kyle cleared his throat and dabbed at the corner of his mouth with his napkin.

"Sebastian," he said, hand finding mine under the table and wrapping it up tightly. "We'd like to talk to you about something."

"Okay," my son said, swinging his feet and chomping on his corn on the cob.

Kyle lifted our hands to rest on the table, smoothing his thumb over mine. He nodded for me to take the wheel then.

"Do you remember when I introduced you to Kyle, and I told you we were friends?" I asked my son.

He nodded, still mostly focused on his food, bless him.

"Well... Kyle and I are actually more than friends. We're... special friends."

Sebastian's legs stopped swinging, his brows folding together. "Like best friends?"

"Yeah, kind of," I said, and I frowned, trying to figure out how to tell him.

Kyle patted my hand, taking over. "I care very much about your mom," he said. "And she cares about me. We..."

His voice faded then, and I wondered if he was thinking what I was.

We love each other.

But that was absurd to think, let alone say out loud. It was too much, too fast.

And yet, I'd always loved him. Ever since we were kids.

"We just want you to know that Kyle will be around more often," I offered. "And that you may see us showing affection to each other the way special friends do. Like this," I said, holding up our clasped hands.

"And I don't plan on going anywhere," Kyle added. "I... I plan to be here, to be a part of your mom's life. And yours. If that's okay."

Sebastian set his corn on the cob down, and I wondered if the seriousness of the conversation was hitting him. Kids always knew. They could pick up even what we tried to cover as adults.

"Are you my new dad?"

I rolled my lips together, emotion strangling my throat. Fortunately, Kyle was still calm and collected.

"I will never take your dad's place," he said.

Sebastian seemed almost sad about that. He nodded, hanging his head.

"But," Kyle added quickly. "What I'd like to do is be your friend. And I want to hang out more, and get to know more about you, and tell you more about me. I'd like to take you fun places, like the zoo and the pool. I'd like to pick you up from camp sometimes, and I hope to be here on my days off. And when the season starts... maybe you could come to a football game."

Sebastian's eyes lit up at that, and he looked at me. "Could I?"

"We'll see," I said. "But, yes, I imagine so."

"That would be so cool!" Sebastian said excitedly.

"Do you have any questions for us?" I asked.

He thought hard on it for a moment before shaking his head, shrugging, and digging back into his ribs. "Nope."

Kyle smiled. "Okay, well... if you change your mind, we're here for you."

"Okay," Sebastian said.

And just like that, the conversation was done.

Later, I walked Kyle out to his car, the two of us deciding that him staying the night might not be the best move on the *first* day we told Sebastian about us. But the evening had gone off without a hitch, and I could feel both of us breathing easier now that we were walking in slow steps toward the future.

"I hate saying goodbye to you," he murmured against my hair as he held me by his car. His lips pressed against my temple before he pulled back, thumbing my jaw line.

"I'll see you soon."

"Never soon enough."

I smiled, leaning into his palm. "That went well," I offered, nodding toward the house where Sebastian was already asleep.

"It did," Kyle agreed. "He's... *God*, he's such a great kid. I really am excited to get to know him more."

"I think he idolizes you already."

"That's a lot of pressure."

"Welcome to parenthood," I said on a laugh.

My voice caught a bit at that, realizing what I'd said, but Kyle smiled wider and smoothed my skin with his palm. "I like the sound of that."

"Speaking of... have you talked to your parents yet?"

He went cool at the mention of his mom and dad, but he still held me, as if I was the force grounding him through it all.

"Not yet, but I plan to. Soon."

I nodded. "I'm here for you when you do."

"Thank you."

"This is kind of crazy, isn't it?" I asked after a while, shaking my head. "How fast everything has happened between us?"

"Don't," Kyle said instantly. "Don't do that."

"Do what?"

"Overthink everything until you make yourself sick," he said with a smirk, thumb gliding over my bottom lip. "Madelyn, you have had to think so hard about everything. For *years* now. You had to go through what happened to us alone. You healed alone. Then, with Marshall, you were the only one thinking about your family. You had to plan ahead for everything for you and Sebastian. You have always had to be the responsible one."

My eyes watered against my will, and I nodded, hating how true that all was, how much it sent pangs through my chest.

"Don't think about this," he pleaded, his blue eyes searching mine. "Just... let it be. Let us have a chance."

I nodded, kissing his palm. "I'm scared," I whispered.

"So am I," he admitted, and then he framed my face. "But I'm sure, too. I'm sure about you. I'm sure about us. I'm sure about *this*."

His next kiss cemented how he felt, the power in it so electrifying I felt as if I could float off the ground and right up into the clouds covering the moon.

Kyle held me for a long while, the two of us too greedy to let go as we leaned against his car. We touched and kissed, eyes wandering over one another as if the other wasn't quite real, as if it all may be a dream and we never wanted to wake.

Somehow, eventually, Kyle found the strength to say goodnight.

But it was only with the promise that he'd see me tomorrow.

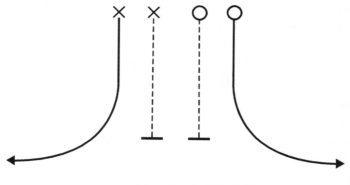

CHAPTER 32

Kyle

My knee bounced like a basketball under the kitchen island of the apartment I was renting, my eyes on the phone clutched between my hands.

The last week had been a whirlwind. Whenever I wasn't training with Braden, I was looking at houses with Madelyn. And any time she'd let me, I was there at her house with her and Sebastian, getting to know them both better, giving her a helping hand.

I didn't know how she did it all on her own.

I hated that she'd had to for so long.

The week had been so busy, we hadn't really talked much about what we were or what came next. Still, it seemed we were both on the same page, and for me, at least right now, that was enough.

We didn't want to let each other go.

We spent every free moment we had together.

She was letting me in, and I was doing the same.

Part of me wished she was here with me now to face

my demons. The other part of me was glad she wouldn't see me like this.

I was going to try real fucking hard not to blow a gasket, but I couldn't make any promises.

I debated booking a private flight out to Massachusetts to face my parents in person, but my common sense wouldn't let me. Because the truth was that I didn't trust myself not to hit my father square in the jaw as soon as I saw him.

And unlike him, I didn't want to resort to violence — no matter how much he might have deserved it.

"Just fucking do it, Kyle," I said to the empty apartment, and then I hit the green phone button next to my mother's name.

As soon as the phone started ringing, so did my ears. My heart leapt into my throat and stayed there even after my mom's voice sang over the line.

"Well, if it isn't our superstar son," she said, and though I couldn't see her, I could hear her smile, could see it in my mind.

She used to be a place for comfort for me in a house of hell.

Now, I felt like she was an accomplice to the worst crime ever committed.

"How's it going out there in the Pacific Northwest?" she asked.

"It's going." I swallowed, wondering if I should indulge her with small talk before I laid into why I actually called. But I didn't have the stomach to even try. "Is Dad there?"

"Oh," she said, surprised — because I *never* asked to speak to my father. "He is. He's in his study."

"I need to talk to him."

steiner

"Is everything okay?"

"No."

Mom paused for a long while. "Are you in some sort of trouble?"

"I know."

"You... *know*?" She sounded confused, and it made me grit my teeth together.

"About Madelyn," I said.

The next pause was different, loaded, heavy with an emotion I couldn't quite place. I heard Mom walking through the house, a gentle knock on the door I could see so clearly in my mind — the one that was shut firmly the last two years of my high school career — and then the muffled sound of her talking to my father with her hand over the phone.

"I love you," she whispered, and I didn't miss that her voice wobbled when she said it.

I knew I didn't need to yell at Mom. She had probably beaten herself up about it since it happened.

But that didn't buy her a free pass in my book, either.

"Hello?"

My father's voice sent a chill racing down my spine, and for a moment, I didn't feel like the six-foot-seven, two-hundred-and-thirty-pound football player that I was.

I felt like a child about to be socked around for fun.

"Let me ask you something," I said, trying as hard as I could to keep my voice even. "Did you hate me as soon as you found out Mom was pregnant, or did it grow once I was born?"

Only a second passed before he scoffed, and I could imagine him taking his glasses off, pinching the bridge

285

of his nose in irritation the way he used to do when I'd want to ask him something while he was working.

"Are you trying to have some sort of therapy session? Because I'm busy and don't have time for—"

"Me? Yes, I'm well aware. But you're going to need to make time for this."

"I don't *need* to do—"

"Shut up!"

I heaved the words, my chest rising and falling with a painful echo through my ribs.

"I have stayed quiet and listened to you all my life," I said. "I've listened to you tell me I'm worthless, heard you spit your vitriol more than a hundred times. I have felt your fist against my face and never once talked back to you. Because you're my father, and I thought that alone deserved my respect. But it doesn't. *You* don't. You never did."

"Is that all?"

He sounded bored, and damn, if it didn't piss me the fuck off.

I sucked in a breath, ready to scream at him, but then realized how pointless it would be. Instead, I forced a long exhale, closing my eyes until I saw Madelyn there behind my lids — calm, poised, strong.

"I thought you were just trying to raise me as a tough man," I finally said, choosing my words carefully. "Not that I loved getting hit, but I thought I understood you." I shook my head. "Now, I feel like I don't know you at all. I feel like... like you're the type of evil Pastor Root used to warn us about."

"So many feelings," he murmured.

I chuffed a laugh.

He was never going to care.

This confrontation... it was for no one else but me.

"I don't expect an apology out of you," I started.

"Good, because I don't have one to give."

"But," I continued. "I need to know. I need to hear you explain."

"Explain what?"

"How you could lie straight to my face about my own *child,* and then move me away from the girl carrying that child, leaving her alone and leaving me in the dark about it all."

For once, I had shocked my father silent.

I heard the distant sound of my mom crying in the background, which told me she could hear everything. Maybe I was on speaker phone. Or maybe she knew just by the look on Dad's face.

"*How,*" I repeated, and my voice cracked before I cleared my throat and forced a breath. "Only a monster could do such a thing."

"Wrong," he said, and to his credit, he sounded so sure of himself, like he really didn't have anything to be sorry about. "Only a *father* who cared about his son's future could have done such a thing."

"My future," I snorted.

"Yes, your future. Are you that daft that you don't understand what would have happened if I *would* have told you?"

"I would have stayed with Madelyn," I said immediately. "I would have been there with her every step of the way to raise my *child.*"

"Exactly!" He roared, and even miles away, the sound made me flinch. "You would have thrown it all away! School, football... do you think you would have had a chance at going to college if you had a toddler to care for? Do you think you would have even been able to play ball through the rest of high school?"

My nostrils flared.

He was right — but I didn't want to say it.

"So what," I volleyed. "So I wouldn't have had football. I would have been okay. I would have figured it out."

"And you would have struggled. *Both* of you."

"So, you were content to just let her struggle on her own?"

"Oh, don't be dramatic. I know she lost the baby, Kyle."

That shocked me as much as a punch to the nose would have.

I blinked, opening my mouth and then shutting it again before I let out a harsh laugh.

"Wow. So, you kept tabs on her?"

"Of course, I did. I'm your father. And whether you think so or not, I had your best interests at heart."

"You were a selfish, horrible father then, and you are still."

Dad barked out his own laugh. "Ungrateful brat. You always have been."

"And Mom?" I said, knowing now that she could hear me. "You... you played along. You loved Madelyn. How could you do that to her, to us?"

Mom wailed harder, and I heard Dad shuffle to stand.

"Don't you dare talk to your mother like that."

"Or what? You going to hit me? Because I hate to break it to you, Dad, but I'm big enough to fight back now."

The garbling noise he made told me he was getting angry, that his face was turning red.

"You want to think you know what's best for you? For you at *sixteen*? Well, when you're a father, you can talk to me again."

"I was a father!" I cried, shaking, my neck heated. "I *was* a father, and you stole that from me."

The silence that dragged on between us was heavy and thick, and for a moment, I thought he might actually *feel* something.

I thought he might actually apologize.

Instead, he sniffed, and leveled his voice when he finally replied.

"Well, I think it's safe to say you shouldn't come home for Christmas."

"I think it's safe to say I never had a home to come back to, anyway."

Mom cried harder in the background, and as much as my heart broke for her, I couldn't forgive her right away, either. I couldn't give her a free pass for playing into this, for not having the backbone to stand up to my father and stand up for what was right.

"Are you done now? Or do you want to keep going until your poor mother is on the floor with grief?"

"Don't put this on me. This is all you, Dad. If Mom is crying, it's because of the terrible lie you forced her to live with." I shook my head. "It's because of the choice *she* made to keep that secret. And here I thought you might actually apologize, that we could maybe work through this as a family." I tongued the inside of my cheek. "But now I know I never had a family to begin with."

"Someday, you'll understand," he said — and the bastard said it with such conviction it made me laugh.

"No, Dad. I'll never understand how you could lie to your son's face about his child. I'll never understand how you could leave a teenage girl on her own. I'll never understand how you could celebrate the loss of your own *grandchild*."

"Then I guess we have nothing left to say."

"I guess so," I mirrored, and then I hung up the phone.

Less than an hour later, I was at Madelyn's door.

I knocked hard four times, a gray drizzle soaking my long sleeve shirt even in July.

When Madelyn opened the door, her brows slid together, and she immediately dragged me inside and into her arms.

I crushed her to me, squeezing my eyes tight as I wrapped her up like she'd disappear if I didn't hold on tight enough. She clung to me just as desperately, and then her lips found mine, and I sighed into her kiss, losing myself, losing the day.

Madelyn dragged her lips over every inch of my neck, my collarbone, along the line of my jaw before she was capturing my mouth again. It was as if she saw the pain before I even said a word, like she was intent on melting it all away with her touch before I could even fully express what I was feeling.

"Sebastian?" I asked.

"Asleep," she answered against my lips.

I lifted her, holding her to me as her legs wrapped around my waist. Then, we were traveling back down the hallway to her bedroom, into her en suite bathroom, and I ran the shower hot without letting her out of my arms.

I didn't drop her until it was time to undress, and I peeled each article of clothing off her while she tugged at mine.

"Need you," I rasped against her mouth each time I claimed it. "Need you so fucking much."

"I'm here," she promised, and when we were bare, she pulled me into the shower, pinning me against the cool tile wall and kissing me hard.

I kissed her unhurriedly, exploring her with my hands and mouth as the water ran in hot rivulets over our bodies.

I never would have left you if I'd known.

I would have stayed.

I love you.

I hoped she could hear the words I couldn't say, and by the way she climbed back into my arms and wrapped herself around me, I knew she could.

With her arms around my neck and mine around her waist, I lifted her enough to place myself where we both needed the connection.

And I filled her.

I slid inside all at once, stretching her, catching her gasp of an exhale with my mouth and holding her to me as I rooted myself deep.

Outside that shower, there were warning signs and hurdles to jump, conversations to have, a cold reality to face.

But under the water, it was just us.

FALSE START

It was just carnal need and unbridled pleasure. It was hands and lips and sighs and moans. It was her surrendering to me, and me kissing unspoken promises along every slick inch of her skin.

I will protect you.

I will love you.

I will never leave you again.

You are mine.

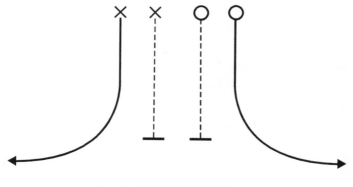

CHAPTER 33

Kyle

"**A**re you nervous?"

The question came out on a grunt as Braden pressed up from his squat, the barbell on his back loaded with weight. I stood a few feet behind him, close enough that I could help him if he needed a spot, but far enough away to give him space.

"About?"

"Camp," he breathed as he lowered, and his face turned red with strain as he pushed the weight back up again.

"Two more," I said, knowing he was close to failure, but he could push a little more.

Braden groaned, but determination slid over him as he gritted his teeth and sank down for another squat. He shook all the way back up to standing, hissing through his teeth when his legs locked.

"Last one," I said.

He looked ready to throw in the towel, but he didn't. He squatted low, and on the way up, his body started to stall. I stepped in just enough to give him the slightest bit of assist, and then with sweat dripping down his neck, he racked the barbell, hanging his hands on his hips.

"No," I said as he rested, and I changed the weight up on the barbell, adding another twenty pounds to each side for me.

"No?"

I cocked a brow at him. "When have you ever known *me* to be nervous."

He rolled his eyes at that, nodding for me to take his place in the torture chamber and get my squats in.

Braden and I had trained together relentlessly over the summer. Now, we were just a little over a week away from training camp starting.

I didn't lie. I really *wasn't* nervous.

But I was unprepared.

We were rookies. We had zero idea what to expect — no matter how we tried to watch tape, learn the playbook, and train until our bodies were weak. The truth of the matter was that we were young, and compared to the beasts who had been playing in the NFL for years, we were weak.

"Are you?" I asked when I got through my set. "Nervous, I mean."

"Fuck yeah, I am," he said. "I want a spot on this team so fucking bad, Kyle. I..." He shook his head, swiping his water bottle from the ground. "I can't fail at camp. I just can't."

I knew without asking that he was thinking about his sister, his parents, about the weight of the world he'd always worn on his shoulders so they wouldn't have to. He was quiet about it most of the time, but every now and then, he'd talk about his sister's illness. I didn't know everything, but I knew he'd been the responsible one in his family for years now. I knew he was the kid his parents didn't have to worry about, that he took it on himself to care for them and for his sister, too.

I knew he had his reasons for not blowing through his signing bonus — no matter how much I loved to give him shit about it.

"You won't," I assured him, clapping his shoulder. "Especially because I'll be there to push your ass."

"Sure you won't be distracted by a certain redhead-ed MILF we know?" Braden smirked.

I punched him hard enough in the arm to make him yelp. "Watch it."

He laughed, holding up his hands. "I'm thinking things aren't so fake anymore with that reaction."

"It's never been fake," I admitted, sighing as we wiped down the squatting equipment and moved over to the bench press.

"Seems like things have gotten pretty serious since the wedding," he assessed, taking his spot under the barbell. I was quiet as he pulsed out his first set, and when he sat back up, he cocked a brow at me, waiting for my response.

I sighed, sinking down onto a bench across from him. "Is it crazy if I admit that's true?"

I knew my answer shocked Braden. His eyebrows slid up into his hairline, his jaw hinging open a bit.

"No, not crazy," he finally said. "Fast, maybe, but..."

I groaned, sliding my hands back through my hair. "I know. It *has* been fast. But... only if you look at this summer. The truth is that I've been gone for that girl for fucking *years*, Braden. And the way I feel about her…"

The corner of Braden's mouth quirked up. "Who are you and what have you done with the Kyle Robbins shithead I know?"

I scowled, winding up my sweat towel and snapping him with it before we traded places.

I pumped out ten quick reps before sitting up again.

"Why aren't we ever having these conversations about *you*," I asked, jabbing him in the chest with my finger.

Braden shrugged, though I didn't miss how the question had sobered him. "You know how it is for me. Football and family — that's where my focus is."

"You know you can be a great athlete, take care of your family, and still have a little time for fun, right?"

He frowned. "It doesn't feel fair."

"What doesn't?"

"For me to be able to have fun, to live a life so full when my sister…"

He swallowed, not finishing the sentence.

"She would want that for you," I said. "She'd want you to live."

Braden considered it for a moment before he was shooing me out of the way, lining himself up under the bar. He was quiet for his set, and then he sat up, wiping his face with his towel.

"I have my role to play," he answered simply.

And with that, our conversation was over, all focus shifting to weights.

Madelyn

"It looks like a banana!"

I covered my smile as Sebastian stood on a step-stool next to Kyle, pointing at his pancake creation.

"That's his mouth!" Kyle argued. "See? These two little pancakes are the eyes, and this is the smile."

"It looks like a banana!"

Sebastian bit back his giggle, eyes cast up at Kyle, and Kyle stood there with his spatula hovering in the air and his eyes narrowing on my son.

"I see," Kyle said. "You think you're soooo funny, don't you?"

Then, he proceeded to tickle Sebastian mercilessly, abandoning the griddle altogether when he picked Sebastian up and carried him over to the couch. Kyle lifted him high before dropping him into the cushions, and my son let out his signature gut-busting laugh when he hit them and bounced a full foot into the air.

It was my favorite sound in the world.

The summer was rushing to an end. Kyle had his first day of training camp on Monday, and though we'd seen each other as much as we could, it still felt like time was whizzing by.

We had yet to find him a house.

We also had yet to talk about what happens next.

It was like we slipped into a normal routine as if we didn't even *have* anything to talk about, like it was all figured out for us. Kyle trained with Braden and some of his teammates when I was at work. We looked at every house that we could find with all his requirements — though I felt like he wasn't seriously looking anymore. He'd pulled back from the hunt, always having some excuse for why a house didn't work.

I spent every hour I could with Sebastian, soaking up the summer while we had it. But now, we had just a month until we'd start the mad dash of getting him ready to go back to school. And between sharing him with Marshall and letting him do camp like he'd begged me to, I knew the time would fly.

But this morning, on a warm Saturday in late July, it was just the three of us and smiley-face pancakes.

I sipped my tea as Kyle walked toward me, Sebastian pretending he was dead from the tickle attack on the couch. Kyle pressed a kiss to my hair that made my heart expand, his hand lingering on the small of my back as he passed by me and back into the kitchen.

In the past couple of weeks, this man had made so much food for us, I was surprised I even remembered how to cook now that he'd all but shoved me out of my own kitchen.

You take care of everyone else. Let me take care of you.

Those were the words he'd said to me when I tried to argue that it was *my* turn to cook dinner last week, and they'd been circling around my head like love-drunk birds ever since.

While pancakes were by far the simplest dish he made for us, they were always Sebastian's favorite. I much preferred when Kyle whipped up bright, colorful dishes with more flavor in one bite than seemed possible — like his prawn and red cabbage summer rolls with cashew butter dipping sauce, or the melt in your mouth salmon he quickly found was my favorite.

Still, I smiled when he slid a blueberry pancake in front of me that looked like Mickey Mouse, complete with the ears, his eyes and mouth made out of fresh blueberries. The little thing had a hat made of whipped cream, and I smothered it with the compote Kyle made that was so delicious I wanted to take a bath in it.

Sebastian liked his pancakes a little more tradition-al — buttermilk style with syrup. Kyle always obliged him, but not without making crazy shapes with the bat-ter. While smiley faces were always on the menu, today, he'd also added a dinosaur and a handful of little star-shaped pancakes, too.

We sat at my small dining table as we ate, Sebastian prattling on about how excited he was for camp while Kyle ran lazy circles over my knee under the tablecloth. When we finished, Sebastian took our plates to the sink before running back to get ready for the day, and Kyle swept me into his arms before I had the chance to start washing.

"I think it's about time you let me take you on a proper date."

My cheeks warmed. "Is that so?"

"Mm-hmm. I was thinking tonight."

"Tonight?" I balked, but didn't have any reason to argue other than I was surprised and couldn't think of a thing I had to wear on a date. Sebastian would be with Marshall tonight and tomorrow before coming back home on Monday after camp. "What do you have in mind?"

"Do you want to pick, or do you want me to surprise you?"

"Surprise," I said instantly.

Kyle smiled like he already knew that would be my answer. "Tired of making decisions all day every day?"

"You have no idea."

He chuckled, tilting my chin before his lips found mine. "I can imagine," he murmured, and then my whole body was tingling, just like it always did when that man kissed me.

Suddenly, the front door banged open, the sound of the springs hitting their max rattling through the house.

And Marshall stormed in.

I jumped out of my skin at the commotion, heart galloping, but I didn't even have time to process what was happening before Kyle had me behind him, his chest puffed and his gaze murderous on my ex-husband. Marshall stopped at the sight, sneering at us both like he'd caught us red-handed in an affair.

"Oh, I'm sorry. Did I interrupt breakfast?"

"As a matter of fact, you did," Kyle said. "I think you should turn around and walk out that door and try again — with a knock this time."

Marshall's jaw popped, and he took a big step toward us, his thick finger pointing at Kyle. "Don't you tell me what to do, you fucking punk. That's *my* wife and child."

"*Ex*-wife," Kyle pointed out.

I ran a shaky hand gently over Kyle's arm, stepping around him to face Marshall with my chin held high. Adrenaline was rushing through me, the memories of similar scenes with my ex's wrath playing out in my mind like a highlight reel. But I held my chin tall, my back straight, shoulders back, eyes assuring Kyle as much as just having him there assured me.

I didn't have to get close to Marshall to smell the alcohol on his breath.

Red beer. I remembered it well. It was his favorite way to start a morning.

"Marshall, you know you're not allowed to show up here unannounced. And you sure as hell are not allowed to storm in like you own the place."

"It was my money that bought it," he shot back, which made me grit my teeth.

All of it was always *his money* when we got divorced, as if I did nothing in the marriage but take up oxygen and give him something to hit.

"And it's my day with Sebastian," he continued.

"Which means you can pick him up from camp, just like we discussed," I said, keeping my voice calm and ignoring his attempts to goad me. "But only if you sober up. And I'd appreciate it if you'd keep your voice down."

"I think I'll keep it raised. Because in what universe did I agree to letting you have another man around my son?"

I tried to settle myself with a long breath. "Marshall, we are divorced. You do not get to dictate who I spend my time with."

"But I get to dictate who my *son* is around. You're not going to be some fucking whore with a train of men coming in and out of his life. I'll—"

Kyle rushed him so fast he was a blur, and then Marshall was being shoved outside onto the front porch.

"Talk to her like that one more time, and you won't have teeth to form the words," I heard Kyle threaten as the glass door slammed shut behind them.

But then, I heard a door creak, and I whipped around to find Sebastian peeking out of his door at the end of the hallway.

"Hey, sweetie," I said, hoping my smile was convincing that everything was okay. I glanced back out at where Marshall and Kyle were obviously in a heated argument on the lawn, but as much as I wanted to know what was being said, I wanted to make sure my son was okay more.

I made my way down the hall to him, and as soon as I made it to his door, Sebastian hugged my legs tight, burying his face in my stomach like he did when he was sick.

Or scared.

I sighed, running a hand through his hair. "Everything is okay," I promised him.

"I don't like when Daddy yells at you."

My eyes shut, and I let out a long breath before replying, "I don't like it either, baby."

"Kyle never yells at us."

Another squeeze of my heart. "No, he doesn't."

"He loves you."

At that, I smirked, dropping down to his level and brushing his hair from his face. "I don't know about that, but I know he cares about both of us."

Sebastian nodded, looking down at his sneakers.

"You okay?" I asked him.

He nodded again, but then shook his head. "Sometimes I have a bad thought."

I frowned. "Well, you can tell Mommy. There's no judgment here. Remember?"

Sebastian swayed a bit side to side, his eyes on his shoes still, and I thought I heard the front door open and close somewhere behind us.

"Sometimes, I wish Kyle was my dad, instead."

I covered my mouth, and when Sebastian looked at me, he seemed worried that I was upset. So, quickly, I smiled and grabbed his arms. "It's okay to wish that," I assured him. "But your dad loves you. And you have fun with him, don't you? You always love going to his house, and when he takes you to get ice cream, or when he takes you to the cool baseball games downtown."

"Yeah," Sebastian said, but he grew quiet after that.

"You about ready?" I asked.

He nodded. "I just need to feed Titan."

"Okay. You go feed Titan and then we'll get you to camp, okay?"

"Okay."

"Hey," I said when he went to pull away. "I love you."

"I love you, too," he echoed. "Mommy?"

"Yeah?"

"I don't want to go to Dad's tonight."

Emotion strangled my next breath. Technically, he didn't have a choice. Marshall and I had shared custody, and tonight was his night.

But he was already drinking, and if I knew my ex-husband well enough, he would continue drinking until he was passed out. I knew I could count on him not wanting to take on any responsibilities come this afternoon. I knew, if I waited and called him after camp, saying Sebastian wasn't feeling well and wanted to come back here — Marshall wouldn't argue.

He'd take the easy way out.

"Okay, baby." I whispered. "You don't have to go to Dad's. I'll get you after camp."

When Sebastian dipped back inside his room, I made my way into the living room and found Kyle standing at the front door looking out at the front lawn. After confirming Marshall wasn't still out there, I slid up behind him, wrapping my arms around his middle.

"Everything okay?"

Kyle's jaw worked under the skin, and he covered my hands with his, angling his face toward mine.

"He threatened to take you to court again," he said, his voice low so Sebastian wouldn't hear. "He... he said he'll go for full custody."

All the blood drained from my face, my body running cold.

I stood there frozen as Kyle turned and pulled me into his arms, searching my gaze.

"He... he can't," I croaked, but even as I tried to convince myself, I knew damned well he could.

He'd threatened it before, but I'd always thought he'd be too lazy to actually do it.

But with Kyle in the picture, with him feeling threatened...

"Oh, God."

I covered my mouth with both hands, eyes pricking with wet heat. Before a tear could fall, Kyle had his hands framing my face, and he lowered his gaze to be level with mine.

"No, he can't," he said. "He won't."

"But he *can*," I said, arguing with myself. "He's a well-respected vet. He has the money, the means to care for Sebastian. He knows how to spin a room. He can make anyone believe that he's the good guy. He—"

"He will be fighting a losing battle if he goes through with this, and so help me God, I will hang him out to dry in front of any judge he dares to force you in front of."

I shook my head. "Kyle, you wouldn't be there. You—"

"Yes, I will be." He swallowed, his eyes flicking between mine. "As long as you say yes."

"Say... yes?"

He wet his lips, and then with a steady gaze and intent so pure I could feel it burning through his hands and into my very being, he dropped to one knee.

"Marry me."

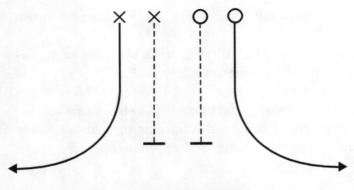

CHAPTER 34
Kyle

"**Y**ou... *what*?!"

Giana was aghast — and judging by the faces of the rest of my friends on our emergency Zoom call, she wasn't the only one.

"I'm pretty sure he just said he asked her to marry him," Holden clarified.

"Without a ring," Riley added.

"Without a *plan*, clearly!" Giana interjected. "Kyle — do you not understand what this means, not just for you, but for her? You are a rookie in the NFL. Camp starts in a few days. We already have you lined up for multiple television and podcast interviews."

"We don't need to put her in the spotlight," I said instantly. "At least... not yet."

"Not *yet* being the key words," Giana said. "Because there is absolutely no way she can stay hidden from the media — not unless you plan to lock her in a castle somewhere and never let her see the light of day."

"How does she feel about it all?" Julep asked gently, her hand wrapped around Holden's arm in the video frame. "Is she okay with this part of you?"

I swallowed. "We haven't really discussed it."

"I can't believe you proposed in the most un-romantic way," Giana said. "Without a ring!"

Clay shrugged next to her. "I think it's kind of romantic," he argued. "Kyle is her knight in shining armor. Marshall is the dragon with bad breath."

"Slay that motherfucker!" Leo chimed in, standing up and doing a weird joust with his arm.

Mary tugged him back down into his seat with her lips in a flat line.

"This is serious, guys," I said, heaving a long breath. "This man is a well-known vet in the area. A doctor. And he's good at manipulating the system to get what he wants." I swallowed. "He's put his hands on her plenty of times without any recourse. But that shit ends now. I will do anything it takes to protect her." I met their gazes. "Anything."

There was a long pause, and then Leo folded his hands together, his brows furrowed. "Kyle, I respect that you want to keep her safe. But... is that the only reason you want to marry her?"

"No."

I said it instantly, as if the fact that he'd even asked it was an insult.

"I just mean, you've only known her for... what? A couple months?"

"I've known her my whole life," I argued. "And yes, while we only recently reconnected, I... I can't explain it."

"Try," Zeke said.

And the way he looked at me, the history he and Riley had... I knew he understood before I even said a word.

"Since the day I met her when I was a fifteen-year-old kid, she's been a part of me. She was just my annoying babysitter at first, but then she was my friend. And back then..." I swallowed. "A friend — a *true* friend — was impossible to come by. She showed me what it was to have someone care about me. She kept *me* safe in a time when no one else even realized I was in danger. She made me stronger. She brought out the side of me that could move mountains. And then... I fell in love with her.

"I fell hard, and fast — the way only a teenager can. And I know she fell for me, too. We fell in the way two people do when there's nothing to lose, when there are no stakes, when it's all just fun and warmth and *of course we love each other*. You know?"

They nodded, their gazes solemn.

"And then, our worlds came toppling down." I didn't need to elaborate — I'd already filled them in on our past. "But even when she hurt me, even when I thought she'd betrayed me, there was still this part of my heart reserved for her. Hell, maybe it was my entire heart. I never could open up to another woman. I never could let anyone in the way I did with her."

"Relatable," Leo murmured, and Mary squeezed his arm with a soft smile.

"When I saw her again earlier this summer... I hated her. At least, I *wanted* to — but the truth was that as soon as it happened, I was already planning how I could see her again, how I could talk to her, how I could get her to tell me what happened all those years ago."

I tongued my cheek. "I am and always have been hers. And being with her again, fighting through what we've had to, surviving what we did... there's no one in this world I could ever want more than her. There's no one who could ever make sense. She's it for me. Period. End of story. She is... everything."

Giana sniffled, dabbing at the corner of her eyes. "So much better than *I love her.*"

That made everyone laugh, lightening the mood a bit, and then Holden leaned toward the camera. "Okay, we appreciate you filling us in. And I think it's safe to say we all understand how love can make us do some drastic things. But... what is it you need from us?"

"I need your help."

"With what?" Riley asked.

I let out a long, heavy sigh. "Pulling off the proposal of a lifetime."

Madelyn

Another yawn stretched my mouth wide as Kyle drove us into the city later that night, one hand on the steering wheel and the other gripping the inside of my knee.

"I see you're so excited for our date," he mused with an arched brow.

I shook off the yawn. "Sorry. I've been so tired the past couple of days."

"Well, that doesn't surprise me, considering you're Super Mom."

"Hardly," I said, but my stomach was tied up in knots.

Just like I'd suspected, Marshall hadn't fought me when I told him Sebastian wanted to be home tonight. All that drunken energy had left him.

But he'd wake up sober, and I knew he wouldn't forget what he'd threatened. I knew he'd follow through.

I knew I was about to have to fight, whether I felt ready to or not.

My head was still spinning from the morning — from Marshall showing up, Kyle protecting me and my son, Marshall's threat, Kyle's proposal...

Literally — a proposal.

That part still didn't feel real. No matter how many times I'd replayed it — his intent gaze, his hand holding mine, his knee hitting the ground, the words slipping from his lips...

It felt like a dream.

He'd hopped up almost immediately when I'd stared at him in shock, urging me not to answer — not yet. He kissed me hard and promised we'd talk more about it all tonight. Then, he'd followed me to drop Sebastian off at camp, making sure I got to my first house showing okay before we split for the day.

There were no words to explain how safe I felt with him, how *whole*.

"Well, I'll do my best not to keep you out too late," Kyle said.

"No, no," I assured him, covering his hand on my leg. "We have a babysitter for the night. I'm happy to be here. I can sleep tomorrow."

Even as I said it, it was through another yawn, which made Kyle chuckle. He folded my hand in his and lifted my knuckles to his lips, kissing them gently.

It was nice being on a date. I couldn't remember the last time I'd been on one. I loved the way Kyle opened my car door for me, how he draped my arm through his and led us into the restaurant where he'd booked us reservations. It was far nicer than anything I'd been to since living in Seattle, the kind of place that had a tasting menu and wine pairing.

We laughed all through it, talking about all the things we missed with each other's lives. He told me more about his time at North Boston University and I told him about the early years of being Sebastian's mom, of how my entire world had shifted when he was born.

When we were caught up on the past, the conversation slipped to the future, and though he didn't bring up the proposal again, it was easy to see that's where his mind was heading.

"Do you like your job?" he asked over dessert — a delicious key lime and graham cracker creation that made me feel like I was on vacation in Florida.

I shrugged. "It's not bad. I like the flexibility it gives me."

"But you don't love it?"

"It's far from my dream job, if that's what you're asking."

"What is your dream job?"

I smiled, twirling my fork in the whipped cream on my plate. "To write."

When I peeked up at him, his smile was genuine and soft, his eyes searching mine.

When the bill was paid and the valet pulled our car around, Kyle held the door for me again, chuckling a little when I slid in with yet *another* yawn taking over me. I couldn't help it. Maybe it was all the excitement from the morning, or maybe it was the ridiculous client I'd shown houses to all day who'd been nothing less than a pain in my ass — but I was *exhausted*.

"I think it's time we get you home," Kyle said when he slid into the driver seat.

I could think of many reasons why I was happy about his decision, and none of them had to do with me being ready for bed.

But instead of driving the way toward my house, he took the highway the opposite direction.

"Um... I think you're lost," I commented with a grin.

He just smirked. "One quick pit stop."

Twenty-five minutes later, we pulled up to a gorgeous home on Puget Sound — one I'd shown him just a few days prior. I didn't need it to be daylight for me to remember how stunning it was — the expansive windows showcasing the breathtaking view of the private beach and the water, the lush garden landscaping, the veranda that transported indoor living space to outdoor seamlessly, the cozy fireplaces, the beautiful pool...

I'd shown it to him even though it didn't quite meet his requirements, since it didn't have nearly the number of bedrooms he asked for. But he'd taken it all in in quiet assessment like he really was considering it before telling me it wasn't the one.

"What are we doing here?" I asked when he parked.

"You'll see."

With my hand in his, Kyle walked us around the house to the back gate, surprising me when he knew the code to unlock it.

"Are we trespassing?!" I hissed under my breath.

Kyle arched a brow at me. "I seem to remember a time when that wouldn't have scared you."

"We were teenagers! We didn't have careers and *children*."

Somehow, the way he grinned and continued walking made me feel like we were fine, even as my heart raced in my chest in warning. If the owners didn't know we were here, if we really *were* trespassing, this would be grounds for me losing my real estate license.

And that somehow calmed my heart.

Because I knew Kyle wouldn't risk that.

When we rounded past the beautiful garden to where the pool was, I gasped, stopping in my tracks and covering my mouth with both hands.

Soft yellow twinkle lights were strung from end to end, casting the pool in a gorgeous glow. Two bottles of champagne were on ice at the edge of the pool, and various flowers drew a trail from where we stood around every inch of that pool — ending at the champagne.

Lilies, carnations, and peonies.

All my favorites.

A familiar song played from a speaker somewhere, "Stay With Me" by Sam Smith.

The same song that had played from Kyle's phone all those nights ago, when we were just two stupid kids in love.

As gorgeous as it all was, that wasn't what made my breath catch.

It was that all around the pool, Kyle's friends stood in pairs, dressed to the nines with soft smiles on their faces and each of them holding a candle or a card.

"Kyle... what is happening?" I breathed, looking up at him.

He smiled, kissing my hand before letting it go. "Follow the flowers," he said, and then he walked to stand where the champagne was, folding his hands in front of him.

I wanted to laugh. I wanted to *cry*. I could feel how big this moment was before it even happened.

My feet moved me forward, my brain too sluggish to keep up until I was standing a couple feet in front of Riley and Zeke. Zeke held a candle and wore a comforting grin, and Riley handed me the card in her hands.

On the front, in Kyle's handwriting, it said *I loved you then...*

Tears pricked my eyes as I tore the envelope open, and then I laughed, pulling out an old, origami folded note that we'd passed back and forth in high school. The pencil marks on it were faded, but I could still make out the words, from where we just talked about our weekends to where we shamelessly flirted and made promises of making out when we got alone.

It broke my heart as much as it healed me to see that again, to remember what it felt like to be that version of myself with Kyle.

We were so young, so innocent, so hopeful of what the future held.

With encouraging looks from Riley and Zeke, I continued walking along the flower path around the pool, coming to Clay and Giana next. Giana held the candle, her eyes brimmed with tears, and Clay handed me another envelope.

I loved you from afar...

My shaking hands covered my mouth again when I saw what was inside — a flash fiction narrative I'd had published in *SmokeLong Quarterly* shortly after graduating high school.

He'd read it.

He'd *printed* it and kept it.

When Giana saw my first tear fall, she broke her composure, shoving the candle into Clay's hand and wrapping me in a fierce hug. I chuckled and held her to me, the heaviness of this moment settling into my bones.

The song changed as I made my way toward Julep and Holden, and now, it was "Thinking Out Loud" by Ed Sheeran — another song that played that night all those years ago.

Julep handed me the third envelope.

I loved you when I tried to hate you...

I laughed at that, thumbing the matchbox from *Rains* where we'd eaten that night I decided to take him on as a client. It felt like just yesterday, and yet like it was years ago, as if we'd lived an entire lifetime already just this summer.

The last envelope was in Leo's hands, and he crooked a grin at me before handing it over.

And I love you now. Still. Always.

I couldn't fight back the tears any longer when I opened this one and found a photo of me, Kyle, and Sebastian. It was one Kyle had snapped on his phone when we'd set up the sprinkler in the backyard and made a day of running through it and tossing water balloons at each other. Droplets clouded the camera and smudged our faces, but Sebastian had his arms around my shoulders and the biggest, toothy grin on his face.

We looked like a family.

In so many ways, we already *were*.

Leo nodded at me when I looked up at him, his gaze shifting to where Kyle waited for me.

My legs felt heavy and sluggish as I walked those final steps, but Kyle stood tall and sure. His fiery blue eyes seared into mine, sealing every promise those envelopes had whispered.

When I reached him, he gathered the envelopes from my hand and set them aside so he could hold onto me properly. Then, he lowered to one knee.

"Madelyn, I knelt before you just like this only hours ago, but it was in haste. It was in desperation to protect you, to assure you that you weren't alone, to prove that you had me by your side." He shook his head. "And while all of those things are true, they're nowhere near the top of my list when it comes to why I want to make you my wife."

His wife.

I nearly melted right then and there.

"In this life of mine, I have only loved you. Even when I wanted so desperately to hate you, it was impossible. You have known me, the true core of me, since I was just fifteen years old. We grew up together. We grew apart. And somehow, in a crazy turn of events, or maybe... fate," he said with a wry grin. "The universe brought us together again."

I sniffed, squeezing his hands where they held mine.

"I love you, Mads," he breathed, and when his jaw flexed with those words, when emotion made him swallow — it nearly broke me. "*God*, I love you fiercely. I love you in a way that would kill me if I wasn't allowed to act out this love every day of my life. I love your passion and your heart. I love your fight. I love your determination. I loved you as a friend, as my first love, as my first... *everything*. And I love you even more now, as a mom, as a woman who has worn the weight of the world on her shoulders."

He shook his head, kissing my knuckles.

"But I don't want you to shoulder that weight alone, anymore. I want to bear it with you. I want your mornings, and your afternoons, and every single night. I want to wake up to your morning breath and fall asleep to the sound of your snores."

I laughed, swatting at his hand.

"I brought you here because I saw the way you lit up when we toured this house, and I'd be willing to bet my life that it was because you saw what I saw." He swallowed. "You saw us. You saw our things in this home, saw us playing with Sebastian here, saw us growing old together. I felt it just as much as you did — and it's what I want. *You* are what I want."

He pulled his hands away, reaching into the lapels of his suit jacket to pull out a black velvet box. When he cracked it open, I covered my mouth, sobbing into my hands.

It was the most dainty, beautiful ring — a white gold band with one brilliant cut diamond.

"I meant what I said this morning," Kyle proclaimed, his shoulders back, eyes on mine. "Marry me, Madelyn. Move in with me. Start a new life with me. I know I come with a lot of fanfare. I can't promise you won't want to throttle the paparazzi sometimes, that the media won't want a piece of you and, yes, a piece of Sebastian, too. But I promise I will protect you from them and only allow as much attention as you want. If you want to watch me play, I'll have seats for you and Sebastian both. If you never want to step foot in a stadium, then I'll rush home to you after each and every game.

"And I don't know what happens next with Marshall, but I know whatever it is, we can face it together. And I can promise you that I'll do everything in my power to ensure that Sebastian is never taken from you.

"More than anything, I promise to love you. With everything that I am. With every breath I have left. Forever. Because honestly, even if you say no, that's the only choice for me. *You* are my only choice."

Kyle wet his lips, holding his chin high.

"Marry me, Mads."

I was already nodding. I was already dropping to my knees and wrapping my arms around him so hard I nearly took us both into the pool. I was already claiming his mouth with mine and clutching him to me, so desperate to hold onto this moment forever.

Somewhere in the background, I was aware of his friends cheering, and I knew without him telling me that this was a show of his love, too. He'd never introduced them to another woman, never welcomed another woman into their family. But this was his public declaration not just to me, but to them.

And it was *their* declaration that I was already a part of their group, that they had our backs, that we would never fight any battles alone.

Kyle stood and swept me up with him, forcing me to break our kiss long enough for him to slide the ring on my finger. But as soon as it was on, my arms were around his neck again, and I climbed into his arms as the cheers around us turned into full-blown hoots and howls.

"I love you, too," I breathed against his lips. "I have never stopped."

"It's me and you now," he said between kisses. "Me. And you."

"Me and you," I echoed.

And somehow, even with Marshall's threat hanging over our heads, I knew I was safe in Kyle's arms. I knew *we* would figure it out. I just knew.

Fireworks went off in my heart, sparking me to life in a way I hadn't felt in a decade.

All the pain was worth it.

And for the first time I believed myself when I said everything would be okay.

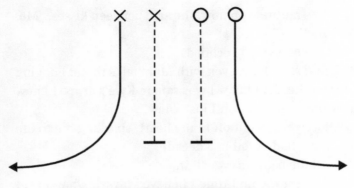

CHAPTER 35

Kyle

"I just don't think he's going to react well to this," Madelyn said as I shut the door to her house behind us, immediately pinning her against it and continuing my assault of kisses along her neck.

"Well, that's too bad for him." I nipped at her bottom lip, and she moaned when I slid my thigh between hers.

"He's more powerful than you give him credit for."

"He's an ass cactus."

That made her laugh, and I breathed the sound in as I pulled her into my arms and carried us toward the kitchen.

I froze when I saw the babysitter on the couch, a book splayed in her lap and an amused smile on her lips.

"Oh shit," Madelyn cursed, slipping out of my arms and fixing her dress and hair as much as she could. "Sorry, Anna."

Anna smiled, marking the spot in her book with a bookmark before she uncurled her legs and stood. "Nothing to apologize for. I was just reading about a kiss like that. I'm a bit jealous."

She reminded me of Giana — except Anna was about twenty years older than us and not quite as spunky as my agent.

"Bas is asleep," she said, tucking her book into a large purse that she slung over one shoulder. "Has been for hours now."

"Thank you," I said as she passed us, and Madelyn gave her a hug before pulling a one-hundred-dollar bill out of her purse to pay. Anna assured her it was too much, but Madelyn wouldn't accept anything less.

Once Anna was gone, Madelyn looked at me with cheeks as red as a fire engine.

"What? Embarrassed you got caught making out with your fiancé?" I teased, sweeping her into my arms once more.

She groaned and shook her head, covering it with her hands. "We probably scarred her."

"Nah, she thought we were cute."

"You think *everyone* thinks we're cute."

"Because we are. You still tired?" I asked as I slid her ass onto the kitchen counter, wedging myself between her legs. My hands slid up the outside of her thighs to the hemline of her dress, shoving it up just a few inches before I stopped.

I wanted nothing more than to take her right now, to hear my *fiancée* whimper before she came undone.

But she had been yawning all night, exhausted from the week she'd had, and if she needed sleep, I'd gladly tuck her into bed and cuddle her.

"Yes," she answered honestly, but her arms wound around my neck, her hands sliding into my hair. "But I don't want you to stop touching me."

I licked my bottom lip, shoving her dress up higher until the fabric snagged where her ass was on the counter. She lifted enough for me to take it higher, over her hips, and I kissed her hard and long and with pure intention as I ran my hands up each of her ribs.

And then that whirring mind of hers took over again.

"I'm just worried he'll take Sebastian from me," she said with a sigh against my lips. "Marshall is—"

"Listen to me," I said, pausing and holding her gaze with my own. "I am about to have this dress stripped over this beautiful head of yours, and once I do, you are forbidden from saying your ex-husband's name."

She let out a huff, but her grin told me she liked what I'd said. Her brown eyes were golden in the low light of her kitchen, her face framed by the strands of copper hair that had fallen from where she'd pinned it all back.

"I will handle him," I promised her, noting the worry still in her eyes. "*We* will handle him. Together. Okay? I promise, I'll try to talk him out of the whole thing. But if he's dead set on taking us to court, then we'll go, and we will eviscerate him."

Madelyn's eyebrows bent together like she still wasn't sure.

"Trust me," I pleaded.

At that, she nodded, leaning in to press a kiss to my lips that felt a whole lot like she was putting all her faith in me.

I wouldn't ever take that lightly.

"But tonight," I continued, sliding her dress up inch by inch as I peppered her with kisses. "You are not allowed to say his name again. The only name I want to hear coming from these pretty lips is your future husband's."

"My future husband," she repeated, airily, like she couldn't believe it.

It felt surreal to me, too.

"Do you remember his name?"

She smiled against my lips as her arms lifted above her head, allowing me to pull the fabric over her chest. "Kyle."

"Damn fucking straight," I said, and my cock jumped at how sweetly she said my name, at the tease and the promise in just those two syllables. "Say it again."

"*Kyle*," she moaned as I slid the dress up over her arms and head, letting it fall somewhere behind me.

And then my mouth was on her.

It was on her lips, her collarbone, the swells of her breasts as I hastily unfastened her bra. It was on her ribs and her hips as I kissed my way down, and along the lace lining of her thong before I peeled it off her and tossed it behind me to join her dress.

I bent at the waist and grabbed her by her hips, tugging her to the edge of the counter to feast. The second I tasted her, she groaned and arched and let her head fall back in ecstasy, and my cock grew even harder at the realization that she was *mine*, forever — that I'd get to taste her and touch her and hold her and *exist* with her for the rest of my fucking life.

I gripped her thighs tighter, spreading her wide for me as I devoured her like it was an audition. I'd learned over the last month what she liked, what she didn't like, and what she *loved*.

I knew that when I ran my tongue flat and hot and slow over her, she moaned and bucked against me begging for more. I knew when I sucked her clit between my teeth and held that pressure, her legs shook. And I knew when I slid one finger inside her to curl into that special spot, when I combined it with my tongue swirling around her — she'd combust.

I almost had her there when she stopped me, her hands flying to my shoulders and tugging me up until she could taste herself on my tongue. Then, she was ripping at my clothes — her hands fussed with my tie as I worked on my belt, and in-between panting kisses, she stripped me out of my suit and hopped down off the counter, dropping to her knees right there in the kitchen to return the favor.

"Mads," I croaked, running a hand through her hair as she looked up at me and gripped my cock in one hand. She knew this was my weakness. She knew just the *sight* of her like this was enough to make me come.

"Yes, *fiancé?*"

I groaned, both at the sound of my new title and the way she ran her tongue from my base to my tip, swirling it around my crown before she planted sweet, wet kisses all along my shaft.

I fisted my hand in her hair, gripping her tighter and helping her move. "Open."

She did as I said, and I noted the way her nipples hardened, the way her knees spread *just* an inch. She loved when I commanded her, when I took control.

She loved bringing me pleasure just as much as I loved doing it to her.

When she opened her mouth, I took over, gripping my cock in my free hand and running my tip over her tongue before I slid just an inch into her mouth. I withdrew, coating myself again before plunging in deeper.

Again, and again, until she gagged and her eyes watered and I said, *"Fuck,"* and she smiled and went in for more. I let her take over then, let her use her hands with that perfect mouth of hers to fuck me until my thighs were shaking and my breaths were shallow and I was fucking *seconds* from busting.

As much as I wanted to watch her swallow my cum the way she did so eagerly, or paint her with my release and watch her drag her fingertips through it with that wicked smile she always gave me after she brought me to this point — tonight I wanted more.

Tonight, she was my fiancée, and I was her future husband, and I wanted to bury myself so deep inside her we'd become one.

I hauled her up and slid my hands into her hair, framing her face and kissing her hard enough to bruise. She pressed up on her tiptoes just the same way I bent to meet her, like we couldn't get close enough if we tried.

"Hands on the counter," I husked, and I spanked her ass for good measure when she whipped around.

Madelyn offered her ass to me like the golden platter of perfection that it was, smiling at me over her shoulder with her lashes dusting her rosy cheeks.

"Goddamn, Mads," I said, biting my lip as I rubbed her round cheeks. I spread them so I could see her pussy dripping for me. "You are so fucking gorgeous."

She preened under the praise, arching more for me so I could position myself right where we both wanted. I hiked one of her legs up until her knee was half-balanced on the counter, that leg supported by my hand, and she shook with the effort of standing on one tiptoe as I slid inside her.

She was so fucking wet, and my cock was still coated from her mouth. The combination made it easy for me to slide all the way in, and we both gasped and cursed and clung to each other at the sensation — me from feeling her tighten around me like a glove, her from having me fill her all the way up.

I swore just from the way we fit together that we were meant for one another, that we were *made* for one another.

"*Fuck*, Kyle," she hissed when I withdrew and pushed in again, and I groaned at the way she said my name, at how she arched and dug her nails into my arm where I held her leg up.

"You feel fucking incredible," I told her, pumping in again, and again, and again. "So tight. So wet. So fucking perfect."

"You're so deep like this."

God, that made me see stars. It was usually me doing the talking, but fuck if hearing those words from her mouth didn't coax my orgasm right to the cresting point.

"Yeah, baby?" I asked, and I pushed in even more, holding deep before withdrawing and finding a slow, steady pace. "I love how you take it, how you take all of me."

Madelyn moaned, and I covered her mouth with one hand and a reminder not to wake Sebastian.

I knew by how she breathed against my palm and rubbed her breasts that she was close.

I leaned over so I could slide my hand down between the counter and where she was pressed against it, finding her slick clit and rolling it with my fingertips.

"*Shiiiit*," she cursed, shaking violently and holding onto me for dear life as I stroked her, drove into her
deeper, and kissed along the back of her neck, nipping at
the skin and begging her to come for me.

She did so with the most glorious break, her cries
of pleasure muted as she fought not to be too loud. I savored every quiet moan and breathless plea of my name
she let loose as I helped her ride out the orgasm. I didn't
stop until she was limp in my arms, until she could barely hold herself up.

"Don't give up on me yet, baby," I said, sucking her
lobe between my teeth. "I'm close."

Those two words ignited her, her strength coming back as she swatted my hand away so she could put
her leg back on the floor. No sooner than she had, she
pushed until I had no choice but to pull out of her, and
then she hopped up onto the counter and pulled me into
her, wrapping her legs around my waist.

"Like this," she pleaded, and that was the only request I needed to do exactly as she asked.

I tugged her to the edge again, slipping inside her
with my cock ready to release on the first fucking plunge.
She was somehow even tighter now that she'd come, her
pussy swollen from release, and I soaked in every soft
whimper she let loose as I found my pace again, kissing
her lips and chin and neck and collarbone with every
thrust.

"Fuck, baby," I whispered as I plummeted inside
her, my hands sliding up her ribs to cup her breasts. "I
love watching these perfect tits bounce when I fuck you
like this."

She moaned and leaned back on her palms, sup-
porting herself so I could knead her breasts and work

between her legs. It was as if they were swollen from release, too. They felt heavier in my palms, and every time I hit the max inside her, those beautiful breasts would ripple in a way that had me cursing and counting my lucky stars for the view.

My orgasm snatched me by the throat, heat tingling at the edges of my vision before it took over my entire body. I called out her name in a quiet grunt when the first wave rushed over me, and then I was kissing her and flexing in deep and fucking her like it was the first and last time. She clung to me, arms around my neck and digging into my shoulders as I rode out the climax, and it felt like the longest, most ecstasy-filled one of my fucking life.

Because this wasn't just some girl.

This was my future *wife*.

That thought spawned my orgasm on and on and on, until I was completely spent, and we were sweat-slicked and holding onto each other with our chests heaving.

"Holy shit," she breathed when we slowed, and I laughed, kissing her nose.

"For the rest of your life."

"Psh — you think you'll still fuck me like that when we're fifty?"

"I'll fuck you even better then, because I'll know you even better."

She laughed as I swung her up into my arms and carried us toward the shower. I had to admit, I loved the thought of my cum inside her, loved how she had to squeeze her thighs together to keep it from dripping out onto the floor as I carried her. I knew the mom inside her was thinking she needed to disinfect that whole kitchen before Sebastian woke up, but it could wait.

We grew quiet in the shower, staring into each other's eyes like the other one wasn't real as we took turns washing one another. She lathered shampoo in my hair, and I gently washed between her legs, doing my best not to let the hot water and soap running over her body turn me on for round two. I knew she was exhausted, and I could see it on her face now that she was ready to collapse.

When we were dry, I helped her into bed, pouring her a tall glass of iced water and watching her drink half of it before she put it on her bedside table. Then, I climbed in behind her, curling her up in my arms and savoring the sated sigh she let out when I did.

"I love you," I whispered against the shell of her ear, and I smiled just as she did.

"I love you, too."

"I hope you know I'll never get tired of hearing that."

"I'll check in on that in ten years."

"Go right ahead. It'll still be true. And ten years after that, and ten years after that, and ten years after that, and..."

"Okay, okay," she said, shimmying into my arms more. "Less talking. More sleeping."

"So bossy when you're tired."

"Get used to it."

I smirked against the back of her neck, kissing her softly and settling in to sleep.

Get used to it.

Yeah, I liked the sound of that.

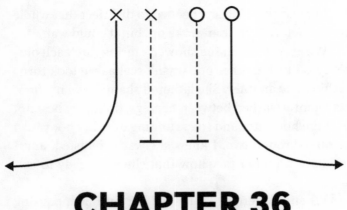

CHAPTER 36
Madelyn

Kyle's face didn't look promising when he came through the front door a week after our engagement, a heavy sigh leaving his chest and that massive hand of his running through his hair. It was a bit longer than when I'd met him, and he looked worn from the week of training camp. The first pre-season game was this weekend, and he'd been pushing hard to get ready for it.

From what he'd explained, these pre-season games would be his chance to seal his spot — and, hopefully, be named as a starter on the team. I hadn't seen him play yet, but if he was anything like he had been in high school, I had no reason to worry about him making it.

Then again, when he was in high school, he was just a kid. He didn't have a care in the world other than football.

Now, he was newly engaged to a train wreck of a woman with a crazy ex-husband and a six-year-old kid.

Boxes littered every corner of my home as we prepared to move into the new house Kyle had purchased for us.

And for reasons I wasn't sure I even understood, he *wanted* this life. He chose it. He chose *me*.

I was trying really hard not to be so surprised by it all. I wanted to be confident, the way I used to be. I wanted to hold my head high and shrug like, "*Of course*, he wants me. I'm amazing."

But the truth was I hadn't felt that way in a long time — not until Kyle looked at me the way he did, and touched me the way he did, and *loved* me the way he did.

Slowly, he was bringing back a bit of who I used to be while simultaneously helping me slip into who I would be in the future. He was showing me what it was to feel safe and cared for, how just those two truths alone allowed me to be more of a human and less of a mess.

He was showing my son how a calm, warm, loving household felt.

He was showing *himself* that he was nothing like his father, that he had more to offer the world than what he ever imagined.

Still, my stomach was in knots as he stepped inside the house, and I felt a wave of nausea wash over me when he slid his hands into the pockets of his joggers and lifted his eyes to mine.

Those bright blue pools were shielded by furrowed brows and a tight-lipped smile that told me we were in trouble.

"Well?" I asked, hoping he was playing a joke on me even when I knew he wouldn't — not in this situation.

Kyle swallowed, shaking his head just marginally.

I deflated.

"We're fucked," I said, falling onto the couch and burying my face in my hands. I actually thought I might throw up.

A warm hand slid down my back as a heavy body sank down next to me, and Kyle kissed my temple, exhaling a long, sad breath against my shoulder.

"I tried to reason with him. I promised we would happily drive Sebastian to him when it was his days, that we would never try to switch up holidays or weekends — no matter what my game schedule looked like. I assured him the school Sebastian is transferring to is far better than the one he's attending now, and that everything monetarily would be taken care of."

"But he didn't care."

Kyle sighed. "I think he feels like he's lost control of the situation."

"Of me," I corrected, letting my hands slap against my thighs as I looked up at Kyle. "He can't stand the thought of me being happy without him."

"Well, that's just too damn bad for him." Kyle's jaw was hard then, his eyes sliding from sympathy to rage. "He wants to take us to court? Fine. Let him. He's going to regret it."

"He has a lot of connections in this city."

"Well, I have the ability to *make* connections in this city," Kyle said firmly. Then, he took my face in his hands, leveling his gaze with mine. "Listen. He's lazy as fuck. He's going to take his sweet time getting things in order."

"I don't know, he might be motivated now..."

"Even still, it'll take a while before we're in front of a judge. And when we are, rest assured, we will be represented by the best attorney I can find. And we will not just argue our case for split custody to remain." He licked his lip like he wasn't sure he should say what he wanted to next. "I think we should take him down."

I frowned. "Take him down?"

"Madelyn, when I saw his handprints on you..." Kyle swallowed so hard his Adam's apple bobbed in his throat. "I've never been so close to committing murder in my entire life. I didn't even think twice about it. The only thing that stopped me was that speech you gave me, when you reminded me that you're strong, and capable, and that you can handle him — can handle *yourself*."

Pride beamed in my chest as much as despair. He was right — I had handled Marshall. While we were married *and* after.

But I hated that I had to.

And I knew Kyle hated it, too.

"But what has kept me up at night lately is the thought that one day, he could hurt Sebastian."

I started to shake my head, frowning, but Kyle spoke again before I could.

"I know you don't think he ever would. He loves his son, I know that. He hasn't shown any signs of physical aggression toward him. But he *has* shown signs of aggression toward *you* when Sebastian is around. He has raised his voice and thrown tantrums. He has toed the line. And as someone who grew up in a household just like that, let me tell you, Mads... there *will* come a day when that pencil-thin line becomes invisible. The first time he hurts Sebastian, he'll apologize and say it was a mistake. The second time, he'll say it's Sebastian's fault, that he did something or said something to make him do it. And the third time..." Kyle's jaw ticced. "He'll say Sebastian deserved it."

My eyes welled with tears so fast the first one slid free and ran down my cheek.

Just the *thought* of that made me want to march down the street to our old house where Marshall still lived and slit his throat.

"I would never make you do anything you didn't want to," Kyle assured me. "But if you'll agree to it... I think we should go for full custody. I think we should expose what he's done to you in the past, and how he's behaved recently, and show the court that he's not safe for Sebastian to be around."

"I don't know that I can take him from his father like that," I admitted on a wobbly voice.

"What if he was getting another father in his place?"

I blinked. "What... what do you mean?"

"I haven't done all the research I need to," Kyle started. "But there's this process. Stepparent adoption. If we can get Marshall to relinquish his rights, or if the judge revokes them... I would adopt him. We would be his parents by law."

"You would do that?"

"In a fucking heartbeat, Mads."

I nearly started bawling. The image of it, of us as a family and Sebastian being able to call Kyle *Dad* the way he told me he sometimes wanted to...

But what about Marshall?

He was a piece of shit, but he was still Sebastian's real father. I knew Sebastian loved him.

Then again, lately, all he'd been showing me was that he was scared of his dad, that he didn't want to be around him.

I was speechless for so long that Kyle started talking again.

"Maybe we work out that Marshall can still see Sebastian, but only in supervised situations. You and I need to be present with him, or something, I don't know. We can talk to our lawyer about it. But Madelyn," he said, folding his hands over mine. "I know this isn't my decision. I would never ask you to do something you don't want to. Sebastian is *your* son and I support whatever you want to do. All I want you to know is that in the past couple of months, I have come to love that little boy like…"

His throat constricted, and when his eyes watered, too, I nearly broke into pieces.

I threw my arms around him and squeezed tight, loving the way his arms shielded me, how I felt so safe there.

"You love him like your own," I finished, my voice tight with emotion.

Kyle nodded into my neck. "I do. And I love you. And I want both of you to be safe and happy and to never have to walk on eggshells again."

"I'll think about it," I promised him when we released the hug. "And thank you… for trying to reason with him. I didn't have much faith it would do anything, but I'm glad we tried."

"Anything for you," Kyle said easily.

And I knew he meant it.

For a while, we just held each other on that couch, Kyle kissing me and soothing me with a hand on my back. When I fell back into the cushions and scrubbed my face, preparing myself to get up and go get Sebastian from camp, Kyle reached for my feet and pulled them into his lap, rubbing the arches with just the right pressure to make me moan.

"Why don't you take a nap," he suggested. "I know this week has been a lot on you. I'll go pick Sebastian up."

"This is your one day off. *You're* the one who has training camp and a game this week."

"I'm perfectly fine," he promised.

"I'm not even working."

Kyle sucked his teeth at that, tickling my feet a bit until I was writhing and giggling. But it was true. As if Kyle hadn't given me enough already — a new home, a safe and healthy relationship, a love like I'd never experienced...

He was also giving me *time.*

He was making space for me to figure out what I actually wanted to do with my life, with my career.

It was so hard for me at first, to relinquish my control and walk away from my job. So much so that for a small moment, I wondered if I actually did like the career I'd started out of necessity. And I suppose a part of me *did* like it — I liked helping other women, other moms in trouble trying to make it on their own.

But at the end of the day, real estate wasn't my passion. It didn't fuel me. It had just been a way to make ends meet, to do what I had to do for me and my son. I was so used to taking care of everything, of every*one*...

Now, I had the precious gift of time, space, and security — of a man who loved me and took care of me for once.

"Don't pull that shit," Kyle said. "Being a mom is a full-time job in itself. And the only reason you're not working is because your brute of a fiancé has seen how tired you've been lately and is forcing you to let him spoil you for a bit."

"And because my brute of a fiancé is giving me the first opportunity to think of what I actually *want* to do for a career."

"My money is still on bestselling author."

I laughed at that, digging my toes into his ribs. "I'd have to finish a book first."

"You will," he said without doubt, and then he lifted my ankle to his lips and kissed it. "And I'll be first in line for a signed copy."

I was still swooning over this man who I was absolutely certain had to be a figment of my imagination and wildest fantasies at this point when he stood, grabbing his keys and wallet before bending to press a kiss to my forehead.

"Rest," he said. "I'll be back in a bit. Maybe Sebastian and I can stop on the way home and get stuff to make homemade pizza."

"He would love that."

"Don't act like you wouldn't, too. I know how my girl feels about pizza."

He winked, heading for the door, and I smiled long after he'd shut it and I heard his car leave the driveway. The strange thing was that I usually *did* love pizza, but for some reason, the thought of it now made me want to...

I bolted upright on the couch, my heart hammering in my chest.

Puke.

It made me want to puke.

I blinked, breathing more and more erratic the longer I let that fact sink in. Alone, it wouldn't have been anything. I would have chalked it up to my nerves being a wreck from the week.

But then I realized how exhausted I'd been, how I'd needed a nap almost every day since the engagement.

I tracked through the week, how I hadn't wanted my tea like usual in the morning, how I had been averse to foods I usually craved.

I thought I was just a mess from everything that had happened — Marshall showing up at the house, Kyle proposing, the offer on the house, going under contract, suddenly not working, my whole *life* changing...

But now, I was blinking rapidly, doing math in my head after a quick glance at my phone to confirm what the date was.

I was late.

Nine days late, to be exact.

My stomach fluttered violently as if it had been waiting for me to put the pieces together.

And as I ran to my car and drove like a bat out of hell to the store, I felt like a mad woman.

Because while I did feel a tinge of worry, a bit of uncertainty, and a dash of *holy fuck, oh shit*...

What I felt *most* was pure, undulating excitement.

Oh, God.

Am I pregnant?

The short five-minute drive to get a test felt like the longest journey of my life.

I couldn't wait to find out.

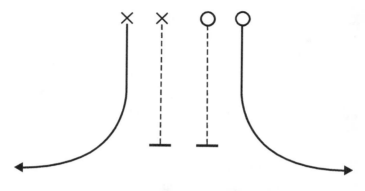

CHAPTER 37

Kyle

"**S**o, your job is to catch the ball," Sebastian said as he tried to follow my explanation, his tiny hands kneading the dough for his own personal pan pizza.

"That's part of it. Think about Titan," I said. "One part of your job is to feed him, right?"

Sebastian nodded, his little tongue sticking out as he stretched the dough.

"What else do you have to do to make sure he's cared for?"

"I gotta clean his aquarium," he said, and I smiled a little at how the *r* in that word sounded a bit like a *w*.

"Mm-hmm. What else?"

"I gotta make sure he's warm enough. Like his lamps and heating pads."

"You sure do. So, the same way there are a lot of jobs for you to take care of Titan, that's how it is for me on the field. I've got to catch the ball, but I also have to keep it safe while I run with it to make sure the other team doesn't steal it."

"That's illegal!"

I chuckled, helping him stretch out his dough a bit before we started adding toppings. I was working on mine and Madelyn's both, and I was ready to make sure hers had lots of pineapple — because she was weird like that.

"It's actually allowed in football," I explained. "There are rules, of course, but if they were to knock the ball out of my hands while I'm running and get it for themselves, then it would be their team's chance to score."

"How do you score?"

I explained that next, along with the many, many jobs I had on the field. By the time we were sitting down to eat the pizzas we'd made, Sebastian was throwing questions at me faster than I could bat the answers back. He was excited, bouncing in his chair with wide eyes the more he understood, and when I took him down the hallway to get ready for bed, he begged me to watch a game with him sometime that week so I could teach him more.

He begged me to let him come to *my* game.

I swallowed, nodding toward the sink for him to brush his teeth. "We'll see. It's a big stadium with a lot of people. We'll have to talk to Mommy about it."

Sebastian nodded, brushing away before he took a moment to spit. "Yeah. Mommy doesn't really like people." He shrugged. "'Cept you, of course."

"And you," I added, digging my fingers into his ribs.

He giggled and wiggled away, and once he'd finished brushing his teeth, he changed into his pajamas and crawled into bed.

His room was stacked high with boxes just like the rest of the house, and movers were coming in just two days. He'd been such a champ about the news of a new house and a new school. That was just the kind of kid he was. Anything new, anything different excited him.

I hoped he held onto that forever.

I read him one of his new books — a space book that I actually found interesting even though it was written for a first grader.

Soon-to-be second grader, Sebastian would often remind me.

He still seemed wired when we finished the book, but he said goodnight and I tucked him in before leaving him to sleep.

When I shut his door behind me, I stood on the other side of it for a long moment, a smile curling on my lips and a sigh leaving my chest. I was exhausted. He was full of energy and taking care of him felt like a full-time job.

And yet, I'd never felt joy like this.

I'd never felt so excited about anything in my life like I did explaining football to that kid. Even my best touchdowns didn't compare to the way it felt to watch his eyes light up when he finally understood something. I'd never felt love like the kind that burst from my chest when he hugged me, or when he kissed Madelyn's cheek and beamed up at her like she hung the moon.

Seeing the world through his eyes was like being reborn myself.

God, all I wanted was to keep him safe.

I wanted him to grow up nurtured and supported. I wanted him to be able to explore and try and fail and try again. I wanted him to know he was loved and safe.

I wanted to keep him far away from his father.

I didn't know if that made me a prick or not, but I didn't care. Marshall had the same evil in him that my father had. I didn't give a rat's ass if he saved kittens and helped cows give birth — he'd laid his hands on Madelyn.

And I knew whether she did or not that, eventually, he'd do the same to his son.

At least, he *would have* — but that was before I came into the picture.

And as long as Madelyn was okay with it, I'd burn that motherfucker down in court and make sure he couldn't ever hurt Sebastian.

Whatever she decided, I'd stand by her side. I just hoped with every ounce of my being that she agreed we should go for full custody. I prayed she'd resist the urge to see the best in her ex-husband, that she'd fight against reason that might have told her that Marshall hadn't done anything to deserve being torn from his kid.

In the end, it wasn't my decision. But whatever path we took, I'd be there to fight for both of them. I'd keep them safe. I'd love them. I'd lay down my life for them if I had to.

They were my family.

The heaviness of that statement surprised me a bit as I walked down the hall toward the living room. It seemed impossible, to feel this much for two people in such a short amount of time. In a matter of months, they'd become everything to me. I couldn't imagine living without them. I couldn't remember what my life had been like before. Partying, drinking, a different girl in my bed every week... who even *was* that man?

I didn't recognize him.

And I definitely didn't miss him.

When I made it to the living room, I leaned a shoulder against the wall, smiling at where Madelyn was seated on the couch. She'd put everything from dinner away and washed the dishes already, and now she was curled up at the corner of the sectional with a journal in her lap.

Her metallic hair was half-tied up in a small ponytail, strands of it framing her face and falling down over the back of her neck. The oversized cream sweater she wore covered her hands and slid off one shoulder, and even under the blanket in her lap, I could see the ridiculous fuzzy socks she'd been wearing all night.

She looked cozy and tired, and all I wanted was to wrap her in my arms.

But she also looked... sad.

Scared.

I couldn't place it earlier. I knew she was off by how quiet she'd been all night, but I assumed it was just because she was tired. After all the shit we'd been through in the past week, how could she *not* be? I hoped me taking over picking up Sebastian and making dinner and getting him ready for bed would alleviate some of that, but I knew the truth was that a mom's job was never done. She would always have something to do, even with my help, and she'd probably have many days where she'd be tired just like this.

Still, there was another layer to those weary eyes. The way her brows tugged inward, the way she chewed at the inside of her lower lip and nervously fidgeted with the pen in her hand...

"I don't know that he'll fall right to sleep, but he didn't fight me on it," I said. "He seems pretty excited from all the football talk."

Madelyn's smile was weak. "He adores you."

"I adore him back."

Her brown eyes watered, lip wobbling as she looked at the pen and journal in her lap.

"Hey," I said, walking over to sit down next to her. I pulled the pen and notebook from her hands and set them aside before pulling her legs into my lap. "Is this about Marshall? Because I promise, he won't be bothering us. I made it clear that—"

"No," she said, cutting me off with a shake of her head. She lifted her eyes to mine only a split second before she was burying her face in her hands. "Oh, God, Kyle. I... I have to tell you something."

"Okay," I said softly, taking her hands in mine and squeezing. "Tell me. I'm right here."

"You don't understand," she whispered, folding her lips together. "It... it's a big something. And I'm *terrified* of how you'll react because I..."

She couldn't even finish the sentence, her eyes wide and filled with horror before she squeezed them tightly and shook away whatever thought was making her pulse race.

And now it was *my* thoughts running wild.

Because I'm a sick fucking bastard, the first thing I thought was that she'd slept with someone. But even before my stomach could fully drop at the possibility, I batted it away. She would never. I knew without an ounce of hesitation.

But then what could it be?

My mind cycled through every scenario it could think of while I waited for her to speak. She was sick. She didn't want to move in with me. She didn't want to move Sebastian. She didn't love me. She didn't want to get married. She didn't want to be together at all.

Sweat trickled down my neck the longer the silence stretched between us, and then Madelyn blew out a shaky breath, squeezing my hands in hers and meeting my gaze.

"I've been so tired lately," she started. "And today, after you left to go get Sebastian, I felt so nauseous I was sure I was going to vomit."

I nodded. Those words didn't take any of the sick scenarios out of my head. She was tired and she was sick. I was doing that to her. I was causing her stress. I was hurting her.

My heart was ready to beat itself to a bloody pulp before she had the chance to.

"I thought it was just my nerves, thought it was just everything that's been going on," she continued, her eyes flicking between mine. "But... then I... I realized... I'm late."

I blinked.

Once, twice, then a few times in quick succession.

Late?

Late for what?

Madelyn searched my gaze and waited for me to react, but I didn't know how to, because I didn't understand what she was saying.

Not until she lifted her brows and dipped her head a bit.

"I'm late," she repeated.

And my stomach fell out of my asshole.

I knew she saw it, the moment I realized what she meant, and that moment was followed by my chest rising and falling more rapidly, by my hands growing clammy where they held hers, my next swallow so hard to take it felt like sandpaper lined my throat.

It took everything in me to remain neutral, to wait for her to keep speaking before I got ahead of myself. I almost wanted to tear my hands from hers and sit on them to aide in my efforts.

Because right now, my heart was thundering with hope that was impossible to tame, and all I wanted was to pull her into me and kiss her and scream and cry and laugh and spin her around the room.

She's pregnant.

Just *thinking* the words made my heart leap into my throat, made a smile impossible to hide bloom on my face.

I tried to wait for her to confirm it. I tried not to get ahead of myself. But *fuck*, it was damn near impossible.

What if she didn't want it? What if this was bad news to her? Judging by the anxiety riddled in every inch of her right now, that very well could be.

I schooled myself as much as I could, waiting for her cue, letting her take the lead and dictate how I should react. Whatever she needed from me right now — I'd be it.

But that hope was inflating in my chest so fast and furious I felt I might float away.

"Kyle," she whispered, sucking in a sharp breath before she let it out slowly through parted lips. "I'm pregnant."

The word hung between us, a softly whispered, life-changing declaration made in a quiet home stacked with boxes. My heart beat once, twice, and I savored the way those words sounded, the way they slid over my senses and embedded themselves deep into the roots of who I was.

I let out one shallow breath.

And then I released the leash on my emotions, and I kissed her.

My hands slid into her hair, pulling her mouth to mine. I kissed her hard and long, her lips surprised against mine at first before they softened. I laughed against those soft, perfect lips. Or maybe it was a sob? I couldn't be sure.

But I held her to me, and I savored that kiss and that moment, never wanting to forget even a single second of it. I committed her to memory — the texture of her hair in my hands, the trembling of her lips against mine, the soft whimper she let out that I mirrored. I vowed to remember everything, from the way my heart raced in my chest to the way the truth raced in my mind.

Pregnant.

She's pregnant.

I'm going to be a dad.

"You're sure?" I asked, pulling back to search her gaze.

She nodded, the tears in her eyes spilling over. She covered my hands framing her face with her own, rolling her lips together. "I'm sorry."

"You—" I frowned. "What? What on Earth are you sorry for?"

"I know this wasn't planned. I... you're about to start your *career*. You're so young. You didn't sign up for this, for *any* of this. You—"

"Woman," I growled, and then I kissed her silent for good measure. "I don't give a flying fuck if this was planned or not. You just... you just made me the happiest fucking man in the world."

"I... wait." She sniffed. "You're not mad?"

"*Mad*?" I laughed. I couldn't help it. "Are *you* mad? As in fucking crazy? How could I ever be mad that you're carrying my child?"

Saying the words sent a river of goosebumps down my arms, and I laughed again, resting one palm against her still very-flat stomach.

"Mads, you're pregnant," I repeated, like she wasn't understanding. "I... I'm *thrilled*. I'm over the moon. I—"

Fuck.

I stopped myself from saying another word, swallowing down the urge and bringing my smile to a neutral expression.

"Are *you* happy?" I asked. "Because if you're not, if you're not ready for this, if you never wanted to have another child, I understand. It's your body and I—"

"I cried when I took the test," she said, her nostrils flaring, eyes locked on mine. "I broke down."

I swallowed and nodded.

The hope in my chest deflated.

But I let myself feel that disappointment for only a split second before I was holding her tight, looking her right in the eyes and letting her know I wasn't going anywhere.

Whatever she wanted, whatever she decided — I would be there.

Her lips wobbled a bit, but they curled into a smile even as her eyes glossed, two silent tears sliding down her red cheeks. "I was so scared to tell you, because it wasn't planned. But I... I was so *happy*, Kyle. I know it's fast. *God,* this whole summer has felt like a whirlwind. It's felt... *insane*. And now to add this to the equation?" She shook her head, and then her hands were framing *my* face, and her smile was enough to put that hope

348

back in my soul. "I was scared to tell you that when I was waiting for the result to show, I was *praying* for a positive. I wanted it. I wanted to be pregnant. God, am I a nutcase?"

"You're *my* nutcase," I said, and I wrapped her into my arms in a crushing hug, lifting her off the couch just like I'd wanted to when she first told me. I spun her around as she laughed, but then she made a comment about throwing up, and I immediately stopped, setting her back on the ground and checking her for bruises like she was a fragile doll.

She swatted me away. "I'm fine. It was a joke."

"Do you need ginger ale? Water? Saltines?"

"Oh, my God, Kyle."

"Shit, did the pizza make you sick? You didn't eat much. What do you need?"

"Shut *up*," she said, and she wound her arms around my neck and pulled my lips down to hers. "I'm fine. I... I'm just shocked, I think."

"Yeah, this was definitely unexpected."

"No, I mean, I'm shocked by your reaction."

"What did you think I'd do?"

She shrugged. "I don't know. I mean, you didn't sign up for this. You're supposed to be fucking models and actresses and living it up as a rookie in the NFL. Instead, you got a single mom with a batshit crazy ex-husband and, now, a baby on the way."

The word *baby* made my face split with a grin. "A baby."

"A baby," Madelyn echoed on a whisper, and she shook her head, burying it in my chest.

And the moment hit us.

I felt it, not just how it slammed into my chest, but how it knocked the breath from hers, too.

This very same moment had been stolen from us years ago.

This elation, this celebration, this immeasurable amount of love had been ripped away from us.

We'd lost our first child — and neither of us had been able to properly grieve that loss.

Madelyn's arms slipped from my neck to wind around my waist, and she squeezed me tight, her brows furrowing as I hugged her and held her to me. I kissed the crown of her head, and we both let out long, slow breaths.

It was the most delicate mixture of pain and elation, that hug shared in her half-packed living room.

I felt the loss of innocence, the loss of another life.

But I also felt the birth of a new one — one that was so far from anything I'd ever imagined, and yet brought me so much joy I wanted to burst with it.

"I have a request," I said after a while, still stroking her hair.

"No, we aren't naming them Madden."

I smirked. "Let me be the one to tell Sebastian."

At that, Madelyn pulled back, her eyebrows sliding together as she looked up at me.

"He's going through a lot of change right now," I said, as if his own mother didn't already fucking know. "I want to make sure he knows that he's supported through that. That it's okay to not feel happy about it all. I want him to know we're a team. And I want to talk to him about being a big brother, about how..."

I swallowed, unsure of how she'd feel about what I was about to say next.

"I want him to know that I see him as my own just as much as this one on the way," I said, floating my hand down to her stomach again. "And for the next nine months, I want him to know he's my priority, and that even when the baby comes, he's needed. And he's allowed to need *us*. And... fuck. Do I sound stupid? Am I failing as a dad already?"

Madelyn was watching me with an amused smile, but her eyes were glossing again. She sniffed, shaking her head.

"No," she whispered. "You're going to be the best dad in the world. To both of them."

I let out a puff of a laugh from my nose. "Holy shit. I'm going to be a dad."

"You already are."

I shook my head, tucking the loose strands of Madelyn's hair behind one ear. "I gotta say... this has been one hell of a summer."

She laughed, tilting her head back, the sound sweet as it reverberated off the empty walls.

"And all because you had insomnia and couldn't resist house shopping at three a.m."

"I think I should lose sleep more often."

"Oh, believe me — you'll lose *plenty* of sleep in about nine months."

"Good thing it'll be offseason."

"Sebastian will be the best big brother," she mused with a watery smile.

"That's because he has the best mom."

"No," she said softly. "It's just who he is."

I smiled, thumbing her chin, and we stared at each other like we couldn't believe the new world we'd just stepped into, and like we couldn't bear the thought of any other possible outcome.

"I love you, Mads."

She leaned into my touch, closing her eyes and nodding on a smile. "I love you, *Daddy*."

One eye peeked open at that, and her smile turned mischievous.

I wet my lips, spanking the side of her ass. "Say that again, and I'm going to put two babies in you."

"I don't think that's how this works."

"Only one way to find out."

I swept her into my arms as she let out another sweet laugh, and I basked in every decibel of it, every centimeter of her lips against mine on our way back to her room, and every moment of stripping her bare and laying her down and sliding inside her until we were one.

She bit my shoulder to muffle her cries of pleasure, and I buried myself deep, marveling at how one seemingly insignificant decision can set our lives on a completely new track.

The life that was stolen from us would never be ours to hold again.

But we *did* hold the power to build a new one.

And I counted my lucky stars that the universe gave us this second chance.

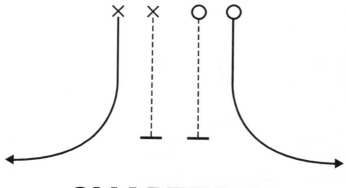

CHAPTER 38
Madelyn

By the middle of October, I finally didn't feel like death.

The first trimester of my unexpected pregnancy had hit me hard. Between the constant nausea — that lasted all day, by the way, not just in the morning — and the extreme fatigue, it was like walking in a fog I just couldn't wait to find the end of.

Add in the fact that I hadn't been working, we'd moved across town, and things were slowly progressing in the court case against Marshall, and you could say I didn't even feel like a real human. Nothing in my life was the same. Everything was chaos.

And yet, somehow, I'd never felt happier in my life.

Because I had Kyle.

Kyle, who doted on me every day as if he didn't have enough on his plate with a full-time job as a professional athlete and the start of his very first season in the NFL.

Kyle, who massaged my back and took complete-ly over cooking, hiring a chef to do it on the nights he couldn't.

Kyle, who wouldn't let me lift a finger during the move, who was reading expecting father books and try-ing every nausea cure under the sun that he could find.

Kyle, who spent all his free time that wasn't devoted to making sure I was okay, to caring for my son, making sure he was loving his new school and settling into his new neighborhood and home.

This man had taken every notion of what I thought a husband was and fast-pitched it out the window.

We weren't even married yet, and he was illustrat-ing what I thought was just a fairytale. He was my part-ner. He wasn't just leaving me to endure this alone. He was there, every step of the way, doing everything in his power to make the first trimester suck less.

I was thankful for the fact that I didn't feel like throwing up or passing out on the first soft surface I could find to get horizontal on as Sebastian and I made our way up to the club level of Lumen Field. Kyle had refused for me to sit anywhere but in a suite for our first game — especially in my condition. Apparently, he and a few of his teammates had reserved a suite together, which had Kyle assuring me I would be welcomed by wives and families.

I didn't feel that comforted.

I was over the moon to finally be able to watch a game live. I was thrilled to have Sebastian with me, whose eyes were so wide as we walked through the sta-dium that I thought they were going to pop out of his head. He'd been glued to the TV during every game of the season, teaching himself the game and asking Kyle question after question when he got home. He was full-on obsessed.

I had a feeling it was a little more because of the man who played the game than the actual game itself.

But still, this was out of my comfort zone. In a matter of months, I'd gone from a struggling single mom real estate agent with approximately twelve outfits in my closet, to the fiancée of an NFL rookie tight end with more money than God.

I didn't feel natural walking into that suite after showing our credentials. I didn't feel like we belonged as we slipped inside the room filled with alcohol and food and chattering friends and family members of the team. I didn't feel confident as we made our way directly to the seats in front of the tall windows overlooking the field, nor as I tucked my purse under the seat and held my son's hand as he pressed up onto his toes and stuck his nose to the glass to watch the players warm up.

Even as my heart raced with the discomfort, I smiled in excitement, too.

Especially when Sebastian pointed near the end zone and said, "There he is!"

And there he was.

Kyle Robbins, number eighty-two on the field and number one in my heart.

He looked more focused than I'd ever seen him as he ran drills along with his team. His tall, muscular frame crouched low, feet moving him side to side in quick steps like a crab before he transitioned to the next drill. He was explosive, working his legs in a quick sprint in place before he'd take off down the field a bit and cut left or right. Then, he was jumping straight up into the air in a feat of magic, soaring impossibly high for someone as tall and heavy as he was.

Sebastian and I watched him like he was the only player on that field.

Kyle's focus was on his teammates and the drills he was running, and I could tell from how he wasn't even clowning around with his teammates that he was getting in the zone. He loved to fool around. He loved to make jokes and lighten the mood in any room — especially when it came to his team.

But this was game time, and if he was serious about nothing else, he was serious about this.

The clock counted down to kick off, and when there were only about ten minutes left, Kyle started jogging toward the tunnel that led to the team locker rooms.

Only then did his eyes skate up to the suite.

My stomach fluttered with butterflies instead of nausea when I saw the smirk climb on his lips, and he lifted a navy-blue glove-covered hand to wave at us.

Sebastian lost his mind.

"He sees us! He waved to us!" Sebastian jumped up and down and waved with both hands like Kyle was a celebrity.

I don't think I truly realized, until that very moment, that he actually was.

The game began after the national anthem was sung, and I felt my nerves disappear more and more as the minutes ticked by.

Well, at least, the nerves about *me*.

Now, all my energy was focused on being nervous for Kyle. I wanted him to win. I wanted him to do well. But more than anything, I didn't want him to get hurt.

And every time a Philadelphia Eagles player crashed into him or slammed him to the ground, I had to fight to stop myself from shrieking.

Sebastian noticed how I'd grip his hand a little too tight, though, or how I was picking at the skin on my lips as I waited for Kyle to pop back up after each play. Sometime before the end of the first quarter, my son smiled at me, stepping between me and the window view of the field.

"He's okay, Mom," he assured me, his voice lilting in a way that told me he was almost embarrassed that I was even worried, as if I were being silly to think he might get hurt by these three-hundred-pound men tackling him to the ground. "This is his job. It's what he does. He's got this."

I blew out a breath and nodded, smiling at my son who was far too smart for his own good before tickling him until he moved out of my way. The first quarter ended with the Eagles ahead seven to zero, and I felt like I was cracking ice off my body as I stood and made my way to get some food and water from the suite's bar for me and Sebastian.

I was plating some hamburger sliders and chicken tenders — which blessedly didn't make me want to hurl — when a familiar face strode through the suite entrance.

"Giana?"

I couldn't hide the surprise or joy in my voice as I set my plate aside just in time to receive a fierce hug from Kyle's curly-haired friend and agent. She squeezed me so tightly, I felt every inch of her now rather large baby bump, and she beamed up at me when we broke away, her smile dazzling.

"I'm so sorry it took me this long to get up here," she said. "Between the pre-game interviews, fielding requests for meetings with Kyle from possible sponsors, and the fact that I waddle more than walk these days..." She shook her head, still grinning. "But it looks like you're settled in! Is everyone being nice?"

"Yes," I answered, which wasn't a lie. A few of the wives had come to introduce themselves, and no one had been anything but kind. "I'll admit that Sebastian and I are sticking to ourselves, though."

"Perfectly understandable. It's all new, after all," Giana said, and she waved to where Sebastian was behind us in the seats.

My son looked ready to climb over those seats to get to the food I was holding hostage.

I told Giana I'd be right back, plated a hearty portion of veggies and fruits along with his slider and nuggets, and delivered it all to him along with a water bottle. Once he was set up and watching the second quarter, I rejoined Giana at one of the cocktail tables.

"Do you want to sit?" I offered, noting how she was rubbing her lower back.

She waved me off. "Trust me — nothing feels comfortable right now. Sitting, standing, walking, lying down. It all sucks. Of course, you know this already," she added with a smile.

"How far along are you?"

"Thirty-one weeks."

I let out a low whistle. "Won't be long now."

"I'm ready. Don't get me wrong, being pregnant has been cooler than I imagined it would be. I'm cute as hell with this little bump," she added, smoothing her hands over her stomach. "But I'm ready for this baby to be on the outside. It's Clay's turn to carry them around for a while."

I chuckled. "I bet you can't wait to meet them."

Giana softened at that. "You have no idea. Well, I guess you do, actually." She shook her head. "I hope this little boy or girl has his eyes. And his smile." She paused. "But I truly hope they do *not* have his smart-ass attitude, or I'm in trouble."

A roar broke out on the field, and Giana and I turned to the television screens just in time to see the end of a monster run from the Seahawks. We were within twenty yards of scoring now, and Giana and I moved to stand behind the seats so we could watch the field through the glass.

Two plays later, it was touchdown, Seattle Seahawks, and the game was tied.

I ran down to celebrate with Sebastian, made sure he was okay, and then kept my eyes on him as I rejoined Giana. There was a family sitting in the seats next to where Sebastian was, and another little boy maybe a few years older than him was pointing to the field and explaining things just the way Kyle had been. Sebastian was all ears, eager to learn like always.

God, I loved him.

I absentmindedly ran a hand over my stomach, which looked more like bloat than anything else right now.

Sebastian would be a big brother soon, and it filled my heart just as it made my eyes brim with tears.

"Okay, I need to get back down there before halftime," Giana said once the noise had died down a bit. "But the whole reason I came up here was to see how *you* are doing."

She smiled softly, petting my arm.

"I'm..." I blew out a breath. "Wow, I'm not sure how to answer that."

"It's been a bit of a whirlwind, hasn't it?"

I nodded. "One summer, and my life has completely changed. I'm not sure what all Kyle has told you..."

Giana held her hands up. "He hasn't said much, and I don't pry. I just ask that he lets me know things that I need to know as his agent and publicist. But obviously, I know that you two just reconnected, and that not even two months later he was asking all of us to get on a plane to help him pull off a proposal." She raised a brow. "I never thought I'd see Kyle Robbins weak for anyone, but girl, he is *feeble* for you."

My cheeks ran hot as I looked down at the floor.

Then, I filled her in on everything Kyle hadn't.

Marshall. The move. The wedding we hadn't even started planning yet.

The Big Secret News.

Giana did all she could to not react, to play it cool and not cause a scene, but when I revealed that I was pregnant, she couldn't help herself.

She burst into tears, clinging to me and proving yet again that her size didn't mean shit when it came to the hugs that girl could give.

"I'm sorry," she whispered when she finally released me, swiping at her face. "These damned hormones. I cry at every car commercial and country song now, too."

"Relatable," I said, and we laughed together, her squeezing my hands in hers.

"Ugh, okay, I really have to go," she said, sneaking a peek at the play clock. "But we will all get together soon. And I'm adding you to the weekly Zoom call with the girls. We have so much to talk about. And so much to plan!"

I chuckled, my heart warming with the most unfamiliar sensation.

It had been a long time since I'd had a group of girlfriends.

"Congratulations, by the way," she whispered. "I can't wait for Kyle's Daddy era."

"Thank you, G. And thanks for not being... thanks for not judging our situation."

She frowned. "Judging? Why on earth would I?"

I shrugged. "I mean, let's be honest... it is all a bit crazy."

At that, Giana sighed and smiled up at me like the sun beam that she was, her hands squeezing mine once more.

"All the best love stories are."

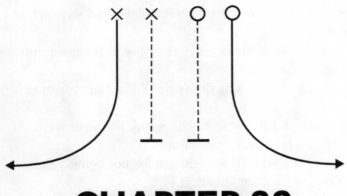

CHAPTER 39

Kyle

Nothing I experienced at the collegiate level could have ever truly prepared me for what I'd experience in the NFL.

I heard the stories from other players about the after-game madness on the field. I remembered Holden telling us all after his first few games how the hits were bigger, harder — the kind that would steal your breath and leave your head spinning. I knew to expect more cameras and interviews, to have higher demands put on me, to have coaches breathing down my throat demanding me to be better.

And yet, here I was, seven weeks into the season, and I still felt like a little kid who just took his training wheels off.

My confidence was building, but slowly, like thick syrup draining down a very small straw. I felt myself getting stronger, faster, and learning my way around my new team and my new opponents.

Still, my stats weren't what I wanted them to be. I only had one-hundred-and-fifty-two receiving yards and one touchdown. We weren't even halfway through the season, and I knew I had the opportunity to have a great rookie showing by the end of it all.

But I hated where I was currently.

I wanted more. I was thirsty. *Hungry.* Ready to devour.

I just needed my body to catch up to my brain.

And while I'd thrived off the media attention and brand deals in college, they felt overwhelming now. I found myself slacking on social media, focusing only on what Giana said was absolutely necessary. I recorded commercials. I posed for pictures for the brands sponsoring me. I took the interviews she or the team's PR coordinator instructed me to.

But at the end of a game, I didn't want to flex or show off — even if we won. I'd lost the desire to take out my phone and film a selfie, or to be front and center at a post-game press conference.

Giana assured me it would come back, once I felt more comfortable.

As it was, the only thing I thought of after a game was getting home to Madelyn and Sebastian.

We'd moved into the new house just before the start of the school year and, in turn, the regular season. And while we might have picked the most chaotic time to make such a change, it was like the most natural shift for all of us.

Sebastian loved his new school and our new home. He *especially* loved his new room, which was twice the size of his old one. Plus, we had a pool, and a hot tub, and an outdoor court to play on, and a huge yard, and a view of the water. Upstairs, we'd made a playroom all for him — complete with an epic case to display his favorite rocks.

And, of course, a lizard mansion for Titan.

Madelyn was having a bit of a harder time, but mostly because she'd been so sick. Maybe that was part of why I wanted to rush home to her after every practice and every game. I would have given up my entire *career* if I could switch places with her, if I could take the nausea and headaches and exhaustion that had taken over her entire life.

But she was strong. *God*, she was strong. And beautiful. Every time I looked at her, even when she looked green and ready to shove me aside to run for the toilet, I found myself struck with how fucking gorgeous she was. She'd laugh and wave me off when I told her as much, arguing with me instead that she looked like death.

I knew it was hard for her, but it seemed almost *harder* to let me help. I knew without asking that Marshall hadn't been a partner to her through her first pregnancy. She'd had to do it all on her own.

Not this time.

I made sure to show up for her, every day, in every way I could, to let her know that we were in this together.

It was what I would have done even when I was sixteen, had I been given the choice.

I didn't let myself ruminate on that, though. I focused on the here and now, on the life we had stretching out before us.

And tonight, we were finally telling Sebastian about his new role in our family.

My body ached like I'd been in a plane crash as I made my way through the back of the stadium, headphones on and my head down. We'd won the game, so I made sure to keep my face pleasant, smiling a bit for the cameras as I walked by, and all their flashes blinded me. I just didn't want to be stopped.

Because for the first time all season, Madelyn and Sebastian had come to the game.

I knew Madelyn wanted to come sooner. I knew Sebastian was *dying* to finally attend. But with Madelyn being sick, I refused to let her put herself through a night of misery for me. It wasn't until we made it out of the first trimester and her nausea faded, that I agreed it was time.

We'd pitched it to Sebastian as a big night out for him. He and I spent the day together before the game, making a big breakfast and swimming in the heated pool. When I'd made my way to the stadium, Madelyn had taken over. They spent time at the park and got McDonald's before she took him to the team store to pick out whatever gear he wanted.

And at home, there was a gift waiting for him — one he'd never forget.

My stomach was in knots as I made my way to the friends and family lounge where wives, kids, and parents gathered after the games to wait on players. I'd been so excited to deliver this news, and yet, I wanted to do it right. I wanted to make sure Sebastian understood how much he meant to us, how much we would *need* him as a big brother. I wanted him to feel loved and feel special.

The last thing I wanted was for this to come like a blow to the knees, to sweep him into a new reality he wasn't prepared for.

I'd talked through it all with Madelyn a million times, and though she'd assured me it would all be okay, I was still nervous as hell.

That kid meant more to me than I could put into words.

He felt like my own.

I hoped he understood that I'd always see him that way, that this wouldn't change anything between us.

My thoughts were shaken loose when I pushed through the door to the lounge. I was greeted by the raucous noise of families reuniting, kids running around, wives chatting, friends cheering. I lifted my chin at a few of the players as I passed them, saying brief and friendly hellos to their families as they introduced me. But my focus was on finding Madelyn and Sebastian.

When I did, my heart stuttered in my chest.

They were in the far back corner with Giana — who was absentmindedly snacking on Cheetos in a bowl that she'd apparently decided was all for her and no one else. Sebastian was wearing a kid version of my jersey along with a Seattle Seahawks hat, and he had a navy-blue foam finger that looked half as big as he was. He looked a bit tired, but mostly excited, his eyes wide and his smile stretching across his face as he told some sort of story to Giana.

And then there was Madelyn.

Her red hair was longer now than when she'd first spiraled back into my life earlier in the summer, the silky strands of it hanging down past her shoulder blades. Her cheeks were flushed, her skin glowing in a way it never had. She wore a loose-fitting green blouse and a navy-blue blazer with cut-up denim jeans that reminded me of when she was my hot babysitter.

It didn't matter that she wasn't quite showing yet, that she looked as if nothing was different at all about her.

I knew, under that blouse, there was a tiny little bump steadily growing more and more each day.

I knew her breasts had swollen at least a cup size, that she had a new sensitivity that sometimes made her writhe in ecstasy when I played with her, and other times made her swat me away and give me a death glare if I so much as *thought* about touching her tits again.

I knew every mood swing she'd had, every tear she'd let fall, and every frustrated growl she'd let loose.

I knew she was carrying our child.

And that knowledge nearly knocked me to my knees every time I thought about it, no matter how many weeks it'd been.

My chest squeezed as Madelyn laughed at something Sebastian was saying, and then as if she felt me watching her, her warm brown eyes searched the room until she found me staring back at her.

Time slugged to a stop, the noise muting around us as her lips curled up into a soft, knowing smile.

Mine.

She was mine.

My rib cage expanded with the thought as I made my way to them, ready to sweep her up into my arms for the whole room to see. But Sebastian barreled into me first, crushing my legs in a hug.

"That. Was. *Awesome!*" he said, bouncing up and down with eyes the size of coasters. "We could see *everything* from our seats! When you ran that one play, the one where you spun and shoved your hand in that guy's face?" Sebastian made a noise I'd never heard, something between a squeal and an evil laugh. "It was the best! I want to come to *every* game!"

I bent down next to him, flicking his hat. "I think you're my good luck charm."

"Next time, you gotta get a touchdown when I'm here."

"What do I get if I do?"

"Hmmm... breakfast in bed! I'll make it!"

"*You'll* make it, huh? So, what am I getting? Cheerios?"

"Froot Loops!"

I laughed, plucking at his jersey. "I like your style, by the way."

"Wouldn't wear any other number," he said proudly with a toothy grin — one that showed evidence that he'd be losing his front teeth soon.

Madelyn squeezed Sebastian's shoulder. "He wanted to make sure he had *this* specific one, too. Not the white one. It had to be the navy."

"These ones are the coolest," Sebastian said matter-of-factly.

I winked at him, and then pulled my girl into my arms, inhaling the sweet scent that was so uniquely her. Tea and ink and citrus. I pressed my lips to her hair, feeling whole again.

"And what about you," I asked. "You enjoy yourself?"

"Eh, it was alright."

She smirked with the tease, but that didn't stop me from digging my fingers into her side and tickling her mercilessly. Giana watched the whole ordeal with a soft smile on her face, like she both couldn't believe what she was witnessing, and like she'd seen it coming all along.

"How did Clay do?" I asked, tucking Madelyn under one arm and Sebastian under the other.

"Beastly. He got an interception that was *almost* a pick six. Sadly, they didn't win, but he seemed in decent spirits."

"You see him tomorrow?" Madelyn asked.

Giana nodded. "Yes, and it still feels like too long. I swear, my hormones make me needy. We both fly home in the morning, and I've got just a few more weeks before I won't be flying at all."

"I can't imagine you sitting still," I remarked.

"Oh, trust me. I won't be. I'll be bossing Clay around to get the nursery painted and organized. If he thinks Coach is a hard ass, just wait until he sees me at thirty-eight weeks pregnant."

We all laughed at the image, and I made a mental note to check in on my soon-to-be-dad friend. I knew he was excited, but I wondered if he was nervous, too. I wondered if he felt the way I did — like he wanted to be the best dad possible, all while understanding that he was for *sure* going to fuck up.

We stayed and visited for a while longer before Giana was ready to head to her hotel, and we were ready to brave the madness of the paparazzi on our way out to the parking lot. I'd asked Madelyn if she wanted to leave separately, if she wanted to avoid the spotlight for a while longer, but she'd wrapped her arm in mine and held Sebastian's hand and said she was done hiding.

Cameras flashed as we made our way through the stadium — though there were fewer gathered now than there had been right after the game ended. I knew Giana would be hounded in the morning, everyone wanting to know who Madelyn was. Sebastian stole the show, grinning and waving at every camera we passed. I had a feeling he'd have no problem with a life that came with a bit of spotlight, but I still wanted to protect him at all costs, to make sure he never felt like his privacy was invaded.

Security escorted us to my Audi. I'd left the Aston Martin at home, since it only had two seats. Madelyn and I both breathed a sigh of relief once we were inside the tinted windows with the doors locked.

Sebastian, on the other hand, let out a whoop of adrenaline, declaring how awesome that was and that he couldn't wait to see his pictures.

He passed out in the back seat less than five minutes into the drive, and Madelyn reached across the console, wrapping my hand in hers.

"You ready?" she asked on a whisper.

I couldn't fight the smile that washed over my face, and I squeezed her hand before lifting her knuckles to my lips.

"Ready."

Madelyn

Sebastian was so tired when we got home that I carried him inside, and I loved that I could still do it. He was teetering on the edge of being too big, and I found myself nuzzling into him for those little boy cuddles as long as I could get them.

Once we were inside, though, he stirred, and a new wave of energy washed over him. He asked me if he could have ice cream, and though I didn't think sugar at midnight was a great idea, it was a special occasion.

So, he and Kyle made little ice cream sundaes — one for each of them, and a *special* one for me, which included more sprinkles than I'd had in all my years of life combined.

We ate at the kitchen island and made a mess with chocolate syrup, Sebastian and Kyle talking about the game while I smiled and listened.

I could see how nervous Kyle was, and it was the most adorable thing in the world.

Here was this beast of a man who had just won an NFL game, and he was shaking in his boots at the thought of telling a six-year-old that he was about to be a big brother.

It warmed my heart.

Once the ice cream was done, Kyle grabbed Sebastian's hand, casting me a weary look over his shoulder. I winked at him with what I hoped was an encouraging smile. With one last breath, Kyle nodded, his resolve set.

"Have you had a good day?" he asked Sebastian.

"The *best* day."

"Well, what if I told you we had one last surprise for you?"

Sebastian's eyes widened, flicking from Kyle to me and back again.

"There's a present for you on your bed," Kyle said. "Think you have enough energy to open it?"

"Yeah!" Sebastian took off in a sprint, and Kyle and I chuckled before jogging along behind him.

We poured into his room just in time to see him ripping into the race car wrapping paper, and he tore at the box until he was holding his present in his hand.

A medium-sized, smoothly polished river rock — engraved with the words *Big Brother*.

Sebastian blinked at it for a long moment, turning it over in his hands with a confused and tentative smile. "It's a rock."

"It is," Kyle said, bending down next to him. "Can you read what it says?"

Sebastian sounded the two words out one letter at a time until he got it.

"Big brother."

We waited for it to click, but when Sebastian just tilted his head to the side, Kyle glanced up at me before sitting on the bed and pulling Sebastian up next to him.

"Tonight, at the game, did you see how me and the other guys on my team worked together?"

Sebastian nodded.

"We all had to work as a unit to get the win. Some of us had to throw or catch the ball. Others had to block so our players wouldn't get hit. Some had to kick. Everyone had a role to play."

"Kind of like a family."

"Exactly like a family," Kyle echoed. "Do you re-member when I took you to Talon's birthday party a couple weeks ago? Remember how she was showing off her new baby brother?"

Sebastian giggled. "Yeah. He kept blowing bubbles with his mouth."

"He did, didn't he?" Kyle smiled, sucked in a long breath, and let it out slowly. "Well, what would you think if I told you that *you* are going to have a new baby brother — or sister."

My son's eyes grew wide, and my hands floated to my mouth as tears pricked my eyes.

I knew that look.

He was excited.

"Wait, really?!"

Kyle nodded. "Really."

Sebastian blinked rapidly. "How? When?"

"Well, I think you can see that your mom and I love each other."

Sebastian smiled at me, and I winked at him. "Yeah," he said.

"We love each other *so* much that we made a baby, and that baby is growing inside your mom's tummy right now — just like you did."

"In her *tummy*?" Sebastian looked at me slack-jawed. "Does it hurt?"

"Sometimes," I said on a laugh, and I went over to join them on the bed. "You know how I've been feeling kind of sick lately? Well, that's because it takes a lot of work to make a baby."

"You're making a whole human!"

"Isn't that so cool?" Kyle asked.

Sebastian nodded emphatically. "And I'm going to be a big brother!"

"You are," I said, squeezing his knee. "The best one ever."

"Can I hug the baby? And play with it?"

"Absolutely. And you'll help me and Mom protect it and care for it. Babies can't do much for a while, so it'll be a lot of work, but we'll make it fun, won't we?"

"Yeah," Sebastian said. But his smile faltered a little then, and his eyes met Kyle's. "Will the new baby call you dad, the way I call my dad?"

"Yes, buddy, they will."

My son swallowed. "Would it be okay if I call you dad, too?"

Kyle's eyes fluttered shut, and I watched him compose himself before he reached down and put both hands on Sebastian's shoulders. "You can call me anything you'd like to. And I want you to know that this doesn't change a thing between you and me. I..." He swallowed. "I love you. And you're always going to be my buddy. In fact, I'm going to need you now more than ever. I've never been a *dad* before," he said the word like it was crazy, and Sebastian giggled. "What the heck am I supposed to do? I need you to walk me through it all."

"But I've never been a big brother, either!"

"Well, then I guess we'll figure it all out together, won't we?"

Sebastian nodded, and then he looked up at me. "We're going to be a great team, aren't we, Mommy?"

"We sure are," I said, kissing his hair.

"So, do I have a baby brother or sister?"

"We don't know yet," Kyle said.

"Can I help name them?"

That question surprised me and Kyle both, and we laughed a little before I swept Sebastian's hair back. "Maybe."

"What would you name them?" Kyle probed, curious.

"Spider for a boy! Or Rockman!"

I rolled my lips together to stop my laugh.

"And for a girl?"

"Flower! Twinkles! Pinky!"

"Yeah, I think we might need to work on these a bit," Kyle said, pinching his side. "But you can definitely be a part of the conversation."

"Okay." Sebastian yawned, and we took that as a cue to get him ready for bed.

All of us were still excitedly chatting about the news as Sebastian brushed his teeth and washed his face. He asked me all kinds of questions, including ones I wasn't quite ready to answer like *how are babies made?* But I was happy he was inquisitive. This was a good sign for my little one. He only got curious about things he really cared about.

When he climbed into bed, Kyle tucked him in. We were just about to turn out the light and leave him be when I noticed him sniffle, his little eyes watering.

"Oh, honey. Are you okay?" I asked, sitting next to Kyle.

"Yeah," he assured us with a nod, but he sniffed again. "I'm just... *happy*."

Kyle smiled, swallowing as he smoothed Sebastian's hair back. "Because you're going to be a big brother?"

"Because we're finally going to be a real family."

Kyle and I shared a look before I leaned down to kiss his forehead. "Oh, sweetie. We're already a family. We always will be, no matter what."

"I was wondering something," Sebastian said.

"What's that?" I asked.

"I know you asked Mommy to marry you," he said to Kyle, all serious-like now. "But I think you should wait until the baby is here. I don't think it's fair for them to miss it."

Kyle looked at me with an arched brow, and I considered for a moment before nodding.

"You know what, that's a great idea," Kyle said. "Let's wait for the baby."

"But I can still be the ring tiger?"

I snorted. "The ring *bearer*," I corrected. "And of course."

Seemingly satisfied with all his questions answered — at least, for now — Sebastian settled deeper into his covers. He wished us both goodnight, and we slipped out of his room and into the hallway.

I looked at Kyle.

Kyle looked at me.

And then we crashed into an embrace.

Kyle held me tight to his chest as I melted into him, the weight of the news lifted off both of us. I knew we still had so much to come our way — pregnancy, birth, a wedding, a court trial. But somehow, it felt like the hardest of all of it was behind us. Somehow, it felt like it was all an easy breezy downhill skate from here.

"I love you," Kyle said, pulling back to frame my face. "So, *so* fucking much. Do you know that?"

"Mmm," I said, nuzzling his nose. "How much do you love me?"

He arched a brow. "What do you want?"

I bit my lip. "Macaroni and cheese."

"Baby, I'm about to make you the *best* fucking mac and cheese of your life," he promised, and he sealed it with a smack against my ass before he was toting me into the kitchen, kissing me every step of the way.

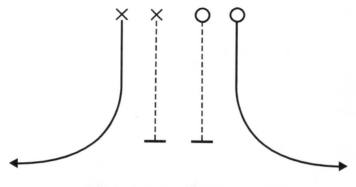

CHAPTER 40

December
Kyle

"**B**ro, you are so soft."

Leo shook his head at Braden — who was currently holding Clay and Giana's newborn with tears streaming down his face.

"Fuck you," Braden sputtered, swiping his face with the sleeve of his hoodie. He cradled the little bundle of blue like a football and stared down at that baby like his entire perspective on life had changed the moment he'd held him.

Honestly, it might not have been far from the truth.

I'd felt that shift several times over the last year. First, when I met Sebastian, when I saw part of Madelyn reflected in his eyes and his smile. That doubled as Sebastian and I got closer, tripled when I told him about his sibling on the way, and quadrupled when he asked if he could start calling me Dad.

And when Madelyn and I had gone to our twenty-week appointment together and seen our baby girl on the ultrasound screen... I was done for.

I didn't dare pick on Braden in that moment, because I knew I'd be even more of a mess the second the doctors placed my daughter in my arms.

"Don't act like you wouldn't bawl your eyes out if I was pregnant," Mary said to Leo, handing him a glass of champagne before taking a sip from hers.

"He bawled his eyes out when you moved out of The Pit," I combatted. "So, yeah, I'm with Mary on this one."

Mary smirked as Leo flicked me in the arm.

December in the Rockies was beautiful. Fresh snow covered the trees and mountains outside the windows of the massive cabin Clay and Giana had found for us, and a fire roared by the Christmas tree as the house hummed with the warmth of conversation.

We were all in the middle of busy seasons. The race for the playoffs was on, and every single one of our teams had a shot — whether we were top seeded or fighting for a wild card slot. But when Giana had Atlas, she'd insisted that we all find time to pause and get together in-between Christmas and New Year's.

We had a new family member, and Giana wanted to set the precedent now that when this happened, we *found* the time whether we had it to spare or not.

Some of us were only here for one night, but we were here.

By the fire, Giana, Madelyn, and Riley were curled up on the couch and chatting, all of them sipping hot chocolate.

Zeke, Holden, and Sebastian were on the floor in front of the girls with their eyes cast up toward the television. They were playing Donkey Kong on the ancient gaming system the cabin had provided.

Julep was in the kitchen washing dishes and smirking to herself as she watched her husband getting far too into the video game, and the rest of us were gathered around the dining table still half-littered with remnants of the dinner I cooked.

"So, how are you feeling, Dad? Other than exhausted," I added, clapping Clay on the shoulder.

His smile was tired but filled with joy I'd never seen as he stared at where Braden still held tight to Atlas — who was now wide-eyed and looking around while his little legs kicked, and soft baby gurgles left his mouth.

"I've never been this tired in my life," he admitted. "Not even during my first semester at NBU when I was trying to figure out how to juggle football and college classes." He shook his head on a smile. "But I've never been this happy, either."

"He's become quite a pro at changing diapers, I hear," Julep called from the sink.

Clay brushed his shoulder off. "I can have him changed in sixty seconds flat."

"Well, you get to show us your record-breaking skills in action," Braden said, wrinkling his nose a little as he passed Atlas to Clay. "Smells worse than the locker room."

"Impossible," Clay said, taking his son into his arms and tapping his nose. "You poop roses, don't you, Atlas?"

I chuckled, taking a swig of my beer as Clay disappeared down the hall to change Atlas. Mary and Leo started in on Braden, asking him when *he* was going to be bringing a special someone to these events, but my gaze had drifted to Madelyn.

She was mid-laugh, absentmindedly rubbing her belly as she listened to Giana, no doubt regaling her and Riley with the water birth story. Where Giana had found it spiritual and beautiful, Clay had been scared to death, his cell phone clutched in his hand should he have to call the ambulance.

But it had gone off without a hitch, their midwife leading the way, and now Atlas was already two weeks old.

Seeing Madelyn laugh made it easier for me to breathe. God only knew the last few months of our lives had been filled with the highest highs and the lowest lows. We had a baby girl on the way — healthy, as far as we could tell from the tests run so far. Sebastian couldn't wait to be a big brother. He was even helping me put the nursery together. And we had enough room at the house that Madelyn's parents had come to stay with us for a few weeks — both to help around the house for the holidays since I was still in full swing for the season, and to be there navigating the custody trial with us.

That had been the source of most of the lows.

If I thought I'd seen Marshall pissed off before, it was nothing compared to when he found out Madelyn was pregnant. He'd threatened to not only get full custody of Sebastian, but to find a way to rip our daughter from us as soon as she was born, too.

I didn't know what fucking planet he lived on where he thought either of those things were possible.

I wasn't the least bit afraid of that punk ass bitch, but Madelyn had years of being on the receiving end of his worst blows. She'd sobbed in my arms, so sure he had something up his sleeve to do everything he promised he would.

When we failed to find an agreement during mediation, I told our lawyer that I was done with Marshall's shit.

I wanted to go for the jugular now.

So, for the last month and a half, we'd endured grueling interviews with both our lawyer and Marshall's. His, of course, tried to pin outrageous accusations on us and trap us into admission — including saying that we abandoned Sebastian for a weekend of partying in Denver over the summer.

However smart his lawyers thought they were, ours was smarter. We were compiling text messages and photographs, and Madelyn was prepared to make a personal statement in front of the judge. We were going for full custody, for stepparent adoption, for everything.

As confident as I was that the judge would see Marshall for the monster he was, it still killed me to see all the stress of the trial wearing on my future wife. She was worried, and nothing I said or did would calm her. She wouldn't rest easy until we had a ruling, and she knew her son was safe with us.

We were just a few weeks from the court date now.

As if she could sense my thoughts, Madelyn blinked, frowning a bit before her eyes caught mine from across the room. I winked at her with a smile and mouthed *need anything*?

She smiled in return and shook her head, holding up her hot cocoa like it was all she needed in this moment. That, and a nod toward where Sebastian was clutching his gut in a fit of giggles after he missed jumping on an alligator as Donkey Kong, and now Holden was tickling him and saying he ruined the mission.

"Here, Dad. Practice time," Clay said, jolting me back to the group. I blinked and set my beer down just in time to have my arms filled with a warm baby boy, who was content for the moment, but looked ready to scream for Giana's boob any second now.

"Think we have a future safety on our hands here?" I asked Clay, adjusting Atlas until we both were comfortable. He was so fucking cute, it wasn't fair. Even this small and new to the world, I could see he had Clay's dimple and eyes. His hair mirrored Giana's — full and curly already.

"Psh, nah," Clay said, waving me off. "QB."

"He's going to need Uncle Holden to show him how to throw a spiral, then," Holden called from the living room. "God knows you won't be able to teach him."

"Got the arm of one of those blow-up noodle dudes in front of the car lots," Braden chimed in, and then he started waving his arms over head and bending in odd directions to illustrate as we all laughed.

"Har har," Clay said, unamused.

"Hey, Dad, can I FaceTime Nana to see Titan?" Sebastian asked, nearly colliding with my legs as he slid over to me in his socks.

I double-checked with Madelyn in a glance across the room, and once she nodded her approval, I told him he could. I dug into my pocket for my phone and offered it to him before letting him take over. He knew what to do, and he ran back to his bedroom with the phone already ringing.

"What about him?" Leo asked when Sebastian was gone. "Think he'll want to play?"

"Maybe. He's been soaking up everything about the game since I started teaching it to him. He mentioned wanting to try playing this summer, but it'll be up to Mama Bear over there," I said, nodding to Madelyn.

She was making her way toward us with three empty mugs in her hands. She dumped them into the sink before looping her arm through mine that wasn't holding a baby.

"We'll see," she said. "I'm not a huge fan of the whole concussion aspect."

"None of us are," Mary agreed.

"It's getting safer each year, with new tackling penalties and helmet advancements. But, yeah, it's always a risk," Leo admitted. "Then again, so are most things in life. I mean, that lizard the kid has could climb out of his cage and eat his face off."

"It's a gecko, not Godzilla," I deadpanned.

Leo threw his hands up. "I'm just saying."

Mary rolled her eyes, and then pulled Madelyn to the side. "Oh! I've been meaning to ask you, I want to add a little bit of you to my tattoo shop. I've got a pole for Julep, books for G, local art for Riley. I was thinking we could incorporate some of your writing, if you're open to that?"

"Oh, yes!" Giana called from the couch. "I love this idea!"

Madelyn was flushing a bright red as Mary tugged her away, and I savored that blush, that smile, that *woman* who was now such a crucial part of my life I knew I couldn't exist without her.

I hadn't heard from my parents since the phone call where I told them I knew what they did.

Not that I expected to, but I guessed a small part of me held onto hope that perhaps at least my mom would have shown up at my door to explain, to apologize, to try to be a part of my life.

As much as it hurt to lose them, to know that, likely, I'd never had much with them to begin with... it healed me to know that I had a family of my own now.

I had Madelyn.

I had Sebastian.

I had a daughter on the way.

I had my teammates and their girls, with a second generation growing already.

Madelyn and I weren't out of the woods yet. We still had many battles ahead of us — starting with Marshall and the impending court date. But one thing I knew for sure was that there wasn't a war we wouldn't fight together, side by side, no matter how dire the outlook.

And I believed with all my heart that we would win in the end.

Later that night, when the house was asleep, Madelyn climbed into bed and curled up to me with her teeth chattering.

"It's snowing again," she said, her voice filled with wonder.

Then, she pressed her ice-cold fucking feet between my calves.

"Jesus, woman!"

I tried to pull away, but she doubled down, tucking herself into my chest and wedging her feet into whatever warmth she could find. "I'm pregnant! You have to keep my feet warm."

"You sure are quick to pull that trump card nowadays," I teased her, but I was already wrapping her up tight and rubbing my legs together to give her feet a little friction.

She shook her shoulders and purred like a cat as I kissed her hair, smiling against it once she was settled.

"You looked pretty hot with a baby in your arms," she said.

"Oh?"

"Mm-hmm."

"Getting wet for me as a dad already?" I teased, and I snaked a hand between her thighs like I was going to investigate.

She swatted me away on a laugh, but then she was climbing on top of me, apparently not worried about being cold any longer. "Don't act like I haven't *always* been wet for you."

"You weren't earlier this summer," I argued, pinning her hips as I rolled my erection against her.

She groaned and fisted her hands in my shirt, leaning down to kiss me as she rocked her hips again.

"Just because I hated you didn't mean I didn't want you to rail me into next year."

"You would have killed me if I'd have tried."

"I guess we'll never know, will we?"

I swatted the side of her ass, and then we were laughing and kissing and shedding clothes despite the frigid temperature outside, and the way the heat in our room struggled to keep up.

Soon enough, we made our own fire in that bed, Madelyn fitting me to her entrance and sliding down as we both groaned and held onto each other for dear life. I'd never had a time I didn't thoroughly enjoy fucking this woman, but watching her ride in the moonlight reflecting off the snow outside with her belly swollen with my child unlocked a whole new kink for me.

I let her ride me long and slow until she found her release, and then I gently rolled her to the side so I could enter her from behind and let my hands explore her heavy breasts, her round stomach, her slender thighs and silky hair and wet, hot mouth.

I came with her name on my lips and a desperate, primal wish in my heart.

That she would be safe and healthy.

That Sebastian and our baby girl would be, too.

And that in a month's time, we'd take her ass cactus ex-husband out by the knees and watch him burn.

Marshall would never hurt her again. He'd never get the chance to hurt my son.

Those were vows I knew I would keep.

One thing I knew for sure was that he picked the wrong motherfucker to test.

And now, Papa Bear was going to rip him to shreds.

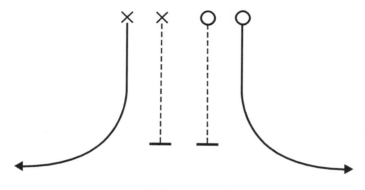

CHAPTER 41

January
Madelyn

I thought my hands would be shaking.

A million times, it seemed, I had played out what I imagined this day would be like in my mind. I had imagined everything from trembling fingers and a weak, shaky voice, to me breaking down into complete hysterics.

But instead, here I was, twenty-six weeks pregnant with a steady, calm heart and clear, focused mind.

I'd survived.

I'd survived hellish failures at mediation, and months and months of being civil with Marshall when he was nothing but nasty to me and Kyle both.

I'd survived Sebastian clinging to my legs not wanting to go to Marshall's house, battling with the love he felt for his father, but the obvious lack of love his father felt for me.

I'd survived holding my son and soothing him after he had to endure on-camera interviews with the judge, his Guardian Ad Litem, and both our attorneys to tell his side of the story, to make his voice heard in this case.

I'd survived the presentation of evidence — everything from text messages Marshall had sent over the years, to photographic proof of him laying his hands on me. Marshall's friends, who swore they were *my* friends, too, had testified against me. His colleagues had attested to his upstanding character. And though *my* parents had testified the opposite, I wasn't sure how that would hold. I couldn't read what the judge was thinking as he listened and watched and analyzed.

I'd survived the cross-examination from Marshall's lawyers, the way they'd tried to twist their questions and my response in tandem to get what they wanted out of me. Fortunately, the lawyer Kyle had hired for us had worked on this with me, and I was prepared.

I also had nothing to hide — unlike my ex-husband, who looked a bit sweaty in his seat as he watched me stand and address the court for the final time.

When I'd asked our lawyer for permission to read a personal statement to the judge, she'd originally nixed the idea. It wasn't traditional. It wasn't how things worked. She didn't want the judge to think we were going for hysterics or fanfare.

But this was the one thing I'd insisted on.

In order for me to read a statement, though, Marshall had to be allowed to read one of his own. He'd done so yesterday, pleading with the judge and making himself tear up and look innocent, like he'd been painted as a victim, when really he was just a good father battling against a selfish mother who wanted to take his child.

Kyle elected not to testify — mostly at my insistence. We both knew my fiancé and the father of the child in my belly wouldn't be exactly trustworthy as a source. He would be entirely biased, and anything he *did* say would likely be taken with a grain of salt.

I knew it had killed him to sit out. But he was still here, front row, right behind our lawyer, and holding hands with my mom, who held hands with my father, who looked ready to kill Marshall if the judge didn't make the right decision at the end of all of this.

Kyle's season had ended earlier than we'd wanted. Unfortunately, Seattle didn't make it to the playoffs. And as much as I hated that for him and for the team, I was selfishly thankful that he could be here for this, that he didn't have to rush off to the stadium for practice or fly away for a game.

I ran my steady, non-shaking hands over my round belly. Our daughter was the size of a head of lettuce now, growing stronger every week. Sebastian was having the hardest time waiting out of all of us. He couldn't bear another day without meeting his baby sister.

I closed my eyes and reached for her in that moment. I asked her to give me strength and poise and confidence. I asked her to help me finally bring this family peace.

"Your Honor," I began, pleased to hear my voice was as even and serene as I felt inside. "I want to thank you for allowing me to address you with this personal statement. I realize this is not traditional, but I hope you can understand that — as a woman who has been silent for many years — I found it of the utmost importance to stand before you today and give the final word on my account."

Judge Hall, an old, bald gentleman with warm brown skin, a black beard tinted with spots of white, and dark eyes that were somehow kind and severe at the same time, nodded in way of acknowledgement but did not give any other emotion away.

I'd watched him listen intently to Marshall the day before, and I hadn't been able to read him then, either. This man had heard both of our stories. He'd interviewed my son. Could he see the truth, or was he blinded by Marshall's squeaky-clean professional record and reputation the way so many others were?

"On my phone, there are hundreds and hundreds of photographs of my son," I said, a genuine smile finding my lips. "There are pictures of him wrapped as a newborn in my arms as I nursed him while running on little to no sleep. There are videos of him using the couch to help himself stand, to navigate walking on his tiny legs for the first time. There are photos of his first day of daycare, his first day of pre-school, his first day of kindergarten, his first lost tooth."

I swallowed, my smile slipping.

"In-between those beautiful memories are photos with a more haunting story to tell. Pictures of bruises on my arms, of the skin above my eye split and angry and bleeding, of me on my bathroom floor sobbing and rocking in pain from being kicked in the stomach — an injury no one could see, but that I felt for weeks."

I didn't have to turn around to know that Kyle was likely squeezing my mother's hand off as he listened to this, that my mother was likely straining to hold *both* men at her sides back from tackling the man I was accusing of doing these things to me.

I also thought I heard a scuffle of some sort from where Marshall sat with his attorneys, like he was ready to defend himself, and they had to remind him to be quiet.

"Now, I know what you must be thinking," I added quickly. "Why didn't I bring these photos to the police? Why didn't I report my husband, who then became my ex-husband? Why did I sit in silence for so long?

"It may seem stupid to you. It may seem calculative. I'm sure there are many names one might think to call me — weak, liar, bitter, scorned. But the truth, Your Honor, is that as much as it pains me to admit it... I was just scared."

I looked down at the worn carpet floor for only a moment before I lifted my chin again, willing myself not to cry as I met the judge's gaze.

"I was scared of what would happen to me if I told anyone. I was afraid of not being believed. I was afraid of being punished even worse for attempting to show my abuse. And most of all, I was terrified of losing my son, my *life*."

I swallowed.

"There are some things you truly cannot understand until you are experiencing them, storms that you'll never fully feel until you are being wind-whipped and pelted with rain and holding onto whatever grounding force you can find with dear life. There were times I thought about speaking up, but every time that thought passed, my ex-husband would remind me in the very convincing way he always did that I would be fighting an uphill battle, that no one would believe that a kind, caring veterinarian would ever do such a thing.

"And it may seem silly to someone like you, Your Honor, who has likely never doubted himself a day in his life. Who has had faith in his strength and standing and position for many decades. But for a single mother without a steady job, reputable education, or anyone other than her own parents to back her — let me tell you, the story my ex-husband painted was a very believable one. And it was one I couldn't risk."

I heard my mom sniffle from the bench behind me, but I kept my gaze focused, the words coming easier now.

"For many years, I felt that I could handle this. I truly felt I was strong enough to deal with the hits, the bruises, the abuse."

"This is bullshit!"

Every head snapped to Marshall, to where his attorney was whisper-shouting for him to be quiet and sit down.

"Mr. Hearst, I will have order in this courtroom," Judge Hall said sternly. "This will be your only warning."

He let that sink in for a long moment before he nodded for me to continue.

I cleared my throat. "I felt this way because, as I'm sure you can imagine, I will do *anything* for my son. He loves his father. And I believed that, though I suffered at Marshall's hands, Sebastian never would." I paused. "Until recently."

I heard scuffling from my left, no doubt Marshall trying to stand and argue his case again before I finished speaking. I assumed his lawyers settled him, though. The judge arched a brow in that direction before slowly dragging his gaze back to me.

"Your Honor, my son has become more and more reluctant to visit his father in the last several months. As he grows older, he can sense things he couldn't as a young child. He has seen the marks left on me. He notices the way I stiffen when I have to meet with his father."

"It's because this bitch brainwashes him!" Marshall cried out, much to the dismay of his legal team. "And you act so innocent. I only put you in your place when you need it."

"Mr. Hearst, that is *enough*," Judge Hall said, glaring down at my ex-husband. "If I hear one more peep from you, I'll have you thrown out of my courtroom."

I didn't know how Kyle was still sitting after that remark. Again, I wondered if my mom was using all her strength to keep him and my father seated.

Judge Hall turned his attention back to me. "Please continue, Miss Hearst."

Hearst.

I hated that I was still tied to him.

But that would change soon.

With a steady breath, I started again. "My son can feel it, Your Honor — all of it. And the truth is, the older he gets, the *bigger* he gets, and the more he starts to think for himself — the less confidence I have that it will only be me who has to handle his father's rage. And I will tell you, in all honesty, that I will not stand for that man putting a single finger on our son. The moment it happens, the *first* time I hear that he hurt Sebastian? Well, it would be the last. And I would be appearing here in a very different kind of trial."

The judge's eyebrows raised in warning over his glasses, and he jotted something down on his notebook in front of him. I assumed he was recording that should I ever be back here on trial for murder, which I accepted — though I was fairly certain our lawyer was likely pinching the bridge of her brow and cursing me for that little slip.

"It was never my intention to take our son from Marshall," I continued. "Not until he started showing me that Sebastian wasn't safe with him. His need to control me has festered into an inescapable wound, one that has taken over him completely now that he sees that I am happy and moving on with my life. Marshall simply cannot handle that, he cannot accept that he has lost his control over me, that I am no longer scared, that he no longer dictates what I do and do not do with my life.

"Marshall wants you to believe that I am an unfit mother, that — should Kyle Robbins decide to leave me — I would be incapable of caring for my children. Well, to those accusations, I will let the evidence and character statements from today serve as proof that that is not the case. I have shown that I will work long, hard hours doing whatever it takes to make ends meet. I have illustrated that nothing means more to me in this *world* than the little boy you interviewed in your chambers, than the little girl growing inside me right at this moment."

Though I willed myself not to, it was impossible not to get emotional with that. My eyes watered, and I sniffed back the tears and let them blur my vision as I stared up at the judge.

"Your Honor, if there is one thing I am sure of in this world, it's that I am a great mother. I was *meant* to be a mother. I know, with my entire heart, that Sebastian is safest with me. That with me and with Kyle and with his baby sister who will arrive later this year, he will not just survive, but thrive. He will love and laugh and learn. He will be surrounded by people who care for him, and who will stop at nothing to see him succeed.

"So, I am asking you to see that truth with me. I am asking you to think of Sebastian and his future as you make your decision. I am asking you to keep this little boy with me, and with my fiancé, and with the home where he feels safe and warm and protected. I am asking you to believe me, even though I was too afraid to speak up before, even though I have been weak in the past. I hope you see that now, I am strong. I am resilient. And if sole custody is to be bestowed to only one parent, it should — without question — be to me, his mother. Thank you."

I kept my head down as I returned to my seat. Our lawyer squeezed my wrist under the table to let me know I'd done well. I turned and found Kyle's eyes shining with tears, the evidence of two of them that had fallen marring each cheek. My mother was drying her own tears. My father was beaming with pride.

"I love you," Kyle mouthed.

"I love you, too," I mouthed back.

My next breath felt cleaner somehow, even though no decisions were made. We sat through the closing statements from our lawyers. Marshall's kept on with the same stories of why I was an unfit mother. I had to bite back an actual laugh when they tried, again, to use the one time I'd used recreational marijuana with Marshall. It was before I was even pregnant, and it was *weed,* for fuck's sake.

When we finished, I expected the judge to call a recess. Our lawyer had warned us it could be a few hours or even a few weeks.

Instead, Judge Hall took his glasses off, rubbed his eyes, slipped them back on with a heavy sigh and spoke.

"Well, I have to say, I'm always disappointed when matters of custody cannot be resolved in mediation. By the time you make it in front of me, there is a lot of animosity and cruelty between people who used to love each other, who once made vows to one another and agreed to make a life. But in this case," he added with a shake of his head. "I believe there has been cruelty and animosity long before this custody battle."

The judge grew silent for a moment, thinking over his words before his eyes met mine.

"Ms. Hearst, I want to thank you for sharing your story with us over the last two days."

Every time I heard that name, it had me counting down the days to when I would change it, to when I would take Robbins as my surname and leave this part of my life firmly in the past.

"I can't imagine how difficult it was for you. And as I'm not one to beat around the bush or get flowery with my words, I just want to look you in the eye right here and now and tell you one thing." Judge Hall took off his glasses and leaned forward. "I believe you."

My nostrils flared, tears pricking my eyes and flowing over my cheek bones before I could stop them. I didn't wipe them away. I didn't cry harder. I just blinked and let those silent tears fall as my heart raced and my next breath racked out of me in a shudder.

I nodded, a silent thank you, a quiet mercy.

"And Mr. Hearst," he said, sliding his specs back into place. He looked down at his notes before shaking his head and lifting his gaze to my ex. "Sir, all I can say is *shame on you*."

I let myself glance at Marshall, let myself take one moment to see his jaw tightening, his face turning a bright red before I drew my attention back to the judge.

"I am very familiar with men like you. I know how you firmly believe your education and profession protect you. I know how you hide behind a public persona when you are nothing short of a monster at home. The fact that you came to this court and tried to convince me that it is, in fact, your ex-wife who is unfit for parenting is quite comical, and in the same breath, absolutely despicable. It is my belief that every man and woman have it within themselves to make changes for the good, but I can tell that you have a long road ahead of you if that is to be your story."

The judge looked down at his papers again, shaking his head before addressing us both.

"In my twenty-two years of serving as a judge, I have never ruled in court during a case such as this. I have always taken at least two weeks to deliberate before coming to my decision." He shook his head, glancing at his notes before his eyes were on the courtroom again. "But, with the evidence presented before me, along with the uncontrollable outbursts from the plaintiff that I witnessed myself, I have made my decision. And I cannot, in good conscience, wait to pass my judgment."

He caught my gaze, a soft smile on his lips before his eyes slid to Marshall. He gave him what I could only describe as the look of a disappointed father before he sat a little straighter in his chair.

"I hereby grant full custody of Sebastian Calvin Hearst to his mother, Madelyn James Hearst," Judge Hall said. "Effective immediately."

Marshall cursed and kicked a chair, which had the judge beating his gavel as my heart worked overtime, all the adrenaline of the day coursing through me.

"I am also ruling that your visitation with your son will be supervised, Mr. Hearst, until you have completed two-hundred-and-fifty hours of anger management courses and have successfully attended weekly AA meetings for one year. Now, I take no pleasure in keeping a father from his son, but I will have you know that I will never stand to put a child's safety in jeopardy. You prove to me that you can be the man I think you have inside you, and you will have your visitation rights invoked. You will not harm that young boy, Mr. Hearst. This is your chance to turn things around for you and for your family. I truly hope you take it. But believe me when I say that should you not, I have no problem doubling down."

"Fuck this and fuck you," Marshall spat to the horror of the entire courtroom.

His lawyers tried without any luck to get him to calm down, grappling at his suit sleeves to no avail.

"If I'm going to have my visitation supervised, I don't even want it."

My heart thumped hard in the silence that followed that statement.

"Be very careful with your actions right now, Mr. Hearst," Judge Hall warned, his patience growing thin.

"I shouldn't have to put up with all this." Marshall turned to where Kyle sat now, glaring. "If you want the kid so badly, you can have him."

"I've had enough," Judge Hall said, his voice booming. "Consider that verbal statement your surrender of your rights as Sebastian's father, Mr. Hearst. I will accept the defendant's request for stepparent adoption."

Marshall flopped back down into his chair with a sneer and a wave of his hand like he couldn't care less.

The rest of the words blurred in my mind, as if my soul had floated up to the top of the courtroom and I was watching everything from above. It was all muted, distorted, distant.

My husband's temper had caught up to him. He'd shown his ass in court like I never thought possible. Gone was his restraint, his fake smile and professional demeanor.

In the blink of an eye, he'd shown his true colors to every person in this room.

The rest of it happened like an out-of-body experience. Eventually, I was being wrapped in a hug by my parents. Kyle was kissing me and taking me by the hand as we walked out of the courtroom, the courthouse, and into the drizzling, cool rain.

Thankfully, due mostly to Giana's gentle maneuvering of the media, there were no cameras waiting for us. She had been a godsend, communicating our desperate plea for privacy during this time, and working some sort of magic to where the press was actually respecting that.

I didn't know how long it was before we were in the car, before we were picking Sebastian up from Braden's condo, before we were sitting at Sebastian's favorite pizza place and explaining everything to him.

There was laughter. There was sadness. There were so many mixed emotions I couldn't name them all.

When we finally made it home, my mom and dad hugged me tight and implored me to get some rest before they made their way to our guest suite out back. I thought I thanked them for coming. I hoped I conveyed how much it meant to me that they were there, that they had been with me and with Kyle and with their grandson.

I couldn't be sure.

It was all surreal, even when Kyle and I climbed into Sebastian's bed on either side of him and answered every question he had for us. We knew he'd go through many emotions after tonight, and we assured him we'd be there for all of it. But tonight, he cuddled us and told us he loved us, and most of his questions were about his baby sister. He wanted to know when she was coming, even though we'd told him several times. He wanted to know how big she was now. He wanted to know what color we would paint her room. He wanted to know if he could help pick out her first toys. He wanted to know what we'd name her.

I had a feeling it was him fixating on something happy to avoid the truth of the day — that, at least for now, he would no longer have Marshall in his life.

If the stepparent adoption really did go through, that would be true forever. Because I knew once Kyle made Sebastian his, he would keep him from my monstrous ex at all costs.

I was content to let my son ride out the emotions in his own time. I promised him I'd be there for him no matter what. Kyle promised the same. In fact, Kyle even asked Sebastian if he'd like to talk to someone who wasn't us about everything that had gone on. He explained it would be a way to talk about everything without fear of hurting anyone's feelings.

At first, Sebastian had shaken his head. But then, he'd shrugged and said he didn't know, that maybe he would like that.

I knew I'd be looking into a therapist first thing in the morning.

I wanted him to survive this and come out stronger on the other side. I wanted him to be able to communicate everything he felt, to have space for the anger and the sadness and the resentment, and anything else he might feel.

By the time Sebastian was asleep, Kyle and I were bleary-eyed and walking like zombies into the living room. Kyle pulled my feet into his lap and massaged them as I moaned and sank into the cushions.

"You were amazing today," he said.

I blew out a breath. "I don't feel amazing."

"It's not easy," Kyle said, and I knew he understood. "But... I wish my mom would have had the strength you do. I wish she would have saved me from..."

His voice drifted, and I sat up, my brows inching together.

God.

I hadn't even thought of this piece of it.

Of course, it would hit close to home for Kyle. Of course, he would see himself in Sebastian, see the possible future of what Bas could have faced had I not stepped in, had we not fought for him.

"Kyle," I breathed, reaching out for his hand.

He slid his palm over mine, squeezing once and lifting my knuckles to his mouth for a kiss before he dropped my hand and went back to massaging me.

"I know it wasn't easy, and I know there will be many other battles we have to fight. Who knows what will happen in a year or two. We may have a time where Marshall has partial custody again, or at the very least, visitation. The stepparent adoption may not go through." Kyle shrugged. "But one thing I do know is that you are the most incredible woman I have ever met in my life, Madelyn." His blue eyes held mine steady. "What you did today, what you do for this family *every* day..." He shook his head. "You're amazing. And I love you. And I'm so thankful for you, I want to write a fucking poem or something."

I laughed at that. "Oh, God, please don't. I remember your notes from high school. You couldn't even spell restaurant."

"Hey, to be fair, that's a really fucking hard word to spell."

We both smiled, a comfortable silence slipping between us.

"How are you feeling?" he asked, nodding toward my swollen belly.

"Okay, actually," I said. "A little tired. My back hurts. But otherwise, I'm okay."

"Hungry?"

"Always."

He smirked, helping me stand and pulling me into the kitchen. He sat me at the island and poured a tall glass of my favorite sparkling grape juice, and then proceeded to make me the best grilled cheese of my life.

I was halfway through it when he leaned over the island with a mischievous grin. "So, energy has been feeling decent lately?"

"If you're asking if I want to ride you, good sir, the answer is *absofuckinglutely*," I said around a mouthful of cheese. "But first, I'm going to finish every bite of this and lick the plate clean."

Kyle chuckled. "Not what I was getting at, but very happy to know where this evening is headed." His eyes were shining in the low light of the kitchen. "I asked because I have a surprise."

"A surprise?" I asked, again, around a mouthful of food. Apparently, I didn't have it in me to put this sandwich down.

"Your parents are staying for another ten days."

I blinked. "Uh... they are?"

"They are. And I have a suitcase half-packed for you in our bedroom, but you'll need to go through it and add anything you might want that I've forgotten. I'm phenomenal at many things," he added with a salacious grin. "But packing, admittedly, is not one of them."

I chewed on the last bite of my sandwich for a long time, washing it down with a gulp of grape juice before I arched a brow at him. "Okay, and what exactly am I packing for?"

"A baby moon."

"A *what*?"

Kyle rounded the island, sliding his hands over my belly before they trailed up to frame my face. *God*, I loved when he held me like that, when his hands cradled my neck, and his thumbs tilted my chin up, when his eyes stared deep into mine.

"I want to spoil you, Madelyn," he said. "I have a pretty good hunch your first pregnancy wasn't exactly rainbows and roses. And so far, this one hasn't been much better. I had the season. We had the court case. We moved to a new house, moved Sebastian to a new school... it's been one thing after another."

He kissed my forehead, holding his lips there a long time before his gaze found mine again.

"And I want a vacation with you. You, and me. Just the two of us. I want to buy you the most expensive massages I can afford, and see your beautiful body relaxing in an infinity pool overlooking the ocean, and make love to you in a bed meant for kings and queens."

"Okay, you have my attention."

He smirked. "Everything happened so fast for us. We never really even got *one* real, traditional date. Granted, nothing has ever been traditional with us —

and you know what, I love that. I fucking *love* that our story is ours and ours alone. But," he added, tapping my nose. "This is the last chance we have to take a moment for ourselves before we become a family of four. And while I can't fucking *wait* for that day, there's nothing I'd love more than to whisk you away to a tropical island and spoil you rotten for a week before we slip into our new life."

"Damn it, Kyle," I cursed, swiping at the tears sliding down my cheeks. "I'm too hormonal for this shit."

He smiled against my lips before kissing me long and slow, his hands massaging my neck and holding me to him.

"Is that a yes?" he asked.

"It's a *hell yes*," I said on a laugh. "But... when do we leave?"

"Well, at first, I wanted to leave in the morning," he said. "But then I thought about it, and I think we should spend a few days with Sebastian first. We can take off on Saturday?"

I shook my head, pulling him in for a kiss and wrapping my arms around his neck. "God, I love you. Do you know that?"

"I do, but I'm very content to let you show me just how much, if you'd really like to," he said with a grin, and then I was in his arms, and his lips were devouring me on the way back to our bedroom.

Our bedroom.

Our home.

Our life.

Finally, the storm was settling, the waters calming, the sun peeking through the gray clouds in the distance.

With the trial out of the way, I saw nothing but pure gold and possibility.

I saw a luxurious week away with my soon-to-be husband.

I saw a pregnancy so unlike the first one I had, one where I was safe and cared for and loved.

I saw the birth of our daughter, the growth of our family.

I saw our wedding.

Each vision filled my heart with more joy than it knew how to hold, and I was nearly bursting with it when Kyle laid me down in the cool sheets and took his time stripping every article of clothing from my body.

He worshipped me like I was a goddess, like every inch of my skin must be touched and kissed and praised before he dared to slide inside me.

All the hell I'd been through, it was worth it.

Because I had firmly landed in heaven.

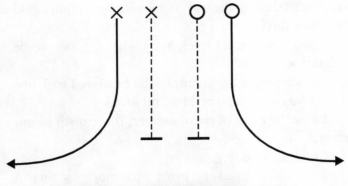

CHAPTER 42

Kyle

There was something about seeing Madelyn in that hammock that put me in a wild state of being.

My eyes had laid upon many attractive women, but none so gorgeous as Madelyn James — because *fuck* if I was ever going to use that man's last name on her again — right here, right now, in this moment.

Her bright copper hair was pulled up into a high ponytail, the edges of it sweaty and greasy from sunscreen. Those strands stuck to her forehead and neck in little swirls of metallic orange. I was particularly drawn to one strand that was clinging to her plump, pink bottom lip. Her skin was freshly bronzed and sporting new freckles — ones I took a lot of pleasure in peppering with welcome kisses each evening when we climbed into bed.

She wore an oversized pair of sunglasses and a black bikini, the triangle top of which struggled to contain her breasts, and the skimpy bottom of which was barely visible under her swollen belly.

And *that* was what turned me on the most.

How fucking cliché, I know.

I'd read it in a dozen baby books already, how expecting fathers have their own hormones running rampant — mostly when they looked at their partners and saw evidence that they'd impregnated them. It was so caveman, so fucking *brute-like* to think that I was being run by an archaic, natural instinct.

But fuck... I really was.

There was nothing sexier than Madelyn growing rounder each day. Any time she wore something tight-fitting or took her clothes off, I had to bite my knuckles and groan at the sight. I always made sure she was open to touching before I attempted — because I know if anyone tried to touch *me* while I was two seconds away from vomiting, I'd fucking deck them.

But the second trimester had been kinder to us, and now we were just entering the third, and Madelyn seemed to want my touches as much as I wanted to give them to her.

I relished every rub of her belly, every little kick I felt against my palm, every smile that graced Madelyn's beautiful face when she saw *me* reacting to our daughter inside her.

I massaged her feet, her legs, her back, her neck — anything I could do to bring her relief. I even watched a fucking YouTube video on how to relieve some of the pressure from the baby. So, my new favorite thing was walking up behind Madelyn and wrapping my hands under her belly. I'd lift and hold the baby, the weight, while Madelyn moaned and sank into me like it was the best gift in the world.

This woman... this goddamn goddess. She was growing a human inside her, all while continuing to care for me, for Sebastian, for our home, for our *lives*.

She was fucking incredible.

I watched her from where I was situating a tray of fruit inside our private, over-the-water villa. The turquoise water of the Maldives spread out before us, making the sight of my pregnant, soon-to-be wife that much more picturesque. She had a notebook balanced on her knees, a pen scribbling lazily over the pages as she tapped her foot to the soft reggae music playing from the speaker I'd put out for her this morning.

This trip was for her.

In fact, I was pretty sure that sometime in the last several months, I'd silently decided that *everything* in my life was for her.

I'd pampered her with massages and facials and sound baths on this trip. I'd made sure she had any and all food she wanted — usually more at my insistence than hers. I'd waited on her as if I worked at this luxury fucking resort, and I didn't care if it was the kind of behavior that would make my teammates call me a simp and rag on me endlessly.

She was literally carrying my daughter, making a human's organs and body, creating a life.

It blew my fucking mind.

And, let's be honest, I wasn't immune to that part of a man who looked at his woman and thought *fuck yeah, I put a baby in her*.

Once the tray of fruit looked like something out of a goddamn food magazine, I carried it out onto our private wooden deck on one hand held high above my head, the other wrapped behind my back as if I were a butler.

"Madam, your afternoon snack," I said, waving my free hand in a flourish before bowing and presenting the tray to her.

Madelyn smirked and sat up as much as she could in the sunken hammock, the netted one hanging just off the side of the wooden deck and over the water. She shut her notebook and slid the pen into the spiral that bound it as I sat the tray on the edge of the dock closest to her. I offered to take the notebook from her, and only once it was safely placed did I grab a chunk of pineapple and tumble into the hammock with her.

She giggled as I rolled down like a kid going down a hill, and I landed perfectly on my elbow, facing her, and waggled my brows as I offered her the piece of pineapple right at the edge of her pretty pink lips.

She shook her head and slid her sunglasses up so I could see her roll her eyes, but then she opened like a good girl, eating the pineapple and wiping the juice from the corner of her mouth.

Instantly, she moaned.

"Good?" I teased.

"Why is fruit so amazing when you're pregnant?" She shook her head, motioning to the tray for another bite. I rolled enough to grab a strawberry and a couple slices of kiwi for her, and thoroughly enjoyed feeding her each one and hearing the resulting groans of ecstasy.

"Why is fruit so sexy when a pregnant woman is eating it?" I countered.

She swatted me with a grin, sliding her glasses back down and resting against the hammock. "It's such a beautiful day."

"I checked my weather app. It's fifty-one and raining in Seattle."

"Suckers."

I smirked, pulling her onto my chest despite her protests that she was gross and sweaty. As if I cared.

"I have a question," I said after a moment.

"Shocking."

I tickled her ribs until she was thrashing, and only once she settled into my arms again did I continue.

"What do you want from life in the next five, ten, twenty years?"

"Wow," she said, sitting up on her elbow to face me. She struggled a bit with the movement in the hammock and her giant belly. I reached out to rub a palm over said belly as she got comfortable. "We're getting heavy today."

"I mean it. Everything between us happened at lightning fucking speed. We skipped over all the shit we would have gone through if we'd dated in the traditional sense, if we'd spent a year or two going to restaurants and movies and on trips before we moved in together and got married."

She frowned. "Does it make you sad that we missed all that?"

"Not even a little bit," I said instantly. "I fucking *love* this, our story, the shit we've been through." I tugged at the string of her bikini bottom, not untying it, but plucking it away from her skin playfully. "I wouldn't change a thing. I love you. I love *us*."

"Cornball."

"You love it."

She smiled, no denial.

"I know a lot about your past because I was there. We've caught up on what happened since then — what you've been through, what I've been through. I know there will be moments when we're just hanging out and a little story will come up and you'll tell me about a drunk night out with your friends, or a funny story when Sebastian was little. And I'll tell you about a wild night out with the team, or the time I almost got expelled because I tried to sleep with my professor to get a better grade."

Her eyebrows shot into her hairline at that. "Excuse me?"

I waved her off. "Not important."

"You are such a menace," she said on a laugh, shoving me away playfully.

But she pulled me right back into her, as if to say silently to that professor *he's mine now, bitch.*

"I want to know what you want from here on out," I repeated, bringing us back to the question at hand. "Tell me your dreams, Madelyn."

She sighed, watching where her finger was drawing circles on my chest. "Well, first and foremost, I want to deliver a healthy baby girl."

I smiled, running my palm over her stomach. "Our little Raven."

"We are *not* naming our daughter after your favorite childhood football team."

"Come on!" I protested. "Raven is adorable. No one will know but us."

"And everyone you brag to."

"Fine," I conceded, rubbing her belly again. "Our little Raylyn."

Madelyn flattened her lips. "Because Ray Lewis?"

"No one would *know.*"

Apparently done with my antics, Madelyn ignored that suggestion altogether and continued answering my question. "After our healthy baby girl — who will not be named either of those things — is born, then... I'm not sure." She shrugged. "I mean, I would love to be home with her and Sebastian for at least a year or two, I think."

"You would?"

She nodded, her cheeks tingeing pink. "Is that old fashioned?"

"Not at all." I held up a pointed finger. "Feminism celebrates the woman's *choice*. If this is what you *want*, then fuck yeah, let's do it. But I also want you to know that if it's *not* what you want, we can hire help. *I* can help — especially in the offseason. We can figure it out."

"Oh, you're definitely helping. Better get diaper duty lessons from Clay."

"Psh, *lessons*?" I sucked my teeth. "He'll need lessons from *me*. I'll be Diaper Dad and Bath Time Dad and Swaddling Dad, too."

Madelyn smiled. "I have no doubts. What about you? What do you see in the future?"

"Nuh-uh," I argued. "This is about *you*. We all fucking know my plan. Play football and be the best for as many years as my body lets me. And use my shark of an agent to get me a mountain of cash for us to live on forever."

I pecked her with a kiss then, just because I couldn't stand *not* to.

"What's next for you? After baby girl is here and you've had your fill of chasing a toddler and wrangling an elementary school kid."

Madelyn sighed again, biting her bottom lip. "Well... don't laugh, but... I've been writing."

"I know," I said instantly. "I see you with that notebook, with your laptop at home. Why would I laugh at that?"

"I've been writing a book."

I blinked, surprised but in the best way. "Damn. You have? What about?"

She cringed like she was embarrassed. "About... life. My life. What happened to us, to *me*. Marshall and that whole ordeal. Surviving. Figuring things out as a single mom. Finding the road back to loving myself, to letting someone else love me," she added, bowing her head a bit and looking at me through her lashes. "I doubt anyone will want to read it but—"

"Fuck you," I said. "*I* want to read it. I'll be first in line. I want the unedited copy. I want to read it *now*."

"You don't count."

"That's not nice."

"I just mean even if this is just for me, I'm really enjoying it. So, speaking big dreams out loud... maybe one day I'll write more. Maybe one day I'll publish."

"You better. Do you realize how many women you could help feel seen with that book alone?" I shook my head. "Madelyn, I *wish* my mom had someone like you in her life when she was younger. Fuck, I wish she had that *now*. Sometimes all it takes is one person, one book or movie or story from a stranger to make the light switch turn on in someone's head who has been stumbling in the dark their whole life."

"You really think so?"

"I know so. I love this plan," I told her earnestly, pulling her hands to my lips. "And *fuck*, I love you."

"You've said that already. Quite a few times just today, actually."

"And I'll say it again. I love you, I love you, I love you," I repeated, kissing her neck in-between each word as she giggled and playfully shoved at me in a way that told me she didn't want me to stop at all.

"Hmm... maybe the words don't make sense to me anymore since I've heard them so many times," she said, dragging her nail down my chest. "Maybe you could *show* me."

Even through her sunglasses, I knew the look she had in her eyes. I knew because my body reacted without even seeing the heated gaze.

"Oh, with *pleasure*, fiancée," I said, already making quick work of the string tie at her hip.

"What are you going to do when I'm your wife?"

I groaned, kissing her hard and rolling my erection into her. "Probably put another baby in you."

"Um, hard pass."

"You say that now..."

She laughed, but the sound died as I slid my hand between her thighs, moaning and sucking the lobe of her ear between my teeth at the same time.

"Maybe we should go inside," she said breathlessly, but she was already rolling against my touch, swollen and wet and ready. She'd been like this so much of the pregnancy — as eager to feel me inside her as I was to be there.

"Nah," I said, kissing behind her ear. "I got the most private villa for a reason."

"There are boats out there," she pointed out.

"Too far to see anything."

"What if they have binoculars?"

"Then let them watch."

Another sweet laugh left her lips before I was stripping the scraps of fabric she had on and flinging them on the dock. I basked in the view of her bare and spread out on that netted hammock, the bright, aqua blue water contrasting against her bronze skin like the most beautiful tropical painting.

"Gorgeous," I whispered, hands roaming, lips tracking lines from collarbone to collarbone, from shoulder to ear, from breast to breast, and navel to hip bone until I was holding her thighs on my shoulders. I didn't even care that my back was arching at a strange angle in the oversized hammock. I wanted her just like this. I needed her writhing in this netting and calling out my name loud enough for the next villa to hear.

She gasped when I took my first taste, fingers curling in the net as she rolled to meet the next lashing of my tongue. I knew exactly what to do now to get her to fall apart, but I took my time, enjoying every kiss and tease along the way.

Before long, her hands were in my hair, guiding me and urging me to give her what she really needed. My lips enclosed her clit, and I slipped one finger inside her, then another, curling them in tandem with the sucking rhythm of my mouth.

Usually, I would have one hand up massaging her breast, too. I'd roll and twist her nipple the way I knew she loved. But with her belly the size it was now, that wasn't an option, so I doubled down on my efforts, tasting her like it was my full-time job, and the reason I got a healthy signing bonus.

She came quietly, whimpering and shaking and fighting back the cries I knew she wanted to let go as her legs trembled around me. I'd no sooner grinned and ran my mouth along the inside of her thigh, something I loved to do every time after I went down on her so she could feel the climax I coaxed from her, before she was grabbing me by the arms and pulling me up to kiss her.

Her moan into my mouth was urgent and needy, like tasting herself on me set her on fire and she was ready for another round. Then, she was struggling and laughing a little at herself as she maneuvered until her hands were on the dock, her knees still in the netting, her sunglasses thrown somewhere, and her pretty eyes cast over her shoulder at me.

I laid on my back and enjoyed that glorious view as I unfastened my swim trunks and slid them down to my knees, ankles, and kicked them to the side. I still didn't move when they were gone, other than to fist myself and roll my hand over my shaft with a groan as I took in Madelyn's beautiful, perfect fucking body.

"Are you going to fuck *me* with that, or am I just meant to stay like this until you finish?" she teased, arching a brow.

"So impatient."

"Always have been when it comes to you."

Carefully, I pushed myself up and ambled over to her, both of us laughing as we fought to steady ourselves and find balance. When I finally had her hips in my hands, I roamed her slick body again, groaning and smacking the side of her ass before I positioned myself at her entrance.

This was her new favorite position. For a while, it was her on top. Then, it was on her side, me spooning her in the early morning. But lately, she'd wanted me just like this.

She gasped and moaned as I edged my way in, and I knew she felt me deep like this because I felt *her* in the deepest, tightest way, too. Once I was all the way fitted inside, we both took a savoring breath, me kissing her shoulder and her leaning her head back to meet me.

Slowly, I began to move, flexing in and out and wishing I didn't have to use my hands to hold us steady so I could grab her breasts and pull her against me and fuck her with abandon.

But there was something even hotter about the restraint, about having to take my time, hold myself up, hold *her* up and work her to another orgasm all at the same time. Every flex inside her was filled with sensation, my muscles working overtime as blood worked its way from each corner of my body right between my thighs.

"Fuck, Mads," I croaked, kissing the back of her neck. "Feels so fucking good."

"Coming," she breathed back at me, and then in a feat that surprised me, she rested her weight on one hand so the other could dive between her legs.

I focused on making sure she was safe and supported as she worked out her second climax, and this time, she didn't hold back. She moaned and screamed and called out my name just the way I'd wanted.

Those sounds alone sent me barreling.

I wrapped one arm around her lower waist, below her belly, and held her to me as I pumped and flexed and curled, over and over, deeper and deeper until power and numbness consumed me in equal measure.

I came with a groan and her name on my lips, with the sun shining bright above us, with the water lapping at the wood of our villa.

With her burrowing deep into my heart, my soul.

With a future so bright and beautiful it nearly made this grown fucking man sob.

Eventually, when we both had calmed, I helped Madelyn out of the hammock and carried her into our villa, into the rain shower, setting her down gently before running the water the perfectly warm temperature.

I washed her hair and her body before I did the same to mine, and then I fed her again and tucked her into our plush bed for a nap before we'd go to dinner.

While she slept, I lay beside her, watching her dream, marveling at how my entire world had shifted since she'd swung back into my life, and wondering what the fuck I ever did before her.

Soon, I would be her husband.

Soon, I would be a *dad*.

No.

I already was.

Sebastian was as much mine as he was Madelyn's, even if not by blood. Even if, somehow, the adoption never went through. Even if we had to deal with that motherfucker ex-husband of Madelyn's for the rest of our lives.

I never understood why people cared so much about their families. When I was in college, I grimaced at pro football players who had their wives and kids at every game. It was gross to me. And idiotic. All that pussy they could be getting, and they settled down with some everyday broad?

Now, I couldn't imagine who that boy was who thought like that.

Because for the first time, I got it.

Family wasn't what I had when I was a kid. It wasn't a father who yelled and hit and demanded, and a mother who sat silent and complacent and scared. It wasn't a home made of eggshells and lies. It wasn't taking refuge in a sport because the more time you could stay away from the place you were supposed to call home — the happier you were.

Family was *this*.

It was a woman who filled every shattered piece of me, who fired up the need I'd never felt before to be a good man, a good caretaker, a good lover.

It was my son and my daughter, the home we would all build together, the one that was already filled with laughter and playfulness and joy.

It was knowing that no matter what came our way, we would hold hands — the four of us — and we would get through together.

And that did it.

My eyes watered so quickly, I couldn't stop the first tear from falling, though I swiped at it as soon as it hit my jaw.

"I will be the best man I can be for you," I whispered to my sleeping fiancée. "And for you and your brother, too," I promised our daughter, gently rubbing the belly where she grew.

It was one of the last quiet, calm moments of my new adult life.

Because fifteen weeks later — our daughter was born.

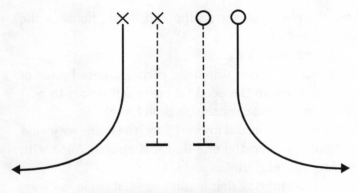

CHAPTER 43

April
Madelyn

"**T**his is honestly the best anniversary gift ever," Julep whispered with a sniff, her eyes watering as she smiled at the screen. Holden was beside her, a gentle smirk on his lips as he wrapped his arm around her shoulders and pulled her closer.

I held my phone, which showcased Julep and Holden in one square, Clay, Giana, and Atlas in another, Riley and Zeke in one, and of course, Leo and Mary in the last one — Leo holding the phone while Mary tattooed something on his thigh in the background.

What *they* saw was not my tired eyes or bird's nest of hair — not that I cared if they *did* see it. But I had the camera turned away from me and pointed at where Kyle sat next to me on the couch, instead.

With Raven Isabel Robbins in his arms.

She was just over seven pounds, with a smattering of soft, fair hair on her cute little head, and eyes that were so bright blue I had a feeling they would stay that way.

Kyle held her in one arm like a football, his free hand adjusting the little headband on her because she kept wiggling it off. Right now, she was fast asleep — which tracked, since the precious little thing had kept us up most of the night.

I didn't mind, though. I would happily be a zombie if it meant I could soak up this time of her being so small, so cuddly, so sweet and innocent. I was pretty much nothing more than a cow right now, existing only to feed her and make sure she was happy. There was nothing quite like newborn exhaustion. But at the same time, there was nothing like this particular brand of joy.

"Raven Isabel," Riley said, shaking her head on a smile. "That is such a gorgeous name."

"I fought it at first," I admitted, sighing a bit at the victorious smirk on Kyle's tired face. "But when she came out, when we held her for the first time... I can't explain it. It was like *she* was telling us her name, and it was Raven. There was no refuting it."

"I love being right," Kyle said.

I dug my toes into his ribs until he yelped on a grin and swatted my ankle away.

"You're going to wake her up!"

"Well, that wouldn't be a bad thing. Maybe then she'd sleep tonight."

Kyle rubbed my leg softly in understanding. He had been there every step of the way, waking up when I did, changing diapers and then handing Raven to me to feed. He'd also taken over so much with Sebastian — along with my parents, who thankfully flew in to help us in the first couple of weeks.

Raven Isabel was born at 7:42 PM on April sixteenth — Holden and Julep's one year wedding anniversary. Labor had been easier for me this time around than it had been with Sebastian. Maybe it was because my body knew what to do. Maybe it was because I was supported and loved through it, because Kyle held my hand and reminded me to breathe and made sure I knew I wasn't alone.

Whatever the reason, Raven came so fast, my epidural hadn't even completely set in. I now knew what it was like to give birth with my *legs* numb, but my uterus still experiencing every contraction.

But it didn't matter — none of it. Not the pain or the discomfort or the annoying headache I'd had for two days afterward.

Because our daughter was here, and everything was right in the world.

"Can I get you anything, honey?" Mom asked, rounding the corner from the kitchen. She was drying her hands on a dish towel, which told me she'd just cleaned up the kitchen after Dad had made us a big lunch.

"I'm good, Mom," I assured her. "Why don't you go rest?"

Mom nodded, looking just as tired as I was. Dad was already in the back room taking a nap since Braden had shown up and offered to take Sebastian to the park. Mom smiled and walked over to where Kyle held Raven, leaning down to stroke her granddaughter's hair and coo at her.

"She's the most beautiful baby girl I've ever seen," Mom whispered.

"Hey, I'm right here," I said, which earned me a laugh from the North Boston University crew still on video call.

Mom leaned down to kiss my forehead. "Next to you, of course."

"No," I agreed. "You're right. She wins."

"It's because she looks like her mama," Kyle said.

He whispered the words, almost to himself, with a glazed smile on his face and his eyes all dreamy as he stared down at his daughter.

Mom and I shared a look — her eyes watering, mine following suit — before she squeezed my wrist and left us be.

For a while, we just chatted with the crew, everyone catching us up on what was new in their world. Atlas was four months old now, and I couldn't believe how much he'd grown since we'd seen him at Christmas. Riley and Zeke were in the middle of launching a new girls' football league in a small town in upstate New York, and every single one of us jumped in with offers to help sponsor any girls who couldn't afford the summer camp fees.

Mary's shop was thriving, and Leo was enjoying the offseason after a playoff run with the Vikings. Holden and Julep were already tending to their garden, rejoicing in spring and all its possibilities while they soaked up every moment of the offseason together.

We all vowed to have a group trip sometime over the summer before training camps picked back up, and just as I ended the call with them, the front door blew open.

Sebastian ran in with wide eyes and pink cheeks, calling out, "WE'RE HOME!" without a care in the world for a sleeping baby. He didn't stop to take off his shoes. Instead, he ran straight through the foyer, past the dining room, and into the living room where we were lounging. We had the windows open to let in the crisp spring breeze, music playing softly on the Sonos, and ESPN on the television, muted.

It was the perfect little quiet spring day.

When Sebastian saw Raven was sleeping, he slowed his steps, giggling a little before he tiptoed over to the arm of the couch and leaned on it so he could look at her.

"Hi, baby sister," he whispered, touching her cheek.

My heart exploded in to a million shiny pieces.

"She sleeps a lot," he added with a toothy grin at Kyle.

"Can you believe *you* used to be this little?" Kyle asked him.

"No!" He laughed like that was a silly notion.

"Well, you were," I said, and I thumbed through my phone until I found a pic to prove it. Sebastian ran over to me and laid his head on my chest while I showed him photo after photo of him as a baby, and he pointed and laughed at the outfits I'd put him in.

Braden looked beat when he joined us in the living room, flopping down into one of our leather chairs.

"Have fun?" Kyle asked.

"That kid has more energy than a hundred Energizer bunnies."

"Makes you feel old, doesn't it?" I teased.

"Makes me feel like I need to get back on the field. Clearly, I'm out of shape if I can't even chase a seven-year-old around the park for a few hours." Braden nodded on a smile over at Kyle. "How's she doing?"

"Sleeping soundly, ready to keep Mom and Dad up all night," Kyle said, booping our daughter on the nose like that was so adorable.

"I'm hungry," Sebastian proclaimed.

"Come on," I said, standing and helping him off the couch. "Mom will make you a grilled cheese."

"You don't have to do that," Kyle scolded. He had clearly displayed his desire to keep me from doing anything close to work after birthing our child. "Your dad just made that skillet scramble. You can heat up leftovers."

"That's cute that you think Sebastian will eat something with mushrooms and green peppers."

Sebastian wrinkled his nose on cue. "Ewwww, mushrooms!"

"Here, you take Raven and I'll—"

"I'm fine," I assured Kyle, pushing on his shoulder before he could stand. I leaned down to press a kiss to his cheek.

Sebastian talked my ear off about the park while I made a grilled cheese, and I stood at the island with him while he ate it, smiling and listening intently. I wanted to make sure he knew that having a baby sister meant he'd have to share us, yes, but that we still had space and time and attention for him.

When he was finished eating, I had him run up to take a bath, promising he could watch *Big Hero 6* for the thousandth time when he finished.

I rejoined Kyle and Braden in the living room just in time to see Braden frowning at his phone.

"Bad news?" I asked.

As if the sound of my voice was a cue that food was near, Raven stirred, crying a bit and making faces that told me she was hungry. Kyle passed her to me, and I set up the nursing pillow under my arm, pulled the nursing cover over my head long enough to free my boob and get Raven latched, and then re-emerged.

Braden didn't skip a beat. "Not bad, just... interesting."

"Do tell," I urged.

"Our PR coordinator wants me to volunteer for the Tacoma Girls Flag Football Jamboree in May," he said. "They're looking for about ten players to go out, and apparently, I'm on their list."

"That's awesome," Kyle offered. "Why do you look like they just asked you to do team laundry?"

"Yeah. Riley and Zeke would be so proud of you if you attended," I added.

"I'm excited for the event," Braden assured us. "I told them at the end of the season to let me know if there were ways I could get involved with the community. It's just..."

"What?" Kyle probed when Braden's voice faded.

"Nothing."

"Nuh-uh," I said, shaking my head as I adjusted Raven to make sure she was actually nursing, and not sliding into another nap with my nipple in her mouth. "No lies in this house. Spill."

Braden let out a heavy sigh. "The cheerleaders will be there."

Kyle and I shared a look, and then Kyle deadpanned, "What a travesty."

Braden glared at him. "Don't be an ass."

"Did I miss something? Why is that a bad thing?" I asked.

"It's not," Braden said, dragging a hand through his hair. "It's just... there's a new cheerleader who just made the squad, and she's kind of a pain in my ass."

This time, the look Kyle and I shared was tinged with curiosity.

"How have you already met her?" Kyle asked.

"I volunteered to be there on finals day, when the squad was selected. I don't know. I was bored," he said instantly, like he knew Kyle would ask why. "Anyway, she just... she's trouble. One of those girls who learns the rules only so she can figure out how to break them."

"I like her already," I mused.

"I have a feeling *you* like her, too," Kyle added. "Which is why you're all weird about the event."

"I'm not weird about it," Braden defended, standing and tucking his phone away. "I'm going. And I don't like her. I'm annoyed by her."

"I think you could use someone to ruffle your feathers a bit," Kyle said. "Someone to get you off your yoga mat and out causing a ruckus."

"Did you just say *ruckus*?" Braden asked.

"Don't change the subject."

"There's nothing more to talk about," Braden said, and he walked over to clap hands with Kyle before nodding at me. "I gotta run, but please don't hesitate to call if you want me to get Sebastian out of the house or take him for a night or two. He's always welcome at mine."

"You're the best," I told him. "Thank you for today."

"Can't wait to hear about the flag football event," Kyle added with a grin.

Braden flipped him off, and then he left, and it was just the three of us.

Kyle scooted closer to me on the couch, draping an arm around me. Raven was finished eating, so I removed the nursing cover and put my boob away — much to Kyle's dismay — before we were both looking down at her like the doting, love-sick parents we were.

"How you doing, Mom?" Kyle asked me, kissing my shoulder.

"Tired," I answered honestly. "But amazing. You?"

"Same." He nuzzled into me. "You're fucking incredible. You know that?"

"I think I've heard you say that a few times over the last week," I mused on a smile.

"Well, it's true. Watching you give birth..." Kyle shook his head. "I'll never forget that experience, Mads. I didn't think it was possible to love you more, but *fuck*, I was wrong."

He captured my chin and brought my lips to his, kissing me with the full intent behind those words. I was still melting into that kiss when the security system notified us there was someone at the gate.

I frowned. "Maybe Braden forgot something?"

"He has the code," Kyle said with a frown of his own. "I'll go see."

He hopped up just in time for Sebastian to run down the stairs, hair still wet, a fresh pair of shorts and his favorite dinosaur t-shirt on. He knew now how to put on the movie by himself, and once it started playing, he curled up beside me and Raven on the couch, leaning his head on my arm.

My whole fucking life was complete.

We weren't even through the beginning bot scene when I heard voices by the front door. Curious, I told

Sebastian I'd be right back, and with Raven in my arms, I made my way toward the noise.

When I laid eyes on Lynette Robbins, I froze in my tracks.

She looked so much older than when we were kids. Her hair was gray now, her face lined and weathered. She was wringing her hands together with her eyes cast up nervously at her son, the two of them talking in hushed voices.

She started to cry.

And then, rigidly, Kyle took her into his arms.

I watched another mother break in that moment, clinging to Kyle as she sobbed, and he held onto her as if he still wasn't sure he should be holding her at all. But there was a tender forgiveness and understanding in that embrace, and when they pulled back, Kyle wiped a tear from her cheek with his thumb.

Then, her eyes found me.

"Oh, Madelyn," she whispered, her eyes flooding again. And when that gaze dropped to Raven, she covered her mouth with her hands. "Is this her?"

I looked to Kyle for guidance, and he swallowed, nodding, promising me with that one look that he'd explain what I'd missed later. Gently, he guided his mother over to where I stood.

"Mom, this is Raven Isabel."

"Oh," she said again, her hands shaking. "Oh, she's beautiful."

I offered a small smile. "Would you like to hold her?"

Mrs. Robbins's eyes shot wide when they found mine. "Could I? Once I wash up, of course," she said quickly, holding out her hands before she was wringing them together again. "Airplane travel and all."

I nodded. "Absolutely. Nothing better for a baby than grandma cuddles."

The look Lynette gave me then was one of disbelief, like she couldn't believe I was treating her with such kindness after what she'd done to me, to Kyle, to both of us.

But if there was one thing I believed in now more than ever, it was forgiveness. It was compassion for people who were just trying to do what they thought was right, just trying to survive. I may never understand why she did what she did, but she was still the mother of the man I loved.

I would respect her always for that, if nothing else.

"Come inside," I said, leading her toward the living room. "We just put on a movie. And I can make you some tea."

"*I* will make tea," Kyle said. "You go rest."

I chuckled, leaning into his kiss when he pressed it against my cheek.

Lynette watched the whole interaction with tears in her eyes.

After she'd washed up and Kyle had taken her bag upstairs to a guest room, Lynette and I sat down on the couch next to one another. I gently handed Raven over to her, making sure her little head was supported as Lynette did her best not to cry once her granddaughter was safely in her arms.

She was quiet for a moment, staring down at our precious new addition to the family before she looked at me.

"You've always brought out the best in him," she whispered. "I'm sorry I didn't stand up for that, for you, when I should have."

I swallowed, covering her hand with mine. I didn't think I'd ever be able to tell her it was okay — because it wasn't. But I nodded. I wanted her to know that she was welcome now, even if we still had a lot to work through.

Kyle brought us both a cup of tea, and then he sat down on the floor next to Sebastian, who had sprawled out in his favorite Lovesac. I laughed as they watched the movie together, both of them reciting the same parts that they knew by memory since this was my son's favorite movie in the world.

And next to me, a woman I thought was out of our lives forever was coming back in, asking for forgiveness, willing to try to be better.

I didn't need all the details right now. All I cared about was that my family was in this house — my parents, my future husband, my son and my daughter. And now, my future mother-in-law, who showed bravery just by coming here on her own. I knew without asking that that hadn't been easy for her to do, that there likely had been a fight, that she'd made a choice — her son over her husband.

Whatever the future held for us, we were family. *All* of us.

I found so much hope and comfort in that fact alone.

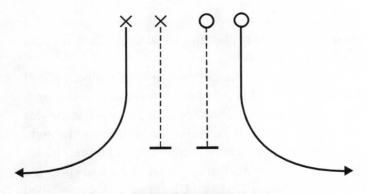

EPILOGUE
One Year Later
Kyle

"I can't believe you managed to wait so long for this," Mom said, messing with the lapels and tie on my suit even though I knew it looked perfect. My guess was she just needed something to do with her hands to keep from crying.

"That makes two of us," I said. "But, then again, I guess it wasn't fair of me to expect Madelyn to want to get into a wedding dress less than three months after giving birth."

Mom chuckled. "The only thing *I* was wearing three months after birth was compression leggings and you. You loved being wrapped up tight to my chest."

She smiled with the memory, her eyes going misty the way they had often over the last year since she'd shown up on our doorstep.

I didn't know if things would ever be *normal* between us — then again, I didn't know what normal was when it came to my parents.

All I knew was that things were *better*.

I knew it wasn't easy for her to leave my father. I knew she was scared out of her mind those first few months, thinking he'd show up and drag her out of my house by her hair. He would have had me to answer to if he so much as tried — and maybe that's why he never did.

Eventually, she flew back to file for divorce, and surprisingly, Dad didn't fight her on it.

That hurt her worse than anything.

He didn't fight to keep her. He didn't fight to have a relationship with me. He was perfectly content to let us both go.

While it broke my mom's heart for us, it broke mine more for *him* — because all that told me was that he was hurt, and he had no intention of healing. I would never know the reasons my father was the way he was. I would never know what happened to him, or what dark secrets he held onto.

But sometimes, that's just the way it is. You can love someone and never understand them. You can care for someone, and also have to draw boundaries with them. You can wish someone well while also realizing that in order for *yourself* to be well, you have to let them go.

"Let's get you to that altar, shall we?" Mom said, tugging on my tie one last time.

I bent and kissed her on the forehead, looping my arm through hers, and then we made our way outside.

The venue Madelyn and I had settled on was simple, save for the views it offered. Nestled atop a cliff on a beautiful gorge with the Pacific Northwest spread out in all its glory, the altar was nothing more than three old pieces of wood nailed together by someone hundreds of years ago. But the view made it grand, luxurious, and breathtaking.

We'd needed only one look at it to know it was the one for us.

It was such a small ceremony, Madelyn and I had opted not to have the traditional bridesmaids and groomsmen next to us. Instead, I walked past my friends seated on either side of the aisle, smiling as they shot out jokes and one-liners at my expense.

Clay and Giana were attempting to wrangle Atlas, who was eager to show off his new skill of walking. Riley and Zeke sat next to them, Riley smiling despite the fact that I was sure she was still battling nausea as Zeke rubbed her back soothingly. She was in her first trimester — a secret she shared with us only so we would know if she ran out of our wedding to puke, that it wasn't because of us.

Holden, Julep, Mary, and Leo sat in the row across the aisle from the previous group. Holden seemed to sit a bit taller now — something I was sure winning the Super Bowl did to everyone. He'd taken a team that had virtually zero chance of even making the playoffs three years ago all the way to the end.

I had a feeling he'd go down as one of the greatest, and I was all too eager to be in the same category.

Just behind them sat Braden and Emily — his arm draped around the back of her chair, and her smirking and leaning into him. She and Mary had spent most of our welcome dinner last night planning out Emily's next tattoo, all while the rest of us reminisced with Braden about the bumpy road they'd had that led to where they were now.

But that's a story for another time.

Once I was at the altar, Mom wrapped me in a light hug before taking her seat in the front row. Instead of sitting on a certain side of the aisle, she sat right next to Madelyn's mom — who had become a great friend to my mom in this trying time in her life.

Other than our parents and the North Boston University crew, we had only a few other guests. There were some women Madelyn met through mommy groups there with their husbands and kids, Madelyn's brother, of course, and his wife. I'd invited a few close friends from the team, who were having a hard time keeping their rowdiness in check before the reception.

All in all, we had less than fifty guests in attendance.

When I turned to face them once I was at the altar, I was thankful for the small gathering. Something about me had turned inward when I became a father. I'd become more private, barely posting on social media once a week, if at all, and *never* with my kids in the photos. They couldn't escape the media — not with my career, and especially since Sebastian wanted to be at every game — but I could at least let them be the ones to decide on their social media presence once they were old enough.

We'd kept the date quiet, somehow able to skirt the media frenzy — likely thanks to Giana throwing reporters off any time they sniffed around asking.

And it just felt *right*, being surrounded by our close friends and family on our big day.

My throat felt tight as I folded my hands in front of my waist and waited for the ceremony to start. I couldn't keep the emotion at bay, no matter how I tried. It was creeping up more and more with every passing moment.

Never in a million years did I think I'd be in this position.

It was unreal, honestly, to think back on who I was two years ago. That version of me was a shell of a man, a shadow of what I was to become. He wandered around aimlessly. He imagined a career in the NFL where the only thing that mattered to him was having the best stats, winning every game, and fucking the hottest women he could find along the way. That man's biggest concerns were what car he drove, and how many likes his most recent post had on Instagram.

I didn't know that man now.

Because now, my entire world revolved around Madelyn, Sebastian, and Raven.

I still loved football. Hell, it was my career, my passion, my driving force to do better and *be* better. It was still as engrained in my heart as ever.

It just had to share, now.

Every night, I went home to Madelyn. Every day, I spent every second I could with my kids. And every morning, I woke with my mind spinning with gratitude. I couldn't believe this was my life, couldn't understand how I'd been so lucky.

How had the universe delivered Madelyn back to me?

How had I managed to get it right, to not fuck up my second chance with her?

How did *we* manage to overcome the tragedy we'd lived through as teenagers, to somehow find love and understanding and forgiveness on the other side?

It felt like a miracle, and maybe it was. Maybe she was *my* little miracle.

Those thoughts were still swirling in my mind when the violin player at the back of the last row began to play a new song, and everyone turned in their chairs to watch the show.

The show being my son carrying my daughter in his arms, doing his best to entertain her and keep her from crying as he did some sort of weird dance-jog down from the lodge and down the aisle.

We all chuckled as he dug into the basket Raven held in her hands, tossing white rose petals left and right. He'd do a few and then wait for her to follow suit, showing her how to grab a handful and let it go. When Raven did it the first time, she giggled with glee, looking up at Sebastian for approval and smiling even bigger when he bounced her in his arms and encouraged her to go again.

My heart tripped inside my chest at the sight.

Sebastian was growing more and more into a young man every day. I couldn't believe he was eight now.

I also couldn't believe he was officially my son.

He would have been even without the paperwork, but there was something about having it made legal, about him taking my last name that cemented a sense of security. And although I knew it killed him a little that his own father never fought for him, that he was so content to let Sebastian go... I also knew he was happier without being forced to spend time with a man who scared him.

As he got older, I would explain everything. I would be there for every question he had. And I'd share my own struggles I'd had with my father to make sure he knew he wasn't alone.

Sebastian would start third grade in just a few months, and in the last year, I'd witnessed him being the best big brother any little girl could ever wish for. He'd taken the role seriously from the beginning, helping us with diaper changes and feedings and bath time just because he wanted to. Now, his favorite pastime was making his sister laugh. He played with her more than he did his rocks and Titan combined.

I didn't know how long that would last, how long he would dote on her before she'd become his annoying little sister who never left him alone. But Madelyn and I soaked up every moment of it while we could.

The only thing Sebastian loved more than his little sister was playing football.

That had been a new development that Madelyn had both loved and hated. I couldn't blame her. With any sport came the possibility of injury, and I knew as a parent myself now how impossibly hard it was to watch knowing there was nothing you could do to keep them safe.

But Sebastian thrived on his team. He was a natural born leader, and with the arm he was developing, I could see him walking in Holden's footsteps one day.

As for Raven?

She looked like her mother — and had me wrapped around her little pinky.

It was true what they said about parenthood. The days were long, but the first year had felt like a blink of an eye. I watched that little girl grow from a soft, sleepy bundle of heat that slept and ate more than anything else, to a curious toddler who was starting to pull herself up and take her first assisted steps. Her wide brown eyes were just like Madelyn's, her smile more like mine, and every day, we watched her explore the world and experience firsts that felt like a bigger win to me than any game I'd ever played.

When they were almost to the end of the aisle, Sebastian carefully set Raven's feet on the grass, holding her hands above her head and helping her walk to me. I swung her up in my arms when she made it, savoring the gleeful giggle that pealed out of her. I kissed her cheek and pulled Sebastian into my side, kissing his hair and telling him how proud I was of him.

Then, he and Raven took their seats next to Madelyn's father, and all eyes swiveled to the end of the aisle.

We'd all been so busy watching the kids, we hadn't noticed sneaky Madelyn making her way out of the lodge.

She stood there like an angel, her copper hair swept back into an elegant bun and her hands wrapped tightly around a bouquet of lilies and roses.

I didn't know what I thought I'd see when I finally laid eyes on her, but nothing in my imagination compared to the long, lacy details of the dress hugging her figure and draping down into the grass behind her. The flowery cream fabric hung from delicate straps over each shoulder, the V neckline hugging her curves and highlighting the slim tapering of her waist. The skirt of the dress flared off at her hips, just slightly, and then fell in beautiful, flowing waves down to the ground.

She looked like something from a fairytale, like a goddess and a princess and a fairy all at once. I half expected the moss and trees and spring flowers to move with her, the birds to float down and land in her hair as she stood there smiling at me.

And *God,* was it the most breathtaking smile I'd ever seen.

I willed myself to hold it together — and not just because I knew the guys had a bet on how long I could make it before I burst into tears.

But because I wanted to be strong for Madelyn, for our family. I wanted to hold my chin high at the end of that aisle and hold her gaze steadily with my own as she walked toward me, toward our future.

All of that went to hell when she took the first step, though.

Because her soft, berry-painted lips curved up, her eyes glossed, and I realized in one all-encompassing moment that she was mine.

So, of course — I fucking lost it.

Madelyn

He was stunning.

I couldn't help the intake of air that I held captive in my throat as we took each other in, the noise of our guests and the violin fading to the background.

My husband-to-be was a vision at the altar, the forest green of his suit with the rich brown accents of his tie and Chelsea boots making him seem as if he'd been born right here in the forest. Even from this distance, I could see the glint of his gold cufflinks, the elegant watch hugging his wrist, the sprig of white flowers pinned to his lapel.

And when I took the first step toward him, he choked on the sob I knew he was trying so hard to hold back, his eyes flooding so fast, he couldn't hide the tears that slid down his cheeks.

I couldn't help but smile even more at him, and he shook his head like he couldn't believe how fast he'd turned to goop. But he didn't hide his tears. He didn't hang his head or swipe them away. Instead, he held his chin high, kept his eyes on mine, and savored every step I took with his bottom lip wobbling.

I couldn't tear my eyes from him to acknowledge our guests as I walked between the rows, but I felt their presence, heard their whispered murmurs as I passed.

"You look beautiful, Mommy!" Sebastian said when I was close to the front row, and I snapped my head in his direction, beaming as tears flooded my own eyes at the sight of him holding Raven in his lap.

I veered off course long enough to bend and kiss them both, and then I handed my bouquet to my mother, and I stepped up to the altar where Kyle stood waiting.

"You're a mess," I whispered on a laugh, swiping my hands over his cheeks and jaw to mop up the tears.

"You make me this way."

I smiled, sliding my hands into his, and I knew he was fighting leaning in to kiss me as much as I was with him. It was silly, to have to wait to kiss the man I shared a bed with every night, the man I quite literally made a baby with.

But I kind of liked watching him squirm with the need to kiss me and not being able to quite yet.

"You are so beautiful," he mouthed, squeezing my hands, his eyes trailing over me as he shook his head. "It's unreal."

"You don't look too bad yourself."

"Wanna skip this part and just..." He jutted his chin back toward his right shoulder, eyes wide like he was ready to sweep me into his arms and run.

I laughed, but before I could accept his offer, the ceremony began.

"Ladies and gentlemen, please be seated," the officiant said, calling our attention to him. "We are gathered here today to witness the union between Kyle Robbins and Madelyn James..."

When we'd hired our officiant, we'd asked him to keep our ceremony short and sweet. I knew from our rehearsal last night what he was saying, how he would tell a little of our story to the crowd that already knew it, anyway.

And so, I let his words fade to the background, let myself live in a quiet moment with Kyle holding my hands and our future stretching out before us.

When it came time for us to read vows, I began.

Writing had always been a passion of mine, and that passion had room to grow and flourish in the last year. Writing my vows had been easy, and I read them without even looking at a card, holding Kyle's gaze and smiling a little in victory when I made him cry again.

Little did I know the joke would be on me in the end.

When it was his turn, he let go of one of my hands to pull a small notebook from the inside of his tuxedo jacket. He held tight to my one hand while he read, his Adam's apple bobbing hard in his throat before he began.

"Madelyn, finding the right words to tell you how much you mean to me, to promise everything I want to promise you... well, it has proved impossible. We all know you're the writer. I had no doubts you would put my vows to shame," he said as the crowd chuckled. "But I happen to know you better than anyone else in the world. And because of that, I know that for you, it's the simple things that matter most.

"I know you love Earl Grey tea when you're tired or feeling down. I know the exact amount of ice to put in your water before placing it on your nightstand each night. I know when I make chicken nuggets and macaroni and cheese for the kids, that I have to make a separate batch of mac just for you — and load it up with extra cheese, bacon, sour cream, and chives."

The guests laughed a little as I covered my face, embarrassed at the truth in that statement.

"I know a lot of other things about you, too," he continued. "Like the two lines that crease on your forehead when you're thinking about the next line you want to write in your book. I know the difference between a real, genuine laugh, and the laugh you give me or the kids when we're walking a thin line between being funny and getting into trouble."

Another laugh sounded from the guests, and I felt my nose stinging, eyes watering at how well this man *did* know me.

"But there's so much more I still want to know about you," Kyle said, his eyes finding mine. "And I know that will never not be true. There is nothing in this world I love to discover more than you. Every day I spend by your side, I peel back another layer. I find something new to love. I find something new to cherish in the woman I never deserved, but will spend the rest of my life trying to be worthy of."

I squeezed his hand in mine, trying to tell him without words that he deserved me and more.

"Madelyn, you have brought out the best in me," he said, and he choked a bit on those words, clearing his throat as I willed my own emotions to stay checked. "I didn't have an example of a father growing up — not one I would ever want to emulate, anyway. But over the past year, through *being* a father, I have learned more about love, kindness, compassion and understanding than ever before. And because of that, I know you really are an angel on earth. Because no one is as kind, compassionate, and understanding as you are.

"You light me up with the fire to live the life I was always too afraid to live before. You make me feel brave. You make me feel limitless. And truthfully, I know there's *nothing* in this world that you and I could ever face that would hold us down. I know we can survive and *thrive* through any test.

"From this moment and until my last breath, I vow to love you, Madelyn James soon-to-be-Robbins." He smiled at that, squeezing my hand as the crowd sniffed and chuckled. "I vow to be the husband you deserve, the father I never had, and the friend you've always been to me. Because though our love is powerful and unending, it's our friendship that has always been our lifeline, the roots that hold our foundation strong."

I nodded, two silent tears slipping down my cheeks.

"I love you. And I will keep loving you until I am taken from this Earth, and long after I am gone, too. Always. That's how long you have me. Forever. That's how long I want you. Infinite, Madelyn — that's what we are."

I couldn't wait any longer.

As soon as the words left his lips, I threw my arms

around his neck and crashed into him, crying even as he chuckled against my mouth. But he dropped the notebook and swept me into his arms, holding me tightly to him as our guests hooted and hollered and made jokes about us not being able to wait.

I thought I heard the officiant announce us as husband and wife.

I thought I heard cheers and felt the dried flower petals we'd given our guests raining over us.

I thought I heard the universe exhale a sigh of relief that we'd finally figured it out.

But none of it registered — not the music or the applause or the smell of the rain moving in.

Because all I could hear, see, and feel in that moment was the most beautiful truth I'd ever known.

I had Kyle Robbins, and he had me.

And we had forever stretching out in front of us, bright and beautiful and unknown.

THE END

Want more of the Red Zone Rivals crew?
Start at the beginning and fall in love!
Riley & Zeke — Fair Catch (https://geni.us/FairCatch)
Giana & Clay — Blind Side (https://geni.us/blindside)
Julep & Holden — Quarterback Sneak
(https://geni.us/quarterbacksneakrzr)
Mary & Leo — Hail Mary (https://geni.us/hailmaryrzr)

Can't get enough of Kyle and Mads? Read this delicious bonus scene! (http://www.kandisteiner.com/bonus-content) Madelyn's book gets published and the girls throw her a release party at Mary's tattoo shop. Plus, Kyle celebrates in his favorite way once they get back to the hotel.

Braden's book is coming!
Sign up for Kandi Steiner's newsletter
(http://www.kandisteiner.com/newsletter)
so you don't miss it.

ACKNOWLEDGEMENTS

My first acknowledgement goes to all the incredible babes who read this first on Kindle Vella. We went on a great adventure together, creating this story TOGETHER episode by episode. Thank you for loving Kyle and Mads as hard as I do, for all your great feedback and guidance, and for making every week so fun while we were in the midst of it all. I'll never forget this experience!

To my husband, Jack – thank you for loving me through this one even harder than the others, as I hit the first trimester of my first pregnancy just as I was ending this book. Some days, it felt impossible to write. But you always believed in me. I love you, and I cannot wait to watch you be the best father to our little girl.

To my momma, thank you for instilling the love of football in me and for always encouraging me to chase my dreams.

Sasha, thanks for listening to me gab about my books even now that I've published thirty-six of them. What an angel you are!

To Tina Stokes, my Executive Assistant and dear friend – there are no words to form a proper thank you. My life is such a joy with you in it, and I can't imagine doing any of this without you. Thank you for loving this story, for helping me promote it, and for being like the big sister I never had. I love you.

A huge thank you to all the amazing women in this industry who have been my writing buddies through various parts of this story, who always encouraged me to write what scared me. Staci Hart, Laura Pavlov, Brittainy Cherry, Catherine Cowles, Lena Hendrix, Elsie Silver, Karla Sorensen – I'm honored to be on this journey with you.

Thank you to the crew at OSYS Studios for bringing these books to life in audio. I always get teary-eyed hearing these stories told through the amazing voices you cast!

To Isabella Bauer – thank you for obsessing over the RZR crew with me and for always being such a bright joy. So happy to have you on the team!

To my beta readers: thank you for looking this one over after I took it from a Kindle Vella episodic story to a novel. I appreciate all your valuable feedback more than I can say. A huge and heartfelt thanks to Kellee Fabre, Sarah Green, Jayce Cruz, Gabriela Vivas, and Carly Wilson. I am so happy to have you all on my team.

And to Jennifer Donnel and Caitie Hey. Thank you for your guidance in the real estate and legal departments, and for taking on this project when you didn't have to. I appreciate you so much!

To the team who helps bring my vision to life: Elaine York with Allusion Publishing, Nicole McCurdy with Emerald Edits, Nina Grinstead, Kim Cermak, the whole team at Valentine PR, Shaye Lefkowitz and Lindsey Romero with Good Girls PR, Ren Saliba – THANK YOU. From editing and formatting to photography and promotion, it truly takes a village. I'm so thankful for each and every one of you.

To my unborn daughter: I found out I was pregnant with you when I was a little over halfway through this book. So much of what I wrote in Madelyn was my own experience, from the extreme fatigue and nausea to the joy I felt when you first moved inside me. And if you're wondering – YES, your father inspired Kyle in so many ways. He cares for me in that same all-encompassing way that makes me count my lucky stars. We are so excited to welcome you into this world, and we can't wait for all the adventures we'll have together.

And to you, sweet, sweet reader. Look at you! You read all the way to the end of the acknowledgements, even! I have been publishing for more than ten years now, and still, it blows my mind to know that you exist – that someone in this world wants to read the words I have written. I am eternally thankful for your support, your love, your reviews and social media posts and shouts from the rooftops to your friends. Without you, I would just be telling myself stories. So, thank you for letting me share with you. And thank you for reading indie.

MORE FROM
KANDI STEINER

The Kings of the Ice Series
Meet Your Match
One Month with Vince Tanev: Tampa's Hotshot Rookie – twenty-four-seven access on and off the ice. The headline says it all, and my bosses are over the moon when the opportunity of a lifetime lands in my lap. Of course, they aren't aware that they're forcing me into proximity with the one man who grates on my last nerve.

Watch Your Mouth
My brother's teammates know not to touch me — but that doesn't stop me from daring Jaxson Brittain to be the first to break the rule.

Learn Your Lesson
Single dad and grumpy goalie Will Perry finds himself wanting to break his own rules when it comes to his new sunshiney nanny.

The Red Zone Rivals Series
Fair Catch
As if being the only girl on the college football team wasn't hard enough, Coach had to go and assign my brother's best friend — and my number one enemy — as my roommate.

Blind Side
The hottest college football safety in the nation just asked me to be his fake girlfriend.
And I just asked him to take my virginity.

Quarterback Sneak
Quarterback Holden Moore can have any girl he wants.
Except me: the coach's daughter.

Hail Mary (an Amazon #1 Bestseller!)
Leo F*cking Hernandez.
North Boston University's star running back, notorious bachelor, and number one on my people I would murder if I could get away with it list.
And now?
My new roommate.

The Becker Brothers Series
On the Rocks (book 1)
Neat (book 2)
Manhattan (book 3)
Old Fashioned (book 4)
Four brothers finding love in a small Tennessee town that revolves around a whiskey distillery with a dark past — including the mysterious death of their father.

The Best Kept Secrets Series
(AN AMAZON TOP 10 BESTSELLER)
What He Doesn't Know (book 1)
What He Always Knew (book 2)
What He Never Knew (book 3)
Charlie's marriage is dying. She's perfectly content to go down in the flames, until her first love shows back up and reminds her the other way love can burn.

Close Quarters

A summer yachting the Mediterranean sounded like heaven to Jasmine after finishing her undergrad degree. But her boyfriend's billionaire boss always gets what he wants. And this time, he wants her.

Make Me Hate You

Jasmine has been avoiding her best friend's brother for years, but when they're both in the same house for a wedding, she can't resist him — no matter how she tries.

The Wrong Game

(AN AMAZON TOP 5 BESTSELLER)

Gemma's plan is simple: invite a new guy to each home game using her season tickets for the Chicago Bears. It's the perfect way to avoid getting emotionally attached and also get some action. But after Zach gets his chance to be her practice round, he decides one game just isn't enough. A sexy, fun sports romance.

The Right Player

She's avoiding love at all costs. He wants nothing more than to lock her down. Sexy, hilarious and swoon-worthy, The Right Player is the perfect read for sports romance lovers.

On the Way to You

It was only supposed to be a road trip, but when Cooper discovers the journal of the boy driving the getaway car, everything changes. An emotional, angsty road trip romance.

A Love Letter to Whiskey
(AN AMAZON TOP 10 BESTSELLER)
An angsty, emotional romance between two lovers fighting the curse of bad timing.

Read Love, Whiskey – Jamie's side of the story and an extended epilogue – in the new Fifth Anniversary Edition!

Weightless
Young Natalie finds self-love and romance with her personal trainer, along with a slew of secrets that tie them together in ways she never thought possible.

Revelry
Recently divorced, Wren searches for clarity in a summer cabin outside of Seattle, where she makes an unforgettable connection with the broody, small town recluse next door.

Say Yes
Harley is studying art abroad in Florence, Italy. Trying to break free of her perfectionism, she steps outside one night determined to Say Yes to anything that comes her way. Of course, she didn't expect to run into Liam Benson...

Washed Up
Gregory Weston, the boy I once knew as my son's best friend, now a man I don't know at all. No, not just a man. A doctor. And he wants me...

The Christmas Blanket
Stuck in a cabin with my ex-husband waiting out a blizzard? Not exactly what I had pictured when I planned a surprise visit home for the holidays...

Black Number Four
A college, Greek-life romance of a hot young poker star and the boy sent to take her down.

The Palm South University Series
Rush (book 1)
Anchor (book 2)
Pledge (book 3)
Legacy (book 4)
Ritual (book 5)
Hazed (book 6)
Greek (book 7)
#1 NYT Bestselling Author Rachel Van Dyken says, "If Gossip Girl and Riverdale had a love child, it would be PSU." This angsty college series will be your next guilty addiction.

Tag Chaser
She made a bet that she could stop chasing military men, which seemed easy — until her knight in shining armor and latest client at work showed up in Army ACUs.

Song Chaser
Tanner and Kellee are perfect for each other. They frequent the same bars, love the same music, and have the same desire to rip each other's clothes off. Only problem? Tanner is still in love with his best friend.

ABOUT THE AUTHOR

Kandi Steiner is a #1 Amazon Bestselling Author. Best known for writing "emotional rollercoaster" stories, she loves bringing flawed characters to life and writing about real, raw romance — in all its forms. No two Kandi Steiner books are the same, and if you're a lover of angsty, emotional, and inspirational reads, she's your gal.

An alumna of the University of Central Florida, Kandi graduated with a double major in Creative Writing and Advertising/PR with a minor in Women's Studies. Her love for writing started at the ripe age of 10, and in 6th grade, she wrote and edited her own newspaper and distributed to her classmates. Eventually, the principal caught on and the newspaper was quickly halted, though Kandi tried fighting for her "freedom of press."

She took particular interest in writing romance after college, as she has always been a die hard hopeless romantic, and likes to highlight all the challenges of love as well as the triumphs.

When Kandi isn't writing, you can find her reading books of all kinds, planning her next adventure, or pole dancing (yes, you read that right). She enjoys live music, traveling, hiking, yoga, playing with her fur babies and soaking up the sweetness of life.

CONNECT WITH KANDI:
NEWSLETTER: kandisteiner.com/newsletter
FACEBOOK: facebook.com/kandisteiner
FACEBOOK READER GROUP (Kandiland):
facebook.com/groups/kandilandks
INSTAGRAM: Instagram.com/kandisteiner
TIKTOK: tiktok.com/@authorkandisteiner
TWITTER: twitter.com/kandisteiner
PINTEREST: pinterest.com/authorkandisteiner
WEBSITE: www.kandisteiner.com

Kandi Steiner may be coming to a city near you! Check out her "events" tab to see all the signings she's attending in the near future:
www.kandisteiner.com/events

9 781960 649270